HATE ME

hate me

THE KEATYN CHRONICLES: BOOK 6

JILLIAN DODD

The Keatyn Chronicles is a registered trademark™ of Jillian Dodd Inc.

Jillian Dodd Inc.
N. Redington Beach, FL

3rd Edition
ISBN: 978-1-940652-22-1

This book is for

Melissa and Mandy

I can't thank you enough for all you do.

Books by Jillian Dodd

Sunday, November 27th

SAY YES.

10:25AM

"YOU CAN'T COME with me. Not right now. You need to go back to school."

"Please, don't shut me out. Tell me what's wrong."

"It's my mom. I told you before. There are some family things going on."

"You did, but you were very vague. You know you can tell me anything, Boots. Seriously. *Anything.*"

"I know."

"I'll come with you and help."

"But you can't."

"Then I'll move to France and see you when you aren't busy."

"Aiden. Please," I plead. "Go back to school." I need him to leave before I start bawling.

"Is your mom sick?"

"Kinda. She's stressed and it's making her sick. I need to help."

"Mentally or physically sick?"

"Both, maybe. I don't really know because I'm not there. And she's sort of shut me out and—"

"I thought your trip home was good?"

"It was, but my mom was, um, sorta distant. Not like herself. And she's lost weight. I'm really worried about her, Aiden."

"What does your stepdad say?"

"He's trying to talk her into taking some time off."

"Do you think she will?"

"I think so."

"Then maybe things will get better on their own."

1

That's what we hoped would happen, I want to say. *But things have not gotten better on their own. They seem to have gotten worse.*

Aiden continues, "I would think your mom would be upset if you left before the semester is over. You won't get any credit for all your work this year. Besides, it's only a few weeks until Christmas break. Come back with me and we'll finish out the semester together. Then we can go anywhere you want."

I back away from Aiden, trying to put distance between us, both physically and emotionally.

He notices and immediately pulls me back into a hug.

I try to stay stiff, but I can't. I melt into his arms. I wish I didn't have to lie to him. Or hurt him.

He looks deep into my eyes and runs a gentle hand across my shoulder. "Don't."

"Don't what?"

"Pull away from me. You're emotionally retreating. It hurts."

"I don't want to hurt you, Aiden. I'm just trying to do what's right." I throw my hands out in frustration. "For everyone."

He slides his hands into mine, holding them tightly. "Keatyn, I know you'd never hurt me on purpose," he says softly.

Tears flood my eyes and I shake my head.

"Is it the forever stuff?" he asks. "Am I freaking you out?"

That's it.

His forever stuff could be my out.

All I have to do is say yes.

That we're too young.

But I can't. I can't lie to him about that.

"I can't promise you forever, Aiden."

"I've never asked you to promise me forever, Boots," he says, the hint of a smirk playing on his lips. "Just promise me tomorrow."

I tilt my head and study him. "Is that your sneaky way of getting me to promise you forever? Because there is always *another* tomorrow."

He laughs in the deep, sexy way I adore. "I didn't think of it that way, but I guess maybe I am."

I notice movement out of the corner of my eye; it's the security guys coming out of the turret with my suitcases.

Shit.

They're going to try to force me to go back.

I mentally scroll through my options. I can run . . .

"Miss Keatyn," Sven's voice comes over the intercom system. "You have a phone call in the main house."

I see Inga walk out onto the deck, waving one of the handsets.

Double shit.

"Um, hang on, Aiden."

As I walk to get the phone, Damian leaves Peyton's side and intercepts me. "What's the verdict?"

"Aiden says if I don't go back then he's not either. But that's the least of my worries now. Garrett's goons packed my luggage. I think they're going to try to force me."

"Whatever you need, you know that," he says, squeezing my shoulder reassuringly.

I give him a big hug. "I love you. It feels good to have you on my side."

Inga clears her throat, so I let go of Damian, go up the stairs, and then take the phone into the house.

I'm mentally gearing up for a battle with Garrett when I answer. "This is Keatyn."

"Keatyn."

Oh, thank goodness. It's just Tommy. "Hey, Tommy," I say cheerfully. "What's up?"

"I just got off the phone with Garrett."

Freaking Garrett. *Shit.*

"Discussing Mom's move to France?" I ask, still hopeful.

"Keatyn," Tommy says softly, "please don't make me worry about you, too."

The desperation in his voice is clear.

"I won't, Tommy. I promise."

"Then go back to school."

"I can't. I'm flying Cooper here tomorrow so we can work on my plan to break Vincent. I have to, Tommy, or this won't end well. For me or Mom."

"Tell me your plan."

My plan.

The plan that has been simmering since I left school and, this morning, as I watched a yacht drift off into the distance, finally became concrete.

"I have to get my friends to the airport. Would it be okay if I call you after they leave?"

Please say yes. Please say yes.

"No," he says firmly. "Because if I don't like your plan, you'll be going with them."

"They can't make me."

"Yes, they *can*. And they *will*. You can't fight them both."

No, but I can run. Right now, when they're least expecting it.

What Tommy doesn't know is that before I came here, I moved money to various bank accounts in the Caribbean. Of course, it was in case I had to run from Vincent, not my own security team.

"Garrett knows about the money, Keatyn," Tommy says, reading my mind.

Fuck.

"I think Garrett and Mom have been keeping information from you," I tell him. I've been suspecting this for a while, but have yet to mention it.

"What do you mean?"

"I think Vincent is still sending stuff to Mom and threatening her. Or, worse, threatening you and the girls. And lying to you is killing her. I think that's why she's getting so thin. Why she was so freaked out when I showed up for Gracie's birthday."

Tommy doesn't answer for a few seconds. "Fucking Garrett," he finally says. "I knew she was keeping something from me. Not only is she hurting herself, she's killing our relationship."

"What?! No, Tommy! Don't let that happen!"

"I'm trying not to. You know how much I love your Mom and our family."

"I know." Tommy has given me so much love and support and never ever asked for anything in return. Ever.

And even though I don't want to do this, even though it's totally going to ruin my plans, I have to do this.

For him.

"How about you focus on getting Mom and the girls to France. Once she feels safe, things will get better. I know they will. Let me deal with Garrett."

"Does that mean you'll go back to school?"

"Yes."

"Good. Once I get to New York, we'll discuss your other plans. Deal?"

"Deal, Tommy."

"I love you, baby."

"I love you too, Tommy."

I hang up the phone and close my eyes.

Shit. What just happened?

How am I going to do what I need to do from Eastbrooke?

And what's Damian going to say when I tell him he can't see Peyton again?

I SET THE phone back in its base, step out on the balcony, and lie. "Hey, Damian, can you come up here for a minute? Your dad's on the phone."

Damian kisses Peyton and comes up the stairs. Aiden is still waiting for me on the beach, so I give him a little wave.

I look down at the clover tattoo I got on a whim. Aiden probably thinks I got it because of him. And, in a way, I did. It's said that warriors used to design their own shields before they went into battle. They included symbols that were important to them, like a family crest or a cross. This tattoo is part of my shield. My hope is that if I can somehow combine chaos with luck, then I might actually survive my battle with Vincent.

But I just screwed everything up.

Damian squints at me. "My dad's not really on the phone, is he?"

"No. I have a problem. I have to go back to school."

At first he looks relieved, but then he glances down at Peyton and mutters, "Shit."

"I know. You're going to have to keep your relationship a secret. Can you do that?"

He rolls his head, considering options. "She knows I have to go back to California."

"Is there any way you could suggest that she not tell anyone about you? I know her. She's going to want to tell the world."

"Yeah, I'll make up something. What's going on? Who was on the phone?"

"Tommy. Garrett called him. Told him that I moved money to some Caribbean bank accounts."

"Did you?"

"Yeah, in case I had to run."

He takes two steps toward me and pulls me into a hug. "I'm in love with Peyton. But, right now, your safety is priority number one."

"And hers."

"Yeah, I guess you're right. This is all just so surreal."

"Tell me about it. Okay, so I have to go tell Aiden that I changed my mind. He's going to think I'm nuts."

Damian smiles and waves a hand at me. "Girls change their minds all the time. He won't think anything of it."

"I hope not."

I START TO walk toward the door, but change my mind, heading for the bar instead. I take a shot glass off the shelf, fill it with Patron Silver, and slam it down.

As the liquid warms my insides, I take a deep breath and try to figure out how to spin this.

Then I make my way down the beach.

Aiden's sitting on a chaise, staring out at the ocean. "Is everything okay?" he asks as I sit down next to him.

"Yeah, everything's fine. My stepdad just wanted to talk to me."

"What'd he say?"

"He sorta changed my plans. He wanted—no, he insisted—that I go back to school. He says my mom will be fine."

I get the blazing smile. "That's good news. On both accounts."

"Yep," I say.

He narrows his eyes at me. "You don't look excited."

"I don't like when my plans get changed."

He tucks his hand under my chin and smiles. "Well, in this case, you should. Think of all there is to look forward to. Basketball season. French weekend. Winter Formal. The first big snowfall. And you'd be in trouble with my sister if you missed the dance competition. And let's not forget French tutoring."

I nod and put on a fake smile. "So, um, I'm gonna go make sure my stuff's all packed. I'll meet you at the car, okay?"

"Okay," he says, giving me a quick kiss.

After he goes in the house, I run to the shed. I take a moment to run my hand across my surfboard and pray that I'll get to use it again. Then I take one of the extra wish bracelets and sneak to the mermaid fountain. I toss a penny in at the same time I tie on the bracelet and make a wish.

WE SAY GOODBYE to Damian, who is taking a company plane back to L.A.

Peyton and Damian's goodbye takes quite a while, so Aiden and I leave them to their kissing and board. When Peyton finally joins us, she's in tears.

I give her a big hug, feeling bad that someone else is hurting because of me.

"I didn't get much sleep last night. I'm going to crash," she says with a little smile. She puts in headphones and seems to be out before we even take off.

"Have you talked to anyone from school since we've been gone?" Aiden asks me, taking what he seems to consider his normal spot, lying across the couch with his head in my lap.

"Just a couple *Happy Thanksgiving* texts. How about you?"

"I texted Logan and Riley off and on."

"How was their holiday?"

"Well, Maggie showed up at Logan's house in tears . . ."

"Wait. Why?!"

"Got in a fight with her parents, I guess. Logan said she didn't want to talk about it, so he's not really sure what happened."

"That sucks. And what about Riley?"

"It was his idea to hijack your plane."

"It was?"

"Yeah, I wasn't sure what to do. I thought the moon . . ."

"I took the moon down. It pissed me off."

"Why?"

"It was mocking me," I stupidly say.

Aiden laughs. "Mocking you? How?"

I don't answer. Just put my head down and knead my brow line with my fingers. "Because I didn't think I'd see you again."

"Are you okay?" Aiden moves my hand off my face, sits up, and looks directly into my soul.

"Yeah."

"You're not very convincing. Do you not want to go back? Would you really have left me without saying anything?"

"I told you goodbye."

"Goodbye for break, not goodbye forever. In St. Croix, you said you're always coming back for me. Did you mean it?"

"I said that I was coming back for you *then*."

"And then I said you better always come back for me. You agreed."

"No, I didn't."

He laughs. "Yeah, you did. You squeezed my hand. I knew what it meant."

I stop smiling and sigh. "Aiden, things are so up in the air. I shouldn't be making promises to anyone."

"Then answer me this. Are you glad you're here with me now?"

His question cuts through all the *What if* scenarios in my brain and speaks directly to my heart. And my heart knows there is only one way to reply. "Yes." I close my eyes, willing back tears.

"Don't cry. No more crying."

"Then stop making me cry." I laugh.

"So, being with me makes you cry?" He chuckles as he clutches at his chest. "Ouch, that hurts."

I place my hand over his and say seriously, "It's the thought of *not* being here with you that makes me cry."

He cradles my face in his palms. "I was serious, Keatyn. Wherever you go, I go. Whatever family stuff you need to deal with, I'll help you. You don't have to face it alone."

I can't say anything. His determination—his belief that we can accomplish anything together—is so touching. I lean forward and thank him with my lips.

AFTER KISSING FOR a bit, he lays his head back in my lap. "You're going to sleep the whole flight, aren't you?"

He gives me a wink, then shuts his gorgeous green eyes.

For a while, I just watch him. The way his breathing slows down. The way his hair lies against my stomach. His long, dark brown eyelashes splayed across his cheeks. I run my hand across his forehead and into his hair, causing him to sigh.

Once I know he's asleep, I grab my phone and get to work.

Starting with a message to B.

> **Me:** We got cut off during all the craziness of your winning, so I didn't get to tell you how proud I am of you. I'm ready to start implementing the takeover. Can we discuss tomorrow night? Say 12:30pm EST? I'm ready to get our lives back.
>
> **B:** Me too, Keats. Things are so up in the air. You know, like, personally.
>
> **Me:** Yeah, I know. B?
>
> **B:** What?
>
> **Me:** I wanna go home.
>
> **B:** Me too. Tomorrow night <3

I stare at the heart until my eyes go fuzzy.

Then at Aiden, who's now sleeping on his side, one strong arm curled above his head and the other hugging my waist.

That's when the guilt sets in.

The guilt.

I feel guilty. Guilty for feeling the way I do about Aiden.

Guilty about the promises I've made to them both.

And guilty for feeling happy about the heart.

I shake my head as I message Garrett, telling myself to take it one step at a time.

> **Me:** Meeting tomorrow. The usual place. 9:30am?
>
> **Garrett:** I'll be there.

I send the same message to Cooper.

Cooper: *On your way back to school under protest?*
Me: *Something like that. Can we meet tonight, late? Say midnight? I need your help.*
Cooper: *See you then.*

After getting all that set up, I do something I should've done on break. I shop for B's birthday presents. Since his birthday is on the fourth, I don't have time to ship them to me, wrap them, and ship them together, so I'll just have them sent straight to his hotel.

I'm not sure what to get.

I end up with a big coffee table book on the history of surfing. On the card, I write, *Surfing's come a long way and so have you. I'm proud of all you've accomplished in such a short time. Happy Birthday, B. Love, Keats.*

Next I decide on a Vuitton passport cover and add another note. *So your passport looks as good as your luggage.*

The last gift I order is a Sector 9 skateboard with an ocean wave design. *For when you're not on the water.*

After getting all that taken care of, I close my eyes and start devising a new plan.

DIFFERENT KINDS OF LOVE.
5:30PM

AIDEN CARRIES MY bags to my dorm, kisses me on the porch, then goes to unpack.

I open the door to my room, still trying to figure out how I'm going to fight Vincent from here, and interrupt Katie and Bryce making out on her bed.

"Oh, I'm sorry," I say, as Katie pulls her shirt down and Bryce fumbles with his pants. "Um, I'm just dropping off my bags! Talk to you later!" I drop my bags, shut the door, and decide to head over to the boys' dorm to see if Dallas or Riley are back. I need a big hug from both of them.

As I walk the short distance to the dorm, I realize it's freaking cold out and I'm not wearing a coat. I wrap my arms around myself and run as fast as I can in my sandals.

I rush down the hall and almost run into Dawson coming out of his room.

"You think you're still on vacation? You must be freezing in that dress."

"Yeah, well, Bryce and Katie were kinda busy in my room, so I didn't get to change."

He grabs my arm and pulls me into his room. "I always end up giving you my sweatshirts," he says as he throws one at me.

"Thank you. How was your break?" I ask while pulling it over my head.

"I think I should be asking you that. I heard about Aiden showing up."

"Yeah, that was a surprise. And an even bigger surprise that I let him come with me."

Dawson pulls his sweatshirt strings in a familiar way, bringing me face to face with him. "You look hot. Tan and hot. But stressed. Still not getting any?"

I back away a little. "I'm not answering that question."

He shrugs. "You don't have too. I already know the answer."

"You going to offer to take care of my stress?"

He smirks at me. "Actually, no."

"Really? Did you meet someone or something?"

"Kinda. Someone I already knew. She was at our club this weekend. Her boyfriend broke up with her and she was upset."

"Did you heal her broken heart?"

"From the inside out," he says with a laugh, pulling me to sit on his bed with him.

I lean against his headboard, bring my knees up to my chest, and pull the sweatshirt down over them. "Really?"

"No, *not* really. She was too upset. It's funny because it kinda reminded me of when we talked at the Cave that first night."

"I wanted to fix your broken heart."

"You did. So aren't you gonna ask me about her?"

I grab his hands like I would one of my girlfriends, bounce on the bed, and giggle. "Yes, tell me all about her."

"So this is what you're resorting to?" Jake says, walking in through the bathroom. "Good thing I'm back so we can talk about all the dirty details."

"Jake! I missed you! But I'm finally warm, so you'll have to come over here and give me a hug."

Jake waves his hands in the air, runs over to the bed on his tiptoes, and says in a high-pitched voice, "Monroe! I missed you too, girl. Did you and Aiden make whoopee yet?"

Dawson and I both laugh. "We're discussing Dawson's love life, not mine."

"So does that mean you told her about Brooke?"

"Brooke?! Really? When she was going to wear your jersey, you told me she was practically married."

Dawson raises his eyebrows. "Apparently, she was more married than he was. She thought they were going to have an amazing Thanksgiving reunion, but he stopped by her house, said he wanted to break up, and left."

"Oh, that's horrible, but I can totally relate. One night my ex took me out for a fancy dinner. I thought he was going to ask me out, but instead he told me he was leaving."

"Girls always think things are more serious than they are," Jake states with a roll of his eyes.

"Well, maybe if guys wouldn't tell girls they love them when they don't really love them that wouldn't be an issue."

"There's lots of different kinds of love," Dawson teases.

"And for most of you, it's the kind of love that wants in their pants."

"That's why I never tell girls I love them," Jake stresses.

"You've never told a girl that? But you're so romantic—well, when you want to be."

"That's because I'm a good actor," he says. "Of course, I can play that part. Speaking of that. I broke the news to my parents that I'm going to NYU. Got the acceptance letter and everything. Me and Dawes both."

"That's where you're going, too? I'm so proud of you," I say to Dawson.

He gives me a sweet grin. And I know that Jake is absolutely right. There are lots of different kinds of love. And I do love Dawson. Jake too, for that matter. "Tell me about Brooke."

"Well, we kissed," he says, actually looking happy about it.

"*Just* kissed?"

"Yeah."

"Whitney and Brooke don't really get along well, do they?"

Jake rolls his eyes again, "Uh, no, they don't. Speaking of that. Does anyone have the scoop on what went down with Chelsea? Is she coming back to school? What she did to you sucked."

"I heard she's coming back," Dawson says. "Brooke said she was worried about how to handle it with the team."

"Oh, I wouldn't wanna be one of the head cheerleaders now," Jake says. "She's got her work cut out for her."

"Honestly, the drama might be just what Brooke needs."

"Why?" Dawson asks.

"Because, it will give her something to focus on besides her boy misery."

Dawson slaps me on the shoulder and Jake says, "Monroe, I think you missed a step. Dawes wants to be the thing she focuses on."

"Oh, well, good for you."

"You're not jealous?" Dawson says with a grin.

"I am so, so jealous. But I will try to hide my grief."

I realize that, in a way, I'm kinda like Brooke. Eastbrooke might be just the thing to distract me, too.

When Dallas and Riley walk through the door, I'm very glad I'm back. I would have missed them terribly.

"Dallas! What did you do to your hair?"

Dallas rubs his buzz cut. "You know everyone at home thinks I'm at military school, right? So I got buzzed on the plane."

I hop up and run my hand across it while he gives me a hug. "You look cute. Older. I like it."

"Well, here's hoping the female population of Eastbrooke echoes that sentiment, because there are eight newly single varsity cheerleaders that may require my attention."

I give Riley a big hug and he whispers in my ear, "I want to hear about your trip."

Dallas overhears him and says loudly, "I think we *all* want to hear about your trip."

"The Cave it is, then. Tonight."

Dawson points to my sweatshirt and says, "Bring a coat, Keatie."

"And here I was gonna suggest she bring some hotties," Jake says with a laugh.

"Oh, that too," Dallas agrees. "That too."

"Wouldn't they expect us to party tonight?"

Jake thinks about it. "Hmm, maybe we should wait a day or two."

"Sounds good, *prefect*. I'll see you all later."

Riley accompanies me upstairs while Dallas stays in Dawson's room to bullshit some more.

"So you and Aiden worked things out?"

"Yeah. I hear that's partially because of you."

He shrugs. "I figured I owed him since I broke his nose. Did he do the dirt?"

"Yeah, he did."

Riley shakes his head. "Why? I told him it was the dumbest thing ever."

"Because he knew I'd love it. I was going to make him leave until he gave me the dirt."

"Girls . . ." he says, laughing and shaking his head again.

"Speaking of girls," I interrupt him. "How's Ariela?"

"I miss her like crazy but, thankfully, she'll be back soon. I want to change my shirt and stuff before she gets here."

"I'm surprised you don't want to greet her shirtless."

"Naw, I want her to rip it off me."

When we get to Aiden's door, he bangs on it, and says in a girly voice, "Aiden, open up. I wanna fuck." And then runs down the hall to his room.

My hand is still up in the knock position when a sexy voice startles me. "Bonjour."

"Aiden, where did you come from?"

"Logan's room." He points to the door between his room and the stairs. "Maggie is in there, unless, *you know*, you need my services now," he jokes.

"You know that was Riley." I laugh.

"Did you get unpacked?"

"No. Bryce and Katie were, uh, getting reacquainted in my room. I just dropped my bag and left."

"Where have you been?"

"I was on my way up here, but Dawson pulled me into his room."

Aiden clenches his back teeth, his jaw tightening. "I see."

"Aiden, he's my friend. And he was telling me about his weekend. And Jake was there, and then Dallas and Riley showed up."

"Well, I'm glad you ended up here."

"Does that mean you're gonna let me in your room?"

He gives me a forced grin. "Only if you take off Dawson's sweatshirt first."

I look down, remembering I have it on. "Better he give me his sweatshirt than offer to warm me up himself, right?"

Aiden pushes his hands under the sweatshirt, purposefully running them up my sides. As he strips the sweatshirt off me, it pulls my dress up in the front and gives Aiden a flash of my thong.

"Aiden!" I yell, my voice muffled by the thick sweatshirt swaddling my head. It's dark and I can't move my arms.

He pulls me into his room, shuts the door, finishes pulling the sweatshirt off, then starts stripping off my dress as he says, "I think I can find a way to keep you warm without a sweatshirt on. Without *anything* on."

I'LL DOUBLE IT.
12:04AM

I'M MEETING WITH Cooper, laying out my plan.

He listens to the whole thing without interruption.

"So, what do you think?"

"If your life weren't on the line, it'd be a great plan."

"Well, that's where you come in. I'd like you to quit working for Garrett and work for me."

"Oh, really?"

"Yeah. Whatever he's paying you, I'll double it."

He raises an eyebrow at me.

"Fine. I'll triple it."

"You suck at negotiation," he laughs.

"That's what agents are for," I laugh in reply.

"Why do you want me to work for you?" He looks at me intently as he leans on his forearms.

"Because I already almost got you fired. And . . . I'm probably going to ask you to help me with some things Garrett may not approve of."

"You've asked me a lot of questions regarding pushing Vincent. Is that part of your plan?"

"Yes."

"And how do you think that will end?"

I fiddle with the string on Aiden's hoodie, the one he pulled over my head as I was leaving, hoping Cooper will forget the question.

"Answer me," he says firmly.

"How do *you* think it will end?" I whisper.

"With one of you dead."

I nod. "That's what I think too. And, either way, it's a win."

"How is you ending up dead a win?"

"Because if he kills me, I know you'll get the evidence we need to put him away for life. Which means my family will be free of him. That's all I want. If I survive, I'll give you a really big bonus."

"I don't want your money, Keatyn. I'd do this for free."

"I know you would, but your life will be in danger too."

He says softly, "I won't let him win."

"There are a lot of ways it could go down. Lots of different endings to the script."

"Like what?"

"He kidnaps me, you come get me, and he goes to prison. Or, he kidnaps me, you can't find me, I escape, and then he goes to prison. Or, he kidnaps me, kills me, and you make sure he either goes to prison for life. Or . . ."

"Or what?"

"I'm going to update my will this week."

He squints at me. "Once I get over the shock of a seventeen-year-old even having a will, I'm going to ask you why."

"If I'm murdered, there will be a provision giving you a large sum of money. I want you to use the money to move your family somewhere there's no extradition. Then I want you to hire a professional to kill him."

Cooper shuts his eyes tightly. "Is there a happier ending? One where you aren't kidnapped or dead?"

I sigh and tell him the rest of my plan.

"When the time is right, we're going to let him kidnap me."

"Are you nuts?"

"Probably. We'll worry about that later. For now, you'll only have to worry when we start baiting him."

"*Baiting* him?"

"Cooper, I understand why your sister didn't want to change her life when she was being stalked. I get it, probably more than anyone. But the difference is she wasn't ready for him. We will be."

He still doesn't look convinced.

I jut my chin out and add, "It's either that, or I go back to Malibu by myself."

He closes his eyes and shakes his head. "I'll give you an answer regarding my employment in the morning. Go get some sleep."

Monday, November 28th
GOT BLOWN UP.
9:30AM

WHEN I GET to the diner, Garrett and Cooper are already sitting at a booth in the back. I skip the hostess stand and join them.

"Hey, Garrett," I say coolly, taking a seat. Be strong, Keatyn. It's time for you to take charge.

"Good morning," he replies.

Cooper rolls tired eyes at me by way of a greeting.

"So, let's hear this plan of yours," Garrett says, cutting to the chase.

"My *plan* got blown up the second you made me leave the island. Look. I want to preface what I'm about to say with a thank you. I sincerely appreciate what you've done thus far in keeping me and my family safe. And you've been especially kind to me." I sigh. "But, when you threatened me—no, worse: when you made Tommy threaten me—it forced me to take a long look at things. You've purposely divided us. And I understand that we shouldn't be in the same location, but what I don't understand is why you haven't been forthcoming about all that's been going on. It's tearing my family apart, Garrett, and I won't allow it anymore. So, starting now, *everything* goes through me. All bills. All plans."

Garrett says, "I have a separate agreement with your mom."

"She'll be calling you to void that later today. I don't want to argue with you. I want to partner with you. And we're going to begin this partnership with you telling me what's been going on with her."

Cooper gives me a little smile over the top of his coffee cup.

"Fine," Garrett says. "You know that everything I do is in *all* of your best interests. The threatening letters didn't stop when your mother moved to

Vancouver. In fact, they have become increasingly worse. Then, there was a small breach at the Vancouver property."

"Breach?"

"The fence surrounding the property was slashed and black roses were left on the swing set."

My heart drops into my stomach.

"You and your mother are a lot alike, Keatyn. She's trying to bear the weight of it."

"Surely, you can see the physical toll it's taken on her?"

"Yes."

"But she won't listen to you, right?"

"Yeah, kinda like when I had to have your bags packed."

"Touché." I blink slowly, then continue. "So, basically, the original plan hasn't worked. You said that if he couldn't find me, he'd lose interest. But the opposite has happened. It's getting worse for my family *because* he can't find me."

Garrett nods. "I'd say that's an accurate assessment."

"Do you think he wants us both?"

"Based on the letters, he only wants you."

"So he's threatening to hurt everyone Mom loves if I don't come out of hiding? Is that it?"

I know by the look on Garrett's face that it is.

"Shit," I say. "That's why she doesn't call me. That's why she was freaked out when I showed up at their house. She was afraid."

"She's pushing you away to keep you safe."

My eyes fill with tears. "But what about the girls? She'd want to . . ." And then it hits me. What she's been doing. "Oh my god."

"What?"

"Mom's plan is just like mine. Only she's using the press to help her."

"I'm not following," Garrett says. His and Cooper's faces are mirrors of confusion.

"The stories in the press. The rumors of the affair with her bodyguard. Tommy and Millie cheating. She's setting it up so that when she leaves Tommy, people will expect it."

"She's leaving Tommy?"

"I think so. Remember when you told me that for witness protection sometimes you make the family believe that the witness is dead? Same thing. I don't think Tommy has a clue. She wants his reaction to be real."

"Why would she leave Tommy?" Cooper asks. "And how would it change what's going on with Vincent?"

"She can't pretend to be dead, so she's doing the only other thing she can. She's leaving them. She'll get the girls to France and then leave them with James. Think about it. *She's scary skinny. Tommy's affair is driving her to drink or do drugs. She's not stable.* She's leaving Tommy and he'll get custody of the girls."

"Shit," Garrett mutters as he quickly recovers from the shock of it. "I knew she agreed to France too easily."

"She wants them safe. But then what?" I ask. "She checks into rehab? Lives by herself? Or maybe even something bolder. Like, maybe she didn't really cancel the *To Maddie, with Love* press tour." I'm thinking out loud, now.

Garrett shakes his head. "I was under the impression she cancelled the tour. If she's going, she won't have security."

"And maybe that's what she wants. She told me it was all her fault. If she wasn't who she is, then her children wouldn't be in danger." I stop and look Garrett dead in the eyes. "I asked Cooper this question, but I'd like your opinion. What do you think would happen if I walked into Vincent's production office and asked to audition for the role?"

Garrett winces. "I really don't think that's a good idea."

"I know, but why? What could he do? Give me the role?"

"Well, if he's caught off guard by it, there's no telling what he would do. Sociopaths like to plan. They are *obsessive* in their planning."

"Right, but what happens when things *don't* go according to their plan?"

"They become more unhinged, mentally."

"Would it cause Vincent to just react? And more importantly, if he couldn't plan, would he start making mistakes?"

Garrett nods. "Their behavior becomes unpredictable. Which is bad. But, yes, if pushed, one would assume he wouldn't be as careful."

"That's exactly what I want. And I'm pretty sure it's what Mom wants."

"Excuse me?"

"I want him to start making mistakes, so we can send him to jail. And I think Mom wants him to kidnap her for the same reason."

Garrett holds his head like he has a headache. "I thought my job was to keep you both safe."

"I know what I'm planning to do is risky. I'm hoping you and Cooper will help to contain that risk."

"So tell me this plan."

"Well, assuming that I'm probably right about Mom, the first thing we need to do is convince her to stay in France. You just can't tell her the part about me."

"What is it with you two?" Garrett says, shaking his head. "I thought you wanted everything out in the open?"

I smirk at him. "Well, maybe not *everything*. So, I have a three-pronged approach. I want to attack Vincent from all sides. He needs to know what it feels like to start losing the things he loves. First, his business. Brooklyn and I are going to work with someone his dad knows to start a hostile takeover of his production company. We'll form a bunch of shell corporations—probably foreign, so that Vincent doesn't know who's behind them. We recently discovered that he's heavily leveraged. And, more importantly, so is his company."

"What will buying his company accomplish?"

"Do you know *why* he's heavily leveraged?"

"No."

"Because he's *personally* financing a large portion of the remake of *A Day at the Lake.*"

"Your mom's movie," Cooper states.

"But he doesn't personally own the options. The production company does."

"And if he loses his company—" Cooper says, as Garrett finishes his thought. "He loses the movie."

"Exactly."

Garrett nods. "I like that, actually. It will give him something else to focus on."

"While we focus on him."

"How?"

"I know you used to follow him, but I want more. I want inside knowledge. So, I looked at his company website last night and I have an idea. His personal assistant is in her mid-twenties and single. Based on her social media, she's a regular at a bar called *Reggae*. I was thinking you might have another employee like Cooper. Young. Good-looking. They become friends. She talks about her job. About her boss."

"Inside information is always good."

"What we learn from her will help me decide how to proceed on the third prong of the attack. Garrett, are you absolutely positive that there won't be any breaches in security at the house in France?"

"We've fenced the perimeter of the property. 24-hour camera surveillance. Armed guards. It's like Eastbrooke, only better."

"Good, because the second prong of the attack will happen organically. The

To Maddie, with Love publicity tour. The worldwide premieres. It all kicks off with the extend trailer premiere during the *Victoria's Secret Fashion Show.*"

"We assumed that's part of what sent him over the edge to begin with," Garrett tells Cooper. He turns to me and says, "So what's the third prong?"

"Me."

"No."

"Yes. We're going to let him see me. Everywhere. When the time is right."

"When will the time be right?"

"I'm going to audition for a role in Tommy's next movie and, if I get it, I'll be filming some scenes in New York City over Christmas break. They can make the crew sign non-disclosure agreements, so no one talks about my role until we're ready. They start filming the big action scenes that I would be a part of in March, so I thought that's when we'd announce it. Do a big press release. Flood the tabloids with pictures of me. I'll become a wild child in the eyes of the press, but it will all be carefully orchestrated. It'll look like I'm out and about all the time. Different guy on my arm in every picture. Drunk coming out of the club. Smoking pot. Skanky photos. *Anything* to get on the cover of a magazine. But all Vincent will know is where I was *last* night. Not where I actually am."

"And where will you actually be?"

"Don't laugh, but Cooper and I will be living on a boat."

"A boat?"

"Well, more like a yacht. There are some details we'll have to work out when the time is right, but no one tracks boats. Not like they do aircraft. So, in theory, I could drive, or maybe even helicopter, to where the yacht is, and sail to a different location. Never a night in the same place, basically."

"You've really thought this through," Cooper states, smirking at me. I think he might be proud.

"And what about Eastbrooke?"

"I promise that I'll stay here until March. So, what do you think?"

Garrett smiles at me. "I will admit, your plan has some merit."

"Oh, I forgot to mention that starting now, Cooper works for me."

"Is that right?" Garrett asks Cooper directly.

Cooper looks him in the eye. Man to man. And says, "That's right."

I breathe a sigh of relief. He hadn't told me his decision yet.

Garrett slips me a forged doctor's note. "Why don't you get back to school?"

I glance at Cooper. "You're going to stay here and talk, huh?"

They both nod, so I grab my keys and head to my car.

WHEN I GET there, I call my mom.

Surprisingly, she answers.

"Hey, Mom. I really need to talk to you. Do you have a few minutes?"

"Sure, honey," she says. "I'm just finishing up some packing."

"I'm glad you and the girls are going to France."

Mom gives me a little, "A-hem," in agreement. I know her. She doesn't like to lie.

"This thing with Vincent has been tough on all of us. You need some time off."

"I'm fine, Keatyn."

"No, Mom. You're not. And I know you planted all the stuff in the press about the affairs and about your health."

Mom lets out a big sigh. "Does Tommy know?"

"Not yet, but he will. Don't let this ruin your relationship. You have to stop lying to Tommy. And me. We can handle the truth. Seriously. And I *am* going to handle it."

"Keatyn, you're just a child."

"No, I'm not. My sisters are children. I met with Garrett today. I know about the breach in security. I know Vincent hasn't stopped sending you stuff. Scary stuff."

Mom starts to cry. "He . . . He . . . left black roses on the swing set. Four of them. One for each of the girls. He sent a photo of Tommy getting out of a car in the city, and it was photoshopped so . . . so that . . . Tommy had been shot in the head. I can't do this anymore. If he wants me, then he can have me."

"But that's the thing, Mom. He doesn't want you. He wants me."

"Well, he can't have you!"

"He's not going to. Garrett and I have a plan that takes you and the girls out of the mix. But I need your help. With the press."

"How?"

"I need you to announce that for your health and well-being, you're taking a break from the movie industry. If they ask where you're going or what you're doing, you'll have no comment."

"They'll ask about Tommy."

"That's an easy answer. Tommy will be filming *Retribution* in New York and you will not be joining him."

"Everyone will assume we're not together anymore."

"That's exactly what you wanted, isn't it?"

"Yes, but then . . ." Mom starts sobbing. "I've been trying to hold it together. But it's so hard. I've missed you so much, Keatyn. But I've been so afraid. Afraid he'd get my phone and find your number. Afraid someone would overhear me talking to you. I needed you to stay safe. You're my baby. And this is all my fault. I thought if I left the girls safe with James and went on the press tour that maybe he'd just take me instead."

Tears stream down my face. I had almost started to think that she didn't care about me anymore.

"Remember New York, Mom? When Vincent chased after me?"

"Yes."

"He was following you, but it was *me* that he chased. It's *me* that he wants. And that means it's time for me to take control of this situation."

"Take control how?"

"Well, to start with, Garrett works for me now. You have to promise, no making up plans of your own, okay?"

"Okay," she says cautiously.

I can tell she hasn't fully committed.

"You and I agree on one important thing, Mom. And that's keeping the girls safe. Go to France. Relax. Eat. Get some sleep. Have fun with the girls. And know that Vincent is going to be busy with other stuff."

"What other stuff?"

"Well, aside from the premieres and press that's due to start on your movie, we're going to mess with his business."

"Does he care that much about his business?"

"His business owns the rights to remake your movie. The movie seems to be the core of his obsession. If he is at risk of losing it . . ."

"He won't have time to worry about us."

"That's the theory, yes."

"I like that. It feels like we're fighting back."

"I like it too."

"Does Garrett really think it will work?"

"Yes, he's completely on board," I say confidently. *Well, okay, like, mostly on board.* "So, are you in?"

"Do you promise me that everything you do will be approved by Garrett?"

"Garrett or Cooper," I reply, not wanting to lie to her.

She exhales heavily, like maybe I've lifted a weight off her shoulders.

"Then I'm in."

"Good. I love you, Mom. I have to get back to school, but call me once you get settled, okay?"

"I will. And I love you too."

YOUR ARM CANDY.
CERAMICS

"WE NEED TO talk about French weekend," Jake tells me.

"What about it?"

"You and me under the lights," he says.

"What are you talking about?"

"The drama department is in charge of the murder mystery dinner theater for Saturday night."

"I know. I think it will be so much fun."

"But you didn't sign up for it."

"I have a date."

"Come on. It's good for your improv skills. And you need to play the movie star."

"But I got the most perfect dress. And I wanna sit with Aiden."

"You and Aiden really need to work on your communication."

"What do you mean?"

"He agreed this morning that you should do it, *and* he even volunteered to play your arm candy. He said something about needing the practice. So I wrote him a part. He'll play your lover slash arm candy. And everyone is wearing their own clothes."

"He really said that?"

I smile, remembering how Aiden came to almost every one of my rehearsals. How he said he'd be my arm candy. How he put his hand on my knee. How he told me I lit up the stage.

"Yeah, he did," Jake says. "We'll all be sitting in the audience with everyone, eating and pretending we're on a riverboat going up the Seine together. Then, when someone gets killed, right before dessert, we start." He holds up a very large clay penis and shakes it at me. "Come on. It'll be fun."

Bryce laughs and makes a naughty comment about coming and penises.

The teacher walks behind Jake, grabs it out of his hand, and swats him on the head with it. "No vulgarity, Mr. Worth."

Bryce and I manage to stifle our giggles while watching the teacher take Jake's *art* to the back room.

"What do you wanna bet she's going to put that in *her* kiln?" Jake jokes.

"Jake!" I screech, laughing.

"Miss Monroe!" My name is yelled from the back room. "Come back here, please."

"Yeah, *come* back there," Bryce says, still cracking up.

I smack Jake on the shoulder as I walk by.

I peek in the back room.

Our teacher is holding my bowl in her hands. "Look!"

"It survived the kiln?!"

She smiles at me. "Yes! And I have a beautiful opalescent overglaze I think you should put on it. It'll add sheen and highlights without distracting from the craftsmanship." She digs through a drawer of glazes then holds up a bottle. "Here it is. See?"

"That is really pretty. I'll work on it tomorrow."

"Keatyn, I'm really proud of you for trying again. The foundation was the key. It's why this new version didn't fall apart."

I look at my gorgeous bowl and think about Aiden.

WHEN THE BELL rings, I grab my phone and text him.

Me: *Meet me at ceramics!! I wanna show you something!!*
Hottie God: *Be right there :)*

After everyone files out, Aiden steps in the classroom. His tie is loosened, one of his shirt-tails is untucked, and his blazer frames his broad shoulders. He looks like he walked straight off the pages of a magazine. He kisses my cheek in greeting.

"What's up?"

"Remember my project? How it didn't survive the kiln because it didn't have a strong foundation?"

"Of course. It was the inspiration for our love mansion."

"Guess what!?"

"What?"

"I made a new one—one with a stronger foundation—and it survived!" I grab his jacket sleeve, leading him to the back room. "Look!" I say, pointing at it.

"Wow, that's really cool. I love the design. All the scrolly pieces. You know what this means, don't you?"

"That I'm amazing at ceramics?"

"It means if you can't take the heat, stay out of the kiln."

"I don't get it."

He runs a fingertip across the top of the bowl, then grabs my hips, pulling me close. "It means we're going to survive the kiln, too. No matter how high the heat."

SLIGHTLY EXAGGERATED.
LUNCH

ANNIE PLOPS DOWN next to me at lunch. "I'm breaking up with Ace."

"What?! Why?" I ask in shock.

"Because he's an idiot."

"Why's he an idiot?" Aiden asks, leaning toward Annie and putting his hand on my knee.

I try to ignore the effect his hand has on my knee. Actually, on my entire body.

"I don't know; maybe I'm the idiot," she says. "Because I know that something happened when he was home. He hardly called or texted me. And since we've been back, he's been different."

"Did you ask him about it?" Aiden asks.

"Yes, and he had no answer. Just sort of shrugged like it was no big deal. I'm sorry, but if you love someone you don't ignore them for four days!"

"Maybe there's an explanation?" I offer.

Jake sets his tray down at the table and says to me, "Did you get in trouble in ceramics?"

"No, she just wanted to show me that my new bowl survived the kiln."

Jake puts his hand up to high five me, so I smack it. "Did she put my sculpture in the kiln?"

"No, but it was just lying there. She hadn't destroyed it."

"I think she wants me."

I laugh at him. "You're silly."

"What'd you make, Jake?" Dallas asks.

"A mold of my dick. Teacher was hot for it."

"Nice," Dallas says.

"If that huge thing was a mold, I wanna sleep with you too," I tease.

Aiden's grip on my knee tightens for just a second. Like a flinch.

Jake rolls his eyes and laughs. "Fine, it may be slightly exaggerated."

"Ha! I knew it!" I laugh with him.

"Can we have a serious conversation?" Annie pleads. "I'm freaking out!"

"What are you freaking out about?" Jake asks her.

She gives Jake the eye. "Do you know what Ace did over Thanksgiving break?"

"Went home?" Jake replies.

"Well, then let me ask you this, Jake. Would you have texted your girlfriend over Thanksgiving break?"

"Uh, sure?" Jake says, not very convincingly.

"What if you didn't? What reason would you have for not texting her?"

"Maybe my phone was dead?"

"What else?"

"I was busy?"

"Exactly!" she says, pointing at him. "That's what I thought! But busy with what—or *whom*—is the question."

"Annie, do you really think Ace cheated on you?"

"I don't know but, as you can see, he's not sitting with me today. Look where he's sitting."

"I don't see him."

"He's sitting by *Chelsea*."

Aiden's eyes get big and his hand finches against my knee again.

And I know.

"Aiden and Logan," I say, "did Chelsea text either of you over break?"

Aiden nods.

So does Logan.

Maggie's eyes get big. "She what? What did you say? Did you reply?"

"Yeah. I told her not to text me again."

Maggie narrows her eyes. "That's all?"

Logan pulls out his phone and shows her.

Maggie reads it. "Oh, nice. She said, and I quote, *We should hook up. You know you and Maggie are never going to work.* That little bitch."

Logan leans his head against hers. "Did you see what I wrote?"

Maggie doesn't read this out loud, but her smile tells us all we need to know.

I turn to Aiden. "What did she say to you?"

"Can we talk about it later?" he says.

"Uh, sure," I say, but I'm not at all sure. In fact, I'm pissed. Because if he said something like Logan did, he would've shown me now.

I move my knee out from under his hand, crossing my legs and turning toward Annie. "It sounds like she is up to her old tricks again."

"I bet she just sent them to Aiden and your friends' boyfriends to get back at you."

"You're probably right." I turn and say, "Bryce, did she text you, too?"

"Yeah, I told her to fuck off. She made a sexual comment about that to which I didn't bother replying."

Katie grins at him and runs her hand down his arm. They're so cute together.

I know I should trust Aiden. I have no reason to doubt him. But it's killing me.

Feasting on my stomach.

I can't eat.

I can't stop wondering what Aiden said to her.

And why he won't tell me.

And I can't even look at him. I just look straight down at my food and pretend to eat.

This is another reason why I shouldn't have come back here. I can't take any more drama in my life.

About halfway through lunch, Aiden reaches under the table, putting his hand back on my knee.

I was pretending to be absorbed in a conversation Jake and Bryce were having and his touch makes me jump.

I bolt upright, grab my tray, and say to the table, "I have to get to class early. See ya later."

I throw my lunch in the trash, deposit my tray, and avoid Chelsea's table.

Whitney says, "Keatyn," as I walk by hers.

I sit down with her, Dawson, Brooke, and Peyton.

"Hey, how was your break?" I ask her politely.

She doesn't answer my question. "Did Chelsea text Ace over break?"

I nod sadly. "Yeah. Logan, Bryce, and Aiden too."

"She wants to get back at you."

"Probably."

"It's because we're divided, so she thinks she stands a chance. In fact, I was thinking . . ."

She leans over and whispers in my ear.

And what she says makes me smile. "You're right. Tomorrow night, it is."

A WEIRD MATCH.
FRENCH

I GET TO French class early, and Miss Praline says, "Keatyn, would you mind missing class today?"

"Not at all!" I practically scream. I really don't think I can stand to sit here with Aiden, wondering the whole time what the heck Chelsea said to him.

"Great. I need someone to go to The Market and choose the picnic basket assortments for the French club to sell. Would you like to take Aiden or Annie with you?"

I shake my head. "Neither one of them is doing very well in class. I'd hate for them to miss it."

"Yes, you're right. You don't mind going by yourself?"

"Honestly, it'd probably be easier to have just one person choose."

"All right," she says, writing out a pass for me. "I'll call them and let them know you're on your way."

I practically skip out the door.

WHEN I GET to the office, Dawson is just leaving.

"Whatcha doing?" I ask him.

"Just dropping off something for my math teacher. What are you doing?"

"Going to choose the picnic basket assortment for French weekend."

"Take me with you? I didn't do my math homework."

"Sure, why not?" I look down at the note. "She didn't put my name on it."

We check out with the office and he offers to drive.

"I saw Brooke was sitting with you today."

"Yeah, and, surprisingly, Whitney was really cool about it. But I guess she's all into Shark. Is it me, or is that kind of a weird match?"

"Shark gets a lot of girls. He's cute."

"Yeah, but . . ."

"I agree. It's kinda surprising. But he complimented her Court dress, and I watched her blush. Shark has charisma. And he's super smart. He's the kind of guy that will go places in life."

"True. And Whitney would like that."

"I don't think that's what they're about though. I think he turns her on."

"Shark kind of reminds me of her dad," Dawson laughs.

"I've never heard about him."

"She doesn't talk about him much. Her parents went through a nasty divorce sophomore year. Her mom told her that her dad never wanted to see either of them again."

"So the guy at Homecoming that looked perfect. That wasn't her dad?"

"Stepdad. Her mom was remarried within six months."

"I didn't care much for her mother. Or her bitchy sister."

"They think their shit doesn't stink. They aren't very nice to Whitney. I always felt bad for her."

"It would suck."

"Speaking of suck," Dawson says with a laugh. "Is it me or does that night at the Cave seem like so long ago."

"A lot has happened since then."

"I'm glad we're still friends."

"I am too. Dawson, did Chelsea text you over break?"

"No."

"Did she text Riley?"

"No. And I think he would have said something because it would've pissed him off."

"She texted Aiden. At lunch, he wouldn't tell me what she said. He said we'd talk about it later."

"And you're freaking out, assuming it's going to be something bad?"

"Kind of. Logan told us what Chelsea said and he let Maggie read what he said back. It made her happy. Aiden didn't tell me that she texted him. And that bothers me."

"Maybe that's why he didn't tell you. Did you have fun together on your trip?"

"Yeah, it was really nice. And it felt like we figured things out. How to communicate better. How not to jump to conclusions. How not to get mad and walk away."

"Does he still speak to your soul?"

"Yeah. And that's why he scares me."

"Keatie, don't let it."

"Does Brooke speak to your soul?"

He shrugs. "I don't know. She's fun to kiss."

I roll my eyes at him.

He smirks. "But, then, you were fun to kiss, too. That's what I loved about our relationship. It was fun and easy. No drama."

I raise an eyebrow at him.

"Okay, there was some drama. But it was outside drama, not drama with us. Until the Whitney thing."

"More like Whitney *things*. Do you think she's changed?"

"I actually think she has. What she did for you was pretty cool. And, today, she didn't say anything bitchy about Brooke sitting with us."

Dawson parks in front of The Market.

"I already asked Brooke to be my date this weekend. I want to impress her with a kickass picnic. You're going to do some extravagant options, right?"

"I am now," I laugh.

NOT AS FUN WITHOUT YOU.
DANCE

"What's wrong, Maggie?"

She's putting her pompoms in her locker slowly and staring at them like she'll never see them again.

She sits down, slumps her shoulders, and drops her head. "I think this will be my last semester at Eastbrooke. I don't know where I'm going to go or what I'm going to do." Her voice cracks. "I haven't told Logan and it's killing me. And I half hoped he would've said something to Chelsea so I could get mad and break up with him. That way it will be easier when I have to leave."

I sit down next to her and put my arm around her. "Maggie! You can't leave! Why would you want to?"

"I *don't* want to. You know how I went to Logan's for most of Thanksgiving break?"

"Yeah."

"I didn't tell him why."

"What happened?"

"You know that my mom got remarried a few years ago?"

"Yeah, you've mentioned that."

"When I go home, I feel like an outsider. Like I don't belong. Last summer was horrible. I was so desperate I wanted to go live with my dad."

"Why would that be desperate?"

She looks down again and starts crying. "My mom comes from a pretty well-off family. She fell in love with my dad but her family never liked him. Said he was worthless. I think eventually he started feeling that way. I remember when we'd go to my grandparents' for holidays. They were never really nice to him. And my dad would always drink a lot. He started using drugs. My mom found out. He was spending a lot of money on them, I guess. I was only eleven when they divorced. Mom got full custody of me, and I'm hardly allowed to see him."

"Did he show up at Thanksgiving or something?"

"No. I don't like her new husband and I'm pretty sure the feeling is mutual. It's all about them and their baby. *Their family.* Apparently their families have known each other forever and my grandparents love him. I don't know why. He's a lazy ass when he's at home. Mom has a nanny for my little brother, so she doesn't have to deal with—and I quote—*the dirty parts of raising a child.* So, of course, I go home and the nanny is off for the holiday. My stepdad was on my ass the entire time. Like it was my job to take care of him. And I was glad to help. I adore the kid. So I fed him, rocked him to sleep, and was right in the middle of texting Logan when he woke up and started crying. When I didn't jump up to get him, my stepdad grabbed my phone out of my hand and blew up. He told me *I* was lazy! While he was sitting on his ass! He decided I was grounded from my phone. I told my mom it was bullshit. She took his side, and I lost it. I got my little brother out of his crib, gave him a kiss, handed him to my stepdad, took my phone back, and marched out the front door."

"And you went to Logan's house?"

"Sorta. I was just crying and driving. Two hours later, I ended up there completely unannounced. His family was amazing. He hadn't told them we got back together because he didn't want them to get their hopes up. I felt more at home there than at my own house. My mom sent me a text and told me that Harry decided they weren't going to pay for me to go to Eastbrooke anymore and not to bother to ask my grandparents for money because they agreed I shouldn't behave that way."

"Oh, Maggie," I say softly, pulling her into a hug. "We'll figure something out."

"I've been on pins and needles waiting to get called to the office and kicked out of here, but right before dance I looked up the tuition policy. They had to pay for this semester in advance and there are no refunds. So at least I know I'll get to finish up the semester. My mom says she's not sending my allowance anymore either, so I'm not sure what I'm going to do. I have some money saved, but not enough for tuition."

"What about a scholarship? I bet they have those."

"They do, but they're given out at the beginning of each school year. I could apply for next year, but not next semester. And my grades aren't that great. Like, I'm a solid B student. Not smart enough for a scholarship."

"You need to tell Logan."

She gets tears in her eyes again. "We just got back together and now I'm going to have to leave him."

I pat her back. "We'll figure out a way for you to finish school here. Stop worrying about it. I promise, something will work out."

"I can't tell him. He'll try to fix it. And his parents already make sacrifices so he can come here. It's not like they can pay for me, too."

"Did you go talk to the dean? Tell him the situation?"

"No. Do you think I should?"

"Yeah. If anyone can help, he can."

"I suppose you're right. I'm embarrassed, you know?"

"Don't be. I'll go with you, if you want."

She nods, then studies me. "Aiden told Logan that you almost didn't come back."

"Please don't tell anyone."

"He said he told you about that night. About Prom."

"Yeah, he did."

"He thought you might hate him."

"I could never hate Aiden."

"That's what I told him. I thought you acted weird when you hugged me goodbye. Would you have really just left like that without telling your friends?"

"I'm having some family issues, too. I thought I might have to go home to help. I'm hoping when I go home for Christmas that things will be better."

She hugs me. "I hope they are, too. And I'm glad you came back. Eastbrooke wouldn't be as fun without you."

"Thanks," I say, and I mean it. A lot.

AS WE'RE WALKING out the door, Peyton says, "Hey, Keatyn, wait up. I want to talk to you about Aiden."

Oh, shit. She knows. Knows that Chelsea texted him. Knows what was said.

"What about?" I say, as calmly as I can, as Shark bumps his hip into mine and joins us as we walk toward the dorms.

"What do you think we should do for his birthday?"

"His birthday? When is it?"

"This Sunday."

"Why didn't he tell me?"

"I don't know."

And already my mind is going crazy. He doesn't want me to know? Does he want to spend it with Chelsea and not me?

No, stop it, Keatyn. Stop doubting him. He's been sweet and amazing.

But why wouldn't he tell me?

"Did he tell you Chelsea texted him over break?"

"No, but I'm sure he told her to go to hell."

"Yeah, probably," I say, less than enthusiastically.

"So, if you're okay with it, I was thinking of inviting some friends out for dinner. I just didn't want to step on your toes in case you were planning something already. But if you didn't know, then you probably haven't planned anything, right?"

"Right. Dinner sounds great. Wait. This Sunday is December the fourth."

"Uh, yeah," she says, looking at me like I'm dumb.

I knew they were both Sagittarians, but Aiden and Brooklyn share the *same* birthday?

Am I in the Twilight Zone?

I look up to the sky and wonder if the gods are done having fun with me yet.

"His birthday is the same day as my ex-boyfriend's. What are the odds of that?"

Shark chimes in. "It's really not that uncommon. About nine hundred thousand people in the United States share any given birthday. Over nineteen million if you count the world."

"Oh, well, that's good to know," I say, thankful that we've reached my dorm.

I HATE THE INTERNET.
5PM

I'M SUPPOSED TO meet Aiden for tutoring in his room.

But I'm dreading it.

Maybe I'll accidentally fall asleep.

Maybe my phone died.

And I am sort of freaking out about the birthday.

Why didn't he tell me about his birthday?

What am I going to get him?

I grab my computer and look up the traits for those born on December the fourth.

If you were born on this day, you are happy, fun loving, and high-spirited. You can be very easygoing, but are often quite ambitious and determined. You have a great attitude toward life. Active and focused, levelheaded and responsible, you are the kind of person who works hard and plays hard. You like your privacy and need a home base to act as your castle. However, you can be opinionated, bossy, and sometimes impulsive.

Your lucky colors are blue and bright white.

In work and money, you have great ambition and should do well in any occupation you choose. You are typically disinterested in finances, which might make you careless with your money. This should subside as you mature.

In the romance department, your soul mate will have to break through your emotional walls to gain your trust and must share your desire for a home base. They must also be able to keep up with your love of adventure and excitement. You have a lusty sex drive. You want to find your true love and will quickly become bored or restless in a relationship that's not up to your standards.

You dream of personal freedom, and you just want to be yourself. You will go to great lengths to achieve this. You don't really set goals; rather, you depend on your gut instincts. You dream of traveling far and wide.

I shut my laptop. I hate the internet.

I mean, except for shopping.

Just not for all the worthless information that doesn't help you in the least.

I get a text.

Hottie God: *Are you running late?*
Me: *No.*
Hottie God: *Then why aren't you here?*
Me: *I don't feel like it.*
Hottie God: *What's wrong?*
Me: *Oh, I don't know. Maybe I'm just mad at myself.*
Hottie God: *You're mad at me?*
Me: *You told me that I'm supposed to tell you how I'm feeling? Right? That we're supposed to talk? Well, here it is. You didn't tell me that Chelsea texted you. And when you finally admitted it, you wouldn't tell me what you said or what she said. And to top it off, I just found out about your birthday. So what else haven't you told me?*

I sit and wait for his reply.

There isn't one, so I throw on my coat and head out the back door.

I wander through the trees, careful to avoid the mud puddles, until I get to the Cave.

I sit down on a stump, close my eyes, and decide to check in on Annie.

"Hey, what are you doing?"

"Just studying."

"Have you talked to Ace yet?"

"Not really. We texted some today. But he's still being weird. Distant."

"I'm at the Cave. Want to come sit with me?"

"Why are you there? Aren't you supposed be tutoring Aiden?"

"Yeah, but . . . he's being kinda distant too."

"He didn't seem that way at lunch. And he seemed upset you weren't in French. But then Miss Praline got a call from the office about you going to town."

"Yeah, they wanted to make sure it was okay I took Dawson with me."

"You took Dawson with you? No wonder Aiden's being distant."

"It was before that. At lunch. He didn't tell me that Chelsea texted him. And he wouldn't tell me what he said. I'm just upset about it. Oh, and his birthday is this week. He also didn't tell me that."

"What did he say about Chelsea?"

"He said he'd tell me later."

"So why aren't you letting him tell you? Why are you jumping to conclusions?"

"Why aren't you going to talk to Ace? Why are you jumping to conclusions?"

She sighs. "Same reason as you probably. I don't want to hear the bad news. I'm giving him until tomorrow. If he hasn't talked to me or tried to explain, I'm breaking up with him."

"I would too."

"On a very weird side note, Whitney was nice to me today."

"How?"

"She's throwing a Victoria's Secret Fashion Show watching party in the school's cinema room. We're supposed to dress in something from the store."

"I heard. That sounds fun, don't you think?"

"Yeah, I just don't understand why she invited me."

"She says if we present a united front, Chelsea might leave us alone."

"You mean leave our boyfriends alone?"

"Yeah, something like that."

"That sounds good to me. And who knows, maybe I'll end up single tomorrow."

"Are you really upset?"

"I'm more pissed than upset at this point. I think I cried it all out over the weekend."

"It's cold out here."

"Go talk to Aiden. Be a big girl."

"Yeah, maybe."

BUT I DON'T. I put my face in my hands, sit frozen in my spot, and try to think positively.

What could he have said to her that he wouldn't want anyone to hear but that would make me happy?

I think.

And think.

And can't think of a positive answer.

And that makes me really sad.

But I decide Annie is right. I need to go talk to him.

I get up and run down the path, being careful not to step in a puddle and ruin my suede shoes. As I come out of the trees, I get knocked flat on my ass.

"What the—"

Aiden picks me up off the ground. I'm soaked and muddy. "I'm sorry," he says.

I look down at my muddy legs and my probably ruined shoes, burst into tears, and run to my dorm.

IN THE BATHROOM, I lock the door, strip off my clothes, turn on the shower to warm up the room, and then try to clean off my shoes in the sink.

I get most of the mud off of them, pat them dry, hope for the best, and then hop in the shower.

I take a long shower, spending more time crying than washing the mud off.

I don't know why I'm crying. I was going to see him. To talk to him.

I'll get dressed and text him.

I wrap a towel around my body, twist one into my hair, and run out in my room to grab some clean clothes.

"Ahhhh!" I scream, dropping my hold on the towel.

I instinctively throw my hands over my lady parts while Aiden chuckles, gets off the bed, and hands me the towel. "What are you doing here? You scared me half to death."

I wrap it tightly around myself while he says, "I'm sorry I knocked you down. Annie told me you were at the Cave. Why were you out there?"

"Because you didn't text me back."

"I heard you crying in the shower. I didn't mean to make you cry."

"Well, you did."

"I wanted to tell you in person."

"I want to trust you, Aiden. I really do. But this feels a lot like when Dawson and Whitney texted. And you liked Chelsea. I just . . ."

He frowns. "You're shaking. Go get dressed."

I realize that I am cold. I run into my closet, throw on some leggings and a sweater, and then go sit on the bed. When he sits on the bed next to me, I quickly move to my desk chair and roll away from him.

He grabs the chair's arms and rolls me back toward him, so our knees touch.

"I didn't tell you about Chelsea because I didn't want to upset you. I wasn't trying to hide it from you."

"What did she say?"

He hands me his phone. "I saved it because I wanted to show you. But then you told me you weren't planning to come back. And I completely forgot about it. I was upset, willing to risk my parents' wrath to be with you wherever you needed to go. Boots, when we jumped off the cliff, you told me you trusted me. Do you?"

His question combined with the pain on his face is why I didn't want to come back. I can't take seeing it. And I can't imagine how it will look in March when I tell him the truth.

"I just didn't understand why you wouldn't show me at lunch like Logan did."

"Because I wanted to tell you in private. And you didn't answer my question. Do you trust me?"

I close my eyes, trying not to cry, and nod. "Yes, Aiden, I do."

"Good," he says, handing me his phone. "I want you to read this."

Chelsea: *Looking forward to everyone getting back from break. You should stay away from Keatyn. She'll be toxic when I'm done with her.*

Aiden: *Don't you dare do anything to hurt her or I'll go to the dean myself.*

Chelsea: *All my friends hate me because of her. Surely, you don't think I'm going to let her get away with it.*

Aiden: *No, all your friends hate you because you were offering sex to their boyfriends. And what makes you think Keatyn did it? There are other people who wanted to get back at you besides her.*

Chelsea: *We'll see . . . Have a nice break.*

"That must be why she texted Logan and Ace. She wants my friends to hate me."

Aiden nods. "I think so. I want you to know that I told you everything about my past on break. Promise me that you won't believe anything she says about me or your friends."

"Okay. But what about your birthday?"

"What about it? I can honestly say that from the time Riley punched me in the nose until now, I haven't even thought about it. But my mom did text me today to say they're coming the week after, both to see the dance competition and to celebrate my birthday."

"Your sister is planning a dinner."

"As long as you'll be there, I'll be there."

"I wouldn't miss your birthday, Aiden."

He kisses me. "Good. Are you hungry? Why don't I order Chinese and we can study French here?"

"That sounds good. I'll go dry my hair."

AIDEN STAYS IN my room until he has to leave to make curfew. We eat, study, snuggle, kiss, and talk about where he wants to have his birthday dinner. I suggest we go back to our French restaurant.

After he showers me with goodbye kisses and heads to his dorm, I grab my laptop and start shopping.

BACK TO SHORE.
12:25AM

I GO INTO the stairwell and make myself at home on a cold, hard cement step. I pull up the video conferencing software and click on B's photo. While I'm waiting for him to come online, I stare at his tan face.

I close my eyes and remember what it was like with him. So different than it was with Cush.

It was never fast. One time, I wanted to do it on the beach—like, quick—and he told me sex isn't about just riding the wave. That it should be the joining of mind, body, and soul. That it's waxing your board, paddling out, floating over the swells, patiently waiting for and preparing yourself for the bigger wave. Then it's all about working your way back to shore.

It never felt like *just* sex with him.

But I know why.

It's because I loved him.

But then I think about Dawson and how hot it was.

How Aiden can make me feel on fire with a single touch.

And I can't help it. I want it all. The connection *and* the heat.

I think about his surfing reference of working your way back to shore. Which is fitting because it's exactly what I'm trying to do. Get back to my family. To him. To my home. To our beach.

I know I can't keep going like this.

I hear him say, "Keats?"

My eyes fly open. "Sorry, I was just thinking about surfing." I start to get tears in my eyes. "God, I miss you. For two years, I saw you almost every day. I feel like a piece of me is missing."

"I feel like a part of me is missing too. I miss everyone. Our beach."

"Are you getting tired of traveling?"

"The flights are a bitch sometimes, and I complain about it. But then I find myself on another amazing beach. Kinda like our summer of waves—all the beaches we discovered. Except bigger and better."

"It was a good summer."

"Yeah, it was. So, I'm sorry, I haven't had time to get together with the guy on the takeover stuff yet. I will, though. This week or next, maybe."

"But, I thought that's why we were talking tonight, so we could get started? We need to start now, B. You don't understand. There are a lot of moving parts to this."

"What do you mean?"

"It has to be timed so that it hits Vincent all at once."

"What does?"

"A hostile takeover alone won't do it. I have to push him from every direction. The publicity for Mom's movie starts this week. We *have* to start this week."

I'm starting to panic. I need this to go according to plan. It has to.

"Oh," he says. He closes his eyes and looks down. I notice he looks stressed.

"I have something I need to tell you."

"Okay."

"Something was delivered to my hotel room earlier."

"What?" I say, instantly on edge.

"A box. In it was a framed photo of me, taken when they handed me the trophy this past, uh, weekend," he stutters again. He's shaken.

"Can I see it?"

"Garrett made me send it to him, hoping for forensics."

"He won't find any."

"Probably not, but I took pictures of it. The ones I texted him when I got it."

"Send them to me."

I watch as he grabs his phone off the table. He gives me a bleak look and I wish I could reach through the phone and brush the lines of stress from his face. They just don't look right on him.

My phone vibrates with the text.

"I know this is going to upset me so, before I see it, I just want to tell you how proud I am of you. How, through all this shit, you've grown and focused and taken a chance on your dream." I put my fingers against the computer screen.

He mimics me, our hands touching tenderly onscreen.

"I was serious when I said I wouldn't be here without you. That night at the Undertow was a turning point in my life."

In both our lives, I think, remembering falling straight into Vincent's arms.

I keep my hand glued to his as I look down and see the photos pop up on my screen. I click on the first one, making it bigger. It's of a plain white gift box, white tissue paper pulled open, and black rose petals sprinkled around an ornate black picture frame.

I look up at him. "I just looked at the first photo with the black rose petals, so I know it's from Vincent. B, have you been keeping anything from me?"

He stutters, "Uh, um . . ."

"Look, it's okay if you have. My mom did the same thing, trying to protect me. So, if you've gotten other things from Vincent, or seen him, tell me now."

"What? Uh, no. He's never been spotted, other than Long Beach. But, except for Hawaii, my tournaments have been out of the country."

"And he's never sent you anything else or threatened you in any way?"

"No. Other than not being able to see you, this whole thing really hasn't affected me that much. Until now."

I look at the second text. This one is a close-up version of the photo inside the picture frame. I can see B holding a trophy above his head in victory. It's exactly as I imagined the scene when I heard it. But then I notice writing on the bottom. I quickly zoom in to read, *I wouldn't be here without you. I love you, Keats.* I smile until I notice the spots. I squint, trying to figure out what they are.

"What are you looking at?"

"Your quote. But I see spots around them and I—" I instantly lose my voice as my eyes focus in on the reason for the red spots. There's a single bullet hole in

Brooklyn's forehead and the whole back of his head is blown away. A horrible special effect frozen in time.

I drop my phone into my lap and cover my eyes with my hand, willing my brain to wipe away what I just saw. No wonder Mom freaked when she got a similar photo of Tommy.

"Keats."

I uncover my eyes, B's face a welcome sight compared to the horrible image in the photo. "What you said about me has put you in danger." Guilt, love, and horror swirl in my brain causing tears to spill down my face and filling me with hysteria. "I'm so sorry, B. I'm so sorry you had to see that. You never . . . should've . . . said you love me."

"Um, about that."

"About what?"

"The *I love you* part."

"That's what made you a target. This photo is for me, not you. He's trying to scare me," I sob. "He's succeeding."

"Keats, look, I just need to tell you something . . ."

"You *have* gotten other stuff from him?"

"No, it's, well, there's this girl . . ."

His words feel like a punch to the gut, knocking the wind out of me.

"No! Don't, B," I beg, covering my eyes again. "*Don't* say it. I can't hear it. Not right now."

"Keats. I know you're seeing . . ."

"No, don't! Just lie to me." I feel like a riptide is pulling me under, drowning me. I'm crying hysterically now. I put my hand against my forehead, trying to calm myself down, but I can't. My heart's beating wildly.

"You need to calm down."

And that sets me off. "Calm down?! Calm down?! The only thing that's getting me through this is the thought of being able to go home. You made me promise you another chance. That we'd be back on our beach. I can't do all I'm about to do if you aren't gonna be back on that beach with me." I sob more. "I just want to go home. He ruined our beach, B. I want it back. I want my family back. You and the beach are part of my home. I. Just. Need. To. Go. Home."

"It sucks, but . . ."

"No buts! What if that horrible picture happens?"

B nods and buries his face in his hands.

Then he looks up at me with a mix of tears and determination in his eyes. "You're right. We have to do this. We have to get our lives back. I'll text you with a time to talk to the takeover guy." He puts his hand back on the screen. I reach up and touch it. "And I promise when this is over, we'll both go home." I nod as he says, "I love you, Keats," kisses his tattoo, and gently closes his laptop.

I shut mine too.

And cry.

I'm sure he's seeing someone. And it's okay if he is, but I need him in this with me. I'm not sure I have the guts or the courage to do it alone.

I love you flits through my brain. I do love B. I just don't know what kind of love it is anymore. And, based on what he says, he doesn't know either. Still, I know he's part of the mix. Of all the people I love. Of my family. Of my friends. Of him. My home. And I know that neither one of us will be able to go forward without going home first.

I sneak back into my bedroom and try to go to sleep, but every time I close my eyes, I see the photo Vincent sent B.

Only I see it in motion.

MY PHONE BUZZES on my nightstand.

> **Hottie God:** You're probably asleep, but I just wanted to tell you I miss sleeping with you.
> **Me:** I'm awake. I miss it too.
> **Hottie God:** Then maybe I should do something about it.
> **Me:** I think maybe you should.

I unlock the window and keep my eyes open until I'm safely wrapped in his arms.

Tuesday, November 29th

PLANNING A MUTINY.
7AM

Social Committee meeting.

I am secretly planning a mutiny due to starting at this ungodly hour.

Although, I shouldn't say ungodly.

Not when there is a beautiful god sitting next to me.

One who keeps playing footsie with me.

And whose smile is definitely worth getting up for.

Whitney and Brad go over what's already been planned.

Whitney says, "Okay, so, Friday during school, we will transform this place into Paris. The dorms will once again be competing for a dress-down day based on how they decorate their houses. Friday night dinner in the café will be steak and *steak frites*. Everyone will be encouraged to attend the basketball home opener. The coffee shops will be open late, serving pastries and drinks."

Brad continues. "Since we're hosting a wrestling match on Saturday, we didn't plan any games, but the café will be open all day, serving French grilled ham and cheese sandwiches—or *croques monsieur*—French pastries, and chocolate soufflés, and will be holding hourly French cooking classes."

"Then, Saturday night," Whitney says, "will be the Seine River Dinner Cruise. I think everyone will be so excited when they find out it's really a murder mystery party. So, Keatyn and Logan, the plan is to let everyone eat their gourmet picnics, and then the cast will get out of their seats and start the play?"

I nod and Logan says, "Yeah, it will be really fun. It's written so that we're all on this dinner cruise, eating the gourmet picnics made by me, Wolfgang Pluck. Then you find out someone has been murdered and who all the potential suspects are."

"Perfect," Whitney says, "and the tables will have to work together to figure out whodunit?"

"Yes," I reply. "Each table will turn in their guess of which suspect did it and the winning tables will get some fun prizes."

"And then Sunday afternoon, students can learn how to play the French lawn bowling game—or *boules,* as it is known—and go to the matinée movie, which will be showing a French film," Brad says.

"That all sounds really great," Brooke says excitedly.

"All right," Brad says, "I think we have this all figured out. Everyone, make sure you work with your liaison clubs so that things go smoothly. We'll meet again Friday morning at . . ." He looks at me. "Let's meet at 7:30. We shouldn't have too much to go over."

I give him a big smile. "You're lucky. I had just decided to mutiny if we had another meeting so early."

Brad laughs, "Let's go get some coffee."

Aiden wraps his arm tightly around my waist, gives me a kiss, and says, "Enjoy your coffee. I have to run down to shop class."

"What for?"

"To oversee the creation of Hawthorne house's decoration."

"Fun. What are you doing?"

"Don't tell her," Brad says to Aiden. "They're the competition."

"Us girls are decorating all our windows to honor Parisian shopping. Is Hawthorne doing that too?" I ask with a laugh.

"Ha. Ours is gonna blow yours away. It's amazing what we'll do to avoid wearing our uniforms for one day."

EMERGENCY FUND.
CERAMICS

I'M IN CERAMICS, glazing, when I hear a *Psst* from the hall.

I turn around and see Maggie. Our teacher is in the back room, so I sneak out to talk to her.

"I just talked to the dean," she says.

"How'd it go?"

"He didn't have good news. All the scholarships for the year have been given out."

"There isn't any kind of emergency fund?"

"He said he would see what he could do, but not to get my hopes up."

I give her a big hug. "It will all work out. He'll find something."

"I sure hope so."

AS I'M PAINTING the overglaze on my bowl, I'm thinking. Trying to figure out how I can help Maggie. Aiden and I watched as her and Logan's lives followed one of my scripts. They're back together where they belong, and I know in my heart they are destined to be that way forever. I'm not going to allow fate to rip them apart.

So, I'm going to intervene.

The question is how?

It'd be easy to just offer to pay for it. Write her a check for next semester. Done.

But what if I'm not here next semester. Or next year?

And I don't ever want her to feel like she owes me.

I finish glazing, look up the annual tuition on the school's website, and then ask my teacher if I can go speak to the dean about some French weekend stuff.

She writes me out a pass, so I leave ceramics, run to my dorm to get my checkbook, and then head to the office.

I give the dean's assistant the same excuse.

She leads me in, tells him why I need his ear for a few minutes, and then walks out leaving the door open.

I follow her, shutting the door, and then sit down.

"We on a top secret mission, Miss Monroe?" the dean asks.

"Actually, kinda. I know Maggie came in and spoke to you earlier and that you didn't have good news for her."

"I'm afraid not. I have some alumni that I could call, but usually the first thing they ask is about the student's grades. Hers are not stellar."

"But she does tons of activities and she still gets mostly Bs."

"I'll do what I can," he says.

"That's not good enough." I lay my checkbook on his desk. "Okay, then, I'd like to start a scholarship fund. One for emergency situations such as this. And I'd like the first recipient to be Maggie. This scholarship comes with a few strings."

"What kind of strings?"

"It's anonymous."

"Many are. That's not a problem. Will this be a one-time scholarship?"

"You mean will it be just for Maggie or will it go on for other students too?"

"Yes, most scholarship funds go on for years, but we can set this up so that it just helps Maggie."

I think about Eastbrooke and how at home and safe I've felt during my short time here. The amazing people I've met. I don't want anyone to have to leave if they don't want to. I don't want them to have to say good-bye to their friends.

"I think I'd like it to go on after Maggie. How would I do that?"

He rolls his chair over to a file cabinet and pulls out a folder. "This is what we give to someone interested in setting up a fund. Typically, they donate a large enough amount so that it supports itself."

"What do you mean?"

"The school invests the donation and the scholarship money is taken out of the dividends earned."

I smile. "I like that idea." Something that will go on long after I'm gone. I flip through the file looking for specific numbers. "I don't see any suggested amounts. What would it take to fund something like this? I want it to be more than just the tuition. I want to include, like, a stipend too."

"Are you really serious about this?"

"Yes, very."

"Okay, well, if you wanted to do it every year for one student, then decide how much of a stipend you want them to receive. If you figure your initial investment to earn a conservative ten percent, that's how you figure it."

I do some quick math in my head. "I want you to be able to use your discretion. I want each student to get this." I write down a number. "Plus have room, board, meals, and activities covered. Which is this." I write down another number. "So that means if I wanted it available for, say, three to five students a year, then I'd need this?"

"Yes, that's right."

"And you promise no one will know who gets the funds? I don't want their friends to know they needed help."

"We'll notify you anytime we have a need. If you want, you can be the one to decide if the need is great enough."

"Would you have given it to Maggie if this scholarship was already in place?"

He nods. "Maggie is a lovely person and an asset to our school, regardless of her grades. She's active socially. Always upbeat. I suspect she will be in the running for dance team captain next year. She'd even be a candidate for prefect if she brought her grades up."

I start to get little tears in my eyes. I'm so happy I'm able to do this. And I know Maggie will be so relieved. I open my checkbook. "Who do I make it out to?"

"Are you sure you are in a position to do this? It's very unusual for a current student to start a scholarship fund."

"I'm not like most students," I say with a sad smile. "When will you tell her?"

"I'll have to do some paperwork to get everything set up, and let the check clear before we can do anything officially. But I'll call the bank to verify that the funds are in place and tell Maggie we've found a solution this afternoon, if you're sure."

"I'm sure," I say, getting up to leave.

"Keatyn," he says, "sit back down. Is everything all right?"

"I'm fine, thank you."

"You don't seem fine. You looked sad just now."

"I have some family issues. They're starting to sort themselves out, but when I left for Thanksgiving break, I wasn't sure I'd be back. I have little sisters and I need to make sure they are . . ." I almost say safe, but stop myself. "Happy. Well taken care of."

"I understand. Family should always come first. How are your boxing lessons going?"

"Haven't had any since we got back. I need to coordinate that too."

"Mr. Steele was in here earlier today."

"Oh, really?"

"He wanted to know if I was okay with him incorporating your lessons into soccer practice for the team."

"How is he going to do that?"

"I believe self defense is going to be part of your workouts several times a week. Really, I'm all for you girls learning how to defend yourselves."

"Wow! That would be awesome! And mean I get more sleep."

"I was going to say give you more time for homework."

"That too," I say as the bell rings. "Thanks. I better get to lunch."

I'M PERFECT.
LUNCH

I SNEAK UP on Aiden in the lunch line and kiss his shoulder.

"Where were you? I went to meet you at ceramics so we could walk to lunch together, but Jake said you left class early."

"I just wanted out of class. And I had a couple things I wanted to okay with the dean about the baskets for Saturday night."

"Did he okay them?"

"Yep. All ready to go."

"Hey, before we sit down, is Maggie okay?"

"I think so. Why?"

"Logan just said she's been acting funny. Really happy one minute, totally depressed the next. And that's not really like her."

"I think it's okay that I tell you. The reason she went to Logan's on Thanksgiving was because she got into an argument with her stepdad and her mom totally took his side."

"So she's still upset about that?"

"I don't know for sure. But I know I would be."

"And how about you?"

"You're standing here with me, Aiden. Right now, I'm perfect."

I get the blazing smile. "That makes me happy. Promise me you'll tell me if anything goes on with Chelsea, okay?"

"I promise."

We sit down at our table and, just as I'm taking a bite of salad, Annie plops down across from me so hard she shakes the whole table.

"He broke up with me! I was going to break up with him, but the asshole beat me to it!"

"What'd he say?"

"He said I was getting too serious. He's the one who asked me out! How was *I* getting too serious?"

Jake says, "He's stupid. Why he'd want a skank like Chelsea, I have no idea."

"Because she's really pretty," Annie says. "And she's easy."

"Easy is not a good thing," Jake tells her.

"Actually, Annie," I say, "you should get glammed up with Whitney, Peyton, and me. We're going to do each other's makeup before the party."

"Sounds fun."

"Good, because Ace will be at the party. And you know what they say."

"What do they say?"

"Looking good is the best revenge."

Annie nods. "I like that. I want him to see me looking all glamorous and want me back."

"Fight fire with fire." I laugh.

"By looking hot?" Maggie asks. "I want in on that too."

"Me too," Katie chimes in. "Bryce, you'll be drooling."

"Of course, it sort of depends on what outcome you want," I tell Annie.

"What outcome?"

"Yeah, do you really want him back or do you just want him to want you back?"

Annie thinks about it for a minute, then says, "No way I'd take him back. Even if it means I end up dateless for Winter Formal."

"I bet you'll have a date before he does," Maggie says.

YOUR GAYDAR IS BROKEN.
FRENCH

MISS PRALINE STARTS right in on a lecture, so I write a note to Aiden and drop it over my shoulder.

I bought you some birthday presents last night. I'm excited for you to open them.

All I want for my birthday is you.

Like all of me? Does that mean you're ready to?

I've been ready, Boots. I want you to be ready.

I know. I appreciate that.

French weekend will be busy. I'm really excited for it. I'm going to try to speak French to you the whole time.

Really?

Ha. Well, I wish, but probably not. I've been studying a few key phrases though.

Like what?

It's a secret.

Are they from the dirty French book?

Nope.

Darn . . .

Next weekend, I told you my parents are coming in for your dance competition and for my birthday. Then, I was thinking . . .

About what?

You're done with the competition on Friday at noon. My parents are going to visit some friends and Peyton is leaving to spend the weekend with Damian. What if we spent the weekend at your loft? We could relax, go Christmas shopping, see the Rockefeller tree all lit up.

Miss Praline finishes her lecture and gives us time to work on our homework, so I turn around. "I'd love that."

Aiden grazes my hand with his finger, giving me instant goose bumps. "*Je veux vos lèvres sur les miennes,*" he says, his voice rough with desire.

Annie rolls her eyes. "Don't be all sexy and say *I want your lips on mine* in French. It's depressing."

"Annie, it's Ace's loss," Aiden says to her. "How do you know there's not someone better waiting for you? He was your first serious boyfriend, right?"

"Yeah," she says, probably wondering where he's going with this.

"See? He was your warm up pitches."

"What do you mean?"

"In baseball, the pitcher gets to throw a few pitches before he faces a batter. Maybe Ace was your warm up and you're ready to start the game for real."

Annie ponders that.

"Is there anyone you think is cute?" I ask, hoping she has a list.

"Well, sure. There are lots of cute guys."

"Any who are single?"

"Well, I mean, Jake is super hot, and he was really sweet at lunch, but I know he was just being nice. He'd never go for me."

"I think you're wrong. But what about Brad? He's not seeing anyone either, and he'll be there tonight."

"Oh, he's really cute too. And he's got those broad shoulders."

"I'm not completely sure," Aiden says in a hushed voice, "but I think Brad might bat for the other team."

"So could I pitch to him too?" Annie says, clearly still thinking about baseball.

Aiden breaks out in laughter, so I clarify. "I think Aiden is saying Brad might be gay."

"Really?"

"I've never gotten a gay vibe from him at all," I say to Aiden, agreeing with Annie.

Aiden whispers in my ear. "Says the girl who dated someone gay for over a year. I think your gaydar is broken."

I stick my tongue out at him, because he's probably right.

He glances at the teacher then grabs my tongue with his lips, pulling me into a very steamy kiss.

STRONG, FIERCE, CONFIDENT.
SOCCER

DURING SOCCER PRACTICE, Cooper announces that the new *Steele Building Workout* will now include two days a week of boxing and self defense training.

"Monroe, come up here."

When I'm standing in the middle of the mat, Cooper says, "I've been doing some private lessons with Monroe here. Learning to defend herself is just one of the perks. She has also greatly improved her core strength, her flexibility, and her overall strength. On the soccer field, you are constantly running into other players. Your ability to hold your ground, to resist getting knocked down, and to have good balance while running are all improved by workouts like these. Show them your stomach," he tells me.

I lift up my shirt.

"Monroe is very active. She surfed, played soccer, did some kickboxing workouts, and danced before she came to Eastbrooke. Here she works out on her own time, as well as with the soccer and dance teams. What's happened to your body since beginning our workouts?"

"Well," I say, "my stomach was always flat, but now I have abs. My core is stronger and my dance kicks are higher because of the increased flexibility."

"What else?"

"Honestly, it makes me feel fierce and it's a great workout when you're pissed off. Gets all your aggression out."

"And that's exactly how I want you all to be on the soccer pitch this spring. Strong, fierce, confident competitors."

"Would you mind demonstrating a little of what you can do?" he asks me.

"Sure, as long as you don't mind if I kick your ass in front of the team."

Cooper turns to the team and says with a laugh. "See? Fierce."

I pull my t-shirt off so I can't get caught up in it, and stand in just my sports bra.

Fortunately for the girls, Cooper does the same.

If he takes off his shirt every time we practice, all the girls in the school will try out for soccer.

I put on gloves and a protective mask and throw the first punch at Cooper.

We begin the choreographed moves that are usually our warm-up.

We connect with a few punches, block a few, and then he grabs me around the waist and throws me to the ground.

I will admit, this part is kinda hot.

Especially when his legs are between mine as he almost pins me.

His face is close to mine, his hard body crushing me, but I manage to get out of his hold and quickly turn the tables, pulling his shoulder in an uncomfortable position.

He taps out and says, "All right. Who wants to try it next?"

I laugh as every hand on the team is raised high in the air.

AFTER SOCCER, I head to dance. Maggie bounds into the locker room, grinning. "Did you hear me get called to the office?"

"Yeah, what did they want? Is everything okay?"

She breaks down and starts crying.

"What's wrong?"

She grabs my hands and jumps up and down, causing me to realize she's crying happy tears.

"It's better than okay! I get to stay!"

"Did your mom change her mind?"

"No, you were right. The dean found me a scholarship. Some sort of special emergency fund for students already enrolled here. And get this. It even comes with a monthly stipend, so with that and my savings I should be just fine!"

"That's awesome! I'm so happy! I was going to talk to you tonight and offer to help."

"That's really sweet, but I just couldn't ask my friends for handouts. That would be awkward."

"Yeah, maybe. But, seriously, you ever need anything else, come to me, okay?"

She hugs me. "I will."

"Maggie, you mentioned a savings account. Are you the only one on the account?"

Her eyes get big. "No, my mom's name is on it too."

"Have you checked it?"

"Shit, no." She grabs her phone, pulls up her balance, and says, "It's still there, but guess I should move it, shouldn't I? It'd be just like them to decide to wipe that out too."

"If you think that will happen, I would."

"How do I do that?"

"Well, you can transfer it to another person until you get an account set up."

"Can I send it to you? I trust you."

"Of course."

She clicks around on her phone. "Okay, I think you have to do something on your end before I can transfer it."

I check my email on my phone, do what's required, and then she transfers the money to my account.

"I'm so glad you thought of that. It's not that much, but still."

"I know. So, how do you think the dance competition will go? I'm nervous. Peyton seems nervous."

"I think we're going to rock it. And speaking of rocking it."

"What?"

"Since I get to stay at school, I don't want to wait any longer with Logan. We were waiting to see if things would work out, but they couldn't be more perfect. I'm nervous, kinda. It's weird. We've done it before, but it's been a while. I don't know why, but I sorta feel like it's my first time all over again."

"I feel that way with Aiden. He makes me nervous."

"It's love, don't you think? That's what makes it different?"

"Yeah, I think so."

53

SEX IN THE ALLEY.
7:30PM

EVERYONE COMES TO my and Katie's room to get ready for tonight.

Whitney assesses our room. "I like how you two have decorated. It's funky."

"Thanks!" Katie says, beaming.

Whitney immediately takes charge. "Peyton, you're best with hair. Why don't you do Katie's hair while Keatyn and I do Annie's makeup. Then we'll rotate."

Annie sits in my desk chair and I wheel her into the bathroom so we'll have better light.

"What do you use on your face?" Whitney asks her.

"Moisturizer and mascara."

Whitney shakes her head. "You're lucky you have such a great complexion. Most girls couldn't get away with that."

She paws through my makeup bag and starts with a primer. "It's good to start with primer," I tell Annie. "It fills in any imperfections and allows your foundation to stay on, so you can use less and still look natural."

"This foundation is too dark for her. Katie's fair. Can we use hers?"

"Yeah, second drawer on the left."

Whitney opens the drawer and tries Katie's. "Oh much better." She uses a damp sponge and blends the makeup perfectly.

Annie tries to sneak a peek in the mirror, but Whitney turns her back around. "No, no. We want you to see it all at once."

I do Annie's eyes in neutral tones, shading and highlighting in all the right places. I add a swoop of black liner and three coats of mascara to her long lashes.

Whitney studies her face, adds a pale pink blush, a little bronzer to the hollows of her cheek, and highlighter to the top of her cheekbones. Then she dabs on a pretty peach lip gloss. "What do you think?" she says to me.

"I think you look gorgeous, Annie. Natural and pretty, and your eyes look huge!"

"Can I see now?"

Whitney shakes her head. "No, wait until Peyton does your hair. Get the full effect."

I touch up my makeup while Whitney does Katie's eyes.

About an hour later, our hair is full and sexy and our makeup is done to perfection.

"What are we supposed to wear?" Annie asks, holding up a pair of pajamas.

"If your goal is to make Ace drool, I'd suggest yoga pants," Whitney says.

"Yeah, boys love yoga pants." Katie laughs. "They make your butt look amazing."

I go in my closet and grab a pair for Annie to try on.

"You have a great figure, Annie. Here, wear this long sleeved V-neck with the pants," Peyton says, tossing a shirt at her.

We all get dressed and let Annie look in the mirror. "Oh my gosh!" she says, studying herself. "I look so pretty! No offense, but I was afraid you'd put a whole bunch of makeup on me and I'd look ridiculous. I look like myself, only better. My eyes look so much bigger. You have to show me how you did that."

"So, you feel good?" Whitney asks her. "Because more than likely Ace will bring Chelsea. You have to be able to handle it. Although, I don't think you'll have much time to worry about it. I think plenty of other guys will be vying for your attention."

Annie stands up straight and tall and says, "Bring it on."

Which makes Katie, Maggie, and me giggle.

Peyton points at Whitney. "We're going to head over there now so we can greet everyone. Annie, you should wait a bit and then make a big entrance."

"With a boy," I say. "A hot boy."

"I don't really know any hot boys."

"I do," Whitney and I both say at the same time. We look at each other and say, "Jake?"

"Yeah. Let me call him." I dial Jake's number. "Hey, favor for you. Would you mind escorting Annie into the party tonight?"

"You trying to piss Ace off?"

"Basically, yes. And Chelsea, too, if she's there."

"My pleasure. What time?"

"Can you come to my room and just hang out? We want her to show up fashionably late."

"Make a big entrance?"

"Exactly."

"I'm on my way, Monroe. And I have vodka."

I call Aiden and tell him I'm ready to run to town for snacks. I'm just heading out when Jake comes in. He stops dead in his tracks and stares at Annie.

He blinks a few times before he says, "You look fantastic. I mean, you always look pretty, but wow."

Annie does a cute little pirouette for him. I love how tight fitting yoga pants and a little eye shadow have given her more confidence.

I look at Jake and pout. He rolls his eyes at me. "You look nice too, Monroe. But Annie, here. She should wear those pants every day. They're like *BAM*. And her hair looks crazy good."

Annie gives Jake a huge smile. "Thank you. I hope I have that effect on Ace."

"Ace will definitely be wondering what the hell he was thinking."

"Okay, so, you two hang out for a bit. I'm going to get snacks and will be back soon."

I RUN OUT of my dorm and find Aiden standing next to his car with the passenger door already open for me.

"Well, look at you," he says, looking more at my body than my face.

"You're supposed to look at my face when you say that," I tease, planting my lips on his.

He grabs my ass firmly. "Forget the fashion show. You should just walk around and let me watch."

I smile and laugh at him, loving how sexy he can make me feel with one touch.

Well, two touches, if you count both his hands.

"I'm wearing workout clothes, Aiden. I'm not even dressed up."

He nuzzles my hair and nibbles on my neck.

"Stop that. It tickles," I screech.

"You really want me to stop?" he asks, his lips grazing my neck.

"No, but everyone is expecting snacks."

He kisses me, then says, "Oh, yeah. I sorta forgot about that."

We get in his car and head off campus. A few seconds later, Aiden has my hand on the stick shift and is roaring through the gears.

"You like to go fast."

"I'd like to go faster, just to see how fast she can go—without getting a ticket, of course. My dad and I always talk about taking her out on a track. We just haven't yet."

My eyes light up, realizing that would probably be the best birthday gift I could give him.

WE STOCK UP on junk food and head back to school.

He parks and pulls me onto his lap. "I'm in withdrawal. I haven't gotten to kiss you nearly enough today."

I know we need to get the snacks to the party, but it's hard to think about such frivolity when a godly, powerful tongue is controlling you.

I love his lips. His tongue.

How he bites down on my lower lip sometimes and pulls at it with his teeth.

But he's not doing that right now.

These kisses are long, hot, deep, full-on tongue kisses.

The kind of kisses that make me want to throw him up against a wall and strip him naked.

Make him model for me.

Do lots of naughty and sexy things.

These kisses make me want to be a very bad girl.

Do the kind of things I've only read about in books.

I mean, it's dark. We're not parked near a light.

Why not?

Aiden's ringing phone interrupts my thoughts. He pulls it out of his jacket pocket, looking as annoyed by the sound as I feel.

"Hey, sis," he says. "Uh, yeah. Sorry. Traffic. We're headed that way now."

He puts the phone back in his pocket and touches my lips. "Your lips are definitely my bliss."

"Oh really?"

"Absolutely. Come on. Annie is about to make her big entrance. We don't want to miss the fireworks."

RIGHT BEFORE I open the door to the cinema room, Aiden gives me a sexy smirk. "Although, I bet there were more fireworks in my car."

As I hand Peyton the bags full of junk food, I notice Ace and Chelsea standing in front of the big screen. The TV is turned on but the fashion show doesn't start for a few more minutes.

All of a sudden, Ace's eyes get huge. I don't need to look to know that Annie and Jake just walked in. But when I do turn to look at them, I'm surprised too.

They're holding hands and laughing.

I start to worry about the vodka.

Oh, please tell me he didn't get her drunk.

But as I study them more, I realize that both their eyes look focused and clear. And when Annie pulls me into a hug, her breath smells more like Jake's cinnamon gum than alcohol.

Ohmigawd!

I grab her hand and pull her away from the food table. "Have you and Jake been kissing?"

She blushes and looks up at the ceiling.

"Annie! Why?"

"Why not?"

"Um, I don't know. Because you're supposed to be in a mourning period or something, maybe?"

"If I recall, when you were *mourning* your relationship with Dawson, you got drunk and kissed, like, five guys in the same night."

"Are you drunk?"

"No, we didn't drink. We were just talking and he kissed me. Just once. Sort of tentatively. Like, he kissed me, then moved his head back and gave me this grin. So I figured, what the heck? I leaned over and kissed him. Once. Pulled back. Smiled. Then he kissed me again and didn't stop until Peyton called. I was a little irritated when the phone rang. I was like, *Ace who?*"

"Ace's eyes about bugged out of his head when he saw you."

"You know what? I don't even care."

"Good for you. Jake is awesome. I mean, as long as you know he's not looking for anything serious."

She nods. "I think I'd prefer it that way."

"Are you two talking about me?" Jake asks, sneaking up behind us.

I start to say no, but Annie surprises me when she smiles and coos, "Busted. Should we find some seats? It's about to start."

"Front row or back?" Jake asks suggestively.

"Definitely back," she replies, giving him a coy smile.

"When did you become such a flirt?" I whisper to her, as Jake grabs her hand and drags her away.

Once he gets her situated, Jake comes back over to get some drinks and popcorn.

"Jake," I whisper. "I know we wanted to piss Ace off, but . . ."

He puts his hand on top of my head and messes up my hair. "Don't worry, Monroe. My kissing her has nothing to do with Ace. She looks smoking hot. I always thought she was cute. She just, she seems more confident now. It's sexy."

Aiden, who was talking to Maggie and Logan, grabs a bag of popcorn with one hand and my hand in the other. "Maggie and Logan saved us seats."

We sit down and watch the show.

The guys are doing a lot of hooting—Dallas, in particular, who is sitting between a couple of the newly-single cheerleaders. Ace is sitting next to Chelsea, but he's not touching her, and he keeps looking back at Annie and Jake, who are cuddling.

Aiden is eating popcorn, enjoying the show, but he's not cheering. Instead, one of his fingers is running along the top edge of my yoga pants. Warmth and desire flow from his fingertip to my soul.

I look at him and smile.

"Your eyes look purple tonight," he whispers. I lean my head on his shoulder, my thoughts taking me to happy far-away places.

"This is it!" Annie says excitedly. "The extended trailer for Abby Johnston's new movie. I heard it's really hot."

I sit up straight, my eyes glued to the screen.

The trailer starts out with Mom sitting at a desk writing *To Maddie, With Love* in a journal. The music moves as painfully slow as she writes. Mom looks beautiful as a brunette, but a little ragged. The slow music is replaced by a techno beat and images flash quickly across the screen. Maddie cutting her wrists. A hospital. Drugs on a kitchen table. Bottles of alcohol. Then back to her writing again. Same desk. Same stress on her face. Then techno. Faster images. Happy Maddie. Dancing. Kissing a man in a dark alley. A flash of Maddie's body. Lips. Hips. Sex in the alley. A bed. Nakedness. Sheets. Smiles. The music changes as we watch Maddie writing again. Then more flashes. Drugs. A club. Dancing on a bar. More men. More sex. The flash of money. Then back to Maddie.

The images are powerful, emotional.

Even though I don't want to see her naked, I want to see this movie. I want to know how Maddie went from a seemingly happy party girl to trying to commit suicide.

"That looks really good," Aiden leans over and whispers to me. "We should go see it."

In front of me, Dallas say, "All I know is Abby Johnston looks fucking hot. We definitely need to go see that one."

"I'm not sure if I'd like it," I say to Aiden.

Dallas' response to the trailer upsets me, and I can see why it upset Vincent. Maddie looks like she lived a very wild life. And I know she did. Mom let me read the script last year when she was considering the role. Reading about it was interesting. Seeing it played out before my eyes is another thing altogether. And I know that the movie, though poignant, is also supposed to be disturbing.

A little bit sick and twisted.

And, right now, I'm feeling a little sick to my stomach. Not because I'm not proud of my mom, but because I know it's images like these that set Vincent off.

I'm so lost in my thoughts that I don't hear the commotion until Aiden startles me by quickly standing up.

I turn around to see Ace standing in front of Annie and Jake, his hands in fists and his body tense.

Whitney quickly steps in between them. "Ace, I think maybe you should leave."

"I'm not leaving unless Annie comes with me."

"Aaace!" Chelsea whines. She puts her hand on his back.

He shrugs it off and says, "Get away from me."

"I'm not going anywhere," Annie says. Her jaw is set, but her eyes are filling with tears.

Jake stands up. He's taller than Ace, but not as broad.

"She's not going with you. Do as Whitney asked. Leave, and take *her* with you," he says with a sneer toward Chelsea. "We're all just here to have some *fun*."

The way Jake says fun makes it sound like he and Annie are hooking up and it sets Ace off. He starts to throw a punch at Jake, but Aiden and Riley are there in a flash. They have Ace's arm pinned behind his back and are out the door in a few seconds.

Once the door slams shut behind them, Whitney says, "It's not a party 'til someone gets in a fight. Enjoy the rest of the show." Then she holds up a few Shark logo flasks and asks, "Anyone care to join me?"

AIDEN GRABS BOTTLES of water for us and sits back down.

"You handled that well," I tell him.

"I have something else I need to handle," he says with a sly grin.

"What's that?"

He picks up my purse. "Is this the bag you took to St. Croix?"

"Uh, yeah."

He starts digging through it and pulls out the glow-in-the-dark moon. "I'm putting this back up. Where do you want it? My ceiling or yours?"

"Where do *you* want it?" I ask. The moon and my stupid wish are kinda the last things on my mind right now.

"Well, I wanted it on your ceiling, that's why I put it there. But I don't want it to mock you." He's trying to suppress a smirk.

"I don't know," I say. Part of me wants to see it on my ceiling every night and part of me wishes I never had to look at the moon again.

Aiden holds up a finger. "Wait. I have a better idea."

"What?"

"I know the perfect place for it. I'll show you later, okay?"

"Okay. Um, I'm not feeling great, Aiden. I think I'm going to head back to my room."

He gets up, looking concerned, and says, "I'll walk you."

WHEN I'M ALONE in my room, I grab my laptop and watch the movie trailer again and again.

Watching it makes me feel nauseous.

It's way worse than I ever imagined. And I know without a doubt that I have to do something about Vincent.

And fast.

I text Garrett.

Me: *I saw the extended trailer.*

Garrett: *Me too.*

Me: *Are you in Vancouver with my mom?*

Garrett: *Yes. And no one knows this, but we've moved up our timeline. We're not waiting until Thursday. We're leaving now.*

Me: *You're going with them?*

Garrett: *Yes, I'm one of many who are.*

Me: *Thank you.*

AN OLD MAP.
12:30AM

Dallas: *Most everyone took Whitney up on her offer, got drunk, and went to bed. You up for a little adventure with Riley and me?*

Me: *Yes.*

I throw on some warm clothes and ease quietly out the window.

Dallas and Riley are waiting for me at the clearing.

"It's cold. Are you sure we want to do this?"

"There is one other place we could go," Dallas says.

"Where?"

"You know how the chapel is always left open?"

"I have to draw the line at smoking in church."

"God made weed, you know."

"I know, but . . ."

"Cool your panties," Riley says. "It's not just the chapel that's open. There's also the social center in the basement, and we think there's some kind of special room there."

"Special room?"

"Cam sent me an old map, a key, and a list of rules."

"What kind of rules?"

"About taking care of the place. Passing on the key to someone worthy."

"Why didn't he give it to Dawson?"

"Dawson may have had a wild summer, but he's a good boy compared to the rest of us."

"So, by worthy you mean someone not afraid to take risks?"

Dallas says, "It's colder than a witches' tit. Can we discuss this later?"

"Wanna run?" Riley asks, both of them taking off before I can reply.

AT THE CHAPEL, we go in the front door, up the side aisle, through a skinny door, down a set of stairs, and through a dark hallway. Once we leave the stairs, Riley starts counting.

"Twenty-seven. Stop. This should be it."

Dallas shines a flashlight in front of us. There's nothing but a dead end. He points it toward the wall on our left. On this wall is what appears to be a memorial stone for a Mary Jane Stockton, who died on April 20, 1920. Dallas points the light toward the other side. Nothing but a blank wall.

"There's a door back there," I say, pointing back. "Maybe you counted wrong."

"Hang on," Riley says, pulling the note out of his back pocket. Dallas shines the flashlight on the note. "See this? I didn't know what this was, but maybe it's a clue."

I move the paper closer to the light. "That's a pencil engraving." I look up at the circular carving above Mary Jane's name and laugh. It's a flower with leaves that look suspiciously like a marijuana plant. "Her name is Mary Jane and she died on four-twenty? This has to be the place."

"So where does the key go?"

I push the flower to the left and find a keyhole. "Here it is!"

Riley puts the key in the lock. We push the big stone door inward, shut it, and then look for a light.

When Dallas finds one and flips it on, I can barely believe my eyes.

We're standing in a huge stone room. The walls are painted in bright colors and there are names and dates written all over them in black marker. There are furry and vinyl beanbags of various shapes and colors littering the floor. Psychedelic posters cover the ceiling. There's a bar running the length of one wall with shelves just waiting to be filled. In front of it is a bar top with stools lined up underneath.

"This place is giving me a hard-on," Dallas says.

"Me too," I reply in awe.

I go behind the bar and find four built-in mini fridges, each bearing their year of donation, and a place to chill and tap a keg.

"I think I'm in love with the class of 2004," Riley laughs. "Holy shit, this place is sweet."

"And warm."

"Look over here," Dallas says, pointing at a foosball table from the class of 1999.

I start reading the walls. "1974 is the oldest I can find. What about you guys?"

"I've got a 1972!" Riley yells. "In fact, I think these are the people who started it."

Dallas and I run over and read the inscription.

All who pass through Stockton's door,
Take an oath of silence swore.
In this place of legend and lore,
Party on, friends, evermore.

Samuel Torpe
Oscar Cullen
Karolyn Thorton
Olivia Newell

Class of 1972

Dallas holds up a joint. "I think we need to toast our forefathers."

We each plop down on a beanbag.

"How is this place so clean?" I wonder aloud. "Shouldn't it be dusty if no one has used it this year?"

"There's probably some secret alumni fund that keeps it clean."

"Yeah, maybe," I agree, taking a hit.

"We need to get the keg down here and fill those bar shelves," Riley says.

"How are we supposed to do that?" I ask.

"We'll figure out a way. More importantly, who will we invite?"

"It'd have to be people we trust not to tell, right?" Dallas asks.

He passes me the joint again and I say, "Could we bring people here without letting them know where it is?"

"What do you mean?"

"I don't know. Blindfold them? That would keep the location safe. And without the key, no one else can get in anyway."

Riley ponders that for a second but then gets distracted by a poster of a hot girl above his head. "This place is sweet."

Wednesday, November 30th
SEX FOR YOUR EX.
ENGLISH

As I'm walking to my seat in English, I get a text from B.

> **B:** *I set up a call with the takeover guy for tonight. 12:30 am EST.*
> **Me:** *Thank you :)*

I stand here for a few seconds, waiting for him to reply, but he doesn't.

Dallas tickles my side as he walks by so I decide to take my seat.

But before I do, I can't help but rub his adorable buzz cut. "Your hair is just too cute like this."

"What is with girls? They all want to rub it. I've starting saying, *If you rub it three times my genie will pop out.*"

"Dallas!" I crack up laughing. "Has anyone taken you up on that? Speaking of which, what ever happened to Panties for the Poor?"

"Still taking donations. Just got a little sidetracked by you-know-who."

"Ha! She's like Voldemort. She's so bad, we can't even say her name."

Dallas laughs. "And right now I'm busy with the Sex for your Ex Club."

"Do I even want to know what that is?"

"I'm offering my services to help newly single cheerleaders get back at their ex-boyfriends."

"You really are an extraordinary philanthropist."

"I know," he says, loosening his tie.

Katie plops down by us. "So, what do you think about Annie and Jake? Ace was pissed last night."

"Good," Dallas and I say at the same time.

We all look at each other and laugh.

65

"Ladies!" our teacher says. "Can we focus on class, please? And Mr. McMahon, kindly tighten your tie so I'm not forced to give you another demerit."

After she turns toward the blackboard and continues to bore us with Shakespearean vocabulary, Katie makes a funny face and I start giggling.

Dallas whispers, "Did you get into Jake's brownies again?"

Which makes me giggle some more.

Or maybe I'm still high from Aiden kissing the hell out of me before class.

"Miss Monroe! Why don't you come up here and pass out the quizzes, since you seem to have so much energy."

As soon as I stand up, Dallas flips the back of my skirt, causing the whole thing to fly up in the air, probably exposing my thong.

"Dallas!" I yell, laughing and pushing it down.

"All right. That's it. You two. Outside."

I freeze and wipe all emotion from my face.

Our teacher motions for us to go and follows us out in the hall, where she chews us out and tells us we're both getting zeros on our quizzes.

Dallas and I slide down the wall, sit on ground, look at each other, and then both start giggling.

"Last night was awesome. Can you believe that place?" I ask.

"It still sorta seems like we dreamed it."

"Could we have all had the same dream?"

"We need to find out more. Wanna go back tonight?"

I think about the text I just got from B. "Probably not. It's only second period, and I'm already tired."

"Come on, we need to go make sure it's real. We'll invite Aiden."

"Maybe."

AN ADORABLE WINK.
LUNCH

COOPER COMES BY our lunch table and hands me a piece of paper.

"Here's a pass to get out of your seventh period class so we can do some physical therapy on that hamstring."

"Um, thanks."

"I'll help you stretch," Aiden says. "You should really do it every day."

My mind immediately goes to *doing it* with Aiden. I don't even try to hide my smirk. "Every day, huh?"

He whispers, "Stretching is what I was referring to, but if you want to . . ."

Jake and Annie sit down across from us and I watch as Jake gives her an adorable wink.

So cute, I think. But then Annie does something that surprises me. The girl winks right back at him.

I decide I like the new, bolder Annie.

They flirt as I pick at my food and try to think about doing it with Aiden as opposed to worrying about why Cooper needs to talk to me.

THE SIDE DOOR.
7TH PERIOD

OPENING THE DOOR to Cooper's office, I take a deep breath and steel myself for whatever bad news he's about to give me.

But when I sit down, he's grinning.

"What's going on?"

"I decided not to wait for Garrett. I got a friend of mine to talk to Vincent's assistant last night. Most of it's boring bar conversation, but there's part of it that might be something. I want you to listen."

"Have you heard anything from Garrett? Did they all make it to France okay?"

"Yes, actually. I got a text from him a few minutes ago. He said all is good."

"Thank goodness."

"Okay, here goes," he says, and presses play.

"My boss? Oh, don't get me started. He's always been really demanding, but now he's almost unbearable. He's obsessed with some girl that he saw in a club. Wants her to star in this film we're producing. You've probably heard about it. The nationwide search for the next Abby Johnston."

"Sorry, I haven't."

"Oh, well, it doesn't matter. What matters is I scheduled a business dinner he's been on me about setting up. With their schedules, it was literally the only night I could make it happen in the next two months. When I posted the date on his calendar, he was furious. Started yelling at me about how I should know he has plans every Thursday night."

I hear her drinking, a mug hitting the bar, and a voice saying, *Another round?* She replies, *Please.*

"Do you want to know what stupid thing he does every Thursday night he's in town?"

"Uh, sure."

"He goes back to the club where he first saw her."

"Club? What is she, a stripper?"

"No, it's a dance club. Some bar with no name."

"The Bar With No Name is the name of the club?"

"No, it literally has no name. One of those places where only the rich and pretty people get in. Or even know about."

"The Side Door," I whisper.

Cooper hits pause. "So now you know where he's going to be tomorrow night. What's the rest of—" He stops, squints his eyes, then continues. "The rest of the stretching plan? Go change, and I'll meet you in training room."

WHILE I'M CHANGING, I remember the first time I met Garrett. It was the day Vincent put the note in Avery's backpack, and he asked about my habits.

"Are there times you go places by yourself?" Garrett asked me.

"Um, I guess I drive to school by myself and dance class, but that's about it."

"You're supposed to go to the club later tonight," Tommy reminded.

"Yeah, but I'm going with Cush."

Mom and Tommy both looked at Garrett.

He said, "I think it's fine if you're not alone. Are you picking him up or is he coming here?"

"I was going to pick him up."

"Let's have a tail on her just to be safe."

"Uh, I don't want some old guy in the club with us."

"It won't be some old guy, and he won't follow you into the club. He'll sit outside, watch Tommy's car, and follow you home after you drop off your friend."

"It's either that or you don't go," Tommy said sternly.

Vincent must have followed me to the club that night. And it may have been just dumb luck that he ran into Vanessa and RiAnne there after I'd left.

In the training room, Cooper pats the table. "Lie on your back," he says loudly, but then he whispers, "The dean is wandering around."

I lie on the table. Cooper pulls my legs so that my butt is down toward the end of it. He pushes one of my legs straight up in the air, letting it rest on his shoulder as he leans his shoulder into the back of my thigh.

"Try to keep your knee straight," he says. "I'll gently push your leg toward your chest until it hurts. Then I want you to push back against me hard."

"And you thought having me in this position would put his mind at ease?" I whisper.

He ignores me. "If you have a friend who could help you stretch before you go to bed, that would help too."

Now I see why Aiden offered to help me stretch. Cooper's practically lying on top of me.

My leg starts to shake, so I push back hard against his shoulder.

After pressing for a few seconds, he says, "Stop," then gently pushes my leg again. I'm surprised that it easily goes farther than it did before.

He stretches my other leg and then says, "I'm going to get you a heat wrap."

He leaves, comes back with a warm wrap, and says, "Okay, he's gone. Come back here."

He leads me into a supply room. "Tell me about The Side Door."

"It's where he tried to kidnap me," I say simply. "Tomorrow night, I'm going back there."

"What?! No, you're not."

"This is the part where you're going to earn that raise."

"Are you nuts?"

"No. I want him to think I'm back home, so he'll stay far away from B and my family."

Cooper keeps shaking his head.

"I'll take care of our flight. Let's plan on leaving here at six."

"Fine. I think it would be best if everyone thinks I'm still here, since you're signing out. I'm going to hide in the back of your car, okay?"

"Yeah, that sounds smart."

HEADING TO THE girls' locker room to get changed for soccer, I run into Dawson.

"Hey, we're all going to Taco Tuesday tonight, even though it's Wednesday. You wanna come?"

"Yum. That sounds awesome."

"Yeah, we thought we'd do that then go to the wrestling match."

A TICKING TIME BOMB.
TUTORING

"HEY, DAWSON SAID the guys are all going to Taco Tuesday even though it's

Wednesday. Are you?" I ask Aiden when I get to his room.

His gorgeous mouth twists into a frown. "I meant to talk to you about this last night," he says, the frown disappearing, "but you kept my mouth busy until curfew."

I blush. "What did you want to talk about?"

"Us."

"What about us?"

"On the beach, when we talked about Brooklyn . . ."

"Yeah?"

"I said I'd take you for now."

"I remember."

"Look, I know you were in a relationship with Dawson, but I feel like until we get past that point, until you decide who you . . ." He stops again. "I guess I'm saying I'm not planning to ask you to be my girlfriend—because, obviously, you aren't ready for that—but that doesn't mean I could handle you dating other people here."

My chest swells with happiness. "I don't want you dating anyone else either."

"Boots, I told you, you're the only girl I've kissed all semester. The only girl I *ever* want to kiss."

I run my fingers through his hair. "I appreciate how understanding you're being about all of this."

"I have a ticking time bomb countdown app on my phone. For your birthday," he confesses.

"Aiden, that's horrible!"

"No, it's not. It's just reminding me that each day I get with you is precious."

"I'm sorry I didn't tell you when I stopped doing stuff with Dawson. It must have been horrible for you when I hung out with him. Now I understand why you acted like such a little bitch sometimes."

"What?!" he says with a grin, grabbing my waist playfully. "I think you just liked watching me suffer."

"No, I didn't, because when you suffered you pretend-punched my head. And pretend-punching someone's head is not nice."

"Better than punching it for real."

"Maybe, unless you *tell them* you're pretend-punching them." I put my finger up to his lips. "And before you say I did that. I did not. You were lurking behind me when you overheard. You told me to my face."

He looks deep into my eyes, the playful mood turning serious with a single look. He doesn't say anything, just kisses me.

And does this kiss ever speak.

It's a kiss that's more emotional than it is sexual. It's a kiss that says all our fighting, all our misunderstandings, our lack of communication, all the hurt feelings, were worth it.

But when his tongue gets involved in the kiss and he pulls me onto the bed with him, and onto his lap, it takes the kiss to a whole other level.

It's emotion mixed with desire.

And I decide that might be the most powerful combination of all.

With every flick of his tongue, with every greedy touch of his lips, with every caress of my face, I know it's not just a silly love potion.

It's what love is supposed to be.

Scary, exhilarating—from the top of the world to the pits of hell—all-consuming love.

I think of his time bomb app, knowing that if I had one, it would be set to go off in March when I'll go public, not August for my birthday. Which means I should follow his lead and appreciate the time we have left.

LIQUIDITY.
12:30AM

I FLIP OPEN my screen to find B waiting for me.

He looks upset. Or pissed at me, I'm not sure.

"Hey. You doing okay?"

"Yeah," he replies, but I don't believe him. Something's off.

"Did something happen?"

"No, it's fine."

"Oh, good. I'm kinda nervous about this call. I know nothing about this stuff."

"Me either. That's why I set you up with Michael. So, conference him in, then I'll introduce you and let you two talk."

"Wait? What? You're not staying on the call?"

"There's really no reason to."

"Yes there is! I can't do this without you."

"Look, finance is not something I really give a shit about and I don't care to learn. As long as I have my board, I'm happy."

"We've had that conversation before, B. It was bullshit then and it's bullshit now."

"Whatever. I'm traveling and I have to practice. I don't have time for it. Do you still want me to introduce you or what?"

I push back tears and force myself to stay calm. "Yes, please."

B goes, "Hey, Michael. Keatyn is on the line, so I'll let you take it from here."

Then there's a little beep indicating that he left the call.

Michael is talking, listing his qualifications, but I'm looking at B. He gives me a sad smile, a little finger wave, and then logs off.

"So, a hostile takeover—how long will it take?" I ask Michael, trying to cut to the chase. I mean, I'm assuming it's not really that hard to buy a company.

"Let's talk about whether it's even possible first."

"What do you mean? Of course it's possible. He's, like, leveraged, right? And that's bad."

"Yes, he is. The company is ripe for a takeover, but you have to be able to make it happen."

"And how do I do that?"

"You offer to buy his investors out. If enough people sell, then you end up with the majority of the stock, which means you control the company. That's what you want, right?"

"Yes. Are there any other benefits?"

"Well, the *obvious* one would be that you vote the current Chairman of the Board out of office."

"Is Vin, um, Mr. Sharpe the chairman?"

"Yes, he is."

"That's perfect. I want to do both. Buy them out and appoint someone else. What will it cost?"

"That all depends on what his stockholders want. I'm emailing you a simple document so you can follow along." The way he says "simple" makes it sound like he thinks I don't have a clue.

I mean, I don't. But still, I'm not loving his attitude.

I don't say anything, though, because I desperately need his help.

"I have the email," I tell him, pulling the document up on my computer.

"His company isn't publicly traded, so it's hard to get financial information. The numbers you see are what I believe it to be worth. And, from the digging I did as a favor to Mr. Wright, I have a list of investors along with their initial investments. Those are below. Do you see them?"

"Yes."

"The next document shows the company's liabilities. And the next is Mr. Sharpe's balance statement."

I scroll through page after page of spreadsheets, trying to keep up. "Uh, huh."

"As you can see, his asset to debt ratio is very high."

"Okay. And why is that important?"

"That ratio refers to his liquidity. He's borrowed money on all of his assets, meaning he won't be able to personally fight a hostile takeover. From on-the-ground intel, he's invested a lot of money in a single movie and is betting the farm that it's going to be a blockbuster."

Mom's movie could financially ruin him?

Wouldn't that be poetic justice?

"But, as you can see from the figures on the last page, acquiring this company will take a substantial amount of capital."

I look at the very big number on the last page. One that would require more than my entire trust. I think about the scholarship check I just wrote.

For a second, I reconsider it.

I quickly shake my head, clearing the thought. I can't take it back and I don't want to.

Besides, B promised his trust to help.

I'll be fine.

"How do you plan to raise these funds?"

"Well, I have my trust fund, and Brooklyn said we could use his for whatever I'm short."

"That's what I thought. *Unfortunately*, Brooklyn doesn't have control of his trust, *nor* will his father authorize the early release of any funds. So, unless you can arrange financing, there's nothing further to discuss."

This is why B didn't want to be on the call.

Freaking chicken shit.

"I can get the money," I say quickly.

"And how is a seventeen-year-old going to do that?" he asks condescendingly.

"I don't know exactly," I admit quietly.

"That's what I figured."

I bite my tongue, thank him for his time, and hang up.

I set the phone down in my lap, feeling paralyzed, like I'm lost at sea with no land in sight.

How am I supposed to do this? How am I supposed to win without B's help?

I can't.

That means prong two of my attack is out, which blows my whole plan to smithereens.

Damnit!

He has to help me. He promised! This was his idea!

I call him.

He doesn't answer.

I hang up and call again.

And again.

And again.

And again.

And again.

I keep punching the button over and over.

BY THE TIME he finally answers, I'm pissed and crying frustrated tears.

"You should have told me yourself if you didn't want to help me! I can't believe you would bail on me like this! I need you!"

"This hasn't exactly been easy on me. I've gotten shit from every direction for what I said about you. God, it was spur of the moment! I *am* grateful that you encouraged me! And I care about you. I *wanted* to help. My dad was willing to help, but he freaked the fuck out yesterday when he heard about the photo. Told me if I have anything to do with you it will jeopardize everything we've worked so hard for. My career. My future. He trashed the takeover idea. Said it was like poking the hornet's nest. Said I can't use my trust. So, I'm sorry, but my hands are tied. And, come on, don't I get some credit for what I've already done? Michael did all sorts of research."

"You should've had the guts to tell me yourself. And without your help I don't have enough money to go through with it anyway! My plan—no, *your plan*—is ruined."

"I'm sorry."

"You just don't get it!" I yell. And as soon as I say the words, I know they're true. I realize that's exactly the problem. Other than one horrible picture, B's life hasn't changed much. He's not in hiding. He's living his dream.

"What don't I get?"

I calm down and use my bitch voice, hoping I can scare him into seeing how important this is. "Every move you make is on the internet, Brooklyn. The tour

74

schedules. The photos. You might think you can just bow out, but you can't. You screwed yourself when you thanked me. And that means *she's* in danger too."

"Don't give me a guilt trip. I know you're seeing someone too."

"Yeah, but the difference is, I'm somewhere safe. *You're not.*"

I hang up on him.

And feel very alone.

I SIT IN the cold stairwell staring at the floor until my phone buzzes, startling me.

> **Hottie God:** *Dallas and Riley want to take me somewhere tonight. You up for that?*
>
> **Me:** *Uh, no. Not at all.*
>
> **Hottie God:** *Are you tired?*
>
> **Me:** *Yes, but I can't sleep.*
>
> **Hottie God:** *Then I'm coming over until you can.*
>
> **Me:** *I'm kind of crabby.*

That's an understatement.

I roll my eyes at myself. I'll just tell him not to come. That I'll see him to-morrow.

> **Hottie God:** *I'll rub your face like I did when you were sick.*

Or not.

> **Me:** *I'll be waiting.*

I sneak into my room, unlock the window, and get under my covers.

A few minutes later, Aiden has his arms wrapped tightly around me, and my face is snuggled into his neck.

"You sound like you've been crying," he whispers.

"Just, you know, family stuff," I say, sort of telling him the truth.

"Tell me. Maybe I can help?"

"No one can help, Aiden," I say pathetically.

He runs his hand over my tense neck muscles, kneading them gently.

"That feels good."

"You're stressed and I want to make you feel better. In the morning, I'll be gone, but I want you to . . ."

Thursday, December 1st

YOU COME TO ME.

7:14AM

I'VE JUST HIT snooze for the third time when there's a knock on the door. I look over at Katie's bed and see she's already gone. I vaguely remember her mentioning a Spanish club meeting.

"Come in."

Aiden walks in carrying a bag and a cup of coffee. He's dressed in a pale green Oxford, making his eyes look even greener than usual. He sits on the edge of my bed.

"Brought you some breakfast."

I sit up, pushing my messy hair out of my face.

He rubs his thumb across my cheek. "You seemed upset last night. I wanted to make sure today gets off to a good start."

I close my eyes and press my face into his hand, which causes him to wrap his arm tightly around me.

"Shit," I say, "it's getting late and I need to get ready. Do you wanna stay here while I do?"

"Of course," he says, sitting down at my desk.

I run into the bathroom, get ready quickly, then run into my closet and throw on a white blouse and my skort. I walk back into my room, looking for my black sweater, and find it draped over the back of the chair Aiden is sitting in.

He stands up quickly, pulls me into a hug, and then kisses me.

The perfect kiss. Soft. Slow. Sweet.

"Do you remember what I told you last night?"

"That you'd help me?"

"No, after that. About what you're supposed to do this morning?"

I shake my head. "Sorry. I must have fallen asleep."

"I thought so," he says, kissing my nose. "I told you to wear the cowboy boots your grandpa gave you. That they're lucky and they'd make you feel better."

A lightbulb goes on in my head. *Grandpa.*

"Ohmigawd, Aiden, you're brilliant," I say with a big grin, running to the closet to grab my boots. "That's *exactly* what I need."

I come out of my closet wearing a smile.

"That's what I like to see. You smiling," he says.

I give him a long kiss, letting my body melt into his. "Thanks for coming over last night, and for breakfast. I really appreciate it."

"I'm gonna have to bring you breakfast more often if I get kisses like that," he says adorably.

"Come on, we better get to class," I say, pulling away.

But he holds me firmly.

"But from now on, when you're upset, you come to me, okay?"

I get lost in his sweet eyes and nod in agreement.

"You and me. That's all we need," he says, giving me another long kiss then leading me toward class.

RILEY SITS NEXT to me in history and says discreetly, "So I talked to Cam last night. Asked how the hell we're supposed to get stuff there. Get this. He told me to go back on Saturday night before curfew and all will be revealed."

"All will be revealed?"

"I guess."

"What did he say about taking other people there?"

"Pillowcase over the head unless you know one hundred percent that you can trust them."

"So who do you think we can trust?"

He looks up toward the ceiling, thinking. "Aiden and Logan."

"I'd agree. What about girls?"

"Girls are tricky. I trust Ariela but what happens if we break up? If it got ugly?"

"I don't know. What about Peyton?"

"Maybe, but I definitely don't trust Whitney."

"Lets keep it small for Saturday night."

"Do sort of a dry run and see how it goes?"

"Yeah, I think that would be smart."

"You know, I was thinking that might be just the place to take Ariela on Sunday night."

"I thought you were coming to dinner for Aiden's birthday?"

"Well, it's our one month anniversary, and I want it to be special. Like, I'm hoping it's *really* special," he says, lowering his voice.

"Ohhh, do you think you will?"

"I think so. And I'm going to ask her to Winter Formal."

"How are you going to ask?"

"I bought her a Hello Kitty purse. Well, no, it's not a purse—more like a tiny purse. Fancy."

"An evening bag?"

"Yes, it's all crystals."

"She'll love that."

"I'm putting a note inside it that says, *Please take Kitty and Riley to Winter Formal with you.*"

"Ahh, that's adorable, Riles."

"Has Aiden asked you yet?"

"No. Do you think he will?"

"Yeah, don't you?"

"I think we'll go together, but I don't know if he'll do anything special . . ." I stop talking and chuckle quietly. "Actually, he will do something special. Everything he does is special."

"You love Aiden," Riley taunts.

I sigh.

"What's the sigh for? Shouldn't you be agreeing with me?"

"Sometimes life is just complicated."

"Well, it's about to get very uncomplicated, because all we're going to be doing is hanging out in the . . . we need a code name for it."

"Stockton's. Remember? Stockton's door."

"Oh, yeah. Awesome. That's where we'll be. *Party on, friends, evermore.* I'm in love with that saying."

I'D MARRY A PIRATE.
FRENCH

BEFORE FRENCH STARTS, I send Sam an email with the changes I want made to my will. The most important change being that if something happens to me, Mom, and Tommy then Damian becomes executor and makes sure my sisters are well taken care of. I also noted the changes I told Cooper about. Taking care of his family if something happens to us both, as well as what to do if I die but Cooper doesn't.

I notice an email from Tommy labeled *Top Secret*.

-Your mom told me everything. All the things she's been keeping from me. How scared she's been. You know, I've been wanting to ask her to marry me for a while now, and I think it's time. A reaffirmation of our love. She won't want to get married until we can all be together, but I need her to know that I want her to be my wife more than anything.

SO, attached are four ring designs. I have no idea which one to choose.

Help!

P.S. The good news: Your mom and the girls are safely moved. The bad news: Bad Kiki came to NY with me.

I open up the first sketch. This ring is beautiful. A huge emerald-cut diamond set flush in a thick band covered in different sized diamond chunks. It's very unique but seems a bit too contemporary for Mom's taste.

"What are you looking at?" Aiden asks, leaning over my shoulder.

"My mom and my stepdad have been together for quite a while, but they're not actually married. He's going to propose soon and wanted my opinion on some ring designs."

"How come they haven't gotten married yet?"

I shrug. "I don't know. Busy with work and life. And, for them, marriage is just a piece of paper. They say all that really matters is their commitment to each other."

Aiden thinks about it and nods. "That is really all that matters."

"Yeah, but my little sisters are at the age where they've started asking why Mommy and Daddy aren't married."

"What do you think of that ring?"

"It's cool, but too unusual for my mom."

I click on the next photo. This setting is very popular now. A large, oval stone surrounded by a circle of smaller ones. What makes this one impressive is that the center stone is over eight carats.

"What do you think of that one?" Aiden asks.

"Too traditional."

"I don't know much about diamonds, but I have seen a lot of rings like that."

"Yeah, me too."

I click on the third sketch. "Oh, she'd love this one!"

I show Aiden the sketch of a large, oval-cut diamond wrapped with trapezoid and round diamonds. It's funky but traditional. I count the round stones. "And there are seven little diamonds for the seven of us!"

"Sounds like you've found the winner," Aiden tells me.

"I like the design the best and the number of stones would make it really special."

"I think so too."

I click on the last sketch. This design literally takes my breath away. It looks nothing like Mom and everything like me. "Wow," I whisper. *Hello, beautifully gorgeous ring that needs to be on my finger.*

"You like that better?"

"What?"

"I asked if you like that ring better."

"Oh, I didn't hear you."

"I take it you like it?"

"I love it, but for me, not Mom. And it's not extravagant enough for my stepdad. Everything he does is big." I stare at the sketch. This ring is so me. A three-carat round canary diamond set on a wide platinum band. The platinum band is completely covered with tiny baguette diamonds. "I'm going to vote for design number three."

MISS PRALINE ASKS Aiden to hand back our quizzes, so I fire off a reply.

-You love that dog and you know it! As for the rings, I'm in love, love, LOVE with #3.

It's big and chunky, but still has a traditional feel.

Did you plan it so there are seven round stones surrounding the main diamond? One for each of us?

That will totally make Mom cry.

(I think #1 is a little too funky and #2 is too traditional.)

Love you!!

P.S. If any boy ever asks for my hand in marriage, show him #4. I'm in love. I'd marry a pirate for a ring like that.

When Aiden sits back down, I tell him that I'm leaving school tonight to go visit my uncle who's in town.

GO FOR BROKE.
6:10PM

AFTER SIGNING OUT, I drive through the gates of Eastbrooke, down the long drive, and out onto the highway.

Cooper pops up from the back seat, where he was hiding under a blanket, and slides into the passenger seat next to me.

"Brooklyn totally bailed on me last night. His dad decided he can't use his trust to help me buy Vincent's company, and he didn't even have the guts to tell me himself. He let the buyout guy tell me instead. That guy was a dick, too. Treated me like I didn't have a clue—or the money—to do a buyout."

"Do you have either?" Cooper asks.

"A clue? Not really. About the money, sorta, but not quite. I was really upset last night, but Aiden came over . . ."

"Kissed it and made it better?"

"He did make me feel better, for sure. But just when I thought prong two of our plan was history, he mentioned my grandpa. And a lightbulb went on in my head. I'm going to call him now."

Cooper nods.

I tell my car to dial Grandpa's cell.

His booming voice fills my speakers. "Well, howdy, hotshot."

"Hey, Grandpa. Do you have a minute? I need some help."

"Of course, I do," he says loudly then whispers, "It's good timing, actually. If I talk to you, I won't have to help your grandma with the dishes."

"I heard that," Grandma yells in the background.

Grandpa chuckles. "So, shoot."

"Do you know much about hostile takeovers?"

"I'd say so. We bought out fourteen companies over the years and none of them were particularly friendly."

"So, if I were to maybe—"

"Keatyn, if we're gonna talk business, you've gotta give it to me straight. No beating around the bush. Tell me what you need and how I can help."

"Um, well, okay." I take a deep breath. "I want to buy Vincent the Stalker's production company. The company owns the rights to make the movie he wanted me to star in. It's at the root of why he wanted to kidnap me, I think. He couldn't get all the funding he needed, so he's leveraged every asset he has, as well as taken on additional investors. He doesn't own the majority anymore, and I was told the company is ripe for a takeover."

"Sounds pretty straightforward."

"Not exactly. I also need to hide my identity, so he doesn't know I'm behind it. I was told that can be done through shell corporations?"

"Yes. What else?"

"B introduced me to a guy who was supposed to help. But he didn't. He assumed I didn't have enough money."

"He wasn't setting up investors for you?"

"No. I was going to spend all my trust but, based on his numbers, I don't have enough, and B's dad won't let him loan me the rest."

"You were willing to risk everything you have to make this happen? Go for broke? Why?"

"Because my family is worth the risk."

"How will taking over his company help your family?"

"I don't know if we actually even *need* to take it over. We just have to make him *think* we're going to. If he loses the company, he loses the movie. I want to give him something to focus on besides threatening the people I love." I have that unsettled feeling in the pit of my stomach. Even though I'm scared of my own plan, I know I have to see it through. "I want my life back, Grandpa. I'm tired of people telling me what I should do."

"Tell you what, why don't I get my old cronies together and have some fun with this. Seems to me you have enough on your plate."

"Are you serious? Ohmigosh, Grandpa, thank you. But before you agree, there's one more thing."

"What's that?"

"I need it, like, yesterday."

"Ain't no roots ever grow under these feet. It'll take some initial investigation, but I already have plenty of shell corporations we can use. This isn't my first rodeo, hotshot."

"I have some information. Who his investors are, their initial investments, Vincent's personal balance sheet. The guy told me this stuff was hard to get because it's a privately held company and not public record."

"Bullshit. You just have to know who to ask. Send me the information and I'll get my guys to confirm. That will give us a head start. I think we could be ready to fire the first shot across the bow by early next week."

"Really? That's amazing. I'll call Sam right now and have him send you the money. I'm short what I think it will cost, but I have some real estate I can sell. I'll put it on the market, take a loss, and get you the rest."

"Hotshot, you let *me* worry about the money. *You* worry about keeping yourself safe. I suffered all the way through that Victoria's Secret fashion show, wanting to see what all the fuss over this movie was about. After seeing the trailer, I suspect Vincent is as fidgety as a whore in church."

"I want him to know what it feels like to lose control of his life."

"I wondered how long it would take for you to fight back," Grandpa says. "Glad to see I taught you well. Just remember, any idiot can poke a rattlesnake with a stick, but a wise man knows exactly how long that stick is."

"Thanks, Grandpa. I'll keep that in mind."

I hang up, pull into the airport parking lot, pull on a wig of chestnut curls, and turn toward Cooper. "I'm really glad you decided to come with me."

"There's no way I'd let you go alone. And I know you would have."

"Yeah, but I may have just figured out a plan that you'll approve of."

"What does it involve?"

"A flashy entrance and a stealth exit. I think I know exactly how long my stick is."

Cooper looks amused. "I don't know how long your stick is, but I will admit, you've grown a big set of balls."

That makes me laugh and also feel a little proud of myself.

ONCE WE'RE IN the air, I turn to Cooper and say, "So, we have homework to do."

"*We?*"

"Yeah. We're going to watch *A Day at the Lake.* I've never really studied the plot."

"*Is* there a plot?" Cooper laughs. "I've never seen the movie, but from what I understand, people only watch it because of all the now-famous actors that got their start in it."

"That's true. But what we have to figure out is why Vincent loves it. There must be something more than her running around in a bikini and screaming that caught his attention."

Cooper shakes his head and chuckles some more. "If he fell in love with her as a teenager, that's *exactly* what caught his attention."

"So you won't mind watching it?"

"Tough job."

AS WE WATCH the movie, I stop it often, rewinding, re-watching, and writing down plot points.

A Day at the Lake

INTRODUCTION – MEET OUR CHARACTERS AND SEE THEM IN THEIR NORMAL LIVES.

* We meet college students, Lacy (Mom) and her hot frat boyfriend, Matt. They are with a group of friends, planning a weekend getaway at a friend's lake house.

* Lacy and Matt seem to be the perfect couple until they argue about her doing a semester abroad to study archeology. *(This scene leaves you wondering if their relationship is just superficial. I mean, he should support her, right? It's her dream.)*

RISING ACTION – WHERE COMPLICATIONS IN THE STORY START TO APPEAR.

* They arrive at the lake house, which is a huge spread in the middle of nowhere. A few people have cell phones, but they have no service. No problem though. The house has a phone line. *(Desolate location? Check.)*

* The party kicks into gear. Drinks are made. Many are consumed. Music blares. A great time is had by all.

* Shot of Lacy walking out of the lake, blowing a kiss to Matt. *(The money shot, so to speak.)*

* Matt and Lacy are making out in the lake when a raft bumps into Lacy's arm. She opens her eyes and screams as she sees Dead Partier #1.

* Everyone is drunk and freaking out. Girls are crying. It's at this point that they discover the house phone is dead. And the boat, although it had been pulling wake boarders all afternoon, suddenly won't start. They are stuck there.

* Drunk boys decide to keep partying, as that's what Dead Partier #1

would have wanted them to do, and figure they can fix the boat tomorrow.

* Matt sends Lacy, who is still in her bikini, to grab a couple more beers. Lacy screams as she discovers Dead Partier #2, a boy who "fell" down the stairs. (*Must have been a small wardrobe budget. They didn't even give her a cover-up!*)

* Drunk partiers decide to be more careful. (*Do your friends typically die when you're partying or are they just accident prone?*)

* Drama ensues as two party girls fight over a boy. Bikini-clad Lacy shows up to save the day, giving them a brief girl-power speech and pouring them tequila shooters. (*Hello, Lacy?! Maybe you should be handing out bottles of water and shotguns instead?*)

* Now bffs again, Bikini-Clad Lacy and the girls head back to join the party, but all scream when they discover Dead Partier #3. She's dead on the bathroom floor, blood oozing from a head wound. Drunk boys surmise Dead Partier #3 must have hit her head on the sink. Someone suggests walking to get help, but is told there are no neighbors for 10 miles. (*And it's dark now.*)

* Remaining partiers decide to sober up—for about two seconds—until Matt makes a poignant speech about their fallen comrades and they all drink to their friends. Partying ensues. (*This scene should be included in a public service announcement about underage drinking.*)

* Matt is all over Bikini-Clad Lacy, things quickly getting hot and heavy between them. (*I will admit, they have good onscreen chemistry and I'm hoping they survive. I'm also starting to scan the remaining partiers trying to determine who is the killer.*) Matt, in the wake of the deaths, tells Lacy that they need to embrace life. (*And, apparently, that means a quick shag in the lake.*)

* Now, Wet-Bikini-Clad Lacy needs to use the restroom. (*She can have sex in the lake, but is apparently too much of a lady to pee in it.*)

* Lacy goes into the dark house, flips a light switch, and discovers that the power is out. (*OMG!*)

* But she must really have to pee, so she creeps up the dark stairs because, obviously, she doesn't want to use the bathroom where Dead Partier #3's body still is. (*Don't. Go. Up. The. Stairs!*)

* While Lacy is peeing, she hears a noise, gets scared, and rushes out of the bathroom without bothering to flush. (*I've heard people play drinking*

games while watching this movie. You drink every time: Lacy screams, Matt says sweet, *or when a dead partier is found. Meaning we'd all be drunk by now.)*

* Lacy tells the boy whose house this is that the power is out. He says, *Happens all the time on the island. Must be a storm.* Lacy agrees with him. *(Even though there's not a cloud in the sky?!)*

CLIMAX – A TURNING POINT IN THE STORY, WHERE MUCH OF THE PLOT IS REVEALED.

* It's at this point that viewers realize they don't know anything about House Boy. He's cute, but seems quiet, and doesn't appear to be drunk.

But when Lacy says, *Vince, do you have some candles?* I about fall out of my seat.

"Ohmigawd," Cooper and I mutter at the same time.

"Is that it?" Cooper asks. "Is it because they share the same name?"

"No. Vincent's real name is Thaddeus Samuel Kingston."

"So where did Vincent Sharpe come from?"

I look at the movie paused on the screen. "I'm pretty sure we know now where the name Vincent came from. But his grandmother was the actress, Viviane Sharpe. I'm not sure when he started going by Vincent Sharpe, but it's the name he uses professionally."

"I'm not a big movie buff, but I know who Viviane Sharpe was. I suppose that name helped him get ahead in the industry."

I nod. "Yeah, probably. Still, it's weird though. Do you think Vince is the killer in the movie? Or the guy she ends up with?"

"I don't know," Cooper says, then rewinds the part we just missed.

We watch as Vince puts his hand gently on Lacy's shoulder.

Are you freaked out by everyone dying? he asks as he hands her a box of candles.

A little, she admits. *You?*

She holds out a candle and he lights it.

(The cinematography on this scene is gorgeous. Dark room, only lit by moonlight. Vince and Lacy's faces suddenly glowing in the candlelight. Mom looks angelically beautiful. And I can see why a boy who thought his mom was a whore fell in love right then and there.)

Vince touches Lacy's hand and says, *Don't worry. I'd never let anything happen to you.*

Lacy places the taper into a candlestick and sets it on the kitchen table.

Then she does what she's famous for. The corners of her mouth form a little smirk, which slowly spreads into her famous megawatt smile.

Thanks, Vince, she says sweetly, blushing.

And you feel it. Something between them. A little spark.

Cooper pauses the movie. "Does it freak you out, watching this?"

"Um, no. Why?"

"That smirk that builds to the big smile. It's like I'm watching you."

I'm flattered, which makes me smile.

"See, you just did it. When you first met Vincent, you were in a bikini, right?"

"Yeah, and in the picture that was missing from Mom's set trailer."

Cooper nods and presses play. "Vince likes her, don't you think?"

"For sure. What you can't tell is if Lacy likes him back or if she's just being nice."

"Let's keep going."

I heard you might not be coming to Egypt. You shouldn't let him hold you back, you know.

I know, Lacy says softly. *But I love him.*

He's an asshole.

We've had this conversation before, Vincey.

"*Vincey?* Does my mom not see the parallels between this movie and life?"

"I think *this* explains why she was planning to leave Tommy," Cooper states. "But she's looking at it from her perspective. I'd say your Brooklyn is in more danger than Tommy."

"Shit." I knead my forehead. "I hope Vincent shows up and thinks I'm back. I need to keep B safe. And I'm so grateful my grandpa is handling the takeover."

"Are you in love with Aiden or Brooklyn?" Cooper randomly asks.

I frown at his question.

"I'm not trying to interfere in your love life, but . . ."

"Anyone I love will be in danger."

"Exactly."

"That's why I didn't want to be at Eastbrooke while we did this."

Have you made a decision?

Yes. I'm not going. I'm sorry. I know you'll have an amazing time without me.

Vince's eyes smolder as he says, *Just answer me this. If he wasn't in the picture, you'd go, right?*

Tears gather in her eyes. *Yeah, probably.*

Vince takes the candles out of her hands, sets them on the table, and pulls her into a hug.

She gives him a sad little smile and then says, *I better get back out there.*

* Not long after this, Still-Bikini-Clad Lacy screams again as Dead Partier #4 is found. It's the girl who was upset earlier. Apparently, she and Lacy were close, because Lacy starts crying and Matt pulls her into a hug. After dead body #4 is found, the four remaining partiers finally sober up.

This is getting creepy, Still-Alive Party Girl #5 says.

"I agree," Cooper says.

I'm starting to think these weren't accidents, Matt deduces brilliantly.

I think you're right, Lacy agrees. She takes a band from her wrist and pulls her hair up into a high, tight ponytail.

I pause the movie and stare at the screen, feeling like I'm looking in a mirror.

The captain announces our decent and asks us to buckle up.

"We'll watch the rest on the way back," I tell Cooper, shutting off my laptop and stowing it.

WE FLY INTO Van Nuys Airport, which is closest to Malibu, easy to get in and out of, and one of the only airports in the Los Angeles area that has no hourly restrictions regarding when flights can take off. We don't have the time to airport-hop, so I did something else to shield our identity. I opened a fractional ownership under Cooper's name and bought a chunk of hours. I figure Cooper Steele kind of sounds like an actor, and he kind of looks like he could be one, too. With my darker hair and our comfortable relationship, we'll easily pass as brother and sister.

Our pre-arranged driver picks us up and shuttles us to Malibu, dropping us off at the Malibu Lumberyard.

"We have time for some fish tacos," I say, suddenly craving them.

"As long as you keep the wig on, I'm fine with it. I'm hungry. Besides, we need to go over your plan for tonight in detail."

The restaurant is crowded, so we sit at the bar. Cooper picks a spot close to the doors to the kitchen. I notice he chooses a seat with his back to the wall, facing the crowd. I sit down next to him.

I look at the tables around us and spy someone I know. "Sand—" I start to blurt out loudly, but Cooper quickly covers my mouth with his hand.

I take a deep breath. "I'm sorry," I whisper. "I forgot for a second."

"You're also wearing a wig."

"Shit," I say, glancing down at my brown curls. I close my eyes and think. "It might be a good idea for me to be seen here. As me."

"If the goal is for Vincent to think you're back in Malibu, I would agree. But we need a plan."

AFTER A BRIEF discussion, I walk out of the restaurant with my head down and go into a nearby restroom, emerging as myself. I quickly go into one of the stores, buy a new outfit with cash, and then wear it back into the restaurant. As I make my way back to Cooper, I purposefully walk by Sander.

"Sweetheart?" he says. I smile, remembering his adorable nickname for me.

"Sander!!" I squeal, throwing my arms around him and causing a bit of a scene. "How are you? How's *Grease?*"

"In the can. Big Memorial weekend release," he says proudly, kissing me on the cheek.

"That's awesome!"

He pushes me out and takes a hard look at me. "You look amazing. Where the hell have you been hiding? I come back and Cush is gone, and you're nowhere to be found." Then he whispers in my ear, "Rehab?"

I laugh. "More like an all-girls school in the middle of nowhere. You heard what happened with Cush, right?"

"Yeah. It's a shame. That boy hit the jackpot when he dated you."

"That's why I love you. You feed my ego." I give him another big hug.

"Join us for a drink?"

"Us?"

With his arm still draped across my shoulder, he turns me toward his group. "Keatyn, this is Danny Woodyard, the choreographer of *Grease*, Dylan George, one of the T-Birds, and Donnie Van Zandt, one of the dancers. Everyone, this is Keatyn Douglas. *Abby Johnston's* daughter."

The boys all ooh and aah over my mom and her acting brilliance.

Gay men love her.

"Can't wait to see her new movie! It's going to be just scrumptious."

"So what's your next movie?" I ask Sander, changing the subject.

"Not sure. I want to choose the right project. My agent called me yesterday wanting me to do a screen test for that remake of your mom's old movie. Hey, we could star in it together. They want me to play the boyfriend. How easy would that be?"

Shit. I need Sander to stay far away from Vincent.

I grab the fruity martini they ordered me, take a big drink, and look toward Cooper. "Oh, wow. I didn't even see him over there."

"Who?" Donnie says, swiveling his head quickly, probably hoping to spot someone more famous than Sander.

"Cooper Steele," I say, drawing his name out. "I'll go get him. I feel bad making him sit over there and wait for me."

"Girl, you should always play a little hard to get," Dylan tells me.

I saunter over to Cooper. "You're going to have to pretend to be really into me, okay?"

"Got it," he says, all business as I grab his hand and lead him back to the boys. But as soon as I introduce him to everyone, he becomes a cad, stealing my martini, drinking half of it, and placing his hand firmly on my ass.

"So, Cooper Steele, where did you get all those muscles?" Donnie asks.

Cooper shrugs like he was just born this way.

"The Steele Building Workout," I say discreetly.

"Sexy name for a workout," Dylan says. "I dance too much. Can't seem to put on any bulk."

"Eat more protein and lift weights," Cooper says. "You need to balance out all the aerobic activity."

"Are you a personal trainer?" Sander asks, sizing Cooper up and noting his hand placement.

Cooper, who doesn't miss anything, keeps his hand firmly in place, but starts caressing my ass with his thumb.

I give a cute little shiver and kiss him on the neck. "Cooper is one of Tommy's stunt men. So, thanks for the drink. It was great seeing you, Sander, and meeting you all. We're going to head out. I'm taking him dancing tonight."

"We were thinking of hitting Plague. Where are you going?"

"To a place that doesn't have a name," I laugh.

"I've heard rumors about that place," Danny says in awe. "Can we join you? Can you get us in?"

I glance at Cooper. He gives my butt a single tap of his finger. "Sure, why not? Can we meet up at your house, Sander?" I look down at my clothes. "Obviously, I need to change."

"Sounds good. Ten o'clock? We can get there before the crowds."

"Sander," I tease. "I'm not going to let you drink with the crowds. We'll be in the VIP section."

Danny claps his hands together and grins. "Even better."

Cooper puts his arm around me as we stroll out of the bar.

"THAT WENT SURPRISINGLY well," he states.

"Hopefully, breaking into my house will go equally well."

"Breaking in?"

"Not breaking in, exactly, but we don't have a car for a reason. Come on."

I take my shoes off and drag him across the street, down the beach, and through the fence delineating the start of the Malibu Colony properties.

"Are we going to get in trouble for trespassing?" Cooper asks after reading the warning signs.

"I live here," I say, then I take off running, feeling free for the first time in a while.

I stop two houses before mine and point. "That one is ours."

"It's pretty here. I can see why you like it."

I nod, looking out at the ocean. "You can sightsee later. We have work to do. No one's around, so let's go."

I take off running again and don't stop until we're standing on the side of my house that's hidden behind the fence. I sneak to the front, push one of Tommy's codes into the keypad, and slip into the garage.

Cooper tries to open the door into the house. "Shit, it's locked."

"I know. Hang on." I walk around Tommy's Ferrari to a shelving unit where he keeps all the car cleaning supplies, pop open a cigar box hidden under a stack of diapers, pull out a key, and let us in.

The house security alarm beeps, wanting me to enter my code. I press in one of Tommy's instead, quickly stopping the beeping.

"Whew," I blow out a breath. "I wasn't sure if they changed all the codes or not."

"Why would they change your code?"

"I didn't enter *my* code. We don't exactly want to broadcast to Garrett that we're here."

"Won't they know Tommy isn't here?"

"I used the code he gave to the guy who details his cars. He has to come inside to get the keys," I say, stepping into the kitchen.

I thought that when I got here I would be able to see all the good times I've had here.

But I don't.

Instead, I'm reliving that night. *The photos dropping out of a manila envelope onto the kitchen island.*

I shake my head to clear my thoughts, and move toward Tommy's closet, sticking to the mission at hand. "We need to find you something to wear."

"What's wrong with what I'm wearing?"

"Nothing, it's just not club appropriate. Hmm, Tommy's a little taller than you."

I open Tommy's closet and step in.

"Whoa," Cooper says. "This is like a store."

"Tommy loves clothes." I move to a section of long-sleeved shirts, pulling out a bright blue one with the kind of sheen you only get from fine cotton. "Try this on."

Cooper strips off his long-sleeved t-shirt and, well, I can't help but enjoy the view. Specifically, the sexy tattoo running across his abs.

He buttons up the shirt and tucks it into his cargo shorts. "Whatcha think?"

"Hmm. The sleeves are just a little long." I unbutton his sleeves and roll them up. "Yeah, that will work. Okay, now we need pants. What size is your waist?"

"Thirty-four."

I move to the wall of pants, find a black pair with a subtle blue pinstripe, and check the label, quickly translating the European size to an American one. "Let's try these."

"Dress pants? Can't I wear jeans?"

"That depends. What size shoe do you wear?"

"Eleven."

I smile. "Yes, if you'll wear a great pair of shoes, I'll let you wear jeans."

"I can live with that."

I throw him a pair of dark jeans and even though I'd like to turn around and watch, I give him privacy and focus on choosing a pair of shoes. One pair immediately catches my eye. I pull the black Pradas off the rack and study the pattern of perforations and the blue undertones, remembering Aiden in the same shoe at Homecoming.

Luck, I think.

Or maybe fate.

Either way, it couldn't hurt to have a little of each on my side tonight.

I look at Cooper. "Hmm, something is missing . . . I know." I grab a large, expensive watch, strap it on Cooper's thick wrist, and nod. "Perfect."

"OKAY, NOW MY turn." I head toward my room, still feeling odd.

I thought I'd walk in here and feel like I was finally home, but I don't.

I feel . . . tense. Nervous. Bad memories keep surfacing.

I wonder if I can even do this.

If it's this bad here, what's it going to be like at The Side Door?

But once I get into my closet, I feel better. It's a happy place, and I've missed my clothes.

I open a drawer and dig through it until I find the pair of shiny black Lurex shorts I want to wear.

Normally, I wouldn't dress quite this skimpy, but if I'm going to do what I want to do, I have to look the part.

I pair it with a neon bra top, fishnet hose, and black patent leather platform boots.

I shoo Cooper out of my closet so I can get dressed.

I also call Troy, but he doesn't answer, so I call Damian.

Thankfully, he answers.

"Hey, it's me. What are you doing tonight?"

"We've been recording all day. Troy's heading out to DJ. I'm probably going home."

"I just tried to call Troy. He didn't answer."

"Why are you calling Troy?"

"Um, you can't tell, but I'm home. Just for the night. Vincent is going to be at The Side Door tonight, and so am I."

"What? Are you nuts?"

"Please just let me talk to Troy."

Damian sighs. "Here's Troy."

"Keatyn, long time no talk," Troy says. "Are you coming to the club tonight?"

"I am and I have a huge, huge favor."

"Whatcha need?"

I make a snap decision to tell Troy the truth. Some of it, anyway.

"I know you've been gone touring, but did you know that I'm not living in Malibu anymore?"

"Uh, no. Where'd you go?"

"An all-girls boarding school out in the middle of nowhere."

"Sounds incredibly boring."

"It is. So, what I was wondering is if you could get me two all-access passes. Something that will allow us to go backstage, get behind all the closed doors."

"Why do you need that?"

I give him a quick version of what happened while he was touring.

"Is that why *we* had so much security?"

"Yeah, he knows I toured with you last summer."

"What's his name?"

I tell him.

"Seriously? He's a VIP. Crazy big spender."

"I know. He comes every Thursday looking for me. He followed me there, you know, before."

"So why would you want to be anywhere near him. Isn't that dangerous?"

"Not if you help me." I tell him the two other things I need.

"Keats, shit. I don't know if I can swing that. The first part is easy. The second part . . ." He trails off, then he says, "Our club security is outstanding."

"And probably easily swayed by a big-spender VIP."

"Hmm, yeah, you're probably right. You'll have to dress skimpy, sexy hot, and a little cheap." He laughs. "That's like a four letter word to you, isn't it? You never look cheap."

"I will tonight."

"Then it shouldn't be a problem. You driving Tommy's Ferrari, like usual?"

"Yep."

"Perfect. I'll leave your passes with the valet."

"Thanks, Troy. I really appreciate it!"

Damian takes the phone back and says, "Don't hang up. I need to walk outside." I hear him walk across a wood floor, the squeak of a door, and then he goes, "Keats, what the fuck?"

"Cooper is with me. This is all well-planned." Well, some of it is.

"I'm coming tonight."

"No! I don't want to risk Vincent seeing us together!"

"Brook told me about the hostile takeover thing falling through. Is that why you're doing this?"

"No, this was my plan all along. And it fell through with B, but not with me. I've made other arrangements."

"I hope you know what you're doing. I've been seeing the movie trailer everywhere. I hate to say it, but your mom looks smoking hot. And bad. Really,

really bad."

"That's part of the plan too."

"Did Peyton tell you she's coming to visit me next weekend?"

"Yeah. It will be a low-key weekend, right?"

"The family will be in New York, so the place is all mine. She'll be lucky if I let her out of the bedroom."

"Damian!" I screech. "But, good. Discretion is key. Especially after the band's write-up in the new *Teen Vogue*."

"Yeah, one of the guys stupidly tweeted about us being in the studio and forgot to turn off his location services. Girls actually started showing up outside. It was freaking crazy."

"All the more reason you have to keep your relationship a secret. Are you picking her up at the airport?"

"Yeah, but she's meeting me outside. I'll be in one of Dad's limos."

"Perfect."

"Keats, be careful."

"I will. Bye."

Cooper comes into my closet. "You've got to be dressed by now."

"I am. What do you think?"

"There isn't much to it," he states.

I shrug. "That's kinda the point. So, I have one more phone call to make and then I'll tell you my plan."

FIREBALL SHOTS.
10PM

I REV THE Ferrari's motor as I pull in next to Sander's purple Lamborghini. I leave Cooper in the car, hoping to get the boys to hurry. We're on a tight schedule.

Sander opens the door, his eyes bugging out. "You're wearing that?"

I raise my eyebrows at him.

"You like nice, you just look . . ."

"Cheap?" I roll my eyes at him. "Standing here, sure, but once I get there, I'll blend in. Oh, before your friends join us, I wanted to tell you something."

"What about?"

"That remake of Mom's movie. I heard that the studio is, like, maybe having some big financial issues. Or, like, about to."

"Where'd you hear that?"

"I overheard Matt Moran talking about it."

"Oh, well, he would know, right?"

I shrug casually. "I would think so."

"I was going to get the script, but now I won't bother. I'm definitely staying far away from that studio," Sander states.

THE BOYS ALL get loaded up in their cars and we caravan to the club.

The valet opens my door, takes my hand, and helps me out of the car. "It's been a while, Miss Douglas. Good to see you."

"Hi, Billy. It's good to be back. Troy was supposed to leave me some passes."

"I've got them right here." He pulls them from his jacket pocket and hands them to me along with my valet claim ticket.

I put the ticket into an envelope with the name of the guy who details Tommy's cars.

I hand the envelope to Billy. "I have someone picking up the car in an hour. Should be a wild night. Figured it'd be better to have a car to take us home."

Sander's car pulls up behind mine.

I turn toward the car and tell Billy, "I brought some friends with me."

"Nice ride," he says.

"Hey, Billy," I whisper. "Do you know Mr. Sharpe?"

Billy rolls his eyes. "Silver Porsche. Douche."

"Is he here tonight?"

"No, but it's Thursday. He'll be here."

"Could you do me a teeny little favor?" I hand him a folded hundred-dollar bill. "When he arrives, will you discreetly let this guy know immediately?" I gesture to Cooper. "He'll be in the VIP section."

Billy looks down at his hand and smiles. "Absolutely."

I move my skimpily clad body just a little closer to him. "And, Billy, under *no* circumstances am I to leave with Mr. Sharpe."

"He bad news?"

"For me, yes."

I GET THE boys happily situated in the VIP section and do a shot with them while Cooper uses his all-access pass to check out the exits. I look down at the dance floor, knowing the door Vincent tried to drag me out of is almost directly underneath me.

When he gets back, Cooper says, "You sure he'll let me know when he arrives?"

"Yeah, I tipped him a hundred dollars."

Cooper pulls me toward the balcony overlooking the dance floor, wraps his arms around my waist, and appears to whisper sweet nothings in my ear.

"I want you dancing there." He uses a mini laser pointer to indicate the spot.

I toss my head back and giggle, playing my role.

"There's an exit here." The red light hits a black spot on the wall. "And here."

"Got it."

My bottom lips pops out in a pout, like Cooper just told me something I didn't want to hear.

Sander says to him, "Aw man, you're in trouble. No one can resist the pout."

"Sander, stop giving away my tricks." I smile at him. "So, the party pooper here has to take a business call. Who wants to go dance?"

TEN MINUTES LATER, Cooper joins me on the dance floor, pulling me tightly into his body.

I grind on him, making sure my ear is close to his mouth.

"Vincent's here. He just left the VIP section and moved closer to the dance floor. As we walk back to the bar, he'll be on your right. I'll be walking on your left. No matter what, I want you to keep looking at me. If you make eye contact with him it will ruin your plan."

"Got it."

I stop grinding on Cooper, close my eyes, and just cling to him for a minute.

"You sure you want to do this?" he asks.

I open my eyes, nod at him, and Party-Girl-Keatyn yells to Sander, "I think we need another drink!"

The small pack of us makes our way back to the VIP section.

Cooper keeps his arm tightly wrapped around me.

Party-Girl-Keatyn gabs loudly the entire way. "So I can't decide what I'm in the mood for. Should we have hypnotic, lemon drop shots, or should we should just keep going with the Don Julio?"

Just as I finish my sentence, I feel Cooper's grip on my waist tighten and I know we're about to walk by Vincent. I keep my eyes locked on Cooper's and stay in my role.

"How about you, sexy?" I say loudly to Cooper. "What are you in the mood for?"

Cooper mumbles something and I laugh loudly. "I think we'd get arrested for that, baby."

"Keatyn, darling, let's do Fireball shots," Danny yells back at me.

"Hot, just like us," Sander and I yell at the same time.

Which makes me forget about Vincent for a second and actually laugh for real.

While Sander is ordering shots, Cooper keeps watch behind me. "It's time to go. He's headed this way."

I pat Sander on the back. "I have a surprise for you boys. Keep an eye out for me."

"Move now," Cooper says, quickly leading me to one of the pass-only doors.

He flashes our pass to the guard, who lets us through.

"I'm still worried about getting you down."

"I know." I lead him to the DJ booth and get Troy's attention.

"Damn, girl," Troy says, giving me a hug. "I've missed you. Not the whiner boyfriend, but I've missed you."

"Brooklyn's not my boyfriend anymore."

"If you weren't our friend, I would have kicked his ass for all the bitching he did. You had fun though, didn't you?"

"I had a blast being on tour."

"Damian says you're going to be in our video."

"If you guys still want me, yeah."

He looks at me again. "We do. So, keep going down the hall. Second door on the left is where all the girls are. They'll tell you what to do."

"Why don't you walk down there, Cooper, and check it out. I'll be right there."

As soon as he's out of earshot, I say to Troy, "Were you able to get it?"

"Are you sure about all this? Damian gave me an earful before I left. I assume you want this guy to see you but not get close?"

"Exactly."

"That shouldn't be a problem. Patrons aren't allowed to touch the cages."

"Still."

Troy sighs. "Fine. It's duct taped to the floor. I put a little spot of glow-in-the-dark paint on both ends of the tape. The safety's on but, Keats, the last thing we need is a shoot-out in a packed club."

"I won't use it unless I absolutely have to."

He musses my hair. "You looked great dancing out there. Wherever you've been has been good for you."

"Thanks. You look like a rock star."

"It's pretty exciting, huh? 'You and Me' has been getting a ton of airtime. The label thinks we'll hit the Billboard chart this week."

"Seriously? Damian didn't tell me that."

"He has some new tail he's after. But I'm not complaining. He's written some seriously amazing shit this week."

"He's in love."

"Apparently. Okay, so get down there. You only have a few minutes."

IN THE DRESSING room with the paid dancers, I get a quick makeover by Marla, the woman in charge. She cakes on more makeup and glues on the huge glow-in-the-dark eyelashes the dancers are known for.

Then she adds glow-in-the-dark paint to strategic locations on my body. Stripes fanning out from my eyes. Four stripes around the clover tattoo on my wrist. A swirly stripe across my left shoulder blade. Filling in numerous diamond shapes in my fishnets.

She stands back and looks at me with an artist's eye, trying to decide where else to put the paint, when she spots my tattoo.

"Oh, I like this," she says, outlining it. "What's it mean?"

"Chaos."

"Love that. We should all have those. I've always said that if they ever give this place a name, it should be called Utter Chaos."

AFTER A FEW words of advice, I'm being locked in a cage and swung out over the now jam-packed dance floor.

I look through the neon sunglasses I'm supposed to wear to start the dance and quickly see Vincent standing in his former spot, his calculating eyes searching the dance floor.

I hang onto the bars of the swinging cage until I'm lowered onto a six-foot-high platform just to Vincent's left.

When all the cages are on the platforms, the music screeches to a halt and a new song plays, causing the Plexiglass bases of each cage to light up, flashing with the beat.

Our cue to start dancing.

THE MORE WE dance, the more people cluster around the cages.

I draw a little crowd, which makes me dance even naughtier.

I use all the moves Peyton told us we could never tastefully do in our dance competition.

Then I remember a move that Vincent will surely recognize.

And one that will probably piss him off.

I bend over, shake my ass, and then blow a kiss over my shoulder, straight toward him.

He immediately stands up and pushes through the crowd toward me.

I put my sunglasses back over my eyes so I can watch him while I shimmy.

He gestures to one of the two bouncers whose job it is to keep drunk boys from trying to climb the platforms.

Vincent hands him a folded bill. I can't read his lips, but I definitely catch the word *VIP*.

The bouncer smiles at the money and says something into a headset as Vincent goes up the steps.

A FEW MINUTES later, my cage starts moving upward.

The girls usually dance in the cage for thirty minutes, then rotate to a VIP lounge platform. Which, obviously, I wasn't planning to do. The dancers, though, love the VIP area, as it's where they earn the majority of their tips.

I notice that my cage is the only one moving.

We're supposed to all come in at the same time.

I glance at the timer that counts down my shift, and see I should still have twenty-two minutes left.

That means Vincent requested me.

I try to imagine what his impromptu plan might be. I'm sure he's planned out what he'd do if he ever saw me here.

But I doubt his plans included me being in a cage.

At least I know I'm safe backstage.

But as I'm being lowered, I see Vincent coming backstage, a bouncer escorting him.

I look in every direction, searching for Cooper, but not seeing him anywhere.

My heart starts to race and I tell myself to calm down. It's not like he's got a van sitting out back every week. The valet told me he drives a Porsche.

The bouncer's job is to protect me. *Look, don't touch* is what they always tell people.

I should have thought about this before. If he found me, how would he get me out of the club?

Then I remember Miami.

He'd drug me.

Slip me a roofie.

Use a needle.

Help his sick friend to the car. *She just had a little too much fun,* he'd say.

Maybe I should go back to the VIP area with him just to see what he'd do.

But then another possibility pulses through my brain. Vincent hurts, drugs, or kills the bouncer. In his slick suit, it would be easy to underestimate his strength.

Where the hell is Cooper?

And why did they let Vincent backstage?

I bend down, pull the duct tape off the gun, and slip it into the back of my shorts.

The bouncer stops Vincent from coming any farther and walks up to my cage.

"I have twenty minutes left. You're going to get me in trouble with Marla."

He lowers his voice. "I know you're new, but the gentleman here is a VIP. *Big* VIP. And he requested you now. You know the boss man is all about customer service."

"Fine. I'll go powder my nose, then I'll head up there."

The bouncer looks back at Vincent, who shakes his head.

"I think now would be better."

"Um, okay." The bouncer opens my cage and takes my hand to help me out.

The second my feet hit the concrete floor, Vincent starts moving quickly toward me.

My eyes get huge.

I point and go, "Um . . ."

The bouncer turns around and says to Vincent, "Go back to the VIP section now. We'll meet you there."

"I just want to talk to her. I'm a producer. This could be her big break."

"I don't want a break," I whisper, putting my hand behind my back and gripping the gun.

Suddenly, Vincent charges toward the bouncer.

Shit!!

I move to avoid getting knocked down.

When I do, the big cage swings, ramming Vincent and the bouncer, knocking them down.

Cooper grabs me, pulls me down the hall, and pushes through an exit door.

The bright streetlights temporarily blind me.

"Which car is it?" Cooper yells.

I hand him the gun. "Here, take this."

"Where the hell do you get—"

I don't answer, just pull him toward a sweet black Ducati.

"A motorcycle?" Cooper panics. "I've never ridden one."

I hop on the bike, pull on my helmet, toss one to Cooper, pop the kick-stand, turn the key, grab the clutch, and hit the start button, bringing the motor roaring to life.

"Just hang on!" I yell as both Vincent and the bouncer barrel out of the exit.

I pop the bike into first gear with my foot, crack the throttle, and speed off into the night.

I make numerous turns through the warehouse district, already having memorized the streets, and then shoot out onto the highway near the Santa Monica airport.

I drive fast, weaving in and out of traffic.

Once I'm sure we're not being followed, I head toward the coast, merging onto the PCH, heading toward Malibu.

I try to stay close to the speed limit now, not wanting to get pulled over and end up a sitting duck on the side of the road.

Before the Malibu city limit, I make a right turn and pull into an unmarked parking lot. Then I hit the remote on the bike's keychain to open a big garage door and pull in, dousing the bike's lights and quickly closing the door behind us.

"I don't think we were followed, do you?" I ask Cooper as I turn off the bike, pull off my helmet, and shake out my hair.

"I don't know how the hell we could've been. You were driving like a mani-ac!"

I roll my eyes at him. "I was only doing eighty on the highway. Vincent has a Porsche. Those things are fast!"

Cooper takes his helmet off and sets it on the bike. "Somehow when you said *stealth out the back*, this was not what I envisioned."

"It worked, though. Come on, we've had our excitement for tonight. Let's get the hell out of here and back the airport."

"What about your wig? Our bags?"

I point to a Mustang sitting in the bay next to us. "It's all in the car."

"What is this? A chop shop? Is this all stolen?"

"No, it's the concierge detail shop that does Tommy's car. They pick up his cars from the house every few weeks, detail them, and put them back under their covers all shiny. He dropped the motorcycle off, picked up Tommy's Ferrari, moved our bags to the Mustang, and already has Tommy's car safely back home. He's also going to drive it around town tomorrow. You know, just to be seen."

"Did he not think it was an odd request?"

"Considering his clientele, probably not. Especially with the rumors of Tommy's affair."

"Oh," Cooper says. "That's smart."

I find the Mustang's keys hanging exactly where I was told they would be and replace them with the keys to Brooklyn's bike.

Even though B knows nothing about it, there's something comforting in the fact that his bike helped me tonight.

Cooper grabs my hand. "You're shaking."

"A little, but I'm fine."

"Adrenaline rush," he states. "It'll stop soon. In the meantime, I'll drive."

ON THE WAY to the airport, I throw the dress I wore earlier over my club clothes, tuck my hair back under the wig, rub off the paint, and gently remove the eyelashes.

"I have to admit," Cooper says, "I'm very surprised you know how to ride a motorcycle."

"That wasn't just any motorcycle. It was Brooklyn's. The concierge service takes care of B's and his dad's cars, too. I knew we were going to have to make a speedy exit, so it seemed like the best option. Honestly, I'm really lucky that he knows me, or I never would've been able to pull it off. I didn't exactly ask B if I could borrow his bike."

"What made you even want to learn?"

"I was fine with just riding on the back. It was fun, felt romantic, you know? But after a couple times of us going somewhere and B needing to take me back home before he was ready to leave, he decided I should learn how to ride it. That way I could take myself home if I needed to."

And once I learned how, he knew he could get high or drink and I could drive us both home. Although at the time that sorta pissed me off, I'm now really grateful I know how.

AFTER WE'VE TAKEN off and gotten to cruising altitude, Cooper says, "So what do you think we accomplished? Seems like all it did was piss him off."

"We made him think I'm back home." I smile. "And remember, a pissed off, out-of-control, mistake-making Vincent is exactly what we want."

"I was there the whole time. In the shadows. Waiting for the right moment."

"I didn't see you."

"You didn't look scared."

"I had protection. Speaking of which, what did you do with it?"

"It's in the bag."

The flight attendant interrupts Cooper to ask us if we would like dinner or a snack.

"Dinner," Cooper says.

"I'll just have some water," I reply. I might not be shaking as bad on the outside anymore, but my insides are still a wreck.

"My sister needs to eat," Cooper tells the attendant. "Bring her a dinner along with her water."

She quickly comes back with plates of grilled chicken in a mushroom sauce on a bed of risotto.

I eat a little and then lean my head against Cooper's shoulder.

Friday, December 2nd

CONFIDENCE AND SWAGGER.
7AM

"YOU AWAKE ENOUGH to drive back to school?" Cooper asks me, putting our bags in the car.

"Yeah, I'm fine."

He sits in the passenger seat until I get about a half mile from school, then he hops in the back and hides.

I go through the school gates, pull into my parking spot, hop out of my car, leaving it unlocked, and then walk to the dorm and straight into my shower.

I'M FORTY-FIVE MINUTES late for our 7 am Social Committee meeting.

"Sorry I'm late," I say, my entrance interrupting Logan.

"That's okay. We're just finishing up," he says.

"You're our last report. Is the French Club ready for tomorrow night? Will the baskets all be ready?"

"Yeah, The Market was happy to do them. They even gave us a nice discount, so the club will earn money for the state competition this spring."

"Perfect," he says. "That completes our list."

Peyton does a little clap. "This is going to be so fun."

Logan holds up his notebook and says to the group, "So, here's to a great event and an entire weekend where we can't get in trouble for French kissing!"

"Hear, hear!" everyone exclaims.

I'm thinking about French kissing Aiden when Whitney says, "Peyton, Keatyn, a word. Alone," she adds, looking straight at Aiden, who is walking toward us.

"We're gonna discuss our periods," Peyton says, teasing her brother.

He winces and says to me, "I'll meet you outside."

Whitney says, "I overheard Chelsea trash-talking you to one of the only friends she has left, and saying that she's going to get even. I think you should start sitting at our table again. It will make her think twice." She holds a single finger in the air as I start to speak. "And before you say anything, Aiden's welcome. Riley, whoever you'd like. The more the merrier. Right, Peyton?"

"Right."

Peyton folds her hands in prayer, begging me behind Whitney's back.

"That's really nice of you," I say to Whitney.

She grins, wraps her arm around me, and says, "Shark's gonna sit with us today too. Try not to have a heart attack."

"I think you and Shark together is awesome. He was totally flirting with you at Homecoming."

"He's been flirting with me for two years and I wouldn't give him the time of day. But then he told me the odds of us getting together were a hundred to one, but that he'd take them any day. It was romantic, in an unusual way. He keeps getting cuter and he just has . . ."

"Swagger," I say.

"Yeah. Confidence and swagger. You can tell he's going to be successful in life. He's already working on building what will be *the* hot new social media website. He'll be an internet mogul by the time he's twenty-five."

"I think all that matters today is what are the odds he's a good French kiss-er?"

"They've been doing plenty of that," Peyton says in a sing-song voice.

"I have a plan," Whitney says. "I need a pedicure and we have," she makes air quotes, "*some French errands to run.* Let's go get pedicures together. Have a girls' morning."

"Sounds great!" I say, mostly because I didn't get my history homework done. "I'm gonna talk to Aiden. Why don't you ask Miss Praline for a note?"

"Already got the note," Whitney replies, waving it in her hand. "We'll go turn it in. Meet us at my car in ten minutes."

I FIND AIDEN in the hall. "How's your uncle?" he asks.

"He's good."

"You look tired."

"We stayed up late talking about my mom."

"What did he say about her? Is she doing better?"

"Well, they just got to France, so it's hard to tell yet."

"What else did he tell you?"

"Uh, well, apparently the Vancouver project was really stressful. A lot of negotiations and stuff. And she was working long hours and spending too much time away from my sisters. So that upset her. And I guess Vancouver sort of, like, consumed her. But the good news is that she's taking a whole month off. At least from traveling. Although, I'm sure she'll work some from home."

Shit. Why did I say that? Next he's going to ask . . .

"What's her next project?" Aiden asks, responding exactly the way I was praying he wouldn't.

Shit.

Uh . . .

Improvise, Keatyn. Make something up!

"Uh, well, part of the reason she agreed to France is because her next job is, uh, it's in the Ukraine."

Where the hell did that come from?

Is the Ukraine close to France?

Do they even have oil in the Ukraine?

"So, that's good, right?"

"Yeah, I think so."

"I'm glad you got to see him while he was in town."

I think of the look on Vincent's face when he saw me at the club. "I'm really glad I got to see him too."

He pulls me in for a sweet kiss. "So, what are you girls planning?"

"Officially, we're going off campus to check on some last minute details for the weekend, but, really, we're getting pedicures. Which is good. My polish is a mess after being in the sand. You wanna come too?"

"Ah, no. I'm busy with the Hawthorne house project."

"What are you doing?"

He flicks his tongue across my neck. "I can't tell. You said you're making your dorm look like store windows. What's going to be in yours?"

"We're only doing it on the front facing rooms, but I helped Maggie plan hers. It will be a springtime in Paris theme. A pretty pale blue dress with a tutu skirt, pastel flowers, and a big art frame to make it look like you walked into a Degas' picture."

"Very creative."

"Are you really not going to tell me what you're doing?"

"You'll see it later. Depending on how it goes. Right now, it's walking a fine line between cool and ridiculous."

"What if I give you a French kiss, *monsieur*. Will you tell me then?"

"Depends on how good a kiss it is," he flirts, sliding his hands into my hair.

I wrap my arms around his neck and move my lips slowly toward his. Then I stick out my tongue and rub it sloppily across his cheek, laughing.

He quickly stops my giggles with his own powerful tongue. Moving it with the grace of a Degas ballerina.

Until the first bell rings.

"I better get going," he says. "What color are you going to get on your toes?"

"What color do you think I should get?"

"A sexy red, maybe?"

"I was thinking a soft pink."

"That would be pretty. Is the dress pink?"

"No, but my bag is."

"Makes sense. Have fun."

"I will," I say, prancing away from him.

But he grabs me by the waist, pulls me back in, and gives me a kiss that leaves me reeling.

ALL THAT SUNSHINE.
8:30AM

I MEET THE girls at Whitney's car and we head to a posh day spa.

We're quickly taken back to a private pedicure room with three chairs.

"What color should I get?" Peyton asks, holding up a bright red and a hot pink.

"I like the red for me and the pink for you," Whitney teases, pulling the red out of Peyton's hand.

Peyton laughs. "That's always what we get. Maybe we should go crazy and switch it up. You get the pink, I'll get the red."

Whiney laughs too. "You're right. We do always get the same thing. Maybe we should get something funky. Keatyn, what would you suggest?"

"What color are your dresses for tomorrow night?"

"Mine is black and Peyton's is an icy blue."

"Oh, pretty." I grab a sparkly, metallic charcoal and hand it to Whitney. "This is for you."

"Really? I won't look Goth?"

"No, dark nails are totally acceptable. Besides, this has glitter, so it will sparkle." I elbow her. "You know, in case Shark sees your toes in soft lighting."

She grins. "I usually make boys wait, but I don't think I'm going to with Shark."

"Really?" Peyton says, turning away from the polish wall and giving me a surprised look.

Whitney shrugs. "Sometimes you just know when it's right."

Peyton, who is standing behind her, pretends to stick her finger down her throat and gag.

I try not to laugh.

"I'm glad you're happy," I say to Whitney. "All right, Peyton, what color for you?"

I stand next to her and stare at the wall of polish.

"Pedicures are supposed to help relieve stress, but choosing a polish totally stresses me out!" she says.

I scan the silver polishes, choosing one that is a soft color but also has an iridescent shimmer to it. "This one."

"Oh, I like that. My shoes are silver, too."

WE GET SITUATED and soak our feet in the warm water.

I turn the massage chair on, lean my head back, and close my eyes.

This feels so good.

"Do you want something to read?" Peyton asks, tossing a paper into my lap before I can respond.

I'm about to throw it back at her when I see a headline at the top with Mom's photo underneath.

I quickly open the paper to the Entertainment section and scan the article.

The headline reads, *Crowds Line Up To See* To Maddie, With Love.

I scan the article.

"This is the kind of rare movie that both critics and fans alike will be raving about," movie critic Tim Steward proclaims.

Fans outside the packed midnight showings were excited to see if Mr. Steward was right. We did our own poll among those exiting the theater, and fans had a lot to say about this film and how Maddie's story touched them.

"Abby Johnston's movies usually make me laugh and fall in love," local resident Alice Truluck said. "This movie made me cry, physically ache, and feel completely uncomfortable. But it still made me fall in love. This is an amazing story of

redemption. Abby has to win an Academy award for this."

Rumors are flying as to why Abby hasn't attended any of the premieres held around the world this week. Also notably absent from Abby's life is her long-time beau, Tommy Stevens. Inside sources say a split is imminent.

There's a photo of Tommy and Bad Kiki getting on a private plane with the caption, *He's moving and taking the dog with him!*

Abby left earlier than planned from Vancouver where the movie she and Tommy were filming together has wrapped. Tommy's publicist said in a statement: "Abby and their adorable children plan to join Tommy in New York, where he will be filming the third movie in the blockbuster Trinity *series."*

But a day earlier, Abby's publicist contradicted that statement. "Like many on the Vancouver movie set, Abby has come down with the flu and won't be attending the premieres." And, when pressed further about the health of the couple's relation-ship: "Abby will not accompany Tommy to New York. She's taking some time away from the movie industry."

Those of us who have seen the frightening photos of a too-skinny Abby hope she's planning on eating during her break.

"I got accepted to Brown yesterday," Whitney says happily, causing me to stop reading. "Did you get a letter, Peyton?"

"No, not yet," she says. "But I don't care. I applied to some more schools this week."

Whitney looks surprised by this. "You did? I thought we were going some-where together? We've talked about it since freshman year. We go to the same college. Join the same sorority. Party it up."

"Yeah, well, I'm not sure the East coast is where I want to be."

"Where else could you possibly want to go?" Whitney says in a snide voice. Like anything other than an Ivy League college would be unacceptable.

"I applied to a few California schools. I'd like to be closer to home."

"California? Seriously? I'd hate to live in California. All that blonde hair and sunshine would piss me off."

I purse my lips in defense of my favorite state and am just about to say some-thing when Whitney turns to me. "No offense."

"I love the feel of the sun shining on my face," Peyton says, dreamily. "And I'd like to trade my car in for a convertible. Drive around with the top down all the time. Never have to deal with the snow again." Peyton sighs. Then she tosses a magazine toward me. This one is rolled open to a certain page.

I flip it over and see a photo of Damian and Troy coming out of a club with a chesty blonde in a tight dress who's hanging onto Damian's arm. *Could this unidentified blonde be the girl to finally snag Damian Moran, the son of mega-hit director, Matt Moran, and lead singer for the band Twisted Dreams, whose studio was mobbed by tweens earlier this week?*

I take my phone out and text her, not wanting to say anything in front of Whitney.

Me: *She's with Troy.*
Peyton: *I know. I was just showing you the pic.*
Me: *California, huh?*
Peyton: *Yes!! We talked about it in St. Croix. I'm so happy!! Stop texting me though. I don't want Whitney to get suspicious.*

"Which colleges did you apply to in California, Peyton?" I ask.

"Pepperdine, USC, UCLA, and Stanford, but I'm leaning toward Pepperdine," she says with a big smile. "It's right across from the beach. How awesome would that be?"

"It sounds amazing. They're all good schools."

"Stanford is pretty good," Whitney says. "But it's the only one I would consider. I'm setting my sights a little higher. Shark already got accepted to Yale. That's where I'm planning to go as well. Just waiting to hear from them. Then I'll make my big announcement."

"What big announcement?"

"Of where I'm going to college," she says in a tone that is supposed to make me feel stupid for asking.

"How will you announce it?"

She gives me a wide smile. "Well, most people just tell their friends. I was thinking of something a little more grand. Like at Winter Formal."

"Cool," Peyton says. "I'm sure the school is on pins and needles waiting to hear your choice."

"I know I am," I say quickly, hoping to distract from Peyton's snotty comment. "How cool to announce it at Winter Formal."

Peyton rolls her eyes at me while Whitney favors me with a wide smile. "Thank you. I thought it would be very cool, too. And Shark is dying for me to reveal my choice, so it will be fun for him."

"That's a really cute way to tell him," I say.

MOST ROMANTIC CITY.
11:40AM

WHEN WE GET back to school, we find that most of the students are out of class, helping their various clubs or dorms.

I'm not really sure if Whitney is trustworthy, but she has been really nice to me, and all of us being friends seems to make Peyton happy, even though I'm not totally convinced that she wants to be friends with Whitney anyway.

And, since it's my fault she can't tell anyone about Damian, I figure it's the least I can do.

Whitney has a long list of things we actually do have to check on for the weekend.

"*Top of the Eiffel Tower, Sunset* is going to be even better than Greek weekend!" she exclaims as we tour the campus.

"Let's go check on the awnings," Peyton says.

We walk to the front of the social center and watch as an alumni-owned rental company adds pink and black striped awnings to the outside of the building and sets up black iron bistro tables and chairs. They've even brought in portable heaters to make sitting outside more comfortable.

"Wow!" I exclaim. "It looks so good! Everyone will love it!"

"You fit right in, too. I love your outfit," Whitney compliments me.

I love my outfit today, too. In honor of French weekend, I have on Louboutin black fringed ankle boots and am carrying their black spiked tote bag. I'm wearing an Alice + Olivia black leather box pleat skirt, pale gray knee-high socks with kitten faces on them, and a white fleece pullover with *Magnifique!* scrawled across the front.

"Thanks, Whitney. It's too bad we couldn't import some French shopping. Chanel. Dior. Lacroix. Gaultier, Louboutin, Chloe, Laurent. All lined up in a row."

"That would be amazing. Maybe instead of going to the beach and partying with boring frat boys, the three of us should go to Paris for Spring Break and do nothing but eat croissants, drink *café crème*, and shop the boutiques and Parisian flea markets," Whitney suggests.

"Oh, that would be fun!" Peyton gushes. "Paris is the most romantic city."

"Yeah, maybe you could meet someone there," Whitney says, getting in a little dig.

Peyton looks at Whitney with puppy dog eyes, but as soon as she turns away

112

she gives me a little wink. She and Damian have talked every single night. He told her that they needed to keep their relationship under wraps for the time being. And, honestly, I probably shouldn't feel too bad because I think the secrecy of it is just adding to her excitement.

The bell rings, signaling the end of fourth period and the beginning of lunch.

"Perfect timing," Whitney says. "We'll check out the café and then get everyone to sit at my table."

We wander into the café.

It's already been mostly transformed into a riverboat with porthole windows showing colorful scenes of the French countryside and Parisian landmarks.

"The drama and art clubs outdid themselves," she says, checking them off the list.

"And you can smell the croissants baking," I add, breathing in the wonderful aroma.

PEYTON, WHITNEY, AND I sit at the table, stopping all our friends and inviting them to sit with us. I never realized it before, but they didn't even fill up a whole table. Now it's crowded and noisy.

And fun.

Particularly when Aiden squeezes next to me and gives me a kiss on the cheek.

"How's the project? I didn't see anything when we walked by your dorm."

"It's not quite finished yet."

He puts his hand on my thigh as he whispers, "When it's done, you'll be the first to see it."

"When will that be?"

"Tomorrow night."

Logan says to Whitney, "We should start the announcements."

They stand in front of the café and Logan clears his throat. "Hey everyone. If I can have your attention . . ." When the room quiets, he continues. "The Social Committee wants to give you a little update on the events for French weekend. The dorms will, once again, be competing for a dress-down day. Entries will be voted for on Sunday. Tonight's café dinner will be *steak frites* and, afterward, everyone is encouraged to attend the basketball home opener. The coffee shops will be open late, serving pastries and drinks, and curfew will be extended to twelve-thirty."

He hands Whitney the microphone. "Since we're hosting a wrestling match on Saturday, be sure to go support our team," she says. "The café will be open all day on Saturday, serving French grilled ham and cheese sandwiches, or *croques monsieur*, French pastries, and chocolate soufflés, as well as holding hourly French cooking classes. Then, Saturday night, everyone will get dressed up for the Seine River Dinner Cruise. Who knows what will happen on the river?!"

Logan finishes up. "Sunday afternoon, you can get involved in some games of *boules* and see a French film at two. Hope you enjoy all the activities we have planned! And a big thank you to all the clubs involved in making this weekend a reality."

After they finish, Aiden whispers, "I need to get back to the shop. Are you going to French?"

"Probably not. I should go back to the dorm and help finish up the windows. Are you coming to dinner?"

He shakes his head. "No. I have to be in the locker room at six and there's no way I could eat a heavy meal like that before the game."

"I'll miss you," I say.

He grabs my hand and gazes into my eyes. "I'll miss you too."

"Will I see you before the game?"

"You gonna wish me luck? Offer up some dances?"

"I don't know. How many points do you usually score?"

"Last year I didn't start and I averaged eleven."

"So, how many will you score this year?"

"Not sure. Twenty, thirty, maybe. Hopefully. It might depend on how motivated I am."

"One of the dancers said that she gives her boyfriend a—" I whisper the word in Aiden's ear. "For every dunk he makes."

Aiden's fingers graze the skin just under my skirt, giving my goose bumps.

I swallow, wishing his fingers would move higher and give me something else.

"Are you offering me that?"

"Can you even dunk?"

"You doubt my skills?" he says with a laugh.

"I probably shouldn't. I don't think there's anything you can't do."

"I can dunk. Never have in a game, though. I don't want sexual favors for my game performance, but if I dunk, what if I get something I want?"

"Uh, what do you want?" I ask, my mind going all kinds of sexy places.

He stands up, pulling me up with him and leading me out of the cafeteria.

Once we're away from everyone else, he backs me up against the wall, his chest pressing into mine, his knuckles pushing my chin up toward his mouth. "I want a night alone with you in my room. No parties. No hanging out. Just you and me dancing before curfew, then you sneaking over to my room after curfew and spending the night. Sleeping with me."

I'm not sure what his definition of sleeping with him is, but I'm totally game.

"I'd do that even without a dunk," I say, pressing my lips to his.

He grins. "I know. Maybe I just want to impress you."

When he goes to the shop, I go to my dorm and order a huge candy gift basket and a whole bunch of chaos glow-in-the-dark temporary tattoos to send to the dancers at The Side Door with my thanks for letting me dance with them.

Saturday, December 3rd

SOME MUTUAL PLEASURE.

5:30AM

AIDEN'S ALARM GOES off at five-thirty in the morning.

He gives his phone a dirty look as I snuggle into his arms.

"No one ever checks on us in the morning. Does your house mom ever?"

"No, and even if she did, Katie would cover for me. I'm still tired. Let's go back to sleep."

He kisses the top of my head and runs his hand down my hair.

"I love when you do that," I say sleepily.

I close my eyes and think about last night.

How he dunked the ball during warm-ups, then blew me a kiss. How he scored twenty-two points. How, when he was on the bench, he'd always catch my eye and smile at me. How his eyes stayed glued to me when the dance team performed at the end of the third quarter. And then how we danced under the twinkle lights to our playlist. How dancing with him makes me feel high. Happy. Emotional.

I can't imagine dancing with anyone else for so long without getting bored.

But things are never boring with Aiden. Especially because he added a fun dance song in the middle of our playlist.

We moved our bodies to the beat, grinding on each other and having fun.

When the slow songs started again, he picked me up, put me on his bed, then lay on top of me and kissed every part of my upper half until I had to run to make curfew.

When I snuck back over later, all he had on were a pair of boxers and a sleepy grin. After some mutual pleasure, I fell asleep in the same spot I'm in now.

116

GRITTY, RAW PERFORMANCE.
3:30PM

AIDEN AND I get up late, have coffee and chocolate croissants, and cheer for Logan at his wrestling match. Now, I'm lying on my bed relaxing before I have to get ready for tonight and reading online reports about Mom's movie.

Christian Protestors Picket Theaters in California

Christian protestors came out in number yesterday to protest the Abby Johnston movie, *To Maddie, With Love*. In Los Angeles, two theaters were shut down after receiving bomb threats. Bomb squads searched both properties and found no incendiary devices. Moviegoers themselves rushed out of one San Francisco theater after smelling what they were afraid was some kind of toxic gas, but turned out to be simply a sewer malfunction.

None of these incidents have effected ticket sales. Box offices are recording what should shape up to be a record-setting weekend. Despite her dismal personal life, it looks like Abby Johnston may finally win an Oscar.

Excerpt from Movie Critic, Bart Wallow

This movie achieves that rare combination of being a big box office hit and having a gritty, raw performance that really shows off Abby's acting chops. That she's damn hot in this movie hasn't hurt ticket sales, either.

Then I start searching for information on the remake of *A Day at the Lake*. I find a small blurb in a trade magazine.

Search For The Next Abby Johnston Falls Short

A Breath Behind You Films CEO Vincent Sharpe has been touring the country, looking for the next Abby Johnston to star in their remake of her cult classic, *A Day at the Lake*. Sources from inside the company say that the search has not gone as planned, and that they will soon have to start looking at more seasoned actresses. Only three roles have yet to be cast. Sources say that Luke Sander, former child star who just wrapped the lead of Danny Zuko in the remake of *Grease* was rumored to be in the running to play the boyfriend. His publicist says he has withdrawn his name from consideration due to a conflict with another project. No word yet on who might play the killer.

I breathe a sigh of relief about Sander.

I also realize that I haven't heard anything from B since I got notification that my birthday gifts arrived at his hotel.

I decide to call him.

He doesn't answer, so I leave him a message.

"Hey, it's me. Just calling to wish you a happy early birthday. I sent three packages to your hotel. It says they were delivered, so hopefully they found their way to you. I also wanted you to know that I'm not mad at you. I understand why your dad doesn't want you to help me. Anyway, um, happy birthday again. Hope you have a great day and we can talk soon. Bye, B."

KNOCK KNOCK.

I'm startled by the loud knock and drop my phone.

"Who is it?"

"Aiden."

I glance at the clock, verifying that it's a little before four, then open the door.

"I need you to come with me," he says, pulling me out the door.

"Why?"

"I need to show you something, but we have to hurry."

"Can I grab my coat?"

"Nope, you won't need it."

"You're being awfully bossy."

He grins at me. "I'm sorry, but we're in a bit of a time crunch."

"Did something happen with the picnic baskets?"

"No, I just need to show you something."

"Is it bad?"

"I sure hope not," he says as he leads me in through the back door of Hawthorne House.

I follow him up the stairs to the third floor and laugh when he goes into someone else's room.

When I catch up to him, I stop in the doorway and stare.

I don't know why he's rushing up here, but I do know I'll remember the way Aiden looks for the rest of my life.

His entire body is bathed in the golden light that's streaming through the window, almost making him glow. They say some people can see the color of your aura, and I know without a doubt that Aiden's must be the purest of gold.

He holds out his hand, so I walk across the room toward him.

"Whose room is this?"

He doesn't reply, just kisses me instead.

His lips press against mine, his tongue slips into my mouth, and I could care less whose room we're in or why.

For a brief moment, I wonder why he dragged me up to someone else's room just to kiss me, but those thoughts quickly evaporate when he moves his hands, one tangling in my hair and the other pulling my waist closer to his.

I slide my hands up the front of his shirt, needing to feel his skin.

I'm getting ready to unbutton his shirt and strip it off him when a loud *HONK* startles me.

Aiden smiles against my lips. "The honk means it's time."

"Time for what?"

He spins me around in a little dance move so that I'm facing the window, wraps his arms around my waist, and rests his chin on my shoulder.

"Time to look outside."

I look out the window and discover the reason for Aiden's bright glow.

The sunset is beautiful tonight.

Gold and red rays of light are fading to pink between layers of clouds.

"What do you see?" he asks.

"An amazingly beautiful sunset."

"You're half right."

He steps closer to the window until I'm almost smashed up against it, moves my hair off my neck and kisses it.

And I could care less about the sunset. I just want to kiss him.

He kisses my cheek, blinks slowly, and then says, "Look down."

"Ohmigosh!" I say breathlessly, not able to believe my eyes.

Now I understand why he brought me up here.

Why the horn honked.

"Top of the Eiffel Tower, Sunset," dreamily escapes from my lips as I look down at his house project.

It's a homemade version of the Eiffel Tower. I can only see the pinnacle from up here, but I know exactly what it is.

"It's beautiful, Aiden." I turn to find him down on one knee.

I swear, I just forgot how to breathe.

He takes my hand in his. "Keatyn Monroe, *vous me faire l'honneur d'être mon jour pour l'hiver formelle?*"

I may have forgotten how to speak, too.

His godly powers are running strong tonight.

I nod.

And keep nodding.

Then I finally mutter, "Yes."

I recover a little, finding my voice, and finish, "I'd love to do you the honor of being your date for Winter Formal, Aiden."

He stands up, takes my face in his hands, and gives me a movie-ending, sweeping-epic-romance kiss.

After the kiss, I open my eyes and smile at him.

"You've had the whole dorm in shop class working on building the Eiffel Tower for the last two days just to get a dress-down day?"

"Not exactly. We've been working on it since we chose French as our next theme. I wanted to ask you to formal at the top of it."

"But that was over a month ago. And when I was still dating Dawson."

Tears start to fill my eyes.

I can't believe he built me an Eiffel Tower.

"What can I say? I was optimistic. And no crying." He quickly puts his lips on mine and makes me forget my name.

He kisses me.

Kisses my neck.

Kisses my nose.

"I know we're supposed to be handing out picnic baskets now, but I was trying to time it with the sunset. I didn't think we'd get it up in time. And I was worried you might have already seen it."

"My room faces the woods. I miss all the good stuff."

"We're going to miss handing out baskets if we don't get going."

"I can live with that," I say.

"Perfect. That means we have time for one more kiss."

ONE REALLY LONG kiss.

Fifteen minutes later, I'm outside, staring up at the Eiffel Tower they built in awe.

From the top, I could only see the metal pinnacle of it, but from down here, I can see that they have covered the metal with flattened soda and beer cases that are duct-taped together. It seems a little odd, seeing brand names emblazoned on the sides of the Eiffel Tower.

I start laughing. "It's like an advertiser's wet dream."

Aiden laughs with me. "Yeah, well, we needed something to help support it.

We couldn't get it to stand on it's own."

"I still can't believe you did this."

"I can't believe it hasn't fallen over yet."

"Do you think we'll have fun at Winter Formal?" I tease.

"I think it will be a night to remember."

WE WALK HAND-IN-HAND down to the Student Center where the French Club is handing out the picnic baskets that everyone pre-ordered.

Annie is already hard at work, and I'm shocked to find Jake with his sleeves rolled up, helping her.

"Hey, Jake." I give him a little elbow to the ribs and a teasing smile. "You join the French Club?"

"I asked him to help," Annie says. "Because I need your help with something else."

"My help?"

"Yeah, come one."

Aiden grabs my hand. "You can't ditch me."

I kiss his cheek. "Apparently, I'm needed."

"What for?"

"Annie?"

"Girl stuff, Aiden. You only have an hour shift and then you can go get ready."

"Just meet me at seven," I tell him.

Jake is wearing what appears to be a permanent grin.

"Annie, does Jake know what we're doing?" I ask her as she grabs makeup and dress bags.

She looks back at Jake and gives him a little wave. "Of course he does. I was kind of freaking out. You guys did my hair and makeup, but wouldn't let me look in the mirror. I need you to show me how to do it so I can do it myself. I've been trying all week and it looks okay, but not as good."

"What are you wearing?"

"I have two dresses. I'm not really thrilled with either. One because I've worn it before and the other because I was supposed to wear it with Ace."

"Have you talked to Ace?"

"He texted me that night after he got mad. Told me he was sorry. I asked him what really happened and he told me the whole story. The stuff Chelsea said to him over break. How he was stupid."

"What'd she say?"

"Sexual stuff. And, you know, I would have been fine with that. He could've apologized and maybe we would've gotten back together. But then he told me that he told her stuff about us. About our sex life. And get this: he told her that I don't give good head! He never once complained! As soon as he told me that, I was completely done with him."

"Wow. That's low."

"Especially since he wanted me to do it to him all the time. Honestly, though, I was doing something—not wrong, really, but I've since learned how to do it better."

"Did you watch videos online or something?"

She half laughs and half coughs. "No. Jake, um, helped me."

"Helped you?"

"Let me practice. Gave me some pointers."

"Annie! I can't believe you're doing that with him already!"

"I know, right? I'm a little shocked too. But I'm having a whole lot of fun. And I just want to look really great tonight. So he's proud to be there with me, you know?"

"I know. I want to look my best tonight too."

"What the heck is that?" Annie says, squinting at the monstrosity in front of Hawthorne's dorm. "Is it supposed to be the Eiffel Tower?"

She takes off running to look at it more closely.

Just as I'm getting to my dorm, she runs back to join me. "That's crazy! Who in the heck's idea was it to make that?"

"Aiden's. He just asked me to go to Winter Formal at the top of it."

"How did you get to the top of it?"

"He took me up to a dorm room, showed me the sunset, and then had me look down."

"Top of the Eiffel Tower, Sunset?"

"Yeah, when I first tutored him, we joked about going to France together."

"I heard they've been working on the project for over a month but I didn't know what it was. You do realize that a month ago you were still seeing Dawson."

"I know."

"Aiden's pretty freaking special."

"Yeah, he is."

ONCE WE'RE IN my room, I make her try on the dresses.

She puts the first one on, and I can tell by her body language she doesn't like it. "Is this what you were going to wear for Ace?"

"No, I wore it last year for something. But I've changed a lot since then." She smiles. "And it's all your and Maggie's fault."

"Our fault?"

"Yeah. I never really cared that much about clothes until I started hanging out with you guys. And you have such a great sense of style. Some of the outfits you put together, if someone else tried to wear them, they would look ridiculous, but on you they just work."

"Thanks, I think. Speaking of Maggie, where are she and Katie?"

"Getting dressed in Maggie's room, then pre-partying with Bryce."

"Cool. Okay, so, what kind of style do *you* want to have?"

"I want to look classic. You dress in classic pieces, classic shapes, but they all have a little flair to them. Then you go crazy on your accessories."

"Actually, the reason my clothes are mostly basics is because I usually choose my shoes first! So, classic. What else?"

"Romantic. A little bit girly. But not frilly."

"Got it. Try on the other one."

The black dress has a little more style, but black really doesn't do much for Annie's pale complexion. I wish she had something in a softer color.

"Oh, I know!" I say, running into my closet and finding a dress that I think will look great on her. "Try this on."

The dress slides over her hips like butter. "This is beautiful," she says. "Wow, I look good in it, and I don't even have any makeup on."

"That's one way to tell if a color is good on you. I wore this dress once when I went to dinner with Aiden, but no one else has seen it. Do you have some pretty black shoes?"

She nods. "The ones I wore to Homecoming."

"Those were cute. They'll be perfect. Okay, take that off and I'll show you how to do your makeup."

AFTER GETTING ANNIE ready, I work on myself. I'm supposed to look like a movie star and my dress is perfect for that. It's tiered black silk organza, similar to one worn in a Miss Dior ad.

I do my hair in big curls, then brush it out into soft waves. The dress has a bit of a twenties vibe, so my hair will match perfectly.

I'm just putting on a pair of black suede Charlotte Olympia cut-out sandals when Aiden knocks on my door.

When I open the door, he hands me a beautiful bouquet of flowers in the palest of pastels. Light fuchsia roses. Pale pink and blue hydrangeas. White lilies of the valley. Dusty pink peonies.

"They're beautiful, Aiden. Are they for me?"

"Who else do you think I'd buy flowers for?"

"They're just so pretty. I thought maybe they're, like, a centerpiece or something."

"They're for you, silly." He sets the flowers on my desk then holds out his arms. "So, obviously, you look crazy beautiful. But how about me? Do I look good enough to play your arm candy?"

I let my eyes slide down his buff body, which is looking totally delectable in a black suit. His hair is perfectly mussed. His angular face is freshly shaven. And his shoes . . .

"You might have more shoes than I do." I laugh. "You look more than good enough to be my arm candy. In fact, I don't think anyone will even be looking at me."

I hold my pink Alexander McQueen appliquéd clutch and look at myself in the mirror again.

Something's missing.

I spy the flowers behind me. "That's what I need!"

I grab one of the pink roses, pin it to the plain black satin ribbon that came with the dress, and tie it around my neck.

"You look beautiful," Aiden says, holding my hands and leaning in for a sweet kiss. He looks at his watch. "We better get to the café."

I glance at his watch too.

"I'm playing the starlet. I'm pretty sure that means I should be a little late and make a big entrance."

"Well, if you're sure," he says, and leans in for another kiss.

TWENTY MINUTES LATER, Aiden is escorting me onto the French riverboat set.

Everyone is seated and opening their picnic baskets.

We make a purposefully noisy entrance and, right on cue, I'm stopped by two different dinner guests who ask for my autograph, which I sign on their dinner napkins with a purple glitter pen.

I stop along the way and give air kisses to a few of the other characters, and it's obvious that the students are wondering what the heck is going on.

Once we're seated, Logan walks out, dressed in a suit and a chef's hat. "I am the great Wolfgang Pluck. It was my honor to prepare your gourmet meals for this evening." He takes a prop glass of champagne off our table and raises it in the air. "I'd like to make a toast to a few very important guests." One by one, he introduces the characters in the cast. "Relax and enjoy the beautiful views out the boat's windows, *Bon appétit.*"

Aiden starts unpacking the picnic basket that is sitting on the floor next to us.

"What'd you get?"

"It's a surprise," he says. "But, since you'll be performing while everyone is having dessert, I thought we'd start with that."

He sets a container of chocolate mousse between us and pulls out two spoons.

"Oh, good call," I say. "It's my favorite."

I let the chocolate melt in my mouth.

He uncorks a bottle of fake wine and pours me a glass.

He clinks my glass and I take a sip.

"Aiden, this is not the fake wine. It's a Merlot, I think."

"Very good. And, shhh, don't tell." He kisses my cheek.

I use my palm to turn his face toward mine.

"I love chocolate, but kissing you is even better," I whisper. "What else is in the basket?"

"Brie, apple slices, some warm sourdough bread, chipotle almonds, and some ham."

"You planned so much for tonight. The Eiffel Tower, the flowers, the wine. It's sweet."

He shrugs his broad shoulders. "Maybe I'm a little sweet on you." Then he leans in close to me, clinks my glass again, and whispers, "In case you haven't figured it out, I'm still trying to woo you."

HAPPY BIRTHDAY!
MIDNIGHT

AT MIDNIGHT, I stop kissing Aiden and yell, "Happy birthday!"

"Thanks," he says shyly.

"We have to go somewhere. Grab your coat."

"Where are we going?"

"It's a surprise."

"For my birthday?"

"Not exactly. But we will be celebrating."

It's really cold tonight, and we don't run into anyone as we make our way to the chapel. Riley and Dallas are waiting for us downstairs, in the hall outside Stockton's door.

"You're late," they tell us.

"I had to wait until midnight, so I could wish Aiden a happy birthday!"

"Happy birthday, Aiden," Riley says with a fist bump.

"What are we doing down here?" Aiden asks.

"Traveling to paradise," Dallas says very seriously.

Riley puts his key in the lock, opens the door, closes it behind us, and then hits the lights.

I'm expecting Aiden to be wowed, but when the lights come on I'm saying *Oh my gosh* right along with him.

"Holy shit!" Riley says, bouncing on his toes like a little kid.

The room has been transformed. It no longer looks empty and unused. The walls behind the bar are stocked with top shelf alcohol and twinkle lights have been strung across the ceiling.

We run behind the bar.

"The keg's full," Riley says joyously.

Dallas opens what looks like a humidor sitting on the bar. You'd swear he just found the Holy Grail. Dallas looks in the box and backs away in awe. "This almost makes me cry," he says. "Look."

There are freshly rolled joints lying in layers in the box.

"Ohmigawd!" Riley screams.

"What?"

"There's a furry rug!"

I run over to a corner of the room, which has also changed. The corner is now mod and plush. There's a huge furry white rug. A sparky little chandelier hung in the corner. New furry purple beanbags and pillows scattered across the floor. A black curtain with holographic beads dangling from it.

"I wonder what's behind the curtain?" I say, pushing it out of the way.

Riley drops to his knees onto the furry rug, his hands folded devoutly, as I reveal a cozy king-sized platform bed wrapped in layers of overstuffed comforters.

"I'm going to kiss my brother on the lips next time I see him," Riley says.

Aiden, who's been standing in the middle of the room in shock, finally says, "What is this place?"

"Heaven," Riley replies as he falls face first onto the bed.

"Come here," I tell Aiden, grabbing his hand and showing him the names scrawled on the wall and the poem from the room's founders.

My phone buzzes in my pocket.

Cam: *How'd I do?*

Me: *It's like the Room of Requirement. Your brother's lying on the bed thinking he's died and gone to heaven.*

Cam: *A word of advice?*

Me: *Please.*

Cam: *Don't EVER invite Whitney. I know she's been nice to you lately, but don't believe it. She's just biding her time, waiting to strike.*

Me: *Okay.*

Cam: *And I love my brother, but I didn't think Dawson could handle it. I'm a little on the fence about his decision making.*

Me: *Other than lunch, I've hardly seen him.*

Cam: *I heard about him and Brooke. Another disaster waiting to happen, don't you think?*

Me: *I don't know. Probably depends if her ex changes his mind.*

Cam: *Exactly. Did Dallas find his present?*

Me: *Yes. He almost started crying.*

Cam: *What about yours?*

Me: *Mine?*

Cam: *The lights on the ceiling.*

Me: *Now I want to cry.*

Cam: *:) You need to leave now. Curfew.*

Me: *Oh shit, we do.*

Cam: *There are multiple exits. You'll bring friends in the front door, but don't leave from there any more. There's a map marking the exits on top of the bar. You can let people leave whenever they want to. Just send them out one of the exits. They are one way and take you to different points on campus. Hit the button on the paneling under the founder's poem. Use that tonight. Have fun!*

"We have to go, guys. It's almost curfew. Cam said to go this way." I press the hidden button and a small doorway appears. Through it is another clean and fairly well-lit tunnel.

"We need to run," Aiden says.

The tunnel is long, and I'm really worried we're going to miss curfew. Only a few minutes later, though, we slide open a door and find ourselves in the basement of Hawthorne House.

While the boys high five each other I tear out an exit door and run to my dorm. I'm late, so I knock softly on the window.

Katie helps me in. I quickly run into my closet, strip off my clothes, and throw on a robe.

A knock at the door causes me to launch myself onto the bed and pretend to be asleep.

I hear our house mom say to Katie, "Is Miss Monroe here?"

I sit up in bed and try to look sick, rubbing my eyes for effect.

"Sorry, I think I forgot to sign in. I'm not feeling great."

She walks over to my bed and observes, "Your cheeks are flushed." She places her hand in my forehead. "You're warm and a little sweaty. Do you have a fever, dear?"

"Uh, maybe?"

"Well, get some sleep, and if you don't feel better in the morning, go see the nurse. We've got two cases of the flu in the dorm already."

"Okay, I will."

A few minutes later, Katie peeks out the door to make sure she's gone. "Whew! That was close! I about died laughing when she said you were flushed."

"Yeah, I was flushed. From running like a maniac!"

"Were you at Aiden's?"

"Yeah."

"Are you going to Bryce's tonight?"

"I thought Shark was having the party."

"No. I'm pretty sure Bryce is."

"Oh, well. I'm probably not going to anyway. It's now officially Aiden's birthday."

"Ohhh, how are you going to celebrate?"

I shrug and smile.

"Have you guys yet?" she asks. "Are you going to for his birthday?"

"We haven't yet. I want to wait. What about you and Bryce?"

"We've done everything but. He needs to ask me to be his girlfriend and go to Winter Formal before I will."

"Has he said anything about it?"

"Not really, but every time someone gets asked, he asks me if I thought the way it happened was cool."

"What do you want him to do?"

"Just something that shows he put some thought into it." She lies down. "I'm going to take a nap. Oh, and if I'm not home in the morning, I'll be at Bryce's."

"Sounds good."

I'm brushing my teeth when my phone rings with a call from B.

"Hey! Happy birthday!"

"Thanks," he says. "And thanks for the presents. The skateboard is wicked sweet."

He's saying the right things, but there's something in his voice. Something's off.

"What's wrong, B?"

"There was something weird delivered today. Before I opened it, I thought it was from you."

"What was it? Was it from Vincent?"

"A Malibu Ken doll. It had a noose around its neck like it had been hanged."

"That doesn't seem like something Vincent would send."

"I don't think it was. I'm neck and neck with a real asshole in this weekend's competition. We have a saying, like when we screw up, that we hung ourselves. I think maybe he's trying to psyche me out. I'm getting ready to go out there. Look, I'm sorry I couldn't help you on the takeover. Um, and, well, there's something else."

"What?"

"I'm pretty sure I'm being followed."

"Did you tell Garrett?"

"Well, the security dudes. They've seen him too. It's just all messing with my head."

"B," I say softly, "do you remember when we were in Biarritz? When those local guys were giving you shit about how big the waves were? Do you remember what you told me before you went out there?"

"That I'd find control in the chaos."

"Exactly. The waves were crashing. The guys were saying you couldn't do it. But you went out there and found a wave you could control. That's what you need to do today."

"Keats, you inspire me in a way no one else can."

"You know in your heart that you can do it. Sometimes you just need to hear someone say it."

I hear his name announced over a loudspeaker.

"I'm up."

I hear him mutter, "Control in the chaos," before he hangs up.

I GET INTO bed, grabbing my laptop and plugging in my headphones so I don't wake Katie, and do something I've yet to do.

I log into the live feed of the surf tournament and watch.

The swells are huge. The sky looks dark, like it could storm.

The announcer is loud. I turn the volume off, watch B paddle out, and quickly pop up on his board.

The wave he chose loves him.

He moves like he's part of a symphony of water, waves, and wind.

He shreds the wave. Owning it. Flipping in the air.

I can't even believe how much he's improved.

He comes out of the water with a huge grin, looking like the Brooklyn I loved for so long.

He gets a great score from the judges and throws his fist into the air.

Then a skinny, leggy blonde excitedly hugs him.

I didn't realize while I was watching him that tears were falling down my face.

And in this moment, I finally get the quote, *A thing of beauty is a joy forever.*

What B just did—minus the blonde—was truly a thing of beauty.

I send him a text.

Me: *For the first time, I allowed myself to watch you surf. You were amazing, B. I've never seen you do some of the things you did. Congrats. And I wish I was there to share some cake with you.*

CONTROL IN THE CHAOS.
1:30AM

KATIE LEAVES FOR Bryce's and ten minutes later I meet Riley, Dallas, and Aiden, who are leading Logan and Maggie up the hill. When we get near the chapel, they put pillowcases over Logan and Maggie's heads and lead them the rest of the way.

We get them centered in the middle of the party room, and Dallas turns off the light.

"Take off your hoods, oh, chosen ones," he says.

Riley continues. "What you are about to see will blow your mind. You must take an oath right now. Maggie, do you promise under penalty of death—"

"Death?" I say, amused.

"Fine," Riley says. "Under penalty of losing all your friends and this amazing place, do you promise not to tell anyone what you've seen here tonight?"

"I promise," she says.

After Logan offers his promise as well, Dallas flicks on the light.

"Holy shit! Where are we?" they ask.

"We're on campus in a secure location."

"This is amazing!" Logan says, running around the room like we did the first time we saw it.

Aiden shows them the founders' poem.

"Alright, people, it's time for a toast," Aiden says. He pours us each a beer from the keg and we raise them together. "To Stockton's. Where membership has its privileges."

"Hear, hear," we all say.

"Aiden, I challenge you to a game of beer pong," Riley says.

WHILE I'M WATCHING Aiden and Riley compete for the title of beer pong champion, Dallas says, "I think it's time to sample the herb."

Aiden lets out a big whoop as he sinks a ping-pong ball in his last remaining cup of beer.

I cheer for him, then look down at my phone, which just buzzed.

B: Remember the cake on your birthday?

Aiden excitedly plops down next to me and sees my phone.

"Shark told me it's the Keats guy's birthday today, too."

"Yeah. I sent him some presents," I say, looking down.

Aiden pushes my chin up. "You don't have to feel bad. I understand he's part of your life."

"I don't want to ruin your birthday."

"Trust me, I'd rather you tell me about it than use my imagination."

"What would your imagination create?"

"The worse possible scenario."

I look into his eyes questioningly.

"You in bed with him," he says, the green of his eyes darkening.

"I watched a live feed of him surfing tonight. I haven't let myself do that before."

"Why?"

I shake my head. "I'm not sure. Too hard, I guess."

"You miss him."

"We talked almost every day for two years, then, all at once, nothing."

"How did he do?"

"He was amazing. Way better than before. He won his round." I bite the edge of my lip and tap my foot.

Aiden puts his hand on my knee. "What else?"

"There was a girl. She ran out of the crowd and hugged him."

"Did that bother you?"

"It's weird. If I had a normal life then that girl would've been me."

Aiden nods, and I can tell the idea upsets him.

So I tell him the rest. "But if I had a normal life, I never would've met you. Which makes me glad my life isn't normal."

Aiden is my control in the chaos, I realize.

He kisses me just like he did the very first time we kissed. When a simple kiss evoked visions of fairies and happily-ever-afters.

Now it invokes even more.

A deep-seated feeling that I'm exactly where I'm supposed to be.

Dallas plops down in a beanbag next to us. "You two are having entirely too serious of a conversation for this room."

He takes a hit and passes Aiden the joint. Aiden takes a few puffs and passes it to me as everyone else joins us on the beanbags.

"This is way better than the Cave," Logan says happily.

"And a lot warmer," Maggie agrees, sliding onto a beanbag next to him.

I get up and change the music from a dance playlist to one with a slower vibe.

"Much better," Dallas says, chilling.

While I'm up, I look at the map of exits curiously, and text Cam.

Me: *The party gods are bowing down to your greatness. But a question. We came out in Hawthorne. Any chance there's one I missed that would go to my dorm?*

Cam: *The founders lived in the Hawthorne and Pennington dorms. They have a long history of fraternization. To answer your question, of course. You know the part at the end where you made the sharp right?*

Me: *Yes.*

Cam: *Go left through a door. You'll end up in the basement laundry room.*

Me: *Awesomeness. You're like our spiritual party guide.*

Cam: *You never know what you'll find there :) Have fun.*

I start to sit on my beanbag, but Aiden grabs my waist and pulls me down on top of him instead.

"We need to plan a killer party here," Dallas says.

"I don't know," Riley counters. "I think we should keep it our little secret."

Aiden says, "I think we should have some parties, but not huge. Maybe twenty or so people, like at the dorm."

Dallas gazes at the twinkle lights like they hold the answers to the mysteries of the universe.

"Where do you think all this stuff comes from," Maggie wonders, staring up at the lights too.

"Yeah," Logan agrees. "How did all this stuff get here?"

"House elves," I say very seriously, and everyone cracks up. "What? I'm serious." Aiden is chuckling in my ear. "So, Aiden, do you have a better explanation?"

He shakes his head as Logan says, "My guess is alumni."

Dallas passes Logan a joint. "Clearly, you are only half baked. House elves for the win. And I hope they brought food."

Dallas and I jump up. He starts pulling chips and popcorn out of the cabinets.

When I open one of the fridges, I find a triple layer chocolate cake. The same kind Aiden brought me as a peace offering. It's even got candles in it.

I pull it out carefully and set it on the counter. "Um, guys, I think this proves that there are indeed house elves. It's a birthday cake for Aiden."

"How do you know it's for Aiden," Logan, the smart ass, asks.

"Maybe because it says *Happy Birthday, Aiden* on top?"

Everyone jumps up to see the cake.

Dallas squints his bloodshot eyes at the cake and then looks at me and says seriously, "House elves."

Maggie lights the candles.

We sing "Happy Birthday" to Aiden, chow down on cake, and throw ourselves back on the beanbags.

Sunday, December 4th

I WANT TO SHOW HER.

8AM

"UH, GUYS, IT'S, like, morning."

Logan is the first to wake up, stretching his arms above his head.

"Logan, don't you have wrestling workouts this morning?"

He jumps up quickly. "Shit. What time is it?"

"A little after eight."

"Fuck, why did I eat all that cake?" He's freaking out. "How do I get out of here?"

I lead him to the door that will take him to the woods not far from his dorm. I'm not sure his popping out of a hidden door in the basement on a day most kids do their laundry is a good idea.

"Get Maggie up. She's supposed to sing in the choir this morning."

I WALK BY Riley, messing up his hair, but he just rolls over and snuggles back into the beanbag.

I give the bottom of his shoe a little kick. "Rise and shine, lover boy. Ariela's going to be wondering where you are."

He sits up and appears startled to find himself still here.

"Where's my phone?"

"I don't know. Your pocket?"

He shoves his hands into his pockets and comes up empty.

I look on the bar counter.

"Jacket," he says, running over to check it.

As soon he stands up, I see it buried in the beanbag. "Here it is."

He swipes it out of my hand. "Whew. Thank goodness. She's not up yet."

I raise my eyebrows at him and smile. "You, my friend, are whipped." He kinda smiles and hangs his head. "And I love that you are."

"Me too." He looks over at the rug. "Do you think Aiden will mind if we miss his birthday dinner?"

"It's your anniversary. He'll understand."

"Speaking of that. I forgot to ask you. What'd you think of the freaking Eiffel Tower?"

"It's amazing. He asked me to go to Winter Formal at the top of it. At sunset."

"Top of the Eiffel Tower, Sunset. That's the theme."

"One of the very first times I tutored him, he said he's going to ask me to marry him at the top of the Eiffel Tower at sunset."

"What'd you say to that?"

"I said I don't even like you. Why would I marry you?"

Riley laughs. "That's funny. Do you think I take good care of Ariela? Like, Logan did the big gesture. Aiden took you dirt. I want to make her feel like that. I don't want to just tell her I love her. I want to show her."

"She loved the way you asked her out and to Homecoming. I think tonight will be special. There are some votive candles in the cabinet. Light a bunch. Turn on just the twinkle lights. Be as sincere as I know you feel. She'll love it."

Riley pulls me into a hug. "Thanks, baby."

"That's the first time you've called me baby in forever."

"I don't want to piss off her or Aiden."

"It doesn't sound right when you call me Kiki. Do you call her anything?"

"Yeah. I call her Kitty. Not very original, but it fits her. She reminds me of an adorable little kitten."

"And you want to pet her?" I ask with a laugh.

"Ha! Exactly."

"I swear, I can almost smell the croissants baking from down here."

"Should we let them sleep?"

"Naw, let's all go get breakfast."

AT BREAKFAST, ANNIE texts me.

> **Annie:** Are you in your room? I need to talk to you.
> **Me:** I'm at breakfast. Come over.
> **Annie:** Can I meet you in your room?

Me: Sure. Is everything okay?

Annie: Everything is wonderful. (Jake and I did it!!!!!)

I read it twice, just to be sure, then message Jake.

Me: Jake!!!?!!!!!!?!!!!!?!!!!! WHAT???!!! THE??!!!! FUCK??!!!!

Jake: I take it you talked to Annie?

Me: I can't believe you would do that!

Jake: Me?! Oh no. She attacked me!!!

Me: Seriously?

Jake: Yes. It was awesome. I'm going to ask her to Winter Formal. DO NOT TELL HER. I want it to be a surprise. And we need to brainstorm. Come up with something good.

When I get to my room, Katie is there, fresh from a shower.

"Annie's on her way over. Her and Jake did it last night!"

"So did me and Bryce."

"Oh my gosh! How was it?"

"Good. I really like him."

"Wait! Does that mean he asked you to go out with him?"

She gives me a big grin, holds up her hand, and shows me a pretty silver heart ring. "He gave me this, too."

"That's so sweet of him."

"I know. I'm so happy. He didn't ask me to Winter Formal yet, but now I know he will. My mission for today is to find a dress. I'm heading to the mall."

Annie walks into our room, beaming. Her arm is wrapped through Maggie's. I don't think I've ever seen her look happier.

"Ohmigosh, Annie!" Katie says, hugging her. "How do you feel?"

"Amazing. Last night was seriously the best night of my life. I'd been almost dreading having sex with Ace. All the talk about when we'd do it was sucking the romance out of it."

"Are you sore?" Katie asks. "I was sore after my first time."

"Not really. It was a little uncomfortable, like, for a quick second, but he was just so sweet."

"Tell them your good news, Katie."

Katie spills about her and Bryce and gets congratulatory hugs.

"Everything is working out for all of us!" Annie says. "Although it's kind of weird that Maggie and Keatyn haven't done it yet."

Maggie purses her lips and looks slightly offended.

"I didn't mean weird like bad!" Annie says quickly. "I just meant that I never expected to have done it before you guys—and with Jake! Like, not even in my wildest dreams did I ever think I could get a guy like him to even look at me. He's fun to hang out with, and he's really funny. I swear, all I do when we're together is laugh. Well, that and kiss. He's a good kisser too. Like, really good. You kissed him, Keatyn. Didn't you think he was?"

"I was drunk but, yeah, he was a good kisser."

"Who was better, Dawson or Jake?" Annie asks.

"I don't know. They were both good kissers. Dawson was hot. When I kissed Jake, they were sort of angry kisses."

"What about between Aiden or Dawson?" Katie asks.

"I stopped having sex with Dawson when Aiden kissed me with his tongue."

"So good," Annie says.

"I can't compare Aiden to anyone."

"What does that mean?" Katie asks. "Sure you can."

Maggie goes, "No, that means he's the one."

"What do you mean?" I ask her.

"If no one compares, if when he kisses you it's so amazing you don't care if you ever kiss anyone else again, if when you kiss it's so good it's almost overwhelming, then that's how you know he's the one. It's way more than just heat and desire. It's the way he affects you. How, with him, you feel a combination of smoking heat mixed with sweet tenderness. And it's not just when you kiss. It's something as simple as him touching your hand or locking eyes with you from across the room. You feel the intensity. The heat. The complete vulnerability that thrills you and scares the shit out of you."

"Wait, why does it scare you?" Katie wants to know.

"Because people tell you you're young and have so much more life to live. So many more boys to meet. But you know you could meet every boy in the universe and it wouldn't matter. He's it for you." Maggie hugs herself while we all sigh.

SO MUCH CRYING.
10:30AM

I HOPE THAT Aiden likes his birthday surprise. I've never planned anything like this before. Although, honestly, it wasn't that hard. I just emailed the track, told them what I wanted, and they were very accommodating.

I walk down to his dorm, stopping for a moment to look at the Eiffel Tower. I still cannot believe they built it. It's gorgeous out today. Sunny and almost sixty. It's supposed to be nice all day, but tonight the wind is supposed to shift and blow a winter storm down from Canada. They expect us to have a lot of snow by midweek.

I completely lucked out that it's dry today.

When I walk down the hall, I stop and knock on Dawson's door. He answers wearing nothing but a pair of boxers and a sleepy grin.

"Did I wake you?"

"Kinda. That's okay, though. What's up?"

"Nothing. I was just walking by your door and realized we haven't talked all week."

"Come in." He gives my outfit a once-over. "You have on jeans. I don't think I've ever seen you in jeans."

"I don't wear them very often. I'm weird, I know."

He gives me a sexy grin as he walks around me. "Oh, but you should."

I roll my eyes at him. "So, what have you been up to? Lately, I only see you at lunch or when you're playing basketball."

"I've been hanging out with Brooke a lot. Alone."

"How's that going?"

He sits on his bed next to me and shrugs. "I don't know. I like her, but a guy can only handle so much crying."

"How long did they date?"

"Since eighth grade. And during all that time, they only broke up twice, for, like, two days."

"Well, her being upset is pretty understandable—especially with the way she was blindsided by the breakup. I didn't date my ex for that long but I still miss him. He was my best friend for two years. We talked almost every single day. You feel like a part of you is missing when that's suddenly gone."

He nods. "She says the same thing. And she keeps trying to talk to him. Tell him she misses him. I told her that she shouldn't because he's probably thinking she wants to get back together, not that she just misses their friendship."

"It's only been a week. Sometimes you have to miss something to appreciate it."

"I told you that after I lost you."

I nod. "I know. So is she friends with anyone he goes to college with? Does she know what the real story is?"

"What do you mean?"

"Has he been seeing someone else? Did he cheat on her? Or does he just want to enjoy being single for a while?"

"I have no idea, but I know someone who can find out."

"You?"

"I could. I'm friends with him too. We played football and soccer together. But if I ask, he'll think she put me up to it."

"But if Cam asks . . ." I say, smiling.

"Exactly."

"Call him!"

Dawson looks at the clock. "I'm really not supposed to call him before noon, but it's close." He dials and puts his phone on speaker.

"What the hell, bro?" Cam answers, his voice gravely.

"You up?"

"Do I fucking sound like I'm up?"

"Hey, Cam!" I say cheerfully. "You're on speaker with me and Dawes."

"What are you two up to?"

"Typical high school drama. Dawson likes Brooke, who is still obsessing over her ex, who is . . . That's the question. We want to know about her ex. Do you know the real reason why he broke up with her so suddenly?"

"Yeah. Dawson, do you want this for your own knowledge, or are you going to tell Brooke?" Cam asks.

"I guess for my own knowledge."

"He called me before break. He's in a frat and you know how that is. Lots of parties. Lots of girls. He had a night where some things happened with another girl. He didn't cheat. Didn't even kiss her. But he wanted to and felt guilty. He decided he wants to have some fun and figures if they're meant to be together, they'll get back together later. She's planning to go to the same college. He wants to have fun until she does."

"That sucks," I say.

"Why does it suck? It's pretty mature, if you ask me. Better to have some fun now before you settle down than regret not having fun later in life and blame your wife for it."

My mind immediately pictures B coming out of the cabana and the leggy blonde hugging him. "Is he going to tell her?"

"I think so. Eventually," Cam says.

"If he wants her to go to the same college, he should. If he did that to me, I'd be seriously reconsidering my choice."

As the words come out of my mouth, I realize I'm not just talking about Brooke.

"Then they aren't meant to be together," Camden says.

Which pisses me off. "Is that really how he wants to live? Throwing his life into the wind and hoping he lands somewhere good? If he really loved her, he'd never want her to be with someone else."

"That's the problem," Cam says.

Dawson understands what he means faster than I do. "So you mean, he wants to have fun, but if she was having fun, he might change his mind?"

"I think if he thought she was moving on it would affect him. Not sure what he would do," Cam replies.

"Why you getting so worked up about this, Monroe?"

"I've just been in her situation before, and it sucks to think that someone you care about can throw away your love so easily."

"I would think if someone threw your love away, they weren't really that in love with you."

Tears spring to my eyes. "What about that stupid saying about if you love someone let them go and if they come back to you it was meant to be?"

"I've never really understood that saying until recently," Dawson says. "It means you have to give the person you love the freedom to make their own choices, even if they don't choose you. You want people to be in your life because they choose to be."

He touches my hand and smiles at me.

We hear Camden sigh. "All right, this conversation is getting just a little deep for me. I'm going back to sleep."

"Is everything okay with you and Aiden?" Dawson asks, after Cam hangs up.

"Yeah, it's great with him."

"Your ex?"

"He's seeing someone."

"But so are you."

"I know. But I'm not the one who made him promise we'd get another chance."

"He made you promise that?"

"Yeah. I thought it meant he still loved me. I mean, I knew he'd be having fun. I think this girl might be more serious."

"Does that upset you?"

"It confuses me more than anything."

"Maybe you should find out."

"What are you going to do about Brooke?"

"Take it slow, I guess."

"And don't be a stranger." I get up, give him a little pat on the back, and head to Aiden's room.

KINDA BOSSY.
11AM

"HEY, BIRTHDAY BOY," I say as I barge through Aiden's door without knocking.

Aiden is sitting in his chair, and Riley is lounging across his bed.

"On that note," Riley says, hopping off the bed. "I'll let you two go have some fun."

"Where are we going?" Aiden asks after Riley leaves. "And what are you wearing?"

I look down at myself. "What I'm wearing is a pair of jeans, boots, a t-shirt with sparkly lips on it, and a fun pastel moto jacket. What you need to be wearing is something similar."

"I don't think I've ever seen you in jeans."

"Dawson just said the same thing. I wear jeans sometimes."

"Not really. When did you see Dawson?"

"I stopped by his room on the way up here to see if he was alive or if Brooke had buried him in her dorm room."

"He hasn't been around much, has he?"

"No, and even when we went to dinner, all he did was text her."

"He likes her?"

"I think so, but he's also nervous about the whole thing. Says she cries a lot."

"Her and Blake's breakup surprised me. They seemed like a great couple."

"Until he wanted to sow his wild oats. I don't want to talk about them. It's your birthday, and I have something fun planned for you. Change, so we're not late."

"You can be kinda bossy."

"And you can be kinda stubborn."

He hops up and grabs me around the waist, almost causing our faces to collide.

I start laughing but he stifles my laughter with a kiss.

I put my palms on his chest and push him away. "No trying to distract me.

We have to go now."

He grabs ahold of my ass. "It's the jeans. I'm not sure I'll be able to keep my hands off you today. Plus, I was thinking since it's my birthday, we'd skip the French movie and just spend the day doing what I want."

"And what's that?"

He glances toward the bed.

Sure, the one day I have something planned, he wants to spend it in bed.

"We can skip it, I guess. If that's how you want to spend your day."

Aiden quickly lets go of me.

"Fine, I'll change." He strips out of the sweatpants that were riding low on his hips, slides into a pair of jeans, grabs a jacket and says, "Let's go."

"Grab your keys. You have to drive."

"Really, why?"

I give him a frustrated look.

He holds up his hands. "Never mind. Getting my keys."

As we leave school, I click the navigation on my phone and give Aiden directions.

"You're not telling me where we're going?"

"I was hoping to surprise you, but I can if you want," I pout.

He holds his hand up to my face. "Nope, your wish is my command. I can't take that face."

"What face?"

"The face you make when you don't get your way."

"It's your birthday. I want to do what makes you happy, but I think—well, I hope—that you're going to love this."

"If you planned it, I'm sure I will," he says, taking my hand and putting it on the stick shift under his.

About thirty minutes later, we're out in the middle of nowhere.

He turns down the radio and says, "Can I guess?"

"Sure."

"Are we seeing something or doing something?"

"Doing."

"Skydiving?"

"No. Oh! See that red sign up there on the left?"

"I can see it, but I can't read it."

"That's where we're going."

As we get closer, his eyes get big. "The Motorsports Ranch?"

"It's yours for the afternoon. A driving coach is going to work with you and then you get to go have some fun. See what your car can really do without getting a ticket."

He breaks into a mega-watt grin. "Are you serious?"

"I'm totally serious."

EVEN AFTER WE'VE checked in, met his driving coach, and he's suited him up, he says, "I can't even believe you did this."

I watch from the tower as Aiden works on cornering, steering, and proper shifting.

AFTER TWO HOURS worth of classes, he comes back in.

The mechanic checks out his car while we have a lunch of hotdogs and birthday cupcakes. The driving coach sits down with us and tells him the car looks good, and he can go out for some timed sessions.

I can tell he's loving every minute of this. I don't think he's stopped smiling since we pulled in the place.

AFTER ABOUT TWENTY laps, they bring him in, go over his times, give him a few pointers, and then send him back out.

While he's driving, I tell the coach about the classes Tommy made me take before he'd let me drive any of his cars. We start talking about the handling of high performance cars.

"You know," he says. "The classes you took are even more advanced than what we're doing today. You should go out and see if you can beat his time."

"Really? That would be fun."

When Aiden gets out of his car, the coach says, "What do you say we make this a little competition?"

"Sure," Aiden says, still grinning.

"I bet you twenty bucks and the rest of those cupcakes that *she* can beat your fastest time."

Aiden looks at the guy like he's crazy, then turns to me. "Do you know how to drive a stick?"

"I think so," I say, trying not to smile.

"Then I guess I'll take that bet minus the cupcake I'm going to eat while I watch," Aiden says.

They shake hands while I slide into a driving suit, shoes, and a helmet.

I hop in the car, buckle myself in, and take off.

I run the first few laps pretty slowly, wanting to get a feel for what the car can do. How it corners. The whine the motor makes when I need to upshift.

Then I work on the track for the next few laps. Which driving lines I should use.

Finally, I run five laps as fast as I can without risking losing control of the car.

Totaling her would probably ruin the whole birthday.

When I pull back into the garage, Aiden helps me out of the car with an amused look on his face. "How in the hell do you know how to drive like that?"

"I sorta took lessons."

He gives me a long kiss. "You were totally in cahoots with him."

"Ha. Maybe. How did I do?"

"You beat my best time."

"Are you going back out there?"

"Heck yeah. I know I can beat you." He puts his helmet on, then flicks up the visor so I can see him better. "Boots?"

"Yeah?"

"This has been the best birthday of my life."

My face breaks into a smile. "I'm glad."

As he goes back out on the track, I can't help but hope that I'm still alive for his next one.

BEFORE WE DRIVE back to school, I give him a present.

"You got me a present too? The track was really enough."

"I bought a couple presents before I decided to do the track, so you're stuck with them."

He leans over the console and kisses me instead of opening it.

A good long, hard kiss.

And even during the kiss, I can tell he's still grinning.

He rips the paper off. "Burberry. Nice." He opens the sunglasses case and pulls out a pair of square, brushed gunmetal aviators. "These are badass," he says as he puts them on and looks at himself in the rearview mirror. "Do I look like a race car driver?"

"You look hot," I reply, totally loving how cute he looks in them. I knew with his bone structure that they'd look great.

On the ride home, he talks non-stop about how much fun he had. How fast the car went. How he can't wait to tell everyone about it at dinner.

WE HAVE A great time at dinner. Jake and Annie, Katie and Bryce, Maggie and Logan, Peyton and Dallas are all here. Peyton got us a small private room, so we're able to be a little loud. Do lots of silly birthday toasts. Eat amazing food. And hear all about Aiden's day.

Peyton brings in a four-tier red velvet cake for dessert. We sing and then Aiden opens his presents, including the other two gifts from me: a pair of tan antiqued leather Prada High-Top sneakers and the deep green cashmere Burberry scarf that perfectly matches his eyes.

I had hoped we'd get a little time alone after, but we get back just before curfew and I have to settle for a sweet goodnight kiss.

I wash my face and get into bed.

Exhausted.

Vibrate.

Hottie God: *I feel like a little kid, exhausted after his birthday party.*
Me: *Doesn't help that we were partying last night and didn't get much sleep.*
Hottie God: *True. You went way overboard on making my birthday special. The Prada sneakers are so cool. I look like a badass in my sunglasses and the scarf is so soft.*
Me: *And it matches your gorgeous green eyes. That gift was kinda for me.*
Hottie God: *You going to borrow it?*
Me: *No, I get to admire you in it.*
Hottie God: *I seriously had the best day ever. And your driving impressed the shit out of me.*
Me: *Well, thank you. And I'm glad :)*
Hottie God: *The jeans impressed the shit out of me too.*
Me: *Is that why you kept touching my butt?*
Hottie God: *I couldn't help it.*
Me: *I still owe you 18 birthday dances.*
Hottie God: *We'll do those at your loft this weekend. I can't wait.*
Me: *I can't wait for the dance competition to be over. I probably won't see you until then anyway. You sister is making us practice until ten every night this week.*
Hottie God: *We have that French oral exam on Wednesday, and I have an away game Tuesday night. I'm going to fail.*
Me: *We'll find some time to practice.*
Hottie God: *I'm loving our conversation but I just dropped my phone on my face because I fell asleep.*
Me: *LOL. Night, Aiden. <3 Happy birthday!!*

Monday, December 5th

THE FEEL OF FUR.
6AM

I'M UP LONG before the ass crack of dawn. Peyton has decided that, since our dance routine is not yet perfect, we are basically going to be practicing every free moment until we get it right.

After we warm up and go through it as a group, she says, "Maggie, Keatyn, a moment."

She pulls us into the locker room.

"Did we do something wrong?" Maggie asks her.

"No, you're about the only ones who have the routine down. What would you think about breaking into small groups? We'll each take a third of the team and work on a portion of the routine."

"I think that's a good idea," I tell her.

"If we get them to do it well, does that mean we won't have to practice tonight?" Maggie asks, her hands folded in prayer.

"Do you have a magic wand I don't know about?" Peyton asks, teasing Maggie.

I have the magic wand my little sister gave me, I think, but I'm definitely not wasting a wish on a dance competition.

"All right, let's get to it," Peyton says.

AT SEVEN-FIFTEEN, SHE finally lets us go. I get ready quickly so I can meet Aiden for breakfast.

In the café, he and Riley are the only ones sitting at our table. I can see they're having an intense conversation.

I'm pretty sure I know what it's about.

I grab some breakfast and join them.

"So, Riley," I say, "based on the grin that's plastered on your face, I'm assuming last night went well?"

His grin gets even bigger. "I want to shout it from the rooftops."

"You gonna break out in song, too?" Aiden teases.

"So you asked her to Winter Formal, and she said yes?"

"She definitely said yes. And the next thing I know, she's naked on the furry rug. Talk about a sight to behold. And the feel of the fur against your skin." He closes his eyes and shakes his head. "Heaven. Seriously."

"Soooo?"

"Are you trying to get me to spill the details of my sex life?"

"No, I'm just wondering if you have a sex life?"

Aiden and I both laugh.

"Yes, I have a sex life now. A very hot one."

Aiden slaps him on the back, like a proud father.

"So, what about you two?" Riley shakes his finger at me and Aiden.

Aiden and I share a glance, then he says, "We want it to be special."

"I'd highly recommend you visit the furry rug."

"I already have something planned," Aiden says.

I look at him, surprised. "You do?"

He gives my hand a squeeze. "Yeah, I do."

"Hmm, on that note, I'm gonna leave you lovebirds alone." Riley picks up his tray and leaves.

"Do you actually have something planned or did you just say that to get him off the subject?"

"I actually have something planned."

"Winter Formal?" I guess.

"Yeah."

"Yeah?"

He grins at me. "Yeah. And I'm not saying anything else. It's supposed to be a surprise."

"How do you even know I want to?" I tease.

He smirks at me, running his hand up my thigh and his lips across my cheek. "Your body talks to me."

Damn his godly powers.

"Oh, it does, does it? What's it telling you now?" I lean away from him.

He follows me, putting his lips on my neck. "That when my lips touch your neck it makes you wet."

"It does not!" I lean farther away from his lips.

I think I'm fairly convincing in my lie, until his eyes catch me in their tractor beams.

I know without a doubt that he can read the desire in them.

The bell rings, saving me from further conversation about the current state of my lady parts.

OR NOT.

When we're outside my history class, he gives me the kind of kiss that makes me want to do him right here in the hall.

He doesn't say anything when he lets me go.

He doesn't have to.

I'LL HIDE BEHIND YOU.
ENGLISH

I'M STARTING TO think Cupid is shooting his arrows a little early. When I sit down in English, Dallas looks at me with hearts in his eyes and mutters a single word.

"Kassidy."

"The cheerleader?" I ask.

He shakes his head. "More like the hottest newly-single cheerleader. And the best part about her breakup is she's not weepy and sad. She's pissed."

"Have you hung out with her?"

"Yeah, last night after curfew. While Riley and Ariela were getting it on at Stockton's, we were getting it on. Guess where." He breaks out laughing.

"Ohmigawd! You didn't!?"

He laughs again. "Oh, but I did."

"Riley's going to be horrified."

Our teacher starts talking but Dallas whispers, "You better not tell him."

"I won't have to. You won't be able to keep your mouth shut about it."

"Ha. I'll spring it on him at the right time. I'll hide behind you when I do, though. I don't wanna end up like Aiden."

"Chicken shit." I laugh.

"So, I'm going to ask her to Winter Formal. How should I do it?"

"Ha! Maybe you should buy her a furry rug."

Dallas' eyes get huge. "You, my friend, are fucking brilliant."

"I wasn't being serious."

"I am. I think she'd love it! She kept talking about how soft it was. Plus, only we would know what it means. She's got a good sense of humor. I think she'd get a kick out of it."

"And if you give it to her in front of Riley, you're gonna get a kick out of it, too."

FLOWERS, AND ROMANCE.
CERAMICS

AIDEN WALKS ME to ceramics class.

"Is your bowl finished?"

"Yes, but you can't see it."

"Why?"

"I decided to give it to you."

His face brightens. "Really?"

I nod. "I have to touch it up today. I wanted to have it in time for your birthday but I missed class because of all the French stuff."

He corners me at the end of the hall, his chest pressing against mine.

"That bowl is special," he says.

"That's why I want you to have it. Something to remember me by."

Shit.

I didn't mean to say that.

"Remember you by?"

"Uh, remember us."

"There's no way I'll ever forget you."

I want to say, *I hope not.* I want to tell him all about the stuff that went down with Vincent—how scared I was standing up to him. I want to tell him that he's a big part of why I'm doing it. "I hope not."

He gives me a single perfect kiss.

"Gonna be kind of hard to forget you considering I'll be with you. Our ten year plan includes college, marriage, and at least a couple of those four kids we're destined to have."

I smile and roll my eyes at him. "You really think that palm reading stuff is true?"

He laughs, deep and sexy. "Maybe. I like my plan the best."

The bell rings, so he gives me one more kiss and rushes off late for class.

I'M BARELY IN my seat when Jake says, "All right. Winter Formal. Me and Annie. Think glitter, flowers, and romance. What can I do?"

"I still can't believe you guys did it," I whisper.

He whispers back, "Last night too."

"Oh my gosh. Did everyone do it last night but me?"

Bryce breaks into a grin of his own.

Jake says to him, "You too?"

Although Bryce doesn't answer the question, his face is one big smile.

"So, when are you and Aiden?" Jake asks.

"When we want to."

"So, you don't want him?"

"Yes, I do. It's just complicated."

"I know you did it fast with Dawson. Why is it complicated with Aiden?"

"It just is. So, how are you going to ask Annie?"

"She's one of those fairy tale girls."

"What do you mean?"

"She wants the fairy tale."

"We all do, Jake. You want to make the big gesture."

"Exactly. Would it be lame if I wore my prince costume from the play?"

"What else are you thinking?"

"I'm not sure. I wish it would snow big. It'd be fun to ask her outside, throw glitter down on her from, like, the dorm window or something. Ride up on a horse."

"It'd be easy to set up on the stage in the auditorium. We could have glitter and fake snow float down from the sky. You could use the castle backdrop. It's too bad we don't hold pep rallies there."

"Wait. That's it. I'll do it at the pep rally."

"Do what?"

"Shhh," he says, as he gets out a notebook and starts making a list.

BROKE ME INSIDE.
SOCCER

I GET COOPER to let me leave soccer a few minutes early, sneak into his office, and call Damian.

I need to know something.

When he answers, I say, "Damian, in St. Croix you were going to tell me something."

"Yeah."

"Was it that B is seeing someone?"

"Yes."

"Are they serious?"

"You know B. He doesn't really do serious. I met her in Japan."

"What was she like?"

"She works for one of his sponsors—selling t-shirts and modeling bikinis in their tent—so she travels around with the tour. She's blonde, cute. Honestly, she reminds me of you. But . . ."

"But what?"

"Don't take this the wrong way, but she reminds me of the old you."

"The old me?"

"She does whatever Brook tells her to do. When you guys were touring with us, when he was complaining, all that mattered to you was keeping him happy. Even if it didn't make you happy. It wasn't until that last night in London that you stood up to him."

"So you don't think it will work out if we got a second chance?"

"I'm not saying that. He's changed too. He's not high all the time. He's more driven and focused. And, for god's sake, he has a Vuitton duffel bag. I about fell out of my chair when I saw that. All I could think about was your argument about good luggage."

"That makes me laugh, Damian."

"Remember what I told you on beach?"

"About living now?"

"Yep. And, selfishly, I'd like you to marry Aiden, so we can be in-laws."

"I saw you on the cover of the new *Teen Beat*."

"And page twelve of *People* magazine."

"Please make sure no one photographs you and Peyton together."

"They won't. It's going to be a long, lonely week. Video chatting just isn't doing it for me. Well, it sorta does it for me. Last night she was wearing a hot little nightie."

"Do you and B talk much?"

"I talked to him on his birthday, but we're both busy and, honestly, what we've always had in common is you. So, not to change the subject, but I wrote a song for Peyton."

"The one we worked on at The Crab?"

"No, that's not finished. This is a new one. I was thinking about singing it to her this weekend, but I don't want her to think it's dumb. If I play if for you, will you tell me if it's lame?"

"Tommy says you know who your true friends are if they'll tell you the truth."

"And I know you will. Hang on, let me grab my guitar."

I wait for a second, then Damian says, "I'm putting you on speaker. Here goes."

"When the stars come out at night,
It's like when you walked in my life.
Burning so bright,
You became my light.

Oh-ooooh-ooooh-oooh,
Burning so bright.
We'll light up the sky,
Like a meteorite.

With our hearts full of fire,
We're pulsing inside.
Sparked by the flames
Of a burning desire.

Oh-ooooh-ooooh-oooh,
Burning so bright.
We'll light up the sky,
Like a meteorite.

The day we said goodbye
Nearly broke me inside.

And the light won't return
Until you're in my arms, girl.

Oh-ooooh-ooooh-oooh,
Burning so bright.
We'll light up the sky,
Like a meteorite.

Oh-ooooh-ooooh-oooh,
Oh-ooooh-ooooh-oooh."

He stops strumming his guitar.

"Damian, I'm in tears. The part about saying goodbye. It's beautiful. And I love the long oohs. Your voice is just so damn dreamy. You seriously amaze me. I don't think I could ever write something so beautiful."

"You wouldn't change anything? Nothing sounds dumb?"

"I wouldn't change a word. Just know that she's totally going to cry. She's a lucky girl, Damian."

"I think I'm the lucky one. I'm glad you like it. Do you think it's good enough for me to share with the band?"

"Hell, yes. Is it harder for you to share the ones about her?"

"Yeah, they're so personal that I lose my ability to be objective."

"You shouldn't. You sang that with so much emotion it gave me goose bumps. Hey, random thought, but make sure there are no pics of our families together lying around when she comes to your house."

"I'm one step ahead of you. All right, I gotta get to the studio."

"Bye, Damian."

I LEAN BACK in Cooper's chair, replaying Damian's song in my head and thinking about B. I know that the day we said goodbye broke me inside.

But I don't really feel broken anymore.

I just need to figure out a way to keep him safe.

And I think I know how.

Me: *I've been thinking about your safety. You should take the photos of me off your Facebook page and start putting up photos of you and her. Maybe if Vincent thinks you've moved on, he won't feel the need to follow you.*
B: *I'm sorry about everything. I think it's good we're seeing other people.*
Me: *You're not jealous?*

B: I'm trying not to be. It's kind of like when I told you I was going on tour. You said you were happy for me, just not happy for you. That's kind of how I feel.

Me: That's kinda how I feel too. I saw her hug you after you surfed. I couldn't help but wonder if Vincent hadn't happened if that would've been me. Or if you'd have been with her anyway.

B: Remember what I told you? That it doesn't matter where you've been, Keats, only where you end up.

Me: I remember.

B: It's where we END UP THAT MATTERS.

Me: I want to be back on our beach.

B: We will be. And we'll figure it all out then. Damian told me what you did. How you danced at a club in front of Vincent. Part of me thinks you're crazy. Part of me thinks you're really brave.

Me: Thank you. I have to get to dance. Congrats on 3rd place this weekend.

B: <3

RANDOM.
10:45PM

DANCE GOES FROM after school until curfew. Peyton only lets us stop to drink water and eat the sandwiches she had brought in for dinner.

Katie and I both fall flat on our backs in bed the second we walk into our room.

"I'm exhausted. How in the world am I supposed to stay up and do homework?" she groans.

"I don't know. I'm tired too."

"The bad news is, I still don't have that tricky footwork in the second part down."

"You'll get to work on it tomorrow morning."

"I can't believe we have to be back at six. It's just wrong."

"We don't want to embarrass our school though."

"That's true. Do you care if I take a shower first?"

"Naw, go ahead. I'm going to call Aiden."

BEFORE I CALL him, I read through all the adorable, random texts he sent me tonight.

Hottie God: *Riley says I need to lie naked on the furry rug in your room. Would*

154

you mind?

Hottie God: *I miss you.*

Hottie God: *I'm going to fail the French test. Annie is as bad at speaking as I am.*

Hottie God: *I wish you could come to our away game.*

Hottie God: *Can't wait until this weekend at your loft.*

Hottie God: *My mom is taking me shopping for my birthday.*

Hottie God: *I miss you.*

Hottie God: *We just took down the Eiffel Tower. All the cardboard was starting to fall off it and we were told it was a hazard. :(*

"Hey, Boots," he answers.

"Hey, yourself. I got all your texts."

"Ha. Random, right?"

"They were cute. And in reply, I would say: you can get naked on my furry rug anytime you want, providing I get to watch; I can't wait until this weekend either; I was sad to see the Eiffel Tower gone; and what are you going to shop for?"

"You forgot something."

"What did I forget?"

"That you missed me too."

"I missed you too, Aiden. It's part of why I can't wait for this weekend. Are you going to tell me what you have planned for after Winter Formal?"

"Nope. And I'm shopping for clothes."

"I wish I could do that instead of the dance competition. I'm starting to get nervous for it."

"Peyton says you and Maggie have the routine down."

"We do. And our small group hip-hop routine is really good. I feel great about that. But I want the whole team to place."

"I'm sure you will. I won't get to see you tomorrow night either," he says sadly.

"I know. Sucks. I'd like to meet you at Stockton's but I'm just too tired."

"Meet me for breakfast?"

"That sounds good. Night, Aiden."

"Night, Boots."

AFTER I HANG up, I decide to skip my shower and do something for Aiden instead.

LOOK OUTSIDE.
3AM

I WAKE UP to the sound of my phone vibrating.

I open one eye and see that Aiden's calling.

"Open your curtains and look outside," he says, sounding way too chipper for whatever the hell time in the morning it is.

"Uh, what time is it?"

"Doesn't matter. Open them!"

I stumble out of bed and, with one eye still shut, pull open my curtains.

"Oh my gosh!" I whisper, seeing both falling snow and Aiden outside.

I push open the window.

"Get dressed and come outside!"

I run into my closet, using my phone as a flashlight, pull on some clothes, and then launch myself out the window.

The ground is covered with a thick layer of snow. There are millions of white flakes falling and sparkling in the moonlight.

"It's so pretty!" I say as Aiden takes my hand.

"Look at the trees. They're all covered in ice."

"Oh, Aiden. I've never seen trees like that. It's like a real life winter fairyland!"

I run over to one of the trees and feel a branch. It's slick and frozen.

"Have you never seen snow before, California girl?"

"I have. This is just different. When I've been to places with snow, the snow was already there. You know, like, you fly into a ski resort and there's suddenly snow everywhere."

I hold my arms out and twirl in a circle, sticking out my tongue and letting the snowflakes melt on it.

Aiden does the same.

As I watch him, I realize that my heart is like one of these snowflakes.

Aiden has been slowly melting it.

He leaves his tongue out and pulls me into his arms, touching the tip of his tongue to mine, so we're catching snowflakes together.

When other students start wandering out of the dorms, he says, "I knew it wouldn't last long."

"What wouldn't?"

"Us being alone out here." He kisses my forehead. "I'm glad you got to experience the quiet of it."

"It's beautiful, Aiden. Thanks for waking me up."

He smiles at me, then grabs a handful of snow and shoves it down my shirt.

"Ahhh!!" I scream. "What the hell?"

"It's tradition. Eastbrooke students always have a huge snowball fight to celebrate the first big snow. It's about to get crazy!"

"Really? How fun!"

I drop to the ground and quickly start stockpiling snowballs.

After about four, though, my hands get cold.

"I need to buy waterproof gloves."

He slips my wet gloves off and brings my hands up to his face. "They're cold."

He takes my hands and puts them underneath his shirt—on his bare skin—to warm them up.

I stare into his eyes and watch the snow fall around him. Then I stand on my tiptoes to kiss . . .

SPLAT!!

A snowball hits me right in the cheek.

I turn toward the direction it came from to find Riley and Ariela grinning at us.

"They're dead," Aiden says.

He takes his snow gloves off, blows warm air into them, and then puts them on me. "Go get 'em!"

I grab my pile of snowballs, hide behind a tree, and launch them at Riley and Ariela, who have taken off running.

I'm bending down to make another snowball when Dallas shoves a bunch of snow down the back of my shirt.

I scream and go running behind Aiden for protection.

The snowball fight continues until the sun comes up.

Tuesday, December 6th

FRAGMENTED MOMENTS.
HISTORY

I'M SITTING IN class watching a movie.

And somehow it's triggered . . . something.

Caused it to gnaw at the corners of my brain.

It's a thought.

Or a memory.

Trying to get through.

I close my eyes for a second, shutting out my surroundings, and I'm quickly back at the Undertow.

Vincent's strong arms are around me. He's wearing a charming smile.

I relive a series of fragmented moments.

The beach.

The ashes and his loss.

Our dinner.

The brush of a hand across my knee.

Words filled with innuendo.

Kisses that lingered on my cheeks.

Standing at the railing of a deck.

Good advice.

A twirl. A hug.

A toast from across the pool.

An offer to go to his room.

Cartwheels in the sand.

His buff chest.

Blowing a kiss.

Then Garrett. Asking me why I never went with Vincent when he offered.

Was I honest when I answered that question?

I'm not even sure.

Besides, I have to look at it from his perspective.

He idolized Mom, but was always sweet.

Never once was there even a hint of animosity.

He sees the photo of me.

The original girl of his dreams.

Me.

He sets out to meet me in person, finding me on the beach.

I remember when he looked into my eyes like he knew me.

Because, to him, I was familiar.

The first photo he took was of Cush and me.

The question is, why?

Did he really already own the film rights?

And, if so, when did he buy them?

Before or after he saw the picture?

Riley knocks my elbow, causing my head to drop and almost hit the desk.

"Wake up, sleepyhead."

"I wasn't sleeping. I was thinking."

"Sure you were. Probably daydreaming about Aiden on the rug."

I close my eyes again.

Was it all just a mistake?

But then I remember the van.

Him calling Mom a whore.

The drugs.

The ropes.

The bell rings to end class, and I'm thinking about ropes as I gather up my books.

Gives a whole new meaning to the term *tied up* in contract negotiations, I think with a laugh.

As I walk out of class, Aiden's green eyes lock with mine, causing me to forget all about Vincent.

YOU'RE SO NAUGHTY!

LUNCH

I CHECK MY phone as I'm walking into the café. I'm anxiously waiting to hear something from Grandpa. I don't want to bug him, but I need to know. So, I send him an email.

-I don't want to bug you, but how's the takeover stuff going?

I scroll through all the emails I get from the places I shop, and my eye pauses on one from Tommy.

-I ordered the ring you liked best. The seven stones make it perfect. Now I need the perfect proposal. I've got a million ideas. Actually been researching proposal ideas on the internet. I'd like to do something low key, but special. I thought about taking her to the beach, letting her find seashells, and writing it in the sand, but I was worried the public would start taking photos. So I really think it needs to happen at the house in France when I'm there for Christmas. Any suggestions?

"Hey, Boots," Aiden says, wrapping his arm around me.

"Have you checked your phone today?" I ask him.

"You been sexting me?"

"Wipe that smile off your face. It's not like that."

"Darn." He laughs.

"I left you a voicemail," I say seriously. "I need you to listen to it tonight on the bus."

His eyes widen. "Are you breaking up with me?"

"We're not going out, remember?"

"Are you worried about Chelsea being at the game?"

"No."

He looks at his phone. "It's an eleven minute message."

"I had a lot to say."

"Why couldn't you just tell me in person?"

"Because," I say, not able to keep my smile at bay.

He tilts his head and narrows his eyes at me. "What are you up to?"

"I stayed up last night and recorded the oral exam for you. I had to do it on my phone like twenty times to get it all perfect. Then I played my recording on your voicemail. You should probably listen and make sure you can hear it okay."

"You did that for me? You were so tired."

"I don't want you to fail."

"Still trying to get me to France with you?"

"Yeah," I say, hoping I'm not lying.

"Boots," he says, his tone of voice causing me to stop walking and turn toward him.

"What?"

He places both his hands on my face, looks deep into my eyes, and gives me a thorough thank you kiss.

The kind of kiss that makes my legs feel like they're made out of rubber and makes me envision a future with him.

"Thank you," he says dreamily. "Dallas told me in math that he's asking Kassidy to Winter Formal at lunch today."

"Did he tell you how he's going to do it?" I shake my head. "Riley is going to kill him."

"Why?"

"You'll see."

WHEN WE GET to our lunch table, Kassidy and Dallas are already sitting at the table with Whitney, Peyton, and everyone else. I notice he's got a big white trash bag with a red ribbon under his feet.

When lunch is almost over, he pulls the trash bag out from under the table and says to Kassidy, "I lied. This isn't a project. It's for you."

"Really?" she asks, confusion on her face.

"Open it."

"Yeah, open it, Kassidy," I say loudly.

She stands up. That, combined with my loud voice, has gotten the attention of a lot of the students—definitely everyone at our table. She pulls the plastic off and finds the rolled up rug, but she looks unsure of what it is.

Dallas says, "Let me do the honors." He puts the rug under his arm, holding it against his body, and tells her to untie the ribbon.

Once she does, he holds it up in front of him, revealing the front of a green fluffy rug with hearts pinned to it spelling out FORMAL?

Kassidy does a little cheerleader-type bounce, gives Dallas a big smile, and jumps into his arms. I hear her whisper, "You're so naughty. I love it."

Everyone watching does a little clap then goes back to eating their lunch.

Well, expect for Riley.

He gets out of his seat and taps Dallas on the shoulder. "Is that my rug?"

Dallas laughs and goes, "Uh, maybe."

"You're dead," he says, but Dallas moves Kassidy in front of him. She's laughing too.

"You're a chicken shit," Riley says to Dallas. "Just remember, I know where you sleep."

Kassidy breaks out laughing even harder. "Apparently, not," she says through her laughter, pointing to the rug.

And with that smart-ass comment, I decide she needs to be my friend.

Aiden's finished eating his four thousand calorie lunch. I still don't understand how boys can eat so many calories and stay buff.

He puts his hand on my thigh. "I think you've started a furry rug trend."

"Riley is obsessed with them. It makes me laugh."

"You have one in your closet at your loft."

His comment sort of hangs there.

My breath catches as I think about us doing it in my closet. Surrounded by my clothes.

"I need to buy more clothes first."

"Why?"

"Honestly?"

"Yes, honestly," he says, leaning closer to me.

I look around at the table, seeing that everyone is engrossed in their own conversations. I cup my hand to Aiden's ear and whisper, "Remember how I told you my closet at the loft is like my closet at home?"

He nods.

"I've always sort of fantasized about having sex there, on my rug."

Aiden's grip on my thigh tightens and he swallows hard. "But not in your loft?"

"My old closet is full of clothes and shoes. The new one is kinda bare. It wouldn't be quite the same."

He nuzzles my hair and whispers back in his deep, sexy voice. "Sounds like we need to do some serious shopping."

WE FINISH UP lunch and head to French class.

"Are you excited for the pep rally?" I ask Aiden.

"I'm more excited about shopping," he says with a smirk.

Jake comes up behind us, steps between us, and puts an arm around each of our shoulders. "I need your help at the pep rally."

"Did you plan it all?"

"Plan what?" Aiden asks.

"Asking Annie to Winter Formal," I tell him, then say to Jake, "What do you need?"

"Do you think the dancers could all throw glitter at her?"

"Where will she be sitting?"

"Believe it or not, Whitney offered to help. Annie is going to be sitting with her and Shark, front row, center."

"Wow. That's cool of her. And that's perfect. What are you going to do?"

He smiles and tells us his plan.

WILL YOU?
FRENCH

AIDEN AND ANNIE are practicing for the test. I go up front and do mine for Miss Praline, since I'll be gone tomorrow for the dance competition.

When I get back, I start brainstorming proposal ideas. Something involving the girls. Something cute.

I doodle on my paper.

Will

You

Marry

Me

?

Lets se marier

Veux-tu m'epouser?

Aiden leans over my shoulder. "Dreaming about asking me already?"

"I thought you were asking me, Mr. Eiffel Tower."

He gives me an adorable grin. "That's right. So what are you doing?"

"Remember the ring designs?"

"Yeah."

"Now, I'm helping with proposal ideas."

"Come up with anything?"

"A few," I say as the bell rings and it's announced that we're supposed to head to the gym for the first pep rally of the basketball season.

"I heard you have new costumes for today," Aiden says, holding my hand as we walk to the field house.

"We do. Hidden under this warm-up is a nice, skimpy little outfit."

"My favorite kind," he says with a naughty grin.

"Are you doing any shirtless cheerleading skits I need to be aware of?"

"Nope. I'll just be standing out there with the team. Cheering you on."

"So you'll be cheering on the people who are cheering you on?"

"More like I'll be cheering about how hot you look."

"You might not even like it."

He laughs. "I'll let you know after the pep rally. Speaking of which, don't you need to come to my room and wish me good luck before I leave?"

"You already have a permanent clover. No reason to draw one on you any more."

"Fine. Maybe it's just an excuse to kiss you."

WHEN WE GET to the field house, I give him a quick kiss and then rush into the dance locker room and strip down to my gold sequined bustier, little black shorts with *Cougars* scrolled across my butt, and pull on the sparkly gold fingerless gloves we're wearing today in place of our pompoms.

We watch as the cheerleaders start the rally.

Peyton peeks her head out the door of our locker room, which leads straight into the gym. "The cheerleaders are wearing their warm-up suits. We're going to look so much hotter. And I am in love with these gloves. All right, girls, listen up. After our dance, we're going to help Jake Worth with his Formal proposal. I expect you to all be very excited about this. Immediately following our dance, Jake will walk out onto the floor, we'll follow him, and then . . ." Peyton tells us the rest.

SHE PEEKS OUT the door again. "We're almost up. I want you to pretend this is the competition. Big smiles. Focused performance. Show them how awesome our new routine is."

We hear our music start playing and all run out onto the basketball court.

There are lots of whistles and screams due to our costumes alone, but as we do the routine, the students really get into it. The music is super upbeat and fun, and the routine itself contains more hip-hop than usual.

When we're done, we run off the court, grab the bags of glitter waiting for us, then line up, forming a pathway for Jake to walk straight up to Annie.

Jake walks onto the court wearing his full prince costume.

Bryce accompanies him with a horn, playing a fanfare to announce him, then says "Now presenting the honorable Jake Worth."

Everyone thinks this is part of the pep rally. The beginning of a skit.

Jake waves to the crowd and walks through our walkway. We all curtsy as he walks by.

He stands directly in front of Annie and addresses the students. "It seems that I'm without a date for the ball." He makes a dramatically sad face. The students—well, the girls—yell things like, *I'll be your date, Prince Charming. Pick me. Marry me, Jake.*

Jake pretends to look through the crowd while Bryce narrates from a note card. "The Prince looked far and wide for the most beautiful girl in the land to be his date for the ball. Women lined up in town after town, hoping to become his princess. But it wasn't until the prince laid eyes on her that he knew she was the one."

Jake drops down on one knee in front of Annie. He takes her hand and says, "Will you go to Winter Formal with me?"

Annie's eyes are the size of saucers. Whitney nudges her shoulder and whispers, "Stand up."

But Annie doesn't. She just stares into Jake's eyes and nods.

Jake stands up, pulling Annie with him and addresses the crowd, "She said yes!"

Everyone claps and cheers.

Jake holds out his elbow for her, like a proper prince would, leading her back through our human walkway. As they walk by, we toss glitter into the air.

THE PEP RALLY resumes, with Dawson and the coach speaking. I hadn't realized he was the basketball team captain, too. The cheerleaders do another cheer. I glance off to the side of the gym and spy Jake and Annie kissing.

I'm so happy for her. Especially after the way Ace treated her.

When the rally is over, I bound over and hug her.

"Can you believe he did that?" she asks me, not letting go of Jake.

"Yes, I can believe it. He's a real life prince."

Jake laughs. "So not true. I just wanted her to feel like a princess. And this is just the beginning. We're talking five-star restaurant, limo, dance, hotel suite. Only the best for my girl. And before you ask, Monroe, you and Aiden are invited to join us. I got reservations for all of us and a party bus for before the dance."

"That sounds really fun," I say.

"But after the dance, you're on your own."

"The night is sounding better and better," Aiden says, walking up behind me.

I give Annie a quick hug and then follow Aiden to his room.

"WASN'T THAT SO cool?" I ask him, once we're in his dorm.

He makes a little frown. "Do you wish I did something more public when I asked you?"

I pull him onto his bed with me. "Absolutely not. Just because I think it was awesome for Annie, doesn't mean I wish it was me. The way you asked me—the way you do everything—is so incredibly perfect and thoughtful. I would never change a thing."

I get a blazing smile, then a deep kiss, which turns into a hot make-out session that almost makes him miss his bus to the basketball game.

THE ROCK STAR.
6PM

IT'S ANOTHER LONG dance practice.

We get a break for dinner, but then have to come right back to practice until ten.

"You're going to kill me before the competition," I tell Peyton.

"Oh, stop being such a baby. You know as well as I do that we need the extra practice."

"I know, but I've had cramps for the last two days. I may die."

She laughs. "I'd suggest some ibuprofen."

"You're heartless," I say with a laugh. "So, will the competition be fun?"

"It's fun. Stressful. Particularly the team competitions. The small group ones are better. You don't have as many people to worry about screwing up. Do you have a minute? I have something I want you to listen to."

She's starting to blush and giggle and I know it probably has to do with Damian. "Sure."

"It's from my favorite person in California."

"Your dad?" I tease.

She gets her phone out of her locker and hands me an earbud. We each put one in our ear.

I hear Damian being interviewed on a radio show.

He answers a few questions about the band.

His famous dad.

Then:

"We hear you've been doing a lot of writing lately. How do you find your inspiration?"

"Well, there's this girl I met recently, and she fills my heart with music."

"So, tell us about this girl. She must be pretty special."

"Oh, no, Ryan. I'm keeping her all to myself."

"Would you like to give her a shout-out, then?"

"Yeah, she'd love that. Pepper, you inspire me, baby. I love you."

Peyton's eyes are glistening with tears but she has the kind of beaming smile her brother gets when he's really happy.

"This is crazy," she says. "And the fact that he wants to keep it a secret is crazy too."

"He's just trying to protect you."

"Oh, I know. And I'm happy about that. At first, my head kept telling me that guys only want to keep relationships a secret when they have other girlfriends or aren't really that into you. But when I listen to my heart, I know it's in my best interest. His life is getting more and more crazy as their songs keep climbing up the charts. They have two songs on the Billboard Top 100 this week."

"I know. I'm so proud of him. I think once you get out of high school and go to California then you can go public with it."

"I'm thinking about doing something crazy."

"Like what?"

"Transferring out there to finish school. I only need one more class to graduate."

"What does Damian think about that?"

"He thinks I should finish here," she says with a pout.

"Well, having a diploma from Eastbrooke is more impressive than getting a GED. And Damian didn't get to go through a senior year or graduate. I'm sure he doesn't want you to miss out on all that."

"He can't come to Winter Formal with me, but he did promise to come to Prom."

"When is Prom?"

"Late April."

I close my eyes for a second to block out the vision I just had of Aiden taking someone else to Prom.

"So, I'm assuming you're Pepper?"

"Yeah."

"Why Pepper?"

"You know when we went to town and shopped? There was a store that had all these ceramic figurines, but when you picked them up they split apart—they were salt and pepper shakers. Damian joked that it looked like salt and pepper were having sex. Then he said, *I'm salt and you're pepper* and pushed them back together. He was being silly. But then after we did it, he laughed and started calling me Pepper."

"That's cute. Do you call him Salt?"

"No," she says, blushing.

"You're blushing. What do you call him?"

She rolls her eyes and smiles. "It's silly, but when we had sex, it was so unlike anything I've ever experienced. It was hot perfection. And so different than it's been with anyone else. When you do it with someone you're in love with you have both the emotional and physical connection." She smiles again and then laughs as she says, "I was teasing him, telling him that he might not be a rock star yet, but that his—you know what—was. So I guess I named his penis. Now even *he* refers to it as The Rock Star."

"Oh my gosh. What is it with guys and their penises? You'd swear it was bigger than them."

"They are pretty proud of them!" she laughs.

"He said he loves you."

"He told me that before we left the island."

"Didn't that seem a little soon?"

"Not really, considering that we're getting married in a few weeks."

My eyes get huge. "You're what?!"

She laughs out loud. "Ha. Gotcha!"

"Ohmigawd. You about gave me a heart attack."

"What's wrong? You don't want me to marry him?"

"I'm fine with you marrying him. Just not yet."

Not until I've dealt with Vincent.

I'd die if something happened to either Damian or Peyton because of me.

THE SECRET PARTY.
10PM

SAME ROUTINE AS last night.

Katie and I immediately drop onto our beds, exhausted.

"Hey, did you get texted the name of your dorm Secret Santa?" she asks, looking up from her phone.

"Let me look." I check my phone. "I did. I know it's supposed to be a secret, but who did you get?"

"I got Sabrina."

"Cool. I got Molly."

"When we get a break, we'll have to go buy candy and stuff for them while we're in New York."

"Yeah. So, we need something for every day next week and then we give them their bigger gift at Winter Formal, right?"

She nods. "Don't you think that will be fun?"

"I think it will be very—"

She interrupts me. "Did you get the text about a secret party tonight?"

I scroll to a text from Dallas.

Dallas: *Stockton's. 12:30. We're going to party and say screw this secret Santa bullshit. Like any of us guys want to hide candy for other dudes. We're doing Naughty Santas. Drawing's tonight.*

I look up at Katie. "Yeah, I did. That sounds fun, huh?"

"Naughty Santa sounds like something the guys thought up."

I laugh with her. "It does."

We take quick showers, set our alarms, and get a little sleep.

AT 12:30, WE go to the meet-up place Katie's message indicated. Aiden greets me with a kiss, then throws pillowcases over most people's heads and leads them to the party room.

Once they all get over the shock of the room and do shots, Riley and Dallas share the Naughty Secret Santa rules.

"So, the rules are: you will draw a member of the opposite sex. You will buy them fun, sexy, smutty gifts that they would be ashamed to show their mothers. One gift a day. Sometime during Winter Formal, you will give your last gift in person and reveal who you are," Dallas explains.

"And you're not to tell anyone who you get," Riley emphasizes. "We want it to be a complete surprise."

"All right. I'm writing down the girls' names," Dallas says. "We've got Maggie, Keatyn, Annie, Kassidy, Ariela, and Katie." He tears each name apart, folds it in half, and drops it into the stocking hat Riley holds out.

He takes it around the room, letting the guys draw.

Then they do the same with the boys.

I smile when I draw Riley. He'll be fun to shop for.

Dallas hands out shots then says seriously, "Memorize your names. Down your shots. Put the names back into the hat."

We all sit on the beanbags, smoke a little, and I ask Aiden to tell me more about his game. He texted me some, but was busy studying for French.

"They were a really good team. Won state last year. But I don't want to talk about that. I think you owe me a whole bunch of dances."

He pops his phone into a speaker, hits a dance mix, pulls me close, and grinds against me.

Wednesday, December 7th

EAGER TO SELL.

9AM

THE DANCE TEAM is up early once again, only this time we're taking the train into the city for our competition.

I check my email, finding a message from Grandpa.

-All is well. We have representatives meeting with two of the investors this week. Both seem eager to sell.

I write back:

-That's so awesome! I hope they do! Thank you, Grandpa. You're amazing!

Then I email Tommy, giving him the idea that I've been kicking around for his proposal.

He replies immediately.

-That's perfect. She'll love it! Love having the girls involved. Hey, any chance you could do a screen test this Friday in NYC at 2:30?
-I'm headed to NYC right now for a dance competition. I absolutely will be there. Text me the address on Friday.
-Will do.

NAUGHTY PUPPY.
NOON

MY MOM CALLS me as I'm getting settled in my hotel room. Maggie went to get downstairs to get some snacks, so she couldn't have called at a better time.

"Mom! Hi! How are you? Are you all settled?"

"We are. Besides Malibu, this is my favorite place in the world. Plenty of room for the girls to play and no cameras anywhere. We've been to the beach, the market, everywhere, and no one even notices us. And the food is to die for. I've had croissants and coffee every morning and not once thought about the calories."

I want to cry, I'm so happy.

"I'm so glad, Mom."

"How are you?"

"I'm good."

"Remember that game we used to play at dinner after your dad died. We were both so sad, but we tried to find something good that happened each day?"

"The sweet and the suck?"

"Yeah. If I was there with you now, what would you tell me?"

"The sweet is that Aiden asked me to Winter Formal. The suck is that I'm lying to him, and I feel bad about it."

"Sweetie, you can't help it."

"I trust him. I would tell him in a heartbeat. I'm just afraid of putting him in danger. Did you hear about what B got?"

"Yes. It sounds just like the photo I got of Tommy. It was horrific."

"Mom, when you met Tommy, how was your personal life?"

"Hmm. My career was great. You and I were doing well. But . . . I missed being with someone. Having someone take care of me sometimes. Being a single parent isn't easy."

"I was kind of a brat, wasn't I?"

"You were never a brat. You've just always known exactly what you want."

"What happened to me?"

"What do you mean?"

"I think it was high school. I got sucked into fitting in."

"When you were used to standing out."

"Yeah. I'm doing better with all that. I feel like I'm me again, if that makes sense. Oh, and guess what? Grandpa is helping me with the hostile takeover."

"He told me. He's pretty excited about it."

"Me too. I can't wait to walk into Vincent's board room and fire him."

"You're not going to do that, Keatyn Elizabeth."

"Oooh, pulling out the middle name," I laugh. "I don't mean me. I just can't wait for someone to do it." Actually, that's I lie. I totally want to be the one to do it.

I hear Gracie yell, "Mommy!"

Mom says, "Gracie, do you want to talk to Kiki?"

Gracie screams, "Yes!"

She does a little cough then says, "Ruff ruff. Has Kiki been a naughty puppy for Daddy?"

"Gracie, it's Keatyn, not Bad Kiki."

"Oh! Good Kiki! We got a tree for Santa and made cookies! Is Kiki going to open presents with us?"

"I can't. I have to stay at school."

"School dumb. I hate school."

"I'm going to send you a lot of presents."

"Can Kiki open presents on the 'puter?"

"That's a great idea, Gracie. We'll open presents together over the computer. Can I talk to Mommy now?"

"No! My Kiki!"

Mom says to Gracie, "Give Mommy her phone if you want to go to the beach tomorrow." That must have worked because then she says to me. "I think you should come to France for Christmas. We have a lot of security."

"I'll have to think about it. I don't want to put you at risk."

"You can fly from New York with Tommy."

"That sounds good, Mom. I'll talk to Garrett about it," I lie again. I'm not going anywhere near them. "I love you."

"I love you too."

Friday, December 9th
ARE YOU AFRAID?
2PM

AFTER THE DANCE competition is over, I grab a cab to the screen test.

Once inside, I quickly recognize Knox Daniel. Not because I know him, but because I loved the sweet roles he played in some of my favorite teen movies. I'll even admit to having a teensy crush on him back then. From what I've seen in Annie's tabloids, he's recently single after a lengthy-for-him two-month relationship with a pop star.

He used to play the good guy. The pretty boy. Now, his hair is a little darker and it's way sexy on him.

The casting of him in this role is great. He's the hot bad guy. The guy who you wouldn't mind kidnapping you.

I close my eyes.

I can't believe I just thought that.

I've been going back and forth about how this character should be. Based on the lines I memorized, I know they want her to be weak, crying, and wrecked about being kidnapped, but with a little bit of *my-dad-will-make-you-pay* spunkiness.

And if I'd tried out for the part when Tommy wanted me to last spring, I would have acted just that way.

But not any more.

KNOX STRUTS UP to me and gives me a once-over. "Who are you?"

"I'm Keatyn. Nice to meet you," I say with a big smile, wanting to make a good first impression.

He scowls at me. "Why did they make me come in for you?"

"What do you mean?"

"I thought they were bringing in someone famous. You look sorta familiar, though. What have you been in?"

"This is actually my first screen test. First audition, really. I mean, unless you count my school play."

"What the hell? Whose dick did you suck?"

I narrow my eyes at him, totally ready to blast this idiot when I hear a loud female voice.

"All right, let's get started."

He turns to me. "Don't screw up—actually, do screw up so I can get the hell out of here."

Other than the girl who brought me in here, no one's really said anything to me.

And I'm disappointed that neither Tommy or Matt are here.

Oh well.

They can see it on tape later, I guess.

I WALK OUT onto the well-lit set. There are people behind the cameras but the off-set area is dark, so I can't make anyone out.

And if I look too hard at the lights I'll end up seeing spots.

I get tied to a chair in what's supposed to be the middle of an old warehouse. As Knox takes his position, a guy says, "Test one. We're rolling."

Knox struts toward me and allows me to drink from a glass of water he's holding.

I drink it greedily, as if I haven't gotten any in a while.

"What happened to your arm?" I ask him, leaning my cheek toward it, since my hands are tied.

Right now it's a perfectly muscled arm, but it will have a large scar of some kind on it during the actual filming.

He leans down in front of me. "*This* is the reason why you're here."

"You kidnapped me because of a scar?"

"It's more than just this. There are some on my chest too. I wouldn't look like this if it weren't for your dad." At this point the viewers will be thinking, I don't care *at all* about some little scar because Knox is smoking hot.

"What did my dad do?"

"I work for Reginald Ramsey," he says proudly. "When your dad took out one of his factories, I happened to be in it. Barely escaped alive. So you should be nice to me because this isn't just a job. It's retribution."

"Will you please untie me?"

Knox whispers to me, "Wrong line."

"You should untie me," I say, deviating from the script again. "Or are you afraid to?"

"I'm not afraid of some girl."

"Then untie me. My wrists are sore."

"Aren't you supposed to beg?" he says, referring to what my lines are supposed to be.

"I'd never beg for anything."

He gets close to my face—either because he's mad at me or because he's improvising.

"Just wait," he says with a bad guy sneer. "As soon as I kill your father, you and I are gonna have some fun." He runs his hand across my collarbone, suggesting exactly what kind of fun we'll have.

"Did it hurt?"

He flinches, pulling away from me. "It did, yes."

"Why were you working for a guy like Ramsey?"

"My younger brother, he got in with a bad group. Starting dealing and using," he says sadly, staring into space.

It makes me want to hug him. He's a good actor.

He continues. "I got involved so he could get out."

"So this isn't the kind of life you wanted?"

He shakes his head, and the bad boy is back. "It doesn't matter. When this is over, I'll be rich and powerful."

I shake my head right back at him. "No, You're nothing more than a pawn. A babysitter."

"Bullshit. When we take over the country, I get New York. When anarchy reigns, I will be a king." He gets in my face. "Ramsey told me not to hurt you, but he didn't say I couldn't scuff you up a little. Maybe we'll have some of that fun now." He kisses my neck obscenely.

This is where the scene is supposed to stop. To make the audience think that if Tommy doesn't find me soon, I'll get raped.

But fuck that. Tommy Stevens' movie daughter wouldn't allow herself to be the victim.

"So, you really don't want to make the world a better place? Face it. All you are is Ramsey's little bitch."

He keeps going too, improvising his lines. "Bullshit."

"Fight me then."

"What?" he asks, his face screwed up.

"Untie me, and if you can pin me, then I'll go for whatever kinda fun you want, *willingly*."

He shrugs, unties me, then says, "Interesting. Let's see what you've got."

I stand up and massage my wrists for a second, while he takes off his shirt.

I touch his muscular chest. "It's really too bad you wanna play bad guy because of a few scars. I mean, they're kinda sexy. Besides, if they really bother you, find a good plastic surgeon. Don't destroy the world."

"I thought you wanted to fight me?"

I take a step back then throw a jab to his face, careful not to connect.

This surprises him, so he takes a defensive stance. "Interesting," he says again, studying me carefully. Then he goes all cocky. "So, you like what you see?" He points to his real chest and, somehow, even though he's staying in character, I'm pretty sure he's talking to me.

He throws a punch back at me, which I easily block with my forearm, returning a quick jab to the chest.

"You hit like a girl."

"I am a girl," I say, stripping off my own shirt.

"What are you doing?"

"Just evening the playing field."

"Sorry, I'm not twelve. You can't distract me with a pair of boobs."

I throw another punch at him, this one landing on his shoulder harder than I meant it to. "Last chance. Turn good guy and let me go."

"No," he says, throwing a kick at me, which I block with my forearm. Then I punch him in the stomach.

Which I'm pretty sure pisses him off a little. He flings himself at me, pulling me into a tight hold.

"It's gonna suck when you die at the end," I say, totally myself now.

"You'll save me."

"I'm going to change the end of the movie. Let you get shot in the knee. Then, when you're writhing in pain, I'll knock you off that cliff myself."

"But I'll grab you and both of us will roll down the hill. You'll land conveniently on top of me. Then you'll kiss me," he says with a grin, moving his lips closer to my face.

"No. You'll kiss me."

"That's what this is all about." Knox is talking to the whole room. "She doesn't even have the part and she's already demanding a rewrite. You know, sweetheart, all you have to do is ask."

"The last thing I'd want to do is kiss you."

"Cut," a voice says.

Knox says to the guy who seems to be in charge, "Where'd you find this girl?"

"We all know where he found you. Under a rock," I quip.

"Everyone knows I was a model well before I started acting. And what's your name? Besides one that no one knows?"

"It's Keatyn."

"Well, *Keatyn*, you need to learn a thing or two about this business. You don't stray from the script like that, especially at a screen test. You're lucky I'm such a professional and went with it."

"The screen test was just to see if we have chemistry. Which, clearly, we don't. Which means they'll probably kill you off even earlier. Heck, maybe they'll let *me* kill you off."

"You just wanted to kiss me."

"If they make me kiss you in the movie, I'm requesting a stunt double."

"You know I'm a movie star, right?"

"How could I forget? Your picture is splashed on every magazine. You with a different girl. Your mother must be so proud. You should take a tip from Tommy Stevens. You know what happened to him after he met Abby?" I make a rocket with my finger. "'From the atmosphere to the stratosphere,' he always says. And what's with you playing the bad guy lately, anyway?"

"Just trying to break the mold."

"You want the big romance action stuff, you need a leading lady."

"Let me guess. You want to volunteer? No one knows you, sweetheart. You just want me to help you get famous."

"I hope you got all that," I hear a familiar voice say. I turn around, but can't see him in the lights.

"Oh, you're in trouble now," Knox whispers to me. "That's the director. Hope you enjoyed your two seconds of fame."

"At least I'm not going to die in the movie," I tell him. Then I turn around and scream, "Uncle Matty!"

I hear Knox say to the casting director, "Uncle Matty? Just who the fuck is she?"

"This, my boy," Matt says, putting an arm around each of us, "Is the girl who not only just saved your character's life, but is also going to make you a very rich man."

Matt turns us back toward the lights, which have dimmed, and addresses his crew. "Meeting in ten minutes. And someone order in dinner. We're going to be here all night doing re-writes."

Then he leans toward me and says, "Go check on Tommy back there. He said he needed a minute."

I WALK IN the direction Matt pointed, suddenly worried.

Did I embarrass Tommy by going off-script?

This is why I never wanted to audition before.

But Matt didn't seem mad. He's even changing the script.

Writing the daughter out of it and giving Knox a bigger role, most likely.

I walk off the set defeatedly and find Tommy sitting in a director's chair with his head down.

"Tommy, I'm sorry I went off-script. I didn't mean to embarrass you."

His head pops up and his eyes are shiny. "Embarrass me?" He stands up and pulls me into a hug. "I don't think I've ever been more proud of you."

I'M NOT READY FOR THAT.
5PM

"HEY." I LET myself into my loft and find Aiden in the kitchen putting away groceries. "I sort of lied to you," I say abruptly, standing in front of him.

"About what?"

"Remember when I told you that I didn't want to act?"

He squints, remembering, I think. "Uh huh."

"Until I did the play, I was really afraid I wouldn't be good enough. And that thing Annie told me about . . ."

"The nationwide search?"

"Yeah. It was for a lead role. I'm not ready for that."

"Trying to be like Abby Johnston would be a lot of pressure for your first role."

"Exactly. So, today, I didn't really have a hair appointment. I had a screen test. It's for a really small part." I'm practically bursting with excitement. "I did good."

"Of course you did."

"Aiden, just because I did well in a little play, doesn't mean I have what it takes."

He shrugs. "Whatever. I know what I saw."

I smirk at him. "And the fact that you maybe had a little crush on me didn't affect your opinion?"

"You're wrong. It was a big crush."

"Oh . . ." I say as his lips crash into mine, giving me such a hot kiss that it makes me want to tell him a secret every day.

Even after weeks of kissing him, I still feel that same crazy flutter in my stomach the second our lips meet. I still feel the god-like power of his lips. I still feel like I should be showered in glitter as a fairy godmother grants me my wish.

But this kiss could not go in a fairy tale. It's way too deep.

Way too passionate.

Like, I'm pretty sure my thong just caught fire.

When his lips trail down my neck, I say, "I think I need to celebrate."

He kisses just under my earlobe and whispers sexily, "I think what you need is a good screwing."

Ohmigawd!

I do.

I *so* do.

And what a way to celebrate!

He takes my hand and places it on his zipper. "This is for you. What do you feel?"

"Hardness," I practically whimper.

"Maybe you should unzip my pants. Get a better feel."

Jeez, this is sudden. I mean, I want to do it, but my hair's probably a mess from the wind and drizzle outside. And I'm not wearing the new bra and panties I'd hoped to seduce him in.

Stop scripting, Keatyn.

He wants to screw.

You want to screw.

Sorta.

Except, I don't. I don't want just that.

I want him to tell me he loves me.

But what the hell?

I give him a sexy grin, slide my hand down into his pants, and wrap my hand around . . . a box.

"What the heck is this?" I ask, pulling it out.

"Open it."

I take the lid off and find a pair of earrings. Beautiful gold earrings, each with an amber stone. Hanging from each stone is a golden screw.

The construction kind.

"I did a little shopping today. Saw them. Couldn't resist."

"Very cute," I say, removing my earrings and putting on the dangling screws. "Just for you, I'm going to wear them every day. So while we're in class, you're gonna see them and think of us *hammering, nailing, and screwing.*"

"I already think about that every day in class. And don't forget *drilling.*"

"So, what do you imagine? Me, naked, right there on my desk?"

I notice that there is new hardness where the box used to be.

"Can you imagine it?" I whisper in his ear. "I'm lying naked across my desk, waiting for you to get done with your French test." I slide my hands down the front of his shirt. "But you're having a hard time concentrating, because *je suis tellement excitée que je me touchais.*"

"Touching yourself?" he gulps.

"I said, *I'm so horny, I'm touching myself.*"

He lets out a big breath, and I can tell I'm not the only one feeling *excitée.*

"That's really hot."

I smile at him, deciding that I want to make him even hotter. I want to do something to him that I've yet to do. At least, not like this. I slowly sink to my knees, diving my hands into the sides of his unzipped pants and pushing them down along with his sliders, until I am face to face with the Titan.

I take a moment to admire it.

And then to tease it a bit with my tongue, and then my mouth.

He seems fine with it at first, but then his hips start rolling toward me.

"You're teasing me," he groans.

I want to make him feel as good as he always makes me feel.

Or better.

I want him to know how much I want him.

And adore him.

And, well, love him.

I pick up the pace and soon feel his weight shift.

He touches my head and says raggedly, "I'm about to . . ."

I nod and keep going, noting that it was really sweet of him to give me the option to pull away.

He shudders and groans, then stays perfectly still for a few seconds.

Then he grabs my hands to help me up and squeezes me to him tightly.

Putting his lips on my neck, he says, "Wow."

"When you talk on my neck it makes me *excitée*."

"Oh really?" he says, doing it again while he stifles a laugh.

"Did you like it?" I pray he did. I'm hoping he thought it was good. No, I'm hoping he thought it was so fucking good that he never wants another girl to touch it. Never wants to have another mouth within a 500-foot radius of it.

He says seriously, "Every kiss. Every touch. Every single thing we do feels a hundred times better than anything I've ever done before. Because it's with you."

I practically want to cry. "But what do you like? Is there anything that really turns you on?"

"Yeah," he says, kissing my nose. "You."

"That's not what I meant."

"I've realized that even though it's hard to wait—pun intended," he laughs. "It's causing us to focus on *other* ways to please each other. To explore each other's bodies. This weekend, I intend to do just that."

"Really?"

"Yeah, starting now." He leans me up against the counter, then gets down on his knees and kisses my stomach. Tiny little kisses just under my bra line.

Then he stops at my side and goes back to where he started, following the same path a few inches lower, over and over until he's kissing across the top of my thong.

I will him to go down farther, my hips jutting toward him of their own accord.

He pulls my thong down, letting it drop around my boots, and continues his slow, methodical kissing.

I feel like I'm bursting at the seams. My body is begging for him.

When his kisses move lower, I start praying to the gods.

Who is the god of the underworld? Was it Hades?

Or is Hades the *name* of the underworld?

Although, as wet as I am now, I should probably be begging for Poseidon to *give me his Triton*.

Aiden's fingers find their way between my legs and feel what he's doing to me. He smiles against my stomach, obviously taking pleasure in the knowledge that he turns me on.

Immensely.

His finger glides across the edges of my thong, and I'm about to start begging.

He stands up quickly and says, "Turn around" in the hottest voice ever. Then he roughly bends me over the counter.

He's acting like a guy out of one of Mom's romance novels. That hot, hard, burning Alpha male. All he needs is a black leather jacket and a motorcycle.

I have no idea what he's going to do next, but I love the way his now-naked chest is pressing hard against my back, holding me in place.

"Oh my god," I breathe out, surprised as his finger dives into me.

I'm torn between silently whimpering and screaming out loud.

My breath is ragged and my heart is beating wildly as he continues the assault.

It feels so good, I want to cry.

I push back against him, willing his fingers to do it faster, harder, to never stop. My hips move in a rhythm completely controlled by him.

Until I moan out, "Oh," and then my Ohs come faster as he pushes me to places I've never been before.

My body goes limp on the kitchen counter.

He kisses my shoulder sweetly. "We doing okay?"

"We're doing fine. Just don't ask me to stand up. I'll just lean on the counter here for a bit."

He gives my shoulder a little nip, laughs, then picks me up and carries me to bed, where he lies on his side next to me.

I throw myself against his hard body, my lips landing on his, kissing him, thanking him, and maybe even asking for more.

Aiden must know intuitively what I want—possibly that is another benefit of being with a god.

His hand finds its way between my legs again. "More?" he asks.

I don't reply.

I just kiss him and kiss him while he makes me feel amazing again.

And again.

SOMETHING UP HIS SLEEVE.
9PM

I MUST'VE FALLEN asleep.

I'm blinking, trying to focus, when something catches my eye. It's that damn glow-in-the-dark moon.

I want to be mad at the moon, rip it off my ceiling and throw it in the trash.

But I can't.

It looks perfect where it is.

I look down at myself. I'm wearing nothing but a cashmere throw and my boots.

I'm wondering where Aiden is when my nose perks up at a wonderful aroma. I wrap the throw around me, wander out to the kitchen, and find him surrounded by a mess of pots and pans.

He looks adorable.

All I want to do is curl up in this moment and never come out. It's moments like this one that give me the strength to keep doing what I'm doing.

I know that Vincent's going to find me eventually.

We can keep the initial filming under wraps, but once they start the big action scenes in March, I'll be easy to find. And once I announce that I've taken over his company and scrapped the movie, he'll hate me even more.

But not until I've taken away everything he loves—then and only then—will we be on a level playing field.

Me against him.

"Whatever you're doing out here smells amazing," I say to Aiden.

"I thought I'd cook dinner, since you were conked out."

"Sorry," I say, even though I'm totally not.

He wipes his hands on a towel, pulls my cashmere throw open, and smiles. "Naked and wearing cowboy boots. That *is* straight out of my dreams." He pulls me into a hot kiss that tastes of red sauce.

"What did you make?"

"Chicken Parmesan. Salad. Cheese bread. Want some wine?"

"I'd love some." I love you, I want to say, but a softly playing song catches my attention and stirs up a childhood memory. "Hey, that song. Can you play it again?"

"Sure," he says, hitting repeat on his phone.

I listen to the lyrics. A man is saying that he should have been a cowboy.

I can see it in my head.

Daddy and me in the barn at Grandpa's ranch. We're brushing his horse after a long ride when this song comes on the radio. Dad is singing it to me and Grandpa is laughing. Daddy picks me up and twirls me around, still singing.

"Earth to Keatyn," Aiden says, startling me and making me realize he's now standing directly in front of me.

"Oh, sorry. I was kind of stuck in a memory. My dad used to like that song," I say, smiling as the singer continues to croon.

I close my eyes again and savor it.

Aiden pushes my chin up, so I open my eyes. "Tell me."

"Every summer, I go to my grandparents' ranch in Texas. When I was little, my dad went with me. This song, I remember him singing it in the barn. Us dancing. Him telling me he loved me and would miss me on his trip. It was . . . um . . ." I take a deep breath to steady myself. "It was *the* trip. The one where his plane went down . . ."

Aiden caresses my face. "What did your dad do?"

"He was a mod—," I say without thinking. "A, um, moderator. He worked for my grandpa."

"Oil and gas? Like your mom?"

Shit. I can't remember what I told him my mom does. What if that's not what I said? Shit. Shit. Shit.

But why would he say that unless it's what I told him?

Then I remember telling him about possible oil in the Ukraine.

I take in a deep breath and change the subject. "Wow. That smell is killing me. Can we eat soon?"

"If you don't want to talk about it, it's okay to just tell me." He smiles sweetly and kisses me. "And, yes, we can eat now."

DURING DINNER, HE toasts. "To your amazing day. Winning first place in your small group dance. A team third place. And your first successful screen test."

"And to a fun weekend," I add, winking.

"I'll toast to that." We clink glasses and sip our wine.

AFTER A COZY dinner at my kitchen island, he says, "Let's go upstairs. We can watch a movie or something."

There's a little smile playing on his lips and his eyes look sneaky. Kinda like they did the day of my speech when he gave me the glass clover for luck.

He holds my hand as we walk through the living room and then gestures for me to walk up the stairs first.

He's totally got something up his sleeve.

But when I get to the top of the stairs, I can barely believe my eyes.

In the corner, all lit up, is a gorgeous Christmas tree strung with the prettiest pastel garland and topped with a silver star.

Tears immediately spring to my eyes as I stare at it. The Christmas decorations have been up in our dorm for a few weeks, and Katie and I strung some lights around our window, but it's just not the same.

This makes my loft look and feel even more like home.

"It's beautiful." I turn around and throw myself into his arms.

He hugs me, kisses the top of my head, and says, "I thought we could decorate it together."

"Did you get ornaments too?"

He untangles himself from my arms, goes behind the tree, and sets shopping bags down next to the coffee table. "You have to open each one. They all kind of have meaning."

"Really? What kind of meaning?"

"You'll see. Open them."

I sit on the couch next to him and open the first box. It's a beautiful, brightly-colored blown-glass fish. "It's so pretty!"

"What do you think it means? For us?"

I think about it. "Um, we ate fish in St. Croix."

"True. Think some more. When did we see pretty fish?"

"When we went snorkeling!"

"And what happened when we went snorkeling?"

"Your back got sunburned?"

"And how did you try to help me with that?"

I laugh and grin. "So, you're telling me that this fish reminds you of the shower?"

"Yep," he says with a naughty little smirk. "That was fun."

"I'm still kicking myself for giving you that washcloth to cover up with." I lean over and give him a kiss. "I think you should put this one on the tree."

I open another box and find a glass Ferris wheel. "Aiden, are all of these going to make me cry?"

He puts his ornament on the tree, then kisses me. "They're supposed to make you happy."

"I'm crying because I *am* happy. And because, seriously, this might be the sweetest thing anyone's ever done for me."

He gives me another kiss. Like our first kiss on the Ferris wheel. Perfectly amazing.

I walk over and put the Ferris wheel high up on the tree, just like we were when he kissed me at the top of it. Then I excitedly open another one. This one is an adorable piece of chocolate cake. "The peace offering?"

He nods.

"That cake was really good. And I like peace with you better than fighting."

He gives me a steamier kiss this time, but I push him away after a few minutes. "I have a lot more ornaments to see! You need to stop kissing me."

Of course, what does he do?

Gives me about ten more kisses.

I open a Santa, a nutcracker, and a nativity scene, which he tells me are just because it's Christmas and every tree needs them. Then I open a Santa taking a bubble bath, the bubbles a pearly pink glass.

"Hmm. Let me guess. Our bubble bath. The one where you wore your swimsuit?"

He laughs. "Maybe after this, we'll take a bubble bath without swimsuits."

"I'm done opening ornaments for tonight," I tease, putting this one on the tree.

"You're bad," he says, swatting me on the butt.

Which was probably the wrong thing for him to do, because it inspires me to jump on him, knocking him flat on the couch, and attack his face with sloppy kisses.

"Oh, ick," he laughs. "This is going to take all night at the rate you're going. No bubbles until the tree is decorated."

"Fine," I pout.

"How does that song go? *You better not cry, better not pout?*"

"Speaking of that, we need Christmas music playing."

He takes a sip of his wine and then says, "You're right. And we should turn on the fireplace."

I jump up and down a little. "Yes. You do the fire. I'll turn on the music."

"Much better," he says, pulling me onto his lap when we've both made it a little more Christmas-y in here. "What do you want for Christmas?"

"You," I reply.

He gets a little twinkle in his eye. "Are you offering sex to Santa?"

"I have been kinda naughty."

"Well, maybe if you're a good little girl, you'll get what you want."

"I lied. I'm always good."

He shakes his head at me. "Santa doesn't like it when people lie."

"Oh," I say, thinking about the boatload of lies I've told this year.

He hands me another box. "Open some more, then we'll put them on the tree. Otherwise we'll never get to that bath."

I stay on his lap and open a Santa in a sleigh, a Santa in New York City—since that's where we are now—and a Santa that's surfing—since I taught Aiden how. The next one is Santa driving an ice-cream truck with a big cone on top of it. "When we went for ice-cream? I'm surprised that's something you want to remember, seeing as you got all pissed off at me."

"All I remember is the sexy way you were licking the cone. Got me all hot."

Then I open one of an adorable pink purse with little peace signs and hearts on it.

"*I fucking love you*. That's what you told me when I gave you the purple purse," he says.

"I was excited."

"I know you love me."

"I know you love me."

"Still not ready to confess your love?" he teases.

"Apparently, neither are you."

Next, I open a trio of colorful cowboy boots.

"Those might be my favorite, Boots."

"I love them. Although when you gave me that nickname, I thought it was kinda dumb."

"Dumb? I'm shocked. It was very original."

"It's still the name of the monkey on *Dora the Explorer*. I didn't want to be a monkey. But now I like it. I like that it has meaning to both of us."

He grins and hands me another box.

I look at the name of it. "The Sugar Shack?"

"Just open it."

In the box is an adorable little gingerbread house covered with candy. "Hansel and Gretel got eaten there."

"That's supposed to be our mansion of love. Don't make fun of it," he says seriously.

"Oh. Well, then it's adorable."

The next one is The Three Little Pigs. "You're on a roll. First Hansel and Gretel and now pork for dinner."

"You're silly. You know what it means."

I get serious again. "It's for a strong foundation."

"Very good."

I grab another box and find a sand castle—my castle on the beach—a Little Mermaid, and a Frog Prince.

"Oh, the Frog Prince is so cute."

"I remember Damian said you used to make him be a frog."

I hug him. Again.

Next, I open a Nutcracker prince.

"That was always my sister's favorite ballet. I thought maybe since you dance, you'd like it too."

"I love it. This will be the first Christmas that I won't get to see it."

He gives me his nearly-blinding happy smile.

"What?"

He tilts his head in the most adorable, aw-shucks way and pulls two tickets out of his wallet. "I got us tickets for Sunday afternoon."

Which makes me start crying.

He wraps his arms around me. "Baby, what's wrong?"

"I haven't bought any presents."

"But we're shopping tomorrow, all day."

"I just feel bad that I haven't gotten you anything yet. And you did all this. All the thought you put into it."

"Boots, my mom and I went shopping when you weren't dancing. I got a bunch of clothes for my birthday and when we were walking out, I saw the huge holiday section and decided to buy you some ornaments. Then my mom asked if you had a tree. So I bought one of the fake ones. It came with the lights on it. All I had to do was put three pieces together, plug it in, and put on the garland."

"But these ornaments. They all have meaning."

"They had a large selection. Seriously, I was like *I want this one, and this one, and this one.* Twenty minutes, tops."

"It's still amazing, Aiden."

He kisses me then murmurs, "I'm glad you like it. That's all I want. To make you happy. Come on, open the rest. And don't feel guilty. This is our tree. The story of us. And I have an ulterior motive. I want to be so far in your life that, come August, you'll never consider anyone but me."

It's much safer to open another ornament than to discuss that, mostly because I don't even know if I'll still be alive in August.

"Awwww! Look at this snowman! His little stick arms are full of shopping bags! That's adorable!"

"I like shopping with you. So, are you going to wear the gorgeous dress I found last time we went shopping to Winter Formal?"

"Yeah, I am. And I found the perfect shoes to go with it."

"I can't wait to see you in it."

I can't wait for you to get me out of it, I think.

The next boxes I open are a cupcake with a clover on top, a mermaid Santa, and a seashell. "So the cupcake is just for the clover?"

"Uh huh."

"And the mermaid—well, I guess technically he's a merman—and seashells. Do those have to do with our wishes?" I touch the shell bracelet still tightly fastened to his wrist. "Are you ever going to tell me what you wished for?"

"Not until it comes true."

"Hmm. Okay. What's next?"

He hands me another box, this one containing a cotton candy machine. "Is this for the same reason as the Ferris wheel? Except we didn't eat cotton candy together."

"No, I dragged you away from Riley when he was licking cotton candy off your hand. So, no. It's because your hair always smells like cotton candy." He leans in and kisses my temple. "You always smell good enough to eat."

I close my eyes tightly, willing away the heat I can instantly feel rising between my legs. I purse my lips and smile at him.

"You have a dirty mind. I like it," he whispers in my ear in the low, husky voice that makes me melt.

"Well, maybe, a little."

I open another ornament, this one a chapel. I think about how I spilled my guts to him. How he stopped during the game and asked me if I was okay. How sad it was when I planned on leaving him. I feel choked up again.

He says, "It reminds me of the chapel at school. Of our spot. Where I promised not to pretend punch your head."

"It reminds me of how nice you could be even when I hated you."

"You never hated me."

"No, but I thought you hated me, so I told myself I hated you."

"We had a rocky start, huh?"

"Yeah, we did. Damn Logan."

"Would it have changed things?"

"Yeah, we'd probably have dated and then broken up by now. So everything was probably for the best."

"You think so?"

"Yeah. I've changed a lot since we first met."

"You're stronger."

"You think so?"

"Yeah, you've been through a lot. Coming to Eastbrooke at the last minute. The stuff that went on with your friend. Your boyfriend leaving you for a year. All the stuff with Dawson. With Whitney. With Chelsea. With me. You're good at hiding it, though. I think Riley and I are the only ones you let in. Besides Damian."

"Yeah. So, next bag. This is the last one."

"And these are some of my favorites."

The first one I open is a red bag with two baguettes sticking out of the top. "What's this one for?"

"French class. Tutoring with food. Our tutoring field trip. The dances in my room when we should have been studying. French body parts."

"I love it." I open the next one. A Santa dressed in pink with the cancer symbol. "For your mom?"

"Yeah. It made her really happy when I won Mr. Eastbrooke. And that's all because of you. I've grown this year too. At least, that's what my mom tells me."

"Well, we know you've gotten taller. That's why you had to shop."

"I don't mean that kind of growth. I mean not sleeping around. Waiting for the right girl. Knowing you're worth every ounce of frustration. Knowing that— well, open another one."

"Um, okay." This one is a street sign that says Sunset Blvd. "Dual meaning? Our sunsets and the fact that California is where we're both from?"

"That you watch sunsets with me. That I even had the guts to tell you why they were special. I've never shared those parts of me with anyone. No one at school even knows my mom had cancer."

"I'm glad you shared those things with me. And we saw the green flash together."

"Close your eyes," he says. "I want you to see these together." I close my eyes and listen to him unwrap ornaments. "Okay, open."

Lying on the table in front of me is a soccer ball, a four-leaf clover, an Eiffel Tower, and two dolphins jumping out of the water. I don't want to be a big baby and start crying again, so I joke, "Hmm. I'm not sure what any of those mean."

He kisses me deeply then says, "Fine. I'll tell you. These are all about luck and fate. It was fate you kicked the soccer ball at my head and made me instantly fall for you. It's fate that I'll ask you to marry me someday. But it was luck that I found a four-leaf clover to give you, and every time we've given each other a clover, it's helped us both be lucky. And it was luck that we got to see the dolphins. You've made me lucky."

"You helped me make dance team. Gave me the glass clover before my speech. And drew one on my leg for the play. You've been sharing the luck."

"So which one are we? Luck or fate?"

"I guess only time will tell, huh?"

He nods. "Yeah, it will. So, only a few more. This one is about me."

He pulls a Santa out of its box. This Santa isn't holding a bag of presents, he's holding a glass of wine and standing behind of a wine barrel with grapes on it.

"Your dream of owning a vineyard. That one I know."

"How about this one?" he says, taking another ornament out. This one is an adorable yellow Labrador retriever puppy.

"You want this kind of dog someday?"

"Yep. You cool with that?"

"Yeah, I love dogs."

"Perfect. Last one. Hold out your hands."

I do what he asks and close my eyes. I'm sure he saved the best for last. He puts it gently in my cradled palms.

I open my eyes and see a flat scene of a sandy beach, a palm tree, the ocean, and the bright sun. "St. Croix?"

"Damian asked our family to celebrate Christmas with his family there. I wasn't sure what your plans are, but I'd like to spend the holiday with you."

"I'm not sure what I'm going to do. I need to talk to my mom about it."

"I know. I just thought . . . I know they've been there before. Maybe your family could go too? I'd love to meet them."

"I'd love for you to meet them, too. Aiden, I . . ."

I almost say it. Almost blurt out the truth. I want to tell him what happened. What's going to happen. But I don't. I don't want to ruin this perfect day. I don't want him to walk out on me.

It's so selfish, I know. But there's another big reason I can't tell him.

He'd want to help, and I couldn't take another photo of someone I love with the back of their head blown off.

" . . . I, um, thank you for the tree. You have no idea how much this all means to me."

"I'm glad. Let's finish decorating."

AFTER WE'VE DECORATED, we turn off all the lights except for the ones illuminating the tree and snuggle on the couch, staring at its beauty.

"TIME FOR OUR bubble bath," Aiden says about a half hour later.

I run the water, loading it up with bubbles, while Aiden goes to refill our wine glasses. He comes back in with a silver ice bucket and champagne instead.

I squint my eyes at him questioningly.

"Gotta have bubbly for the bubbles, right? I just corked the rest of the wine. We'll have it tomorrow night."

"Yeah, but if we're gonna have champagne . . ."

"Wait, don't finish that sentence." He runs out of the bathroom and comes back with a little plate of chocolate truffles.

"It's official. I do fucking love you," I say.

"I fucking love you too. Now, let's get naked."

Saturday, December 10th
LIED MYSELF INTO A CORNER.
6PM

WE SHOP ALL day and then head back to my loft. We had a ball picking out a bunch of crazy puppets for my sisters, secret Santa gifts, and all sorts of presents for our families and friends.

Aiden wouldn't let me see what he was buying for his naughty Santa, but I will admit, I peeked at his list. Part of it was written in some sort of godly code, but there was an M next to the naughty Santa, so I know he drew Maggie.

I can't wait to see what he got her. Well, mostly to see what he considers naughty.

I was fortunate that when I had packages shipped to France, I was able to say that I didn't want to have to travel with them. I told Aiden that I'm spending Christmas with my family, but I'm not.

I shouldn't be anywhere near them. I mean, if I were Vincent, I would assume that Christmas would be the one time I'd be almost guaranteed to spend with my family. I feel bad that I lied to my mom, too. But I just can't risk it.

IT SUCKS BECAUSE I've basically lied myself into a corner. I told Aiden I was going to France. That my mom needs me. I can't just be like, *Hey, I think I'd rather come to St. Croix with you.* I can't think of any logical reason why I wouldn't go home. And because there's no way I'll actually go to France and put my family in danger, it means I'll be spending Christmas here. In my loft. Alone.

But, on the bright side, I get to film some of the movie with Tommy before he leaves. I wish I could bring Tommy to my loft, but I'm afraid someone would follow him.

Then I'd be screwed. And not in the good way that Aiden's earrings suggest.

Aiden goes to change into something for tonight while I'm putting my purchases away. He sweet-talked me into letting him keep some of his clothes here. I know his goal is to help me fill up my closet, but I told him to put his clothes in a guest room closet. As much as I'd like to have all his clothes hanging next to mine, all I can picture is me dead and Aiden coming here to get them. At least if they're not in my closet, maybe it will spare him some pain.

He won't even have to come into my room. Won't have to see where we've slept. Where we've taken bubble baths. Won't have to see all the clothes I've been saving for the rainy days that will never come.

Okay, Keatyn.

Stop with the whole death thing. It's slowing your roll.

Like, if I was on a roll.

Whatever.

I need to be positive that the plan will work, and I'll get my life back.

But, just in case, I told Aiden to keep the key.

He gave me a big smile and a sweet kiss, acting like we'd gotten engaged or something. Like the key made us official.

And, evidently, I looked freaked out by this, because he touched his hand to my heart and said, *As long as we're in each other's hearts, we don't ever have to label our relationship.*

And, yes, the irony of that did not escape me. All I wanted last summer was for me and B to be official so I could shout it from my social media. Now I realize they're both right.

It does only matter what's in your heart.

The problem is that more than one boy resides there. One who is all wrapped up in my journey home. The other who is showing me that home is where you make it.

Aiden and I are going ice skating, to see the Rockefeller Christmas tree, and then to a trendy restaurant.

And after the hotness that went down last night—pun definitely intended—with me not in the undergarments I wanted, I'm going all out tonight. I start with a pink bra and panty set with black scalloped lace and opaque black thigh highs.

Over it, a shimmering flirty skirt in a gorgeous ice pink patterned lamé and a silk chiffon Rebecca Taylor sweatshirt. It will be adorable for skating—provided I don't fall down and scuff the lamé—and still nice enough for dinner. I pull on the most awesome Lanvin boots—black, ornately brocaded, and thigh high—

and slide on an Henri Bendel crystal bangle. I grab cute black mittens with a heart graphic and my shiny pink Miu Miu bag.

Now, if I can just manage to ice skate gracefully.

WHEN I COME out of my room, ready to show off my new outfit, I am literally stopped in my tracks at the sight of Aiden.

He's playing pool, wearing a plain white t-shirt, dark jeans, a scrumptious black leather Burberry Prorsum motorcycle jacket that I recognize from an ad, and the gunmetal Burberry aviators I got for his birthday.

He looks bad.

Do-me-on-a-motorcycle bad.

He looks so good it's practically criminal, especially since he hasn't shaved in a couple of days. That scruff is perfection.

It revs my motor just looking at him.

He pushes the glasses down his nose and checks me out.

"You look different," I stutter out.

I get a smile and the result is devastating to my insides. A bad boy with a brilliant smile and gorgeous, blinding white teeth.

He sets his pool cue across the table, holds his hands out, and looks down at himself. "You don't like it?"

"Oh, I like. Why don't you dress like that for school?"

"Because we can't?" he says with a smirk. Then he struts over and touches the tops of my thigh highs, his hand brushing under my skirt and giving me a thrill. If I didn't know him, I'd so be running the other way.

After I did him. Probably.

Doesn't every girl need a bad boy at least once in her life?

"These are such a turn-on. It kills me when you wear them with your uniform skirt. All I can think about is . . ."

"Is what?"

"Getting under it." He tilts his head at me. "It's cold out."

"Uh, yeah, it's been cold all day."

"It's warmer here," he says, both his hands sliding up my skirt.

And it does suddenly feel very warm, like I stepped into a sauna of the hotness that is Aiden. I swear, he looks amazing in everything he puts on. Suit, school blazer, football pads, white shorts, sliders, and nothing at all. But this—this almost beats nothing at all.

So hot.

No, so fucking hot.

"So, you don't want to ice skate?"

"How about a game of pool first?"

"Sure, but I'm warning you. I suck at pool."

He lets out a throaty laugh that starts out as a cough. "Even better," he says, his eyes holding mine as his hands continue to wander. He slides his knee between my legs and his firm chest pushes into mine. "I was going to suggest a friendly game of strip pool."

I quickly calculate the number of articles of clothing it will take to get him naked. Two shoes, jeans, sliders, t-shirt, jacket, watch, maybe sunglasses. Seven. For me, two boots, two thigh highs, skirt, top, underwear, bra, necklace, bracelet, and, if I wear my mittens, that'd be twelve. Pretty good odds.

"Sure, why not? But I'm leaving my mittens on if you get to keep your glasses on."

"You can even put your coat on, if you want." He waggles his eyebrows.

I roll my eyes. "Don't tell me you're as good at pool as you are at every other sport?"

He shrugs. I start to move away from him, eager to get started, but he grabs me tightly and kisses me hotly, his stubble rough against my chin.

"No sampling the goods just yet," I say. "You have to win first."

He gives me a smoldering look, then says, "You're so going down."

I think about how I went down last night. "Is that what we're playing for?"

"What?"

"Going, um, down?" I say, glancing at his pants and thinking that if he says yes, I'm going to cheat.

He pushes he glasses back into place, covering his eyes. "Sounds fair to me."

"This isn't poker. Your eyes aren't going to give your hand away."

"I think you like the glasses."

"I like the whole package," I say, then gulp, realizing what I just said.

"You like my whole package, huh?" he teases.

"You talk too much. I'll rack," I say as I line the pool balls up. "You break."

He bends down, slides the cue across his fingers, and blasts the balls apart, sending two in, both stripes.

"Oh, you can't do that," I say.

"Can't do what? Be awesome?"

"No. If you sink two balls of the same kind on the break it's illegal. You have two options. Replace a solid with the stripe or just add one back to table. Which do you want to do?" I say, messing with him. I hold both striped balls in my hand, rubbing my thumbs across them for effect.

He licks his lips, looking at me like I'm a snack. "Leave it off the table, and I'll only make you take off your shirt."

I shrug. "That's cool." I slide my silky sweatshirt over my head, tossing it to the ground.

"Red, corner pocket," he says, effortlessly sinking another and stifling a grin. "Take off your skirt."

Shit. I'm in trouble.

"No one said that you get to choose. I'm taking off a mitten." I pull if off and toss it on the table.

He takes two big strides, his face now close to mine, and says very seriously, "My score. My choice. Take off your skirt." Then he takes my mitten and throws it into the other room. He pushes me back against the pool table. "You lose that one for disobeying. Time for me to shoot again. You're going to be naked in no time."

He quickly sinks another ball.

"That didn't count. It's supposed to be my turn," I quickly say, grabbing his cue stick from him.

"No, it's *mine*."

"Nope. You just made a bunch in a row. It's my turn."

"Since when? Have you never played pool before? You have a pool table."

"Yeah, because I thought it would be fun for parties and stuff. Guys like to play pool. And I've played. Sort of. A few times."

"And how did you do?"

"Honestly, usually when I got to play, I'd shoot a few times, and my boyfriend would make me quit."

"Because you were so bad?"

"No! Because he said all his friends were looking up my skirt. He was a gentleman."

"He the gay one?"

"Shut up!"

He squints at me. "On second thought . . ." He slowly pulls my other mitten off. "Leave the skirt on."

"You know, it's also probably illegal to play strip pool without doing a few shots." I'm feeling strung out. Like a crack addict badly in need of her next fix. Plus, I'm nervous.

And freaking excited.

And nervous.

I already said that.

"So, what did you do at parties when you weren't playing pool?"

"Well, once my ex got drunk enough that he didn't care what I did, then I'd dance on the bar."

"Were you drunk?"

"Naw. I'd have a few shots, have some fun, but that was it."

He pushes his chest tightly against mine, half kisses and half licks my cheek, and says, "Don't go anywhere."

I watch his godly hotness stride over to the bar.

I mean, imagine it. A demigod. Hot, buff, golden boy, wrapped in a designer motorcycle jacket. It's like one of the gods plucked us from the sky and placed us together.

The. Most. Perfect. Boy. For. Me.

But, curse Aphrodite and her vindictiveness, they thought it would be fun to put us together under the worst possible circumstances. I knew she shouldn't be the goddess of love. More like the goddess of spite.

Bitch.

AIDEN HANDS ME a double shot of tequila.

"Nice pour," I say as we clink glasses and drink.

"Well, I'm hoping you'll dance on the pool table for me later."

"I'll dance on the pool table for you now."

"No way. You're just trying to avoid the inevitable. Me whipping your ass."

I really need to start plugging my ears when Katie reads me the naughty parts from her erotic romance novels, because I don't want to lose the game, but the first thought that popped in my head was *Forget date me, love me, and adore me. I want spank me, attack me, fu—*

"Are you gonna shoot now?"

"Hmmm? Oh, yeah."

I remember that he made me keep my skirt on for a reason. Maybe I can use that to distract him.

I lean way over the table, knowing my skirt is totally riding up.

Aiden has shifted to my side of the table. He even sits in one of the low slung leather chairs to get a better view.

I move my hips from side to side, pretending to get comfortable in my stance before I shoot.

I turn around and catch him staring at my backside. "Shouldn't you be standing up and making sure I don't cheat?"

He glances up. "No, I can see the table just fine. Shoot already."

"I can't decide which ball to hit."

He stands up and leans against my back, bending over me, his hips touching my ass in an attempt to line up a shot.

I almost whimper.

"Hit that one right there into the corner. But hit it softly so the cue ball doesn't follow it in."

I slide the cue across my fingers and completely miss the ball.

"Shit."

"Looks like you lose again."

"No. That was a—I don't know what it's called—but it's like when the volleyball hits the net. I get a do-over."

"I shouldn't be helping you," he says as he leans back over me, guiding the cue for me. One of his legs is between mine, I'm bent at the waist, and I'm trying not to close my eyes and just sigh.

He slides the cue gently though my fingers, sinking the ball cleanly in the pocket.

"We did it! Got it in the hole," I say excitedly, but all of a sudden pool seems as sexual as basic construction. "I mean, I sunk it."

Oh, gosh. Sticks. Balls. Holes. Hitting it hard. Breaking. A boy totally made up pool.

Aiden doesn't move even though my shot is clearly complete. He keeps me bent over the table and kisses my neck. "What do you want me to take off?"

"Since you illegally helped me, you have to take off two things."

"No way."

"Fine. I'll compromise. Take your jacket and shirt off, but then I'll let you put your jacket back on."

Surprisingly, he doesn't argue. He slides out of the jacket, hands it to me, and pulls his shirt over his head. Luckily for me, he does this slowly, and I get a clear view of flexing muscles.

He looks hot shirtless but when he slips his jacket back on, I about have a spontaneous orgasm.

Like, if that were possible.

I admire him for a few seconds; even lay a few kisses across his chest.

Then I remember I have another shot.

And, suddenly, I'm very motivated.

I find an easy to make shot and line it up, really focusing.

As I shoot, my cue gets hit from behind and knocked out of my hand.

I turn around to find Aiden wearing a smirk.

"Tough shot," he says. "My turn. You know, you should've put some chalk on the tip. It works better that way."

Oh god. There's another one.

And now I'm wishing I could chalk his stick.

"See?" he says as another ball falls in the pocket. "Hmmm. Skirt for sure, this time, although, I will say the view was nice. I can see why even your gay boyfriend would be jealous of that view."

"I swear to god, if you ever meet him, he's not out. And I promised to tell no one."

"You didn't tell me. I guessed. Skirt."

I roll my eyes, unzip my skirt, and let it fall to the ground.

He surveys my pink and black lace and says, "It's halftime. Do you want another shot?"

"Please."

We down another shot and then he says again, "It's halftime."

"Pool doesn't have a halftime, silly," I tell him.

"Our game does." He hits a couple of buttons on my phone, which has been playing through the speaker system, switching over to a very appropriate song about bad boys. "Get up there and dance," he says as he takes a seat.

"I can't. These heels would tear up the felt."

He stands back up, grabs the cue, and quickly sinks two more shots. "I'll take the boots, Boots."

He picks me up, plops me on the table, unzips my boots and slides them off my feet, leaving me in my thigh highs, bra, panties, and jewelry. Then he holds my hand to help me up on the table.

Ha!

Dancing in a cage for a bunch of horny drunk guys did end up helping me out later. I'll have to tell Cooper that.

I look at Aiden's hungry eyes.

Uh, maybe not.

I move slowly and sexily to the song, close my eyes, and let myself go.

Touching my chest, my hips, and totally caught up in the beat.

When the song ends, I hear Aiden say, "Eight ball, center pocket."

He shoots the eight ball between my legs and wins the game. Which means I get to . . .

Aiden takes my hand and helps me off the table. His lips immediately land hard on mine, and I can feel how much he liked my dance.

I reach for his pants.

He stops me.

"Panties. I win," he says as he rips them off me, sets me back up on the pool table, and sinks his head between my legs.

Oh my god.

His mouth. The source of his power.

That magical tongue is . . .

And the scruff is . . .

Infusing the rest of me with love potion, I think—no that tongue is very capable of inducing lust because . . .

Just because.

Or maybe he's cursing it.

Ruining this part of me like he ruined my lips.

And the scruff is . . .

When someone gets in trouble, Grandpa always says they got a good tongue lashing.

This gives a whole new meaning to that phrase.

And I *so* want trouble.

I'm making promises to myself.

To always dance on the pool table for him.

To always suck at pool.

To . . .

Holy shit.

I grab his hair, because I can't help it. I let out a sound that's almost a scream.

Every bit of cool is gone, and all I can do is react to the way he's rocking my body.

Thank god I don't have close neighbors.

I also pray to the gods that Garrett didn't put in any video surveillance. Or else, somewhere in Indiana, someone is getting an eyeful.

Waves of pleasure roll through my body.

I remember telling him at rehearsal about using that scruff.

I feel like the baddest, sexiest, naughtiest version of myself.

And I like it.

He's relentless.

Only stopping or slowing down to let me catch my breath.

AFTER A WHILE, my throat is dry, and my voice cracks as I say, "Water."

He kisses up my stomach. "Don't you dare move."

"Okay."

He brings me a glass of water, which I gulp down. He steals it from me before I finish and takes a long drink.

"In case you were wondering, you dancing just for me was *the* sexiest thing I've ever seen."

I lean back on the table, stretch out, and make a contented sound.

"That almost sounded like a purr," he teases. But then he says, "Here kitty kitty," and proceeds to convince me that it's not his lips that are my bliss.

It's his tongue.

And the scruff.

BY THE TIME he's done with me, I feel like a meteor, burning hot, shooting through the sky, burning as I hit the atmosphere, then free falling and crashing into the ground. Nothing is left of me but a pile of atomic ashes.

JUST WHEN I think I can't take any more, he kisses me, pulls me off the table, and picks my underwear off the floor.

"Probably not wearable anymore," he says with a sexy laugh, eyeing the trashed pair.

"Probably not," I giggle, leaning against his warm chest.

I close my eyes and breathe in the intoxicating scent that is Aiden mixed with the smell of the new leather.

It's like heaven.

He kisses my forehead and then my nose. "We still have time to make our dinner reservation, if you're up for it. You're outfit is hot. We should go out."

"Plus, you're starving, right?"

"Naw, I already ate," he says teasingly.

"You're bad. Give me a minute to touch up my makeup."

He takes his jacket off and puts it on my shoulders to keep me warm.

Which sorta makes me swoon.

Because he's hotter than hell and the sweetest boy ever.

I run into the bathroom, throw on a sorta matching pink thong, touch up my makeup, and look at my no-longer-stick-straight hair. The back looks mussed and sexy. Rather than straightening it, I tease the rest of it, making it big and hopefully as sexy-looking as I feel.

WHEN I GO back out to the living room, Aiden has his shirt back on and has picked all my clothes off the floor. I slide the thigh highs back on, zip up my boots, and throw on my skirt.

Aiden smiles. "Maybe you should just stop there."

"Just wear my bra and your jacket to dinner?"

"You can have anything of mine you want."

"Anything?"

"Yeah. If you want."

I do want.

I so want . . . but yet.

I just can't.

Maybe before I leave school in the spring, I'll tell him everything.

We'll sleep together. Then . . .

Wait.

Rewrite.

Sleep with him first. Unleash that Titan. Then tell him. That way, if he hates you, at least you'll know if it was everything you thought it would be.

That's the real reason I haven't yet. When we do, I don't want there to be any more lies.

I want to tell him I love him. I want him to know the real me.

As he slides his jacket off me and helps me put my shirt back on, I realize how badly I want that.

One boy to know and love all of me.

Aiden knows part of me. The me I've become.

But part of me is my home and my family.

B knows the old me. He knows my family and understands my life.

Neither one of them know all of me.

As the shirt goes over my head, Aiden gives me the kind of kiss that makes me feel like it doesn't matter with him. Like he knows my soul. Like he wouldn't care who my family is.

What'd he say last week? *You and me against the world. Always.*

And when he holds my hand and leads me out to our waiting car, I feel like it's enough.

But then I remember how I felt so in love with B.

How he loved me, but still left me.

I'm afraid Aiden will, too.

And I'm afraid it will destroy me.

That's the other reason I didn't want to come back to school. It's just going to make it more heartbreaking.

His voice flits through my memory. *A heartbreakingly beautiful kind of love.*

In any good script, there are elements of foreshadowing. A tense score. A dark, scary place. I wonder if what he said was foreshadowing in the story of my life.

A love so beautiful it will break both our hearts.

He puts his arm around me and whispers, "You okay?"

"I couldn't be more perfect, Aiden. I'm with you."

AFTER WE'RE SEATED, served drinks, and hear the long list of specials, Aiden orders a steak and I get blackened salmon.

The waiter brings us out a free appetizer of spicy shrimp. As I bite into it, I can't help but think of being with B at Buddy's and wonder how serious he is about the girl he's been seeing.

Although I was really upset that he didn't help me as promised, I can understand. I might have done the same thing if I got a picture like that.

I think of the one Mom got in New York that was stabbed everywhere.

Aiden rubs my hand. "You're quiet all of a sudden."

"I'm just mellow. Relaxed. Kinda tired."

"How about after dinner, we have the driver take us by the tree and then we go snuggle up in bed?"

I smile. "That sounds perfect."

"So, tell me more about this movie, superstar. Remember, I got your first autograph. It's gonna be worth something someday." He takes my hand in his. "Not that I'd ever sell it."

"It's a small role in an action film. I play the daughter of the badass main character. I get kidnapped at the beginning, have one little scene where they prove I'm still alive, and then a scene at the end where I'm rescued. And half of that may end up on the cutting room floor during editing."

"It's a good start, though, right?"

"Yeah, it's a good start. The scenes are important to the movie, so a lot of people will see my face even if they don't really remember me after."

Aiden runs his hand from my temple to under my chin and says, "Smile."

"You are awfully bossy tonight. That jacket must have come with a dose of cockiness."

"Smile for me. It makes me happy," he says.

And I can't help but smile. I want to make him happy.

"That's what people are going to fall in love with. That smile. It's, well, the only word that really accurately describes it is intoxicating. Everyone in the theater will be instantly love-drunk."

"What about you? You put your picture on your wine. Shirtless. Wearing that jacket. Stuff could taste like crap and women wouldn't care."

He laughs. "You're silly."

"So, what else did up your mom buy you for your birthday? I may need to inspect your purchases if they are going to crash at my house."

He runs his finger across the top of my hand again. I can tell having this stupid table between us is driving him nuts.

Just before our food is served, he says to the waiter, "Can we move to that booth?"

We switch tables, the cozy, round booth allowing us to sit close together. He lays his hand across my leg, sometimes just holding my knee and other times playing with the tops of my thigh highs.

We eat dinner, drive by the beautiful and insanely huge Christmas tree, and then get dropped off at home.

I throw on some pajamas, wash my face, and then dive into bed with him.

All he has on is a pair of soft cotton boxers.

He snuggles me into his arms and kisses the top of my head. "When you told me about the ice cream dream, I should've stayed and listened."

"I know why you got mad, but there's always more to a story than meets the eye."

He nods, snuggles up with me, then immediately starts breathing deeply.

I can tell he's already asleep.

I look at the clock.

11:30.

I don't have any phone calls to make.

No midnight meeting with Cooper.

No flights.

Nothing to think about except how safe I feel, here, in Aiden's arms.

Sunday, December 11th

OUR.

10AM

I WAKE UP to the smell of bacon.

My room feels chilly. I bump the heat up a few degrees, brush my teeth, and wrap myself in a long cashmere robe.

"I was just coming to wake you."

"Have you been up long?"

"About an hour. I made chocolate chip waffles."

"That sounds yummy."

I watch as he adds another waffle to a huge stack in the warming drawer.

"You feeding an army? Or did you invite the football team over?"

"Actually, my parents should be here any minute. I hope that's okay. They went to visit friends in Vermont after the dance competition, but are flying home from here. They'll be home for a few weeks."

"Is something wrong?" I immediately assume something is, based on Aiden's body language.

He pours more batter onto the waffle iron. "Hopefully not. This time every year she goes in for tests, and we impatiently wait to find out if the cancer has come back. She's lost weight since I last saw her, so I'm worried."

"Aiden! Why didn't you tell me?"

"I'm telling you now."

The intercom buzzes. "Shit! I'm in my robe!"

"It's okay. My parents are laid-back."

"Maybe, but you aren't in a robe."

"I've got on sweats and an old t-shirt. Don't worry about it."

"It's no wonder I can't think straight. Your shirt is way too tight and your sweats are way too low on your hips."

"That's because they've gotten too short and look dumb if I don't pull them down." He walks over and kisses my nose. "I like that you can't think straight. You go get dressed. I'll let them in."

I run into my closet, throw on a pair of stretchy jean leggings, an oversized Foreigner t-shirt, and a pair of Ugg slippers. Then I run a powder brush across my face and give my lashes a few swipes of mascara.

I'm back out by the time they have their coats off and are sitting down at our kitchen table.

I stop in my tracks.

Our.

Our kitchen table?

I look at Aiden hugging his mom and smile at him.

As soon as his parents see me, I'm greeting with hugs too.

I try not to hug his mom for too long, but I can't help it. I miss my own mom.

"It smells wonderful," she says, taking her seat.

"Aiden made it all," I admit. "I just woke up."

"Late night last night?" Aiden's dad asks.

"No, we—I mean, I was asleep by like eleven. Aiden," I point toward a bedroom, "has his own room."

I have no idea if they're cool with sleeping with someone before marriage or whatever. I don't want to offend them.

Or for them to think we're having sex when we're not.

I mean, actual doing it. As opposed to the hotness that was the pool table last night.

I glance at Aiden, whose nostrils flare as he suppresses a smile and rolls his eyes adorably.

I figure food is a safer topic of conversation and eating is even safer, so I put a waffle on my plate, throw a few extra chocolate chips on top, and pour melted butter over it all.

"I hear you're all going to St. Croix for Christmas. You'll have the best time," I say.

Aiden says to his parents, "I haven't told you yet, but I'm going to spend New Year's Eve with Keatyn."

"You are?" His eyes meet mine and he nods. I lower my head and pretend to be very interested in cutting my waffle into precise pieces while I fight back tears.

I can't let him leave his family, so I say, "I was actually going to ask how long you're supposed to be there. I was thinking about coming for part of the break."

"We're waiting for Damian to firm up the schedule," his mom tells me. "So, we're not sure on the dates yet."

"You'll love Damian."

Aiden's mom says, "Well, Peyton seems very taken by him. That's part of why we were hoping to have breakfast with you."

His dad smiles. "Yeah, we'd like the 411."

Aiden cringes. "Dad. No one says that anymore."

His dad rolls his eyes exactly like Aiden does, which makes me laugh. "Aiden seems to approve of him."

"I never said I approve," Aiden counters. "I said she's happy. The happiest I've ever seen her."

"He's a great guy. One of the good ones, you know. Smart, respectful, extremely talented, creative, fun, and he has an amazing voice. I think you will love him," I tell them.

"And his family?"

"His dad is remarried and they have little kids. That keeps get-togethers casual and lots of fun. And the house is St. Croix is the perfect combination of luxurious and relaxed."

Aiden adds, "And the food is amazing."

"Well, that sounds perfect," Aiden's mom says. "What are your holiday plans, Keatyn?"

"Um, I'm probably going to France to celebrate with my family."

Aiden narrows his eyes at me. "Probably?"

"Oh, not probably I'll be with my family. I meant probably France. It's hard to say. My mom might decide to go to St. Moritz, or Annecy, or somewhere instead."

"But not to St. Croix?"

"No, not this year."

"Peyton told me that some celebrities might be coming for their New Year's Eve party."

"They have a great party space and, because of his job, Mr. Moran does know a lot of celebrities. I haven't been there on New Years for a couple of years."

"Well, you should come. We'd love to ring in the new year with you and Aiden."

"Maybe. I just have to get things firmed up with my parents."

"What are your parents' names, dear? As much traveling as it sounds like they do, I wonder if we have any mutual friends," his mom asks.

"You probably don't. My mom works a lot."

"And what does she do?"

"Oil and gas leases. With countries."

"And what was her name?"

"She never said," Aiden's dad replies.

"Oh, um, my mom's name is Kathryn," I lie, using her middle name. "For work, she uses the last name Monroe, like mine, but my stepdad's name is Tom, uh, Hart. So, even though they aren't actually married, a lot of people would think of her as . . ." Shit. What did I say her first name was? ". . . Mrs. Hart. Maybe, Mrs. Tom Hart. Kathryn Hart. She'll answer to just about anything, really."

Aiden's mom puts a finger to her temple. "Hmmm, Monroe sounds familiar. I know. George and Elizabeth Monroe. They're from Scottsdale. Any relation?"

"No, most of my relatives are in Texas."

Aiden thankfully stops the Arrington Inquisition by clearing plates and asking his parents if they'd like to see the rest of the loft.

While he shows them around, I make myself busy with the dishes.

When they go upstairs, I grab my purse and add more lies to my ever-growing list. It's no wonder I can't remember half of them anymore.

They finish up the tour, join me in the kitchen, and Aiden asks, "Will Abernathy and Fritz be there?"

"Who?"

"The couple you and Damian were talking about. The love-at-first-sight couple."

"Oh, I don't know. I haven't seen a guest list because I'm not going."

Jeez, does he ever forget anything?

"Abernathy. That's an unusual name," Aiden's dad comments. "Isn't there a Scotch with that name?"

"No, that's Aberloure," Aiden tells him.

His mom changes the subject. "Your Christmas tree turned out beautifully. I thought Aiden went a little crazy on the ornaments, but it was the perfect amount."

"Thanks," I say. "He did go a little crazy."

Aiden leans against the kitchen island in the exact spot he was in when I got down on my knees and unleashed the Titan. I tilt my head and look dreamily at him.

He smirks at me, then looks down. I know he knows exactly what I'm thinking about.

I hear his dad say, "This loft is incredible. Aiden told us about its former life as a concert hall."

The answer to my previous question: no. Aiden clearly never forgets a thing. Damn that godly brain.

"That's why I love it. The history and character."

"And your closet is beautiful, too. Aiden said you have one like it at home?"

"Uh, yeah."

Ohmigawd, people. Please, no more questions.

But they don't stop.

Aiden's dad asks, "Do you have plans for today? Do you want to go do something?"

"We have tickets to see *The Nutcracker* this afternoon. Do you want to see if I can get a couple more?"

"Oh, no, we should probably get to the airport. I start my testing on Tuesday."

"I hope that all goes well," I say. "That must be scary."

Aiden's dad looks at the floor, but his mom says, "Better to know the truth so you can deal with it."

AFTER THEY LEAVE, Aiden pulls me into a hug. "Sorry for the twenty questions."

"It's okay. I didn't mind," I lie.

"I want to spend New Year's with you. Wherever you are."

"That would be nice."

"What would you think of spending the week here? I've always wanted to watch the ball drop in person."

"That would be amazing. But maybe we can go to a party? One that overlooks the ball dropping, instead of standing outside in the cold."

"That sounds even better. Dancing all night. You in a sexy little dress. Kissing at midnight."

"It's a date," I tell him. "Can we make some hot chocolate and go upstairs, so I can stare at the tree before we leave? It's so pretty."

"Perfect. We'll relax for a while before we have to go. Why don't I finish cleaning up while you go put your robe back on."

"You want me back in my robe?"

"Yes, it's soft and you'll be naked underneath."

WE SEE *The Nutcracker*, have dinner, and then take a late train back to school.

I finish doing the homework I didn't do all weekend—while Katie tells me all that happened while we were gone—and am just getting ready to go to sleep when my phone buzzes.

Hottie God: *ifly<3*

Me: *Are you telling me you're fly? LOL*

Hottie God: *I totally am, but no. ifly = I fucking love you.*

Me: *Oh :) Well, then, ifly too <3*

Hottie God: *Leave your window unlocked. I'm not sure I can sleep without you.*

Monday, December 12th
THAT MANY TIMES.
7AM

ANNIE COMES RUNNING into our dorm room laughing while Katie and I are still getting ready. "Look what I got from my naughty Santa! Hold your hand out!"

Katie does as asked. Annie holds up a cute little plastic reindeer, hits a button, and the reindeer poops a chocolate turd into her hand.

"Oh, that's gross!" Katie yells.

"But it's chocolate!" Annie counters, which causes Katie to look closer at the reindeer poo and then pop it into her mouth.

"That's good!" Katie says.

"Did you both sleep in?" Annie asks.

"Yeah," I say. "I was tired."

"Did Aiden wear you out?" Annie teases as she plops on my bed. "Tell us what happened."

"It was more the whole week that wore me out. Dance practices, then the competition. Aiden and I shopped all day Saturday. I got all my Christmas shopping done, though. Speaking of wearing someone out. What did you and Jake do this weekend?"

"Partied a little. We did one night with everyone in Bryce's room and then Riley took us to Stockton's on Saturday night. Jake got a little drunk. He was so cute."

"Cute when he was drunk?"

"He was more like tipsy, I guess. He just said some really sweet things to me."

"Drunk words equal sober thoughts," Katie says as she whizzes by us throwing books into her backpack.

"What does that mean?" Annie asks her.

"It means," Katie replies, "that when you're drunk you say things that you would be too chicken to say sober. For guys, that's usually how they feel about you."

Annie's eyes light up. "Really? Ohmigosh. That makes it even better."

"What did he say?" I ask.

She pulls her arms into her chest and hugs herself. "That he's falling in love with me. And the best part about it is he isn't just saying it to get in my pants."

"Because he's already in them," Katie laughs.

I finish loading my bag and then sit on the bed next to Annie. "Are you both being careful?"

"We've used a condom every time," Annie says. "I have too many life goals to risk getting pregnant. I also made an appointment with a women's clinic in town so I can go on the pill."

"That's smart."

Katie is sort of fidgeting. "Katie, what about you?"

"Well, Bryce doesn't really like to use them, so usually he just pulls out."

"Katie!" Annie and I both say together, horrified.

Annie continues. "That's like playing Russian Roulette! Do you want to get pregnant?"

"No! But . . ." Katie starts to say.

"No buts," Annie snarls. "I'm making you an appointment. We'll go together."

"I'm a little worried, actually. The other night he waited too long."

Annie covers her eyes with her hands. "Katie!"

"Don't chew me out. It's not my fault."

"It will be your fault if you get pregnant. It's your body and your responsibility to protect yourself. We're going to the pharmacy after school and buying you condoms. You will tell Bryce no condoms equals no sex. And pray that you're not already pregnant."

Katie lowers her head and nods. "Okay."

I glance at the clock. "We better get to class."

As I run out the door, I trip over a present lying there, wrapped with a pink bow.

"Open it quick!" Annie and Katie yell. "We want to see what it is!"

I tear open the paper to find a G-string made out of candy.

As we're rushing to get to our classes, Annie says, "I like your present."

"Yeah, it's cute."

"Does Aiden like candy?" Katie teases.

"Doesn't everyone like candy?" I reply.

AIDEN IS WAITING for me outside my history class and greets me with a kiss.

"Do you even remember me sleeping with you last night?" he whispers.

"I remember you getting in bed with me but that's about it. I was tired."

"You kissed my neck and told me it was your favorite place. The rest of my body is jealous."

I laugh. "You're silly. Did you get a naughty Santa gift this morning?"

"I did. What about you?"

"I did too. What did you get?"

He pulls dice out of his pocket and lays them in my palm, flipping them and reading. "Lick, suck, blow, kiss, nibble, tease. You roll this dice first. Then you roll for the body part you have to do it to." He puts the other die in my hand. "Neck, lips, ear, toes, chest, and player's choice. Wanna test them out tonight? Or should we save them for this weekend?"

"Tonight. After we get our homework done."

"What'd you get?" he asks.

"Remember those candy necklaces you used to get when you were a kid?"

"Yeah."

"I got a G-sting made out of it."

He raises his eyebrows. "So I can eat the candy off you?"

"I think that's the idea."

"You win."

"Win what?"

"We'll use yours tonight. Stockton's? Riley's used that place almost every night. I think he should share." He places his palm on the wall above my shoulder and leans his chest against mine. "I can just picture it. Candy thong and a pair of boots. Nothing else."

"Mr. Arrington," my history teacher says, "you need to get to class."

Aiden gives me a quick kiss on the lips and keeps ahold of my hand. He holds it until he has moved too far away from me to keep holding it, looking reluctant to let go.

He's so adorable.

As soon as I sit down in class, my phone buzzes. I cross my legs and hide it under the desk.

Hottie God: Remember the pool playing we did this weekend?

Me: Yes. You cheated.

Hottie God: I won fair and square.

Me: Yes, you did, but the rules were that the loser had to do something, um, nice for the winner.

Hottie God: The rules were made before someone was dancing half naked on the pool table.

Me: The halftime entertainment was your idea.

Hottie God: And a fucking brilliant one at that.

Me: Riley just told me Logan and Maggie have dibs on Stockton's tonight, but we can have it tomorrow.

Hottie God: Logan got six condom lollipops this morning.

Me: I thought they were waiting until after Winter Formal.

Hottie God: Maggie told him she wants to use all the lollipops tonight.

Me: Wow. That's a lot for one night.

Hottie God: We'll need more.

The second I read his text warmth spreads through my body. Thoughts of what he did to me on the pool table are quickly overshadowed by thoughts of what else he wants to do to me.

Riley drops a note over my shoulder and into my lap.

I glance at the teacher before opening it.

#1. I don't know who my naughty Santa is, but I'm in love with her already. I got pink furry handcuffs. Do you think the house elves will know and install an appropriate headboard?

#2. Did you and Aiden do it this weekend?

a.) he seemed very chipper today.

b.) he wants Stockton's for the two of you.

c.) is playing pool your secret code word for sex?

#1. I think house elves know everything.

#2. We didn't, but we had fun. We played pool. Strip pool. He won.

What'd he get?

Not telling.

Tell me!

Let's just say he has a talented tongue.

Ha! I knew it was something!

Hottie God: *You haven't replied.*
Me: *I've never done it . . . like that many times.*
Hottie God: *Me either, but I know once we do, we won't want to stop. I've wanted you since the first day I saw you. I seriously had never seen someone so beautifully perfect until that moment.*
Me: *I have to admit, I'm nervous.*
Hottie God: *Why?*
Me: *What if it sucks?*
Hottie God: *No fucking way. What you should be prepared for is the fact that you're never going to want to be with anyone else ever again.*
Me: *That scares me too.*
Hottie God: *It does me too.*
Me: *You make me feel like no one else ever has.*
Hottie God: *And you're waiting for something bad to happen?*
Me: *I'm afraid it's too perfect.*
Hottie God: *Has anything about us been easy?*
Me: *Not really.*
Hottie God: *In six and a half minutes, I'm going to kiss the hell out of you. Just saying.*
Me: *Aiden?*
Hottie God: *What, baby?*
Me: *I think it's going to be amazing with you, just like everything else is.*

Hottie God: *Me too <3*

I send a quick text to Camden.

Me: *Any chance the house elves can install something your brother could attach furry handcuffs to?*
Cam: *House elves?*
Me: *We decided that house elves were responsible for forecasting our every whim.*
Cam: *LOL. They are :) I hear my brother is giving the place a proper workout. What about you?*
Me: *Winter Formal is coming up :)*
Cam: *Will Aiden be "coming up" there?*
Me: *I think so.*
Cam: *Bout time. How's P? Something's up with her.*
Me: *She met a guy.*
Cam: *Where?*
Me: *Beach over break.*
Cam: *Hmm. What about Whitney?*
Me: *She's dating Shark.*
Cam: *That is a match I bet even Shark wouldn't have bet on.*
Me: *They seem really happy. She seems happy.*
Cam: *And Dawson?*
Me: *One word: Brooke. Hardly ever get to see him.*

I'm walking down the hall toward English when Aiden struts up to me, puts his hands around my neck, and kisses me, exactly as promised.

STRAIGHT OUT OF A MOVIE.
DRAMA

I GET A text from Cooper.

Cooper: *You need to get a really bad cramp now. Go to the nurse. Make her call me out of class.*

I do as he says, make my way in fake pain to the nurse's office, and talk her into calling Mr. Steele.

I know by the look on his face when he walks into the nurse's office that something is wrong.

Is Vincent on his way here? Is he already here?

No. If that were the case, he wouldn't care about pretending to be a teacher anymore.

Which means he has news.

Bad news.

"Is my family okay?" I ask him as I pretend limp down to the Field House.

"Yes," is all he says.

ONCE WE'RE SAFELY in the training room, he says, "The guy who talked to Vincent's assistant is a cop friend of mine. He just sent me something."

"Did he talk to her again? Get something good on Vincent?"

"No, he's a detective. A *homicide* detective."

"Is Vincent dead?!"

"No."

"Is his assistant dead?"

"No, um . . ."

"Just say it, Cooper."

"One of the dancers from the club is dead. She was reported missing by her roommates when she didn't come home from work Thursday night. They found her body on the beach in Malibu." Cooper glances back at his phone. "In front of a restaurant called Moon Beams."

My heart stops beating.

"That's the restaurant Vincent and I had dinner at. We sat on the deck overlooking the water. Which girl was it?"

"She's new. Only been working there for about two weeks. She was off the night we were there."

"So, she was murdered?"

"Yes. Her place of employment caught his attention, so he texted me earlier. Then he sent me this." He holds up his phone, showing me a photo of a thin, tan waist with a glow-in-the-dark chaos tattoo just below the hip.

"I sent a bunch of custom glow-in-the-dark chaos tattoos to Marla. She liked mine because she thinks if they ever name the club it should be called Utter Chaos. Tell me this is just a coincidence."

"You know what Garrett says."

"He doesn't believe in them."

"Is it my fault she's dead?" Cooper is being very careful with his words, and I realize there's something he hasn't said. "How did she die?"

"It's not your fault, Keatyn."

"How did she die, Cooper?"

He sighs then says, "Cause of death was asphyxiation."

"She was strangled?"

"Yes."

I swallow hard. "Was she raped?"

"No."

"Cooper, what are you not telling me?!"

"After her death, she was stabbed numerous times. This type of stabbing is unusual to see on a woman."

"Why?"

"Typically when a body is mutilated after death it is for one of two reasons. Usually, it's out of rage. Like what you would see when a jealous ex commits the crime. In this case, the victim doesn't have a jealous ex. Her boyfriend is devastated and has a solid alibi."

"What's the other reason someone would do it?"

"To send a message to the living. Like when a drug dealer wants to remind people not to cheat him, for example. The choice of weapon was also unusual. It's a weapon usually used by women, but the depth of the stab wounds suggest a male killer. And the picture I showed you, with the tattoo, was of the only part of the victim that was not stabbed."

"What was she stabbed with?"

"Scissors."

My vision blurs.

My face feels hot.

A wave of nausea hits me.

My legs feel weak, causing me to sway.

Cooper grabs my arm and keeps me from falling, setting me down in a chair.

I put my hand across my forehead.

"You look like you're going to faint. Look at me."

I look up at him.

"Tell me," he says.

"Vincent is sending me a message."

"How so?"

"After he chased me in New York City, a picture of me was delivered to my mom's hotel room. The picture had been stabbed with scissors. Have you told Garrett about any of this?"

"No, I just found out."

"Call him. I have to go."

"Where are you going?"

"I just have to get out of here," I say. The training room suddenly feels very claustrophobic. "Get some fresh air."

"Don't leave campus," he says then tries to give me a hug.

"Don't, okay? I'm fine. It's fine. Everything will be fine."

Except it's not.

It's not fine.

At all.

I run out of the Field House, the cold air hitting my lungs and forcing me to suck in a big breath.

I wander aimlessly across campus, feeling numb.

Thinking about that poor girl.

About her poor family.

Her roommates.

Her friends.

And, mostly, that she's dead because of me.

I FIND MYSELF standing in the chapel.

No one is here, so I walk straight to the front, drop to my knees, and pray.

Pray for forgiveness.

Pray that it was a mistake.

That it had nothing to do with me.

That she didn't suffer.

I pray for her family.

For my guilt.

Then I go sit in the back.

I should be crying.

But I have no tears.

I pull my feet up on the pew, wrap my arms tightly around my legs, and rock back and forth.

MY PHONE BUZZES.

I robotically take it out of my coat pocket and look at it.

Hottie God: *Heard you went to the nurse's office with a hamstring cramp. You need me to help you stretch?*

My hands shake as I text him back.

Me: *i*
Me: *need*
Me: *you*

I put my phone down and hug my legs.
Not crying.
Not moving.
Not feeling.
There is nothing.
Just.
Emptiness.
Loneliness.
Despair.

KEATYN.

I hear my name softly spoken, the noise breaking into my thoughts, but sounding very far away.

"Keatyn!"

I remain motionless, only moving my eyes toward the noise.

Aiden shakes my shoulder. "Keatyn!"

I don't move.

Instead, I start sobbing.

And sobbing.

Aiden puts his arm around me and rubs my back. "What's wrong? Are you in pain?"

I sob some more.

"I went to the field house first, but Coach Steele said you left. I texted you to find out where you were, but you didn't reply. I checked everywhere."

I can't speak.

I just keep crying.

A deep, emotional, guilty cry.

Aiden grabs my chin, roughly turning my head and forcing me to look at him.

"She's dead," I whisper.

"Who's dead!?"

"Girl . . . Club . . . Stalker . . . Friend."

"Keatyn, look at me! You need to tell me what happened!"

I shudder.

He presses his lips into my temple and whispers, "It's okay, baby. Shhh. I'm here. It's okay."

His words calm me. I shudder again, but the sobs slow down.

"Tell me what happened," he says quietly, his lips still against my face.

"Girl . . . Murdered . . . L. A."

"Did you know her?"

"No . . . She danced at the club . . . The birthday party . . . Almost kidnapped."

"Is this about your friend? Is she okay? Is she still safe from the stalker?"

"Yes, but. But . . ."

I sob again, unable to say it.

"Shhh," he whispers again. He gently pushes my hair off my face, his lips never leaving my temple. "But what, baby?"

"After my friend left . . . Accidentally saw mom. Both shopping. New York City. Stalker was following Mom. Chased."

"Chased your friend?"

"Yes. Cabs. Streets. Fast. Got away. Later. Mom. Package. Photo of friend. Stabbed with scissors."

"How awful."

I nod, completely agreeing with him. "The girl who . . . was killed. Like my friend."

"And?"

"My friend did something."

"What'd she do?"

"She went back. To the club. Knew stalker would be there. Danced. For him."

"Why would she do that?"

"Tired of hiding. Trying to push. Get him to make a mistake."

"I still don't understand why your friend thinks it's her fault a girl was killed. Sadly, murders happen in big cities like L. A. all the time."

"Girl . . . stabbed with scissors."

"Oh my god. That's awful."

"And . . . and . . . and." I start crying again. "And . . . it was all my idea."

"Take my hand," he says, reaching out to me.

I'm still on autopilot, but my hand moves into his and he squeezes it tightly.

"Listen to me. It's not your fault. You couldn't have known it was going to happen. Everything will be okay. I'll help you."

Somehow his squeezing my hand does make me feel like everything will be okay.

"I'm supposed to be somewhere. Class? Dance?"

"You're in no shape for it."

AIDEN TAKES ME to his room, where I lie on his bed and snuggle into his pillow, which smells just like his neck.

A few minutes later, Riley is sitting on the edge of the bed. "Cooper asked me where you are. He seemed worried."

"I was with him—getting my hamstring stretched—when I . . ."

"I told him all about it," Aiden tells me. "I have to get to basketball practice. Riley is going to stay with you until I get back, okay?"

He kisses my forehead and is heading toward his door when Riley squints at me. "Wait? So both you *and* your friend were stalked?"

Aiden freezes, turning around quickly. "What do you mean?"

My lies are unraveling before my very eyes.

"When we were in Miami, there was a guy who tried to grab Keatyn," Riley says to Aiden.

I get tears in my eyes. Now, not only do I have to lie, but I have to lie about my lies.

"Riley, I lied."

"Why?"

I put my hands in my face trying to figure out a new story, but my brain is fried.

Thankfully, Aiden sits back on the bed and starts telling Riley what I told him.

About my friend.

"Why didn't you tell us?" Riley asks, pushing my chin up so I have to look at him.

It's easy to tell the truth to that question.

"I was shocked. I mean, it all happened so fast, and I was told—no, warned, sworn to secrecy—that if I told anyone about the stalker then he could find her."

"So, where is she?" Riley asks.

I close my eyes again. "She's lost," I say, simply stating how I feel.

"No one knows where she is?"

"They put her in witness protection, but she didn't feel safe anymore, so she left. She can't tell me where, but she's tired of being away from everyone she loves. Her family. Her friends. She wants her life back."

"But what does that have to do with you?"

"It's sort of another reason why I didn't get to stay at my old school. She has this personal security firm that helped. They were worried that all her close friends could be in danger too. That he might hurt us to find her. It just worked out that Damian was away on tour and Brooklyn was leaving to surf. I had the option of coming here or going with my family. I chose here because I was worried about my sisters. She and I were really close. I'd be the natural target if he couldn't find her. And, now, I'm responsible for a girl being dead because I told her it was time to stop running and fight back. My friend told me about the girl. Says she can't handle it. The guilt. The fear."

"Keatyn, you didn't do anything wrong," Riley says. "You're just stronger than she is."

"What do you mean?"

"I mean, if it were you, you'd fight back. You wouldn't just sit around and wait for something to happen. You'd make what you want to happen, well, happen. It's like what we just learned in history. How you never know what people will do when faced with danger. How they react like animals. Fight or flight."

"Fight or flight?"

"He's right," Aiden says. "Your friend chose flight, but not you. You'd fight. You wouldn't let this stop you." He wraps his hands around my fists and squeezes.

I smile at him. "You're right. And you just gave me an idea."

"What's that?"

"Instead of her going to dance this week, I will."

Aiden and Riley share a worried glance.

Aiden kisses me. "Stay here with Riley until I get back."

THE SECOND AIDEN closes the door, Riley narrows his eyes at me and says, "So, which one of us are you telling the truth to?"

"What do you mean?"

"Your story. It's full of holes."

"I know. I don't want to lie to you. I just had to lie about this. I'm sorry."

"That's all you're lying about?"

"Yes. I hate to lie. But I promised. And the lies are only for protection, so I hope you understand."

"I understand. Now, move over. If you're going to do something dangerous, I'm going to help you script it."

I move over and lean against his arm while we brainstorm.

WHAT WE END up with is a scene straight out of a movie.

Which is pretty fitting, if you ask me.

FEELING HORRIBLE.
5:45PM

AIDEN COMES BACK from basketball with takeout food from the cafeteria. Potato soup for me and chicken fajitas for him.

He does our homework while I mostly just lie on his bed feeling horrible.

He makes me stay with him until it's time for curfew, then walks me to my dorm and gives me a comforting goodnight kiss.

AS SOON AS Katie is asleep, I go into the stairwell, call Troy, and tell him what I think happened.

"Oh, wow," he says slowly. "I didn't even put that together. Do you really think it was him?"

I tell him about the picture.

"Wow," he says again.

"So, I need to know. Did he get one of the bouncers to bring him back there? Give her a card? Anything?"

"Uh, I don't know. Let me check and I'll call you right back."

TEN MINUTES LATER, he calls me back.

"Yes. He asked one of the bouncers to give her his business card. Said he was a producer and would be interested in doing a screen test with her. From what I understand, this isn't unusual for him. A lot of the girls admitted to doing screen tests and many have hooked up with him. They say he's charming and a perfect gentleman."

"Is the bouncer willing to tell all this to the police?"

"He will. He feels responsible because he helped her get the job."

"Troy, if he isn't arrested this week, I'm coming back Thursday to dance again. I want to honor her in a big way. Do you think the club and the girls would be willing to help?"

"Absolutely. We're all still reeling. And we've been trying to figure out something to do for Leighton."

"Leighton was her name?"

"Yeah, Leighton Wall."

I close my eyes. Somehow knowing her name makes it even worse.

"I'm going to have a bunch of packages delivered to the club with your name on them. What time does the club open?"

"Ten."

"Can you have all the employees there at nine?"

"Will do."

"And Troy?"

"Yeah?"

"Don't tell Damian. I want to keep him as far away from this mess as possible."

I KNOW COOPER will probably have a fit about this, but I don't care.

I toss and turn in bed, trying to sleep, but visions of Vincent, cages, and scissors haunt me every time I close my eyes.

I know there's a very good chance that I might not come back from this trip.

That my fate might be the same as Leighton's.

Aiden sneaks in my window sometime after curfew and pulls me into his arms.

I still don't sleep, but I do realize there's something important I need to do before I go back to face Vincent.

Just in case I don't come back.

I slip out of bed, grab my phone, sneak into the bathroom, and send Sam an email with a very specific set of instructions to be carried out in a very short amount of time.

I end the email with a directive to meet me on Thursday afternoon.

Then I use the notes function on my phone and start writing.

Tuesday, December 13th

KISS ME HERE.

7:40AM

AIDEN MEETS ME in my dorm room with coffee and donuts.

"How are you feeling this morning?"

"Better. Thanks for always being there for me, Aiden. I really appreciate it."

"There's nowhere else I'd rather be," he says, setting down the food and taking me into his arms. "What's that?"

I turn around and see a wrapped tube with another pink bow. "It must be from my naughty Santa. Katie must've put it there when she left for her Spanish Club meeting."

"Do you want to open it?"

"Yeah," I say, eager to stop talking about yesterday. I rip the paper off the container to find a game called Sexy Truth or Dare. I take off the lid and Aiden pulls out one of the long sticks out and reads it.

"How fun," he says. "You have the option of answering a truth about sex or you have to do the dare on the back."

"That would be fun to play with our friends!"

Aiden shakes his head and holds out a stick with one of the dares, which is definitely something you wouldn't want your friends to watch you do.

"Maybe it's more of a couple's game," I say. "Did you get another gift this morning?"

"Yeah, I think Maggie might be my Santa. She was in our dorm, supposedly picking up Logan, but he always meets her."

"I don't know who anyone has except for Katie. She's bad at keeping secrets."

"Who does she have?"

"Dallas. Yesterday she gave him a six-pack that she decorated so that each beer bottle looked like a reindeer. Today it was a t-shirt with a porcupine that says *Do I make you thorny?*"

"That's funny," Aiden says. "Wanna see what I got?"

"Sure."

He untucks his shirt and pulls it up.

"Ohmigawd." I laugh at the downward pointing, pink arrow-shaped sticky note he has stuck to his stomach. "Kiss me here, huh?" I ask, reading it.

He gives me an adorable grin. "I wanted to give you first dibs."

I pull the sticky note off and put it on my notebook. "I better be the only one you're offering dibs on the Titan."

"The what?"

My eyes get big, realizing what I just said.

Shit.

"The, uh . . ."

Aiden gives me a panty-melting smirk. "You named it?"

"I didn't mean to tell you. Now you're going to get a big head."

He chuckles, playfully pulls me into his body, and puts his mouth near my ear. "If it's called the Titan, it must already have a big head."

"I got my Greek mythology screwed up when I named it."

He glances at his watch, noting that we need to get to class. "We're going to finish this conversation tonight."

HAWTHORNE'S SWEETHEART.
CERAMICS

JAKE LEANS OVER when our ceramics teacher goes into the kiln room and says, "You're going to be Hawthorne's Sweetheart, Monroe."

I squint my eyes at him. "What's that?"

He shakes his head. "I always forget you're new. You know how for Homecoming and Prom we choose royalty?"

"Yeah."

"We don't for Winter Formal. Instead, each dorm chooses a girl to represent their house for the upcoming year. To be their Sweetheart. It's a big honor."

"Who's the Sweetheart now?"

"Peyton. Why do you think she won Homecoming Queen? Our whole house voted for her."

"I didn't know that. What does she have to do?"

"Be friends with the guys."

"Ohmigawd, Jake. Tell me it's not because I've kissed a lot of the boys in your dorm!"

Bryce laughs at me but Jake says, "That's not at all what it's about. It's an honor. We choose a girl we think is cool. Someone the younger guys can look up to. A hot big sister. Someone they can come to if they're having girl troubles. Stuff like that. It was between you, Maggie, and Ariela. Ariela is super pretty, but she's a little too reserved. Maggie is awesome, but she slept with her ex's best friend. As the prefect who makes the final decision, I just have a problem with that."

"I almost slept with you to get back at Dawson."

"But you didn't. Even drunk, you didn't. We all know that."

I have a flash of Aiden and me being crowned Homecoming King and Queen.

But it's a fairy tale that will never happen. I won't be here next year. I won't even be here for Prom.

And that makes me sad.

I wish we could have the Prom of our dreams after the kind of Proms we both had last year.

I close my eyes for a minute and breathe.

We'll just have to make sure Winter Formal is special.

And I need to talk Jake into choosing someone else.

"I'm not sure if I'd give good advice."

"You will. I'm sure of it," Jake tells me. "And when you win, act surprised."

SO DAMN STUBBORN.
SOCCER

BEFORE SOCCER PRACTICE starts, Cooper inquires about my hamstring.

"I think maybe I should sit out today. Could I go in your office and make some phone calls?" I ask.

"What for?" he whispers.

"Can we talk about it after practice. I have something I need to tell you."

"Why don't you go take a whirlpool and then we'll stretch after practice," he says loudly so that my teammates can hear.

"Thanks," I say.

AFTER PRACTICE, HE meets me in the training room.

"So what were the calls about?"

"We're going back to Malibu on Thursday."

Cooper's face turns a shade of pissed-off red. "Are you fucking nuts?"

"Calm down!" I whisper softly, but firmly. "I have to do something. I can't let what happened stop my plan. I also need to go back to honor her."

"You're not going to the funeral."

"No, that wouldn't be right, since I didn't know her. We'll be honoring her at the club."

"No. No fucking way are you going back there. I'll quit before I'll allow that."

"Fine. Then I accept your resignation."

Cooper bangs his fist on the table. "Oh, you are so damn stubborn."

"I know. I'm sorry, Cooper. I have to do something. I can't let him get away with it."

"He might not get away with it. The police are going to question him."

"That's awesome news. He deserves to go to jail. But knowing him, he'll get off. And knowing him, he'll be back at the club on Thursday to see if I have the balls to show up."

"I want to know your entire plan now. We can't go out the back again. We have to have a different plan. Something . . ." Cooper says.

"More dramatic?" I laugh, knowing my plan is just that.

"No, I was thinking safe."

"We're going out the front door, Cooper. I just need you to make sure I get there and then to . . ."

I tell him my escape plan.

Cooper slaps his forehead. "You seriously have a flair for the dramatic."

"Think it will work?"

"It's not like he'll be able to follow us. But you told me that when you were in Miami he had a gun. The photos he's sent to your mom and Brooklyn involved shooting. What if he decides to start shooting? Creates a distraction to get you out. Or, worse, to clear a path to you."

"I think—well, hope—that he'll be too shocked to do anything. And by the time he realizes what's happening, we'll be gone."

"Let me think this through, okay."

I nod, shutting up.

"It sounds more like a movie than real life," he finally states.

"That's why it's perfect. He'll never expect it. And if you can get your friends to help, I'll stay safe."

Cooper shakes his head at me. "I'll see what I can do."

THE ONE CRYING.
6:15PM

SINCE THERE'S A home basketball game tonight, we eat pizza and get ready in the dance locker room.

Once I have my dance uniform on and my hair fixed, I text Aiden.

Me: *Good luck tonight.*

Hottie God: *Thanks. Tonight is a big game, but I have to admit, my thoughts are on you wearing candy. Did I mention I have a sweet tooth?*

Hottie God: *And tongue.*

Whew. Is it hot in here?

I use a pompom to fan my face.

Me: *I like your tongue.*

Hottie God: *It likes you too. I have to go. What outfits are you wearing tonight? Are they nice and short?*

Me: *Very skimpy as usual.*

Hottie God: *Perfect.*

The game is very back and forth. It's also really rough. Dawson has already fouled out and Ace is close. Aiden makes a great defensive play, stealing a pass and running down the court for the fast break score. But as he goes up for the ball, he's badly fouled and falls down on the ground hard.

I hold my breath as he lies on the ground, holding his ankle and writhing in pain.

The trainer runs out onto the court and helps him limp off. He isn't even able to shoot his own free throw.

He sits on the end of the bench and the trainer tries to remove his shoe.

Aiden winces in pain and shakes his head, so the trainer takes him to the locker room.

Dallas is sitting low in the bleachers ogling Kassidy, so I try to catch his eye. That doesn't work. So I figure, screw it.

I get up and march over to Peyton. "I'm going to the boys' locker room."

"You can't go in there," she tells me. "I'm sure he's fine. Probably just a twisted ankle."

I stare at her.

"Okay, fine," she finally says. "Run down and get all our glitter gloves."

I smile at her. "Thank you."

I go out a side gym door, race down to the locker area, barge into the training room, and find Aiden getting his shoe cut off.

"Are you okay?" I ask panicked.

"Not sure. Sprained my ankle for sure. It's so swollen that we can't get my shoe off."

"That's good right? Usually they aren't broken when they swell up that fast?"

"I've never heard that," the trainer says.

I can see the pain on Aiden's face. I want to make it go away.

"I'm fine," he says, gritting his teeth as the trainer cuts away his sock.

I peek at his ankle. "That looks like it hurts," I say, stating the obvious.

"What do you want to do, Aiden?" the trainer asks. "We can do RICE or take you to the hospital now for an X-ray."

"What's RICE?" I ask.

"Rest, Ice, Compression, Elevation," Aiden says. "Let's go with that. And some ibuprofen, please."

The trainer walks into the storage room, so I move to Aiden's side. "It's really swollen."

He holds my hand. "I'm okay."

Tears start to fall from my eyes. I know it's stupid. I know he's not seriously hurt.

He reaches up and wipes away my tears. "Shouldn't I be the one crying?"

"I don't like to see you hurt, Aiden."

"I'll be fine. It's not the first time I've twisted an ankle."

I know what he's saying is true, but he looks just like he did that day in the chapel. And the day at the pep rally. And it breaks my heart to think I'm going to cause him more hurt soon.

Leaving him.

Telling him I've been lying to him.

The trainer comes back in the room, hands Aiden some Advil and water, wraps his ankle, and says, "The game's almost over. Why don't we get you set up in your room before everyone starts coming out of the gym."

ONCE THE TRAINER gets Aiden into bed, with a pillow propping up his foot, he gives him a few more instructions and leaves.

"I have some pain pills left from when I got stitches. Do you want one?" I ask him as I gingerly sit on the corner of his bed.

"Let's see how the Advil works first, but I might take you up on that later." He makes a sad face.

"What's wrong?"

"We're supposed to go to Stockton's tonight."

"We can go there any night, Aiden. The candy will wait."

I move closer to him and run my hand gently through his hair.

He leans back on his pillow, closes his eyes, and falls asleep.

Wednesday, December 14th

IFLY.

5AM

AIDEN TEXTS ME, waking me up.

> **Hottie God:** *I'm going to get X-rays this morning. Swelling is better than last night, but I can't put any weight on it. Sorry if this wakes you up. I can't sleep.*
>
> **Me:** *Does it still really hurt?*
>
> **Hottie God:** *Not as bad, unless I try to stand.*
>
> **Me:** *Text me and let me know what they say.*
>
> **Hottie God:** *I will. ifly.*
>
> **Me:** *ifly too, Aiden.*

THINGS HEAT UP.

FRENCH

I LEARN ABSOLUTELY nothing in class this morning. My mind is too busy worrying about both Aiden and my trip tomorrow.

When Aiden walks into French class with a boot on his foot, I almost want to cry again.

"You didn't text me," I say.

"Sorry, I forgot my phone."

"Should you be walking on it?"

"That's what the boot is. A walking cast."

"It's broken?"

"No, just sprained. The boot will help support it, and I won't have to deal with crutches." He laughs. "Now we're both Boots."

I look more closely at his eyes. "Did they give you pain medication?"

"Yeah, I feel pretty good right now. About ready to fall asleep, though."

"I don't think you should be in class."

"I wanted to see you."

"Why don't I see if Miss Praline will let me take you to your room."

He raises his eyebrows at me. "That sounds even better."

I tell Miss Praline that Aiden isn't supposed to be in class because he's drugged up and ask if I can take him to his room.

Thankfully, she gives me a pass.

I BARELY GET Aiden situated on his bed before he's pulling me onto his lap and kissing me hard.

Things heat up very quickly and soon he's taking off my blazer and unbuttoning my blouse.

"I should probably lock your door," I tell him, getting up quickly to do just that.

When I get back, he's got his pants unzipped and the Titan unleashed.

I have to say that I never really thought boy parts were particularly attractive. Until now.

But, then again, everything on Aiden's body is perfection.

In my eyes, at least.

He pulls me back onto his lap and resumes his hard kisses, his hands simultaneously finding their way under my skirt and pushing my panties aside, so that . . .

I can barely even describe it, I'm so overwhelmed.

But my parts are touching his parts.

All I would have to do is push up a little, then slide back down on top of it and we'd be doing it.

When Mom had surgery a couple years ago for tennis elbow, they told her not to make any big decisions when she was on pain medication. Not to sign anything. That her judgment could be impaired.

Would it be bad of me to take advantage of Aiden while his judgment is impaired?

As he's sliding me back and forth on top of him, I don't care about his judgment. I just want to do it.

But then I look deep into his eyes.

I feel the heat.

The hunger.

But not the connection.

His eyes don't have the focus they usually do.

And I can't do that to him.

I want him to remember every single detail of our first time.

Which means I have to get the heck off him or it's going to happen by accident.

Like accidentally on purpose.

I roll so that I'm lying on the bed next to him, take the Titan in my mouth, and do what he enjoyed at the loft.

AIDEN'S SO DAMN cute afterward.

You'd think I just gave him a million dollars, let him watch porn, and made him a sandwich. The grin on his face is so contagious that I can't help but smile too.

"We almost did," he says. "You stopped it. I didn't think you'd stop it."

"If you weren't all drugged up on pain medication, I wouldn't have."

"I made the trainer stop at the store so I could buy us a movie to watch tonight," he says, the drugs obviously causing him to flit to a random topic.

"You did?" I say, humoring him. "What did you get?"

"*Clash of the Titans,*" he says, suppressing a laugh. "I also got the sequel, *Wrath of the Titans.*"

"Oh," I say, realizing he's still sharp as a freaking tack.

When I'm with Aiden, I never know whether to curse the gods for making him or praise them for doing so.

But for this, I'm going with damn the gods.

I'm just saying.

"Are you going to tell me about the name? And, more importantly, has it lived up to its name so far?" I can tell he is both teasing and serious.

I might as well tell him now. Maybe he won't remember it.

"Do you know the story of the Titans?"

"Sure. They were the first gods before Zeus and all of those guys took over."

"Right. So you know that I called you the God of all Hotties when I first met you."

"I'm still in your phone as Hottie God."

"Yes, you are. I thought you were so beautiful that you must be part god. You also seemed to always have this power over me."

"What kind of power?"

"Like, I couldn't think straight. Sometimes I thought you could read my mind. I'm pretty sure you're infused with love potion. And when you kissed me . . ."

"When you kissed me, I was done for. Ever since that first kiss on the Ferris wheel. Totally and completely your love slave."

"You didn't act like it."

"I was trying too hard, I think. But you were like uncharted territory. I had to make my own map. I was serious when I said that I did stuff for you that I've never done for anyone else, but I also know that, had I done it for any other girl, she would've been ripping her panties off for me. Instead, everything I did just seemed to piss you off."

"Because I heard you were a player. I was still getting over B and, the way you made me feel, I was afraid of setting myself up for heartbreak."

"And what do you think now?"

"That I'm setting us both up for heartbreak."

He places his hands possessively on my cheeks, exactly the same way he did in St. Croix. Like he desperately needs me.

He gives me a single long kiss.

The kind of kiss that always affects me the same way.

Deep within my soul.

Telling me that we can make it through anything.

That we can survive the kiln.

Which, if I do what I'm thinking about doing, is going to get very hot very soon.

"So, tell me the rest of the Titan story," he says, changing the subject again.

"Remember that day, when you got mad at me about wearing Dawson's jersey?"

"Because I said you were dumb?"

"Exactly. And then you went all Alpha Aiden, threw me across your desk and attacked me."

"Alpha Aiden?"

"Yes, you finally took control. Showed me how you felt. It was hot. Like the kitchen counter. The pool table. Anyway, my legs were spread apart and I could feel you were excited. And the way you were kissing me, I thought maybe we'd do it, you know. Then and there. And I wanted to. I don't know, my brain just thought *Unleash the Titan* in the heat of the moment."

"I wanted you too. But I didn't want to be . . ."

"I know," I say, rubbing his hand. "I'm glad now that we didn't. And I was so freaking happy that you finally kissed me with your tongue that I didn't care. But, see, if we watch the movie tonight, you'll know that I got it wrong. The Titans wanted to unleash the Kraken, so that the people would hate the gods, which would, in turn, make them less powerful. So, technically, that should've been its name."

"But in the heat of the moment you couldn't think straight?"

"Exactly."

"I like Titan better than Kraken."

"I do too."

"Have you ever named a guy's," he gestures toward his crotch, "before?"

"No."

"Even better," he says with a grin.

WRITING THE SCRIPT.
6:25PM

I ORDER AIDEN some Chinese food, give him a pain pill, and stare at his beautiful face as he sleeps.

And I know.

Know what I have to do.

Know that I can't lie to him any more.

That I can't wait until March to tell him the truth.

That I'm going to tell him after the dance.

In our hotel room.

And that I'm going to do it *before* we go any further.

I know there's a definite chance that he'll hate me.

That he'll walk away.

That he won't understand.

But I can't do it with him until he knows all of me.

I want him to know all of me.

So I spend the rest of the evening writing and rewriting the script.

THE SETTING: HOTEL SUITE AFTER WINTER FORMAL.

AIDEN

(Opening a bottle of champagne)

KEATYN
(Lighting all the votive candles Aiden brought)
(They kiss)
I need to tell you something.

AIDEN
(Sits on the edge of the bed)
What?

KEATYN
(Stands in front of him)
I've been lying to you. Actually, I've been lying to everyone about something. And I need you to know.

AIDEN
(Looks concerned)
Okay.

KEATYN
I came to Eastbrooke because I was being stalked. My last name isn't Monroe. Well, technically, it is because it was legally changed, I think. I'm not really sure about that. I used to be Keatyn Douglas. And my mom doesn't work in oil and gas. But she is in France. And her name is Abby Johnston.

AIDEN
(Stands up in shock)

When I get back to my dorm, I find another present wrapped with a pink ribbon.

I open it and find a teeny pair of boy short undies with two words written across the butt.

I smile at them, now certain Riley is my naughty Santa, and pack them in my bag to wear tomorrow night.

Then I work on a special gift for Vincent.

Thursday, December 15th

FOR BEING YOU.
7:25AM

AIDEN STOPS BY my dorm before he goes to breakfast.

He sees me dressed in normal clothes as opposed to my uniform and says, "I forgot you're going back to California today. Are you sure it's safe?"

"Yeah, I'm sure."

"Do you want me to come with you?" he asks sweetly.

I smile at him, remembering the last time I saw my dad. I wonder if he would've done anything differently if he had known it would be the last time he'd ever see me.

"No, Aiden. But I want to thank you."

"For what?"

What do I say? What are the last words I want him to remember?

"For being you, Aiden. For being *everything*." I turn away, pretending to look for a bracelet because I'm not able to look into his beautiful green eyes.

He turns my chin toward him. "You're coming back, right?"

"I sure hope so," I say with a grin, trying to making light of it.

"I hope so too," he says, kissing my forehead.

I hug him tightly, kiss him passionately, and then watch as he limps up the hill toward class.

I go back into the privacy of my room and make a few more phone calls.

IT'S PERFECTLY PERFECT.
10:30AM

COOPER TEXTS ME as I'm en route to the airport.

> **Cooper:** I don't like this. I should be going with you.
> **Me:** I'm meeting Sam. Just have to sign papers dealing with this takeover. He has power of attorney, but it's limited and doesn't cover this.

Okay, so I'm lying to him, but only about *why* I'm meeting Sam.
But why I'm meeting him is too personal to share with Cooper.
He'd say I'm admitting defeat.
But I want to be prepared.
Just in case.

> **Cooper:** Still . . .
> **Me:** Your flight lands in L.A. before mine does. I'm wearing the wig and the flight is booked under your name. I'll see you when I get there.
> **Cooper:** You swear to me you're going to see Sam?
> **Me:** I swear. Plus, I don't think it would be smart to both miss school on the same day.
> **Cooper:** True. All right. See you tonight.

On the plane, I look at a magazine that Peyton gave me last night at dinner. On page eight is a spread about Damian, including two pictures of him and Peyton. In one they are coming out of a trendy restaurant and in the other coming out of a club. Obviously, he didn't keep her busy in the bedroom the whole time.

Shit.

But then I look at the caption and realize that you can't clearly see her face in either photo.

Damian Moran, lead singer of the hottest new band on the planet, Twisted Dreams, was seen this past weekend with another blonde on his arm. And this blonde apparently held his attention for the entire weekend. Who is this gorgeous mystery girl? Can she tie down the playboy? And, come on, Damian, how about some equal opportunity for us brunettes?

I'm really thankful they're spending the holiday in St. Croix, where there are no photographers.

And I pray Damian will keep their relationship a secret until March.

I roll the magazine up and carefully put it in my backpack next to the brunette wig.

I'm not wearing the wig for this part of the journey.

I'm just me.

I have to be.

I close my eyes and listen to music during the long flight, arrive on schedule, and hop in Sam's rental car.

We drive for about thirty minutes through what I think is one of the most beautiful parts of the country.

Hilly. Lush. Green. Blue sky.

Sam turns onto a dirt road, winds up a hill, and says, "This is the spot."

I nod, understanding and taking it in.

He stops the car on a large flat area. "Is this what you were envisioning?"

I get out of the car and walk toward the view of the ocean.

And smile.

"You did good, Sam. It's perfectly perfect."

"I got lucky," Sam chuckles.

"No," I say. "It was fate."

I spin around, taking in the beautiful view in every direction.

"You've done everything exactly the way I requested, right?"

"I followed your instructions to the letter."

"And you'll do whatever it takes from a price and timing standpoint? We don't have much time."

"The current owners are aware of your timeline and if the offer is what they expect, we'll have the deal closed on Monday." He looks at me closely. "Are you sure this is what you want? To be cremated? To have your ashes spread here?"

"Yes. I'm positive."

He shakes his head, but all he says is, "Then I just need your signature." He holds out a clipboard, hands me a pen, and points to the places I should sign.

"Thank you so much, Sam. I love it." I pull an envelope out of my purse and say, "And here's this."

He takes it from me and places it safely in his briefcase.

I look back at the ocean, smile again, and feel an overwhelming sense of peace.

I close my eyes.

Say a prayer.

Then get driven back to the airport.

Cooper: *The police questioned Vincent today. He admitted to giving her a business card. When they asked if he knew she was dead, he acted surprised. He asked if they thought he had anything to do with it. They said they were just trying to piece together a timeline of her last hours alive. He said that he only saw her in the club and had hoped to hear from her this week. He even offered to take a lie detector test because, he said, for business reasons, he didn't want his name to be associated with a murder investigation. He had an alibi and passed the lie detector test.*

Me: *He once told me that the key to lying is to convince yourself it's the truth.*

Cooper: *That's also the key to passing a lie detector test.*

MADDER THAN A WET HEN.
7:30PM

I LOG INTO the airplane's Wi-Fi and get a message from Grandpa.

Grandpa: *Been digging into the history of this company. Here's an interesting fact. Vincent inherited a decent chunk of money when his mother and stepfather were killed, which he then immediately used to buy out a small production company. Guess which one it was?*

Me: *I have no idea.*

Grandpa: *The one that made* A Day at the Lake. *Remember, when it was first made it was pretty low budget. So in buying it, he automatically had the ability to do a remake. But based on what I've been told by the investors we've bought out, his decision to do the remake came this spring. I'm assuming that coincides with when he met you.*

Me: *Wow. How many investors do you have deals with?*

Grandpa: *Four out of the six. Those four were pretty eager to sell. They believe this movie has become an obsession. They were also worried because he's not investing in as many movie futures as he used to. He's well-known in the industry for being golden in selecting them.*

Me: *When will he find out that his investors have sold?*

Grandpa: *He found out today when we delivered a letter of intent to take control of his company. I wish I could've been a fly on the wall for that.*

Me: *Me too. Thanks, Grandpa. I love you.*

Me: *And Grandma. Please tell her I love her. Like, in case something should ever happen to me. You know?*

Grandpa: *If something happens to you, I'm killing the bastard myself. You have* *my promise. He won't get the luxury of jail time. But I'm definitely glad you're hidden away at school while this is all taking place. He's going to be madder than a wet hen.*

Me: *A wet hen?*

Grandpa: *If you'd ever seen one, you wouldn't have to ask.*

Me: *Believe it or not, that makes me feel better. At least I won't worry about him getting out of jail someday and hurting my sisters.*

Grandpa: *Exactly. And I love you too, Hotshot.*

Grandpa: *Wait. Sam just messaged me and said he met you in California today.*

Me: *Yeah.*

Grandpa: *Says it was confidential.*

Me: *Yeah.*

Grandpa: *Damian called me yesterday.*

Me: *That's nice of him.*

Grandpa: *Are you going back to the club tonight? After that girl was killed?*

Me: *Yes.*

Grandpa: *There's a reason you wear camouflage when you're hunting, Keatyn.*

Me: *I'll be wearing it tonight. And I'll be in a duck blind.*

Sorta.

Grandpa: *I don't want to end up owning some stupid movie company because you went out and got yourself killed. You understand me?*

Me: *Yes, sir.*

Grandpa: *I admire your courage, Hotshot. Text me when it's over and you're safe. I'll stay up.*

Me: *Grandpa, thanks for understanding that I have to do this.*

Grandpa: *We're cut from the same cloth. And don't worry, I WILL NOT be mentioning this to your grandmother.*

Me: *Thank goodness.*

Cooper meets me at my plane and introduces me to two of his friends. Both are cops who will be joining us tonight. They'll be following Vincent when they're off duty to make sure nothing like what happened to the girl from the club happens again.

Before we go into the club, I tell Cooper, "If something goes wrong—like if he takes me—promise me you'll come and get me."

"I'm going to do more than promise." He points out my locket to his friends. "Tracking device number one." Then he clamps a surprisingly stylish thick bangle bracelet around my wrist and says, "Tracking device number two. It operates in a different way, but if he scans you, he will find that and your locket easily."

"Do you think he would?"

"Hard to say, but we want to be prepared. And this little beauty," he says, holding up what looks like a little blister pad, "is the best one. Top dollar, espionage kind of stuff. Bend at the waist and flip your hair over."

I follow his instructions and feel him stick it right by my hairline.

"Okay, flip back over. Guys, did you bring the scanner?"

One of the guys nods and hands him a small scanner. He runs it across me and quickly finds both my necklace and bracelet, but when he runs it across my shoulders it doesn't go off. The guys all nod.

WE GET TO the club and meet up with the staff. They all know that we're planning to have a memorial for Leighton tonight.

"We just want to give a big *Fuck you* to whoever did this to her," Marla, the woman in charge of the dancers, says. "Also, ladies, *do not* go out with anyone you meet here. Even if they are a VIP. Not until her killer is caught."

The girls all nod. Some are crying.

Marla speaks to the doormen. "Every person who walks through the door tonight will get stamped with the chaos symbol. For those of you who don't know, Leighton was wearing a temporary tattoo on her hip and it was one of the few places she wasn't stabbed. I think you all know my pet name for this place is Utter Chaos, even though I can't get the boss man to give it an official name. So, we're going to celebrate that. Now, let's have a silent moment for Leighton."

Everyone lowers their heads for a few moments.

Then Marla claps her hands and says, "All right, everyone to work."

ONCE I'M DRESSED and ready, I talk to Troy, who won't go in the DJ booth tonight until the program starts.

"This is going to be like New Year's Eve on steroids."

"I hope so."

"You look very hot."

I'm wearing a neon pink push-up bra, which is peeking out from my teeny black dance top. And, with it, an ass-skimmingly short flirty black skirt. "All the girls are dressed this way."

"I sure hope he shows up."

"Me too. Although, if he does, he's going to be pissed. He was notified today that four of his six investors have been bought out and that he's probably going to lose control of his company."

"That your doing, too?"

I smile. "Shhh."

"Keats, do you ever do anything small?"

"Not anymore. Wait until you see the ending."

"Ending?"

"Well, the big finale, so to speak. Provided all goes as planned."

"That's the part I'm worried about. What if it doesn't go as planned?"

I pat him on the back. "Do me a favor and think positive. Also, I have a big favor to ask you."

"Another one?" Troy laughs.

"Yeah. Do you know someone who either works for a delivery service or would be willing to pretend to?"

"One of the valets does."

I get a package out of my bag. It's addressed to Vincent Sharpe at his office. "Do you think he could deliver this tomorrow? At, say, four?"

"Sure. What's in it?"

"Just a photo."

Troy is getting ready to ask more questions when Cooper comes backstage and tells us it's time.

Which means Vincent is here.

"Oh, good. I was afraid he wasn't going to show up."

"All right, girls. Take your spots. Cage girls, get loaded up," Marla instructs.

I get in the cage as it is hoisted into the air and swung out over the dance floor. The eight cage dancers sprinkle a few black rose petals over the dance floor.

I watch as a few people dancing look up to see where they're coming from.

RIGHT BEFORE THE cages start their decent, the music completely stops and the lights go out.

Troy speaks into the microphone. "A few days ago, one of our dancers was brutally murdered. She left work and never made it home. Everyone, please be vigilant when you leave any club and never go home with a stranger. Tonight, we're going to honor her life, starting with a moment of silence for our friend, Leighton Wall."

The place goes completely silent.

After a few moments, Troy yells, "Leighton, girl, R.I.P. This utter chaos is for you!"

The cages hit the platforms, causing the bases to suddenly light up, tonight in her favorite color: neon pink.

Pink beams of light shine down, spotlighting each cage and the spunky crazy song I chose starts playing.

I start dancing like I've never danced in my life.

Each dancer's skin is covered in artistic neon pink scrolls and numerous glow-in-the-dark chaos tattoos.

The song is upbeat and sassy, about a trouble-making girl.

Partway through the beginning of song, I notice Vincent near my cage trying to get a closer look at me.

When he gets close enough, I bend down, grab a handful of black rose petals, and throw them out of the cage directly at him.

Then I grab more and let them fly out of my fingers as I spin around.

Vincent plucks one out of the air and studies it.

Yeah, asshole, those are for you. A black rose petal warning, because you and your company are going down.

When the song gets to the part about flipping off the world, I raise both my middle fingers into the air and salute Vincent, which gets the crowd cheering.

I dance more.

I love this song.

Suddenly, nets in the ceiling open up and thousands of black rose petals fall like confetti over the dance floor.

Once all eyes in the vicinity are back on me—particularly Vincent's—I blow the crowd a kiss, then bend over, flip up my skirt, and reveal the big block letters running across my naughty Santa underwear.

When the crowd reads the slutty *FUCK ME* message on my shaking ass, the guys jump up and down, scream, whistle, and cheer.

And make some very naughty comments.

It's awesome.

And, finally, I see the response I was hoping for: pure rage in Vincent's eyes.

That's right, be mad at me. Just me. No one else. I'm going to be way more than trouble, Vincent. I'm going to be your worst nightmare.

A hurricane of problems.

When the song finishes, a hush spreads through the crowd, except for a little murmuring as they try to figure out what's happening next.

The spotlights leave the dancers and a single pink light shines on six men dressed in black, who are now filing into the club.

You hear gasps and cries from girls as they walk by, and everyone else is straining their necks to see what's going on.

The men work their way through the crowd, carrying a coffin, and come to a stop in front of my cage.

When the spotlight shines back on me, I'm on the floor of the cage, my eyes shut and my body still.

I hear the cage open and feel Cooper's strong arms pull me into the coffin.

I lie motionless as he makes the sign of a cross, folds my arms over my chest, whispers "All's good" to me, and then shuts the coffin lid.

If things go as planned, they will lead a processional of bouncers, waitresses, and clubgoers out the front door.

I lie still in the coffin, trying not to be creeped out.

This was the perfect exit for me. There's only one way Vincent could get close to me tonight.

And that's to start shooting people, which was Cooper's worse-case scenario.

I'm just praying I don't hear any shots.

I would never forgive myself if a gun fight started in a crowded place like this.

The sound I do hear is a big relief.

The beating of helicopter blades slicing through the air.

I finally let out the breath I've been holding as I feel the casket being loaded into the chopper.

ONCE THE DOOR shuts, Cooper opens the lid, so I can roll out of the coffin. I stay on my knees and sneak a peek out of the window, quickly spotting Vincent in the crowd.

As the helicopter lifts into the air, pink, red, and gold fireworks shoot into the sky.

The combination of the cheers, the fireworks, and the helicopter is deafening.

I watch the fireworks and pray that Leighton knows how sorry I am.

That I never meant for anyone to get hurt.

"That was freaking nuts!" Cooper says. "And safe. He didn't even have a chance to touch you."

"He looked mildly irritated when I threw the black roses at him, mad when I flipped him off, and completely pissed when the guys started cheering at the message on my underwear."

"Message on your underwear?"

"Yeah. I didn't mention that to you."

Cooper narrows his eyes. "What'd they say?"

"Fuck me."

"Oh, Keatyn. Jeez. We want to make him uncomfortable, not homicidal."

"He's already homicidal."

"Yeah, you're right. It was a good plan."

"And honored her, I hope."

The cop says, "I heard there was a very large anonymous donation made to the family's fund today."

"I heard that too." I smile. "Oh, Cooper! Do you have my phone? I did something else," I say, while firing off a quick text to let both Aiden and Grandpa know I'm okay.

"What?"

"How long do you think it will be before he'll want to leave?"

"If I were him, I'd be getting the hell out of there and never coming back," Cooper states.

"You should have seen his face when Cooper closed the lid on the casket," the cops says. "If I weren't armed, I would have been scared."

My phone dings with a text from Billy the valet.

I read his message and laugh. "It seems that Mr. Sharpe's Porsche is *somehow* missing from the club's parking lot. He just about blew a gasket."

Cooper and the cop both start laughing hysterically, part of which is probably just a release from the stress of tonight.

I giggle too. "Gosh, that felt good. To finally feel in control. I'm still worried he's going to hurt someone, though. Are you sure they're watching him 24/7?"

"Yes, a two-man team. Off duty cops."

"Do the cops know there's also a two-man team from Garrett's company watching all of them?"

"Naw," Cooper says, "I didn't think they needed to know."

A few minutes later, the helicopter sets down on the roof of the Moran Movies headquarters and lets us off.

Damian is waiting for us at the rooftop door.

He sighs with relief, gives me a big hug, and I introduce him to Cooper.

He looks at Cooper and squints. "You've got to be the hot soccer coach."

Cooper and I both laugh.

"It all went well. And his Porsche went missing for good measure. I mean, just in case the coffin and all wasn't enough for him."

Damian shakes his head. "I'm glad I wasn't there. I wouldn't have been able to watch you get put into a coffin."

"If it weren't for all the adrenaline," Cooper says, "I wouldn't have been able to either."

THE REST OF THE MOVIE.
10:30PM

ON THE FLIGHT back home, Cooper and I are both too pumped up to sleep.

"Let's watch the rest of the movie."

"Maybe we should just fast forward to the end. I mean, more people are gonna die and all that will be left is Matt, Lacy, and Vince."

"Yeah, you're probably right."

We watch in fast motion as the dead bodies pile up, Cooper stopping on a scene where Lacy and Matt are in a storage shed.

"It's Vince that's killing everyone. He wants you to go with Egypt with him, doesn't he?"

Lacy sobs into his chest. "I think so."

He pushes her away, holding her at arm's length. "We're leaving now. Running. We'll find someone somewhere."

"He said there isn't anyone for ten miles."

"He's been killing everyone, Lacy. Wake up. He's a liar. I'll keep you safe, baby. I promise. And if you want, I'll go to Egypt with you."

Lacy smiles through her tears and leans in to kiss him.

WHAM!

Vince hits Matt in the back of the head with a shovel.

Matt falls to the ground.

Dead.

Lacy screams as Vince starts moving toward her.

"It's just you and me now," Vince says creepily.

Lacy takes a step back, picks a life jacket up off a counter, and tosses it at him.

Vince moves sideways, avoiding the jacket and taking another step toward her. "When you first told me you might not go, I asked you if you wanted this as badly as I do. You told me yes."

"Wait, stop!" I shout.

"What?" Cooper says, almost jumping out of his seat.

I place my fingertips on my forehead, like it will help me remember. "Play that again."

"When you first told me you might not go, I asked if you wanted this as badly as I do."

"He said that exact line to me. About making his movie. *You want this as badly as I do, don't you?"*

"That's creepy," Cooper says as he rewinds and presses play.

". . . You told me yes."
Lacy screams, "Well, I changed my mind!"
She takes another step backwards.
"No! Don't give me that bullshit. Matt changed your mind! You came crying to me about it! I told you to figure it out."
Lacy has a flashback of telling Vince she didn't think she was going to study abroad and indicating that Matt wasn't very supportive. Vince offers to take her for a walk to discuss it.
Lacy laughs. "I don't think you can solve my boyfriend troubles, Vince, but thanks."
Vince says, "Maybe you need to solve them yourself."

And I have a flashback of my own.
I'm standing on the deck at a party, turning down a walk on the beach. "Thanks for the offer, Vincent. It's sweet of you, but I don't think anyone can solve my boy problems."
"Maybe you need to solve them yourself."

The movie keeps playing.

Vince is yelling at her, taking another step toward her, backing her into a corner. "But you didn't fucking listen to me. You listened to him."
Realizing she's trapped, she pleads, "Don't do this, Vincey. Tell me what you want and I'll do it."
He doesn't stop moving toward her.
And he doesn't reply.
He grabs her by the neck and starts dragging her out of the shed. "I want you, and I'm going to have you. All to myself."

"Holy shit," I mutter, another scene flashing in front of my eyes.

Vincent is dragging me and I plead, "Stop. Please, Vincent. Just tell me what you want, and I'll do it. I promise I'll make the movie with you. Just please don't do this.

Please."

He doesn't stop.

And he doesn't reply.

He just keeps dragging me, closer and closer to the door.

When we're almost to the door, he says, "I want you, and I'm going to have you. All to myself."

"Keatyn, what?"

"He did the same thing, said the same thing, as he was dragging me out the door. That he was going to have me all to himself."

Cooper takes his jacket off and lays it across the top of me. "You're shaking. Stop thinking about it."

"I'm glad you're here, Cooper. Thank you for everything. For going along with my crazy schemes."

"Somehow I doubt Garrett would have gone for the cage dancing." He smiles at me and pats the top of my hand. "I'm really proud of you."

"Thanks, Cooper. Let's keep watching."

Just when you think Vince is about to take her out the door, Matt stands up and staggers toward him.

Matt is holding a boat anchor that he swings up into the air and then slams into Vince's head.

Vince drops to the ground, bleeding profusely.

But he's not dead yet.

He says, "We're still going to Egypt together, Lacy." His voice starts to fade as he nears death. "And it will be perfection."

"You've got to be kidding me! Did he memorize the whole damn movie?"

"Did he say that to you?"

"At some point, yeah. Actually, no, I think it was in the note with the photos."

Lacy helps Matt stagger outside.

She suggests they try the boat again.

It still doesn't start, so Lacy lifts the motor cover. "Just the battery cable." She pops it back on and starts the boat. "Let's get out of here!"

"Before we do, Lacy. I'm sorry. If you really want to go to Africa, we'll figure out a way to stay together. I don't want to lose you, and I don't want to stand in the way of your dreams."

"You are my dreams, Matty." Lacy throws her arms around him, smothers him with kisses, and then they drive off in the boat as the sun is rising on a new day.

The End

Cooper shuts my laptop. "So, in this, Vince is the bad guy who dies. Do you think he changed that in the new script?"

"He said he was changing a lot of it. Special effects, stunt scenes. He made it sound like the new Lacy was supposed to be some badass heroine, but if she were, she'd save all her friends. And if she saved them, there'd be no story. No plot. I remember him saying something about getting someone ugly to play my boyfriend and not having any kissing scenes. I suppose young Vincent was jealous of Matt."

"Because he wants Lacy for himself."

"I think we need to get a copy of that script."

"How are we going to do that?"

"That's another thing agents are for."

Friday, December 16th

DARE TO THINK.
7AM

I GET BACK to school just in time to curl my hair, touch up my makeup, and put on my day outfit for dance. There's a home basketball game tonight and although we don't have a pep rally today, the cheerleaders declared it a black out game. Meaning all the students need to wear black to the game. Which is sort of funny, since the cheerleaders don't have black uniforms, only red or gold ones.

But the dance team, in supposed solidarity, is wearing our black yoga pants with long sleeved T-shirts that say Black Out the Badgers in gold glitter paint. And tonight we'll be wearing our gold glittery spandex dresses and using our black and gold pompoms instead of the red and gold ones.

The competition between the cheerleaders and the dance team is kind of stupid to me. Next year, if I have any say, we'll work together more.

I stop in my tracks.

Next year.

Did I really just dare to think that?

That I could spend my senior year here?

I shake my head.

The excitement of last night must have me on some sort of high.

Once I'm ready, I sit down and type a message to my mom's agent at the Warren Taylor Agency.

-Is there a way you could discreetly get a script for The Day at the Lake *remake? I might know someone interested in it.*

I'm shocked to get a quick response, especially since it's 4:30 in the morning on the West coast.

-Any chance that someone might be you? I'd be surprised, honestly, if Vincent Sharpe hadn't asked you yet.

I reply with:

-You're up awfully early! And, no, it's for Luke Sander. Apparently, they are interested in him for the boyfriend role, but he's worried because he heard the production company is having some financial difficulties. He's also maybe looking to switch agents and I thought of you.

Yes, that's sort of a lie. The part about the agent. But I could probably talk Sander into it, if necessary. He's told me on more than one occasion that he felt like he'd outgrown his current agent.

-I'm in New York this week meeting with Tommy about your mother's sudden leave of absence. Is she doing okay? I haven't heard about the company's finances. What did Sander hear?
-She's fine. Just needs a break. And he heard that someone is buying out the company's investors and a hostile takeover is imminent.
-Really? Interesting. I did hear the investors were rumbling about the amount of capital he's sunk into that movie. If that's the case, Luke Sander should stay far away from the project.

Shit.

-Can you get me the script anyway?
-Of course, darling.
-Thank you. And give Tommy a hug for me.
-We should have lunch when I'm back in town. Tommy told me last spring that he expected you to follow in your mother's footsteps. I could get you some roles very easily.
-Thank you. I'll think about it. Either way, lunch would be great.

Then I text Cooper, realizing I forgot to tell him this part of my plan.

Me: *I forgot to tell you part of my plan last night.*
Cooper: *Forgot? Or purposely didn't tell me?*
Me: *Forgot. I'm having something delivered to Vincent's office today at 4. I thought maybe your friend who met up with his assistant might text her and ask*

her out for Happy Hour. Like if he got her number.

Cooper: *He has her number. What did you send?*

Me: *A photo I found of him from when he was doing the national search for the next Abby Johnston. I photoshopped the special effect of B's head being blown off onto his head, put it in a picture frame, and boxed it up with some black rose petals.*

Cooper: *And purposely didn't tell me because I would have told you not to?*

Me: *Really? No, I thought you'd love the idea. And I was going to ask your friend myself last night, but forgot with the excitement. I'd really like to know how he reacts.*

Cooper: *I think it's important we know how he reacts. I'll call him later today.*

Me: *Be sure to have him wait to text her until after it's delivered.*

Cooper: *Will do.*

Me: *Have you heard anything from them? Like what he did last night?*

Cooper: *He was furious about his car. Filed a police report. Took a cab home. Stayed there.*

Me: *Thank goodness. I don't want anyone else to die because of me.*

Maggie comes in our room to get a ponytail holder. Her hands are laden with gifts.

She lays two on my bed and one on Katie's.

"I feel like I only see you at dance." I give her a big hug.

"Logan and I have been spending a lot of time alone lately. Making up for lost time, I guess."

"You mean having sex."

"Not just that. We haven't every night." She rolls her eyes. "Okay, so we have. But we've been talking a lot too. About senior year. About our future. College. All that."

"That's good. Have you gotten any fun naughty gifts?"

"Yes. I don't know who my Santa is, but I'm in love with him. I've gotten a pink vibrator, a bottle of cookie dough vodka, chocolate body paint, and nipple tassels."

"Nipple tassels? I heard about Logan's condom lollipops. Did you actually do it eight times?"

"No. Only three." She smiles. "I'm not complaining though. Open your presents!" She holds up a Christmas bag.

I pull the tissue paper out, finding a bottle of cotton candy vodka and two pink silky scarves.

"I think the boys are working together to give us what our boyfriends would want us to use," she laughs. "And get us drunk. We'll take our vodka to the party tonight!"

"I get the vodka, but pink scarves? How it that naughty? I mean, these aren't going to keep me very warm."

Maggie starts laughing hysterically.

"What?" I say.

"I think those are for tying you up."

"Oh . . . I didn't even think of that."

"You will now."

Katie bounds out of the bathroom, sees the chocolate Santa on her bed, says, "Cool," and tosses it in her backpack.

HOT NOT SWEET.
7:45AM

AIDEN MEETS ME at my dorm to walk me to class. He seems much more clear-headed this morning. "So, last night, how did it go?"

"As planned. I'm glad I went."

"And I'm glad you're back here safe."

"Me too. What'd you do last night?"

"Tried to catch up on homework. Passed out at nine. I'm a wimp."

"It takes a lot of energy to heal, Aiden. You're not a wimp."

"I was able to put some weight on it when I showered this morning. I'm hoping not to have to wear the boot for the dance."

"I suppose it would be hard to dance with it on."

"Not if we're slow dancing."

"True. I hope we get to do a lot of that."

"Me too," he says. "And, more importantly, I'll be able to take it off later. That's the real reason I begged them not to cast it."

"It's sweet you'd even think of that when you were in pain."

"What was even sweeter was you on top of me the other night."

Before I walk into my class, I smile at him, give him a kiss on the cheek, and whisper, "There was nothing sweet about it. It was pure hotness."

"TONIGHT'S CHRISTMAS PARTY is going to be a blast," Riley tells me. "I'm hoping you ladies bring some of your naughty Santa gifts. Make the night more interesting."

"Aiden should bring his dice. That would be a fun thing for couples to play."

"What dice?"

"They say things like lick, suck, and blow on one dice and then you roll the other die for which body part to do it to."

"Are they naughty?"

"They are pretty clean, but there is a player's choice, so you could make it that way. So, other than the furry handcuffs, I haven't heard what you've gotten."

Riley grins. "I have a secret crush on whoever my Santa is. I got the pink furry handcuffs. Still waiting to use them. Let's see, a spinning beer pong rank. Gonna destroy Aiden tonight. Body parts bingo. Already had some fun with that game. A Tuggie . . ."

"What's that?"

"Oh, it's the fuzzy sock that warms your co . . ."

"Never mind! I think I saw that when I was shopping. Have you tried it? Does it keep it warm?"

"Don't know, but it's leopard print. And I got a matching leopard baby doll outfit for Ariela to wear. Rawr."

"You're funny. What else?"

"Edible body paints."

"Nice."

"What about you?"

"Honestly, I'm pretty sure I know who my Santa is."

He plays dumb. "Really?"

"Riley, I know it's you."

"I wouldn't tell you if it was."

"I know. It was a good idea. And a lot more exciting than my dorm secret Santa. Although Katie and I have been enjoying all the candy."

Our teacher comes in with a big tray of homemade cinnamon rolls in the shape of Christmas trees. "Yum. All we're going to do in class today is eat. Best day ever," Riley says.

IN ENGLISH CLASS, Dallas is also going on about his naughty Santa.

"This morning I got this little red bong. Can't wait to use it tonight. This party is going to be epic."

Katie takes the chocolate Santa out of her backpack. "This is what I got. Can't wait to get this thing in my mouth."

She undoes the foil from the top and brings it to her mouth.

"Katie!" I yell, realizing that the Santa is really a large chocolate dick.

Dallas starts laughing. Rolling-on-the-floor, tears-coming-out-of-his-eyes laughing. "Ohmigosh, you just said you couldn't wait to get it in your mouth."

Katie looks confused. Then she holds the chocolate out in front of her. "Ahhh!" she screams, which, even though we're having a Christmas party in this class too, gets the attention of our teacher.

She's marching back toward us.

"Put it away!" I tell her.

Dallas is still laughing so hard he can't talk.

"Katie!" our teacher exclaims. "If you have candy, you need to share it with the class."

At which point Dallas really starts crying. "Share it with the class, Katie."

I think Dallas' laughter is contagious because all of a sudden, I can't stop either. I still keep picturing Katie almost putting it in her mouth. And I can picture her walking around to each desk breaking off a piece of it for each student.

"Is it solid or cream filled?" Dallas screams.

"Mr. McMahon, I don't know what's gotten into you," our teacher says. Then she actually sees what's in Katie's hand.

"Suck on it. Let's find out," he continues.

"I'm not sucking on it," Katie says. "Not if I have to share it," she adds naughtily.

"Alright, you three. You can take your naughty chocolate down to the dean's office."

"Do we have to share it with him?" Dallas asks, still dying with laughter.

As we're escorted out of class and head toward the office, I say to Katie, "You're gonna have to bite off the tip."

"Suck it off. Suck it off," Dallas chants.

"We'll get in trouble if you don't bite it off. With the tip gone, it looks like a chocolate Santa."

She tosses it to me. "No, you bite it."

"I'm not biting it." I try to give it to Dallas. "You bite it."

"Oh, no. Not me," he says. "No, wait. I have a plan. Wrap it back up."

I wrap the Santa back up, making it look like it had never been opened.

Dallas takes it from me. "Watch this."

He walks into the dean's office and says to the secretary, "Mrs. Potter, do you have all your Christmas shopping done?"

"Almost," she says. "What are you doing out of class?"

"Mrs. Major sent me down. She handed out chocolate Santas to our class and had an extra one. I offered to bring it down to you."

"Oh, well, isn't that sweet?" She gives him a conspiratorial grin and says, "I'll have to tease the dean with it."

Katie and I bite our lips to keep from laughing as Dallas says, "I'm sure the dean would love that. Merry Christmas!"

We all walk out of the office, run around the corner, and collapse onto the ground in a fit of giggles.

"Ohmigawd! I can't believe she said she'd tease the dean with it!"

Dallas says, "She loves chocolate. I bet she has it open in three, two, one . . ."

"Ahhhhhh!!!" we hear her scream as the bell rings.

I'M A BIG GIRL.
DRAMA

WHEN I COME offstage after my improvisation exercise, I check my phone.

Damian: *Question, since you're still alive.*

Me: *Not funny. It was a good plan.*

Damian: *Troy just told me all the details you wouldn't tell me. Sounded more like a script for an action film than a plan.*

Me: *Well, Riley and I scripted it out.*

Damian: *You told him the truth?!*

Me: *Part of the truth. He thinks it was my best friend who was stalked. That her dancing in a cage a couple weeks ago was my idea. And he knows about the girl that got killed. I couldn't hide how upset I was. He knows I went back there to take her spot and that it was kind of dangerous. Honestly, I told Riley a different story in Miami. So I had to lie about lying. The lies are starting to pile up. Getting hard to keep them all straight.*

Damian: *So the video Riley did of you on the plane.*

Me: *Yeah?*

Damian: *Our label hired this guy who is supposed to be a creative genius to do our video. He sucks. Like really, really sucks. Wanted to make it a piece of art as opposed to a music video that goes with the song. The video is supposed to release on New Year's Eve. Even with my connections, I can't find anyone who's willing to shoot it for us over the holidays. So I was wondering if Riley might be interested in trying his hand at it. We want it fun, campy, like something we'd have shot ourselves, just better edited. And, of course, you promised to be in it.*

Me: *I did. I just didn't realize it would be so soon. Maybe you should ask Peyton.*

Damian: *She's gorgeous, but I don't think she'd be good in front of a camera. She freaked out when the paparazzi jumped us last weekend.*

Me: *She'll have to learn to deal with it. Thank goodness they didn't get a clear* *shot of her face though. You could have put both of us in a lot of danger.*

Damian: *I know. I'm sorry. I'm still not used to being followed around. But back to the video.*

Me: *If my name wasn't listed anywhere, in theory, the people who know me as Keatyn Douglas, would know it's me and wouldn't be surprised since we're friends. The people that know Keatyn Monroe, I'd just tell them that I did it. It's not like anyone is going to talk about me that much, right?*

Damian: *I think they will talk about you. But I think you're right. And would it sort of fit into your plan of letting Vincent see you some? Are you planning more trips back home or to the club?*

Me: *I don't know yet. But probably. Let me think through it and I'll let you know.*

Damian: *So do you think Riley would be interested?*

Me: *I think Riley would be thrilled.*

Damian: *We got invited to play during the MTV New Year's Eve party overlooking Times Square. I have a bunch of tickets that I could sort of repay you both with.*

Me: *You don't have to repay us, but the party sounds like fun. I'd love to.*

Damian: *I heard you're not coming to St. Croix for Christmas.*

Me: *I can't. I sort of lied myself into a corner. I told Aiden I have to be with my family. But I can't actually be with my family. And I can't think up a good reason why I wouldn't go see them, since all I've done is complain about how much I miss them. I'm filming with Tommy and your dad next week, so I'll get to see them. I'll stay at my loft. Aiden bought me a tree. And you'll all be back the next week!*

Damian: *Still, it's Christmas. I don't want you to be alone.*

Me: *I have to be, Damian. I'm a big girl. I'll be fine. I promise.*

GIRLS DANCING.
1:30AM

WE ALL MEET up outside the chapel and get everyone into Stockton's for the party. I brought my cotton candy vodka and Maggie brought her cookie dough vodka as well as some chocolate cookies she got from her dorm secret Santa.

When we turn the lights on, we find a Christmas tree decorated with boas, mini airplane bottles of alcohol, and condom packages.

"This is going to be the best Christmas party ever!" Logan declares.

Aiden is standing behind me, his arms wrapped around my waist. "A little different from our Christmas tree, huh?"

"Yeah, a little," I laugh. "Did you bring the dice game? I think that will be fun to play after we drink a little."

"You told me you used to get on the bar and dance. You gonna do that tonight?"

I look at the long bar, knowing it wouldn't take much convincing to get the girls up there with me. "Do you want me to dance for you, Aiden?"

He spins me around. "What do you think?"

"I think you liked it."

"Yeah, I did."

"And you won't get mad at me?"

"Why would I get mad at you?"

"Other guys will be looking at me."

Aiden puts his hand behind my neck, moving my face close to his. He kisses the tip of my nose and says, "They can look all they want. They just can't touch."

"You're pretty cool," I tell him. "But maybe you should get up there and dance for me?"

"Hmmm, I would," he points down. "But I have this bum leg. And I'm trying to get it healed for tomorrow night."

"Are you going to tell me about tomorrow night?"

"Maybe after a few drinks."

I go behind the bar and pour a round of shots. "Shot time!" I yell.

Everyone takes a glass and holds their shot in the air.

"Everyone do a toast," I say. "I'll go first. Here's to a very naughty Christmas."

Dallas says, "Here's to giving the dean's secretary a chocolate dick."

Annie holds her shot up high and says, "Here's to trying new things."

Jake wraps his arm around her and kisses her while Riley says, "Here's to pink furry handcuffs that I can't wait to use." He grabs Ariela's ass and goes, "Grr, baby, grr."

Ariela raises her shot higher. "And here's to a leopard print Tuggie I can't wait to laugh at."

"And strip off me," Riley yells.

"I think we need to drink this. Drink!"

Everyone downs the shots. We pour more and continue our toasts.

Logan says, "Here's to Stockton's!"

Aiden clinks Logan's glass and says, "And to girls dancing on the bar!"

The guys look up at the bar and then at us. Aiden grins at me.

Riley says to Aiden very seriously, "Are there dancing girls coming tonight?"

"Keatyn is going to dance on the bar. Maggie, too."

"I am?" Maggie says.

I grab her and pull her up on the bar with me.

"Music?"

Logan blasts some dance music and Maggie and I start dancing.

AFTER A FEW songs, Aiden walks up to the bar and holds his hand out to me.

I smile at him and jump off the bar. He leads me back behind the black curtain to the bed. "I told everyone that it's hard for me to sit with the boot on, so Riley suggested I lie down here."

"So, you just want to lie down?" I ask, closing the curtain and crawling on top of him.

"No. I'd like to do what we did the other night. Before you moved off."

"Here?"

"You asked what I wanted to do. That's what I want. But I don't want to do that here. And the party is just getting going. We can't really leave yet."

"Aiden, tomorrow night after the dance. You want to, right? I mean you don't have to give away any surprises about what you have planned, but I also need to be mentally prepared. Like if you don't want to, it's okay, but I don't want to think you do and then be disappointed if we don't. But if you tell me now that you don't . . ."

Aiden puts his finger up to my lips. "Shush."

"I'm kind of freaking out about this."

He moves his finger and shushes me with his lips. When he stops kissing me, he says, "I definitely want to."

"I do too," I say, laying my head on his shoulder. "And I can't wait."

THE PARTY, FILLED with beer pong, naughty dice, smoking, and a lot of fun, continues until almost dawn. Aiden keeps yawning, so I pull him on the bed with me and go to sleep.

Saturday, December 17th

TRYING TO HANG ON.

11:30AM

WE WAKE UP around ten, go back to our dorms, and start packing up for winter break.

"It seems like we just got here," Katie says sadly. "I can't believe it's already Christmas."

"I know. It's gone so fast."

"I love it here," she says.

"I do too. Are you and Bryce doing anything over break?"

"Yeah, he's coming to my parent's cabin after Christmas to ski and spend New Year's together. What about you?"

"Aiden's going to the Caribbean with his family, but we're spending New Year's together." I grab my suitcase and some shopping bags full of gifts. "I'm going to run these out to my car."

I load them up and then head back to my dorm. Cooper is standing outside.

"I just texted you," he says. "My friend texted Vincent's assistant. She said she couldn't leave early. That her boss had just gotten a horrible threatening photo and had thrown it against the wall, then made her clean up all the glass."

"So he was mad. Then what did he do?"

"Left his office and had dinner with two of his investors. Trying to hang onto his company."

"We need to plan what we're going to do next. I'd like to go back next Thursday but with filming, I can't."

"I think the company takeover stuff is enough for now. Your mom's movie is still getting a ton of buzz. So, you're going to the dance tonight, then going to a hotel with Aiden, then going to your loft on Sunday morning?"

"Yeah, he's staying with me until the twenty-third, then leaving for St. Croix with his family."

"And what are you going to do after that?"

"Stay at my loft. Everyone thinks I'm going home. I won't go out, so don't worry about me."

"It's my job to worry about you. What if you came home with me for Christmas? My parents would love it."

"Really, Cooper?" I blink away tears.

"Yes, really. I don't want you to be alone and I know you can't go home."

"That would be nice. I'll get to see Tommy but it just isn't going to be the same."

"I know. Have fun at the dance tonight."

"Have fun chaperoning."

He rolls his eyes at me. "Yeah, right."

FOLLOW MY SCRIPT.
6PM

I'M GETTING READY for Winter Formal.

Curling my hair and then twisting it into a side braid that will show off my dress. Putting makeup on. Touching up my pedicure. Painting my nails.

My dress and shoes are already loaded into my Range Rover.

Aiden and I caravan to the boutique hotel where we're spending the night, so we can drop off all our bags. After the dance, school is officially out for break.

And, since we have quite a few bags, we decide to get dressed at the hotel.

HE HOLDS MY hand as we enter our beautifully perfect suite, our heels clicking on the worn oak floors. Center stage sits a modern black four-poster bed dressed in a fluffy comforter and pillows. The linens are all white except for a golden throw draped at the end of the bed. There's a huge fireplace stacked with wood just waiting to light the room with a golden glow. A thick, white, fluffy rug that's dying to be curled up on. A chaise to lie on. Champagne waiting to be chilled. The bathroom features golden marble, a modern free-standing tub, and a jetted shower.

As I look at each element of the room, I'm envisioning all the places we're going to do it.

JILLIAN DODD

Tonight is finally the night.

And even though I wrote my script to tell him right when we get back to the room, part of me wants to wait until after.

The chicken part of me.

But my heart knows that I need to follow my script. Tell him the truth before I commit to him in that way. I don't want there to be any lies between us when it finally happens.

I'm just worried that he won't follow my script.

That he won't understand.

But you have to trust the people that you love.

So I gaze again at the beautiful surroundings, wiping the negative thoughts from my mind and letting warmth fill my heart.

Knowing that things are going to be perfect.

I make Aiden get dressed in the bathroom while I put on my dress and shoes in the bedroom.

He yells, "You ready yet?"

"Yeah, I'm ready."

He walks out of the bathroom wearing a classic black Gucci tuxedo.

Just think, Keatyn, you get to undress him tonight.

My perfect boy.

I'm wearing a pretty Catherine Deane strapless, silk-organza gown. The gown's sweetheart neckline features polished metal beads, appliqués, and picot-edged overlays. I feel like a winter fairy. Soft and flowy, with just a little sparkle.

Aiden says, "You look stunning."

"You look pretty stunning yourself. Love the tux."

I pull up the skirt of my dress and show off my deep gray Nicholas Kirkwood suede pumps that are covered in pale multi-colored swirls of crystal.

"You were right," he says. "Those are the perfect shoes for the dress. You ready to go?'

"Not really," I say. "I want to go, but I kind of wish we could just stay here."

He kisses me and says, "We'll leave early."

"Deal."

WE HAVE FUN dancing with our friends.

Sneaking into the bathroom for sips of whiskey.

Mostly, I have fun being close to Aiden.

Having him whisper to me how it drives him nuts when I grind on him. The husky, desire-filled sound in his voice.

The way he smells.

The way he looks.

The way my dress floats around me like a dream when he twirls me.

Around us, other people are dancing, but it feels like the room, the dance floor, the whole night, was made just for us.

WHEN WE TAKE a break, I decide to give Riley his final present.

He picks me up and hugs me when he opens a high definition video camera. The kind he could actually shoot a real movie with.

"You're my new best friend," he says.

"I've always been your best friend," I tease.

"Naw, it was Dallas, but between him defiling my rug and your gifts, you win."

I hug him back. "Be nice. And, for the record, I'm going to miss you."

"We'll only be apart for about a week. Besides, I'm not up for being nice. Tonight is all about being naughty. Did you find out who your Santa is?"

"No, I thought it was you. And I haven't kept track of who has revealed theirs already."

"I think some people are waiting until later. Bryce said he's having a party in their hotel room. Doesn't he want to be alone with Katie?"

"I think they've been alone about every night this week."

Riley laughs. "I'm not going to party. Are you?"

"No. Did Aiden tell you about our suite?"

"Yes, we're staying at the hotel, too. Thought we'd meet up for lunch before we leave, so we could talk more about this video for Damian."

"That sounds perfect."

THERE'S A BREAK in the dancing as the house Sweethearts are announced.

Hawthorne is the last to go.

Aiden whispers, "I think it's going to be you."

Jake, who is now onstage, announces my name, and calls me up.

I receive a beautiful bouquet of flowers and a little tiara that says Sweetheart.

THE MUSIC STARTS back up again.

I'm so ready to leave now. To get to our room.

It's been a perfectly scripted night.

Lots of slow dancing.

A gorgeous dress that swirls around my body like a snowflake.

The date of my dreams.

Everything is perfect.

Even though my life is so far from it.

I'm tempted not to stay for the Social Committee presentation. Whitney's doing it all. No one would miss me.

Aiden pulls me into his arms as a slow song plays.

I'm seriously considering dragging his ass out of here this second, telling him the truth, and then making mad, passionate, amazing love all night long.

And although that's how I scripted it, I will admit, I'm still debating about doing it, like, once—or maybe twice—before I tell him. So that if I was completely wrong and he hates me for lying to him, at least I'll have experienced the Titan and won't spend the rest of my life wondering what it would have been like between us.

His arms are wrapped tightly around my waist, and he keeps kissing the side of my face as we dance.

He says quietly, "I think we should start in front of the fireplace on that soft rug, then move to the chaise."

"I noticed the bench at the end of the bed too," I whisper.

"And the jetted shower, the tub. Eventually, maybe the bed too." He lets out an adorable sexy chuckle. "I have something I need to tell you first," he says.

"What's that?"

He leans back and pulls a long white feather out of his jacket and holds it in front of me. There's a little hot pink ribbon curling off of it, just like there has been on all my other gifts.

"You're my naughty Santa?" I say in shock.

He nods.

"Seriously? I thought for sure it was Riley." Then I grin at him. "The stuff you got me. Um, did it have a purpose?"

"What do you think?"

"I think you're tricky is what I think. You wrote an M on your list. I thought you had Maggie."

"You looked at my list? You're a bad girl. And, just for the record, I stole all your gifts out of your car. They're at our room waiting for us."

"I think maybe we should get the hell out of here now."

He whispers, "That's why I fucking love you, Keatyn Monroe."

"I fu—" I start to say, but Whitney grabs my elbow, pulling me away from Aiden.

"Hey, you ready to go onstage?" she says with a big smile. "End the night and officially kick off our winter break?"

"Um, we were just thinking about leaving."

"No way. Not before this. Plus, I decided I want you and Peyton up there with me."

Aiden gives me a smoldering look and puts the feather back inside his jacket. "Go ahead," he says. "Then we'll leave."

"Should I go round up the Social Committee?"

"No. I want just you two," she says, grabbing Peyton from where she's dancing with Brad.

We hold hands and make our way up to the stage.

"Attention, everyone," she says after taking a microphone off the podium and tapping on it. "I have some exciting news to share. And I'm so happy that my two best friends are here on stage with me."

I smile at her, knowing that her surprise will be the announcement of her college of choice. She's gotten all her acceptance letters back and has been playing coy about where she's going. Even though I know it will be Yale with Shark.

Really, I'm surprised I'm even standing up here.

That she would consider me a good friend after our rocky start.

But coming to Eastbrooke allowed me to find myself.

To do the things I wished I had done at my old school.

To use my conscience and do what's right, regardless of what's popular.

To stand up for myself.

And I think I've had a good effect on Peyton and Whitney too. They seem to be on even ground, and, since Whitney started dating Shark, she hasn't acted like the bitchy Alpha she once was.

I think he's good for her.

She sets her laptop on the podium.

After her little speech, we're going to show the video Riley made for the Social Committee highlighting our year so far. The Welcome Back carnival and dance. The Homecoming festivities. The Greek and French weekends.

She starts with, "I'd just like to say a few words from the Social Committee and then I have something fun planned for you."

She goes on to thank the Social Committee members, the supporting clubs . . .

I tune out her voice, because I know her speech by heart.

She made us listen to it over and over.

Instead, I'm staring at Aiden.

Okay, really, I'm staring at his fly.

Imagining.

Anticipating.

"Before the presentation starts . . ."

My ears perk up as Whitney deviates from the script.

"I hate to have to do this, but something has come to my attention, and I feel compelled to share it with you, as is my obligation, per the Eastbrooke code of conduct."

She uses the remote to make the screen behind us roll down from the ceiling.

Now she has my full attention, because this suddenly feels a lot like the day at lunch when she sent the texts to all of Chelsea's friends.

Only it's a lot more public.

The dean and most of the faculty is here.

A few of the parents.

Is she going to do something else to Chelsea?

Whitney flips open her laptop and Peyton, who is still holding my hand, digs her fingernails into me.

I glance at her and see that her face has gone completely white.

I follow her eyes toward the podium.

Ohmigawd.

Ohmigawd.

Ohmigawd.

No.

I can't believe this is happening.

I look at the pictures Whitney is getting ready to flash across the screen.

No.

Not now.

Not tonight.

Not here in front of everyone.

My heart sinks, and I get a horrible feeling in the pit of my stomach.

I remember what she said to me that day at the lunch table.

How Peyton surprised her.

Peyton lets out a little whimper as the screen finishes unrolling.

Whitney was only nice to us because she was planning to destroy Peyton the way Vanessa destroyed Mandy.

Peyton is nothing like Mandy. She didn't do anything mean and calculating. She was hurt and needed comfort when she turned to him.

I look out into the crowd and see the boys' soccer coach and remember how

Whitney specifically asked him and his wife, who is now five months pregnant, to chaperone.

She wants to destroy them both.

Right here, in front of everyone.

I can't let it happen.

I can't let intimate sexual photos of an underage Peyton be flashed across a screen in front of the whole school.

Not to mention what it would do to Coach Kline's life and his wife's.

Just as Whitney is ready to start the slideshow, I move quickly, dropping Peyton's hand and grabbing the remote out of Whitney's.

And it's at that moment that I know what I have to do.

Even though I shouldn't.

Even though it will ruin everything for me.

I have to do this for my friend.

I turn to a stunned Peyton. "Why don't you take Whitney's computer and put it somewhere safe? Photos aren't necessary. I'll tell everyone the truth."

Peyton gives me a confused look, then takes a shaky step, grabs the laptop, and walks offstage.

I'm left with a crowd of students wondering what I lied about.

Whitney opens her mouth in protest, so I take the microphone from her too.

I notice a small group of reporters have moved in front of the stage.

Not only was Whitney going to tell the school, she brought in the local press.

I start telling every lie I've told since I got here.

I look at Riley and confess. "My name isn't Keatyn Monroe."

Then I find Aiden's eyes in the crowd. "I did recognize you as the goalie that day when you asked."

Then Dawson. "I didn't leave my Mercedes at home because of the snow."

Then Maggie and Annie. "My parents didn't move to France or delete my social media. I didn't get in trouble at home, and my photos didn't get lost when I synced my new phone."

I speak directly to Annie. "I have seen every one of Abby Johnston's movies. We do have the same mannerisms, and our voices are so similar even Tommy can't tell them apart. And that's because I'm her daughter."

Cameras start flashing, so I hold my hand strategically in front of my face.

"I came here because . . ."

I want to tell them why. But I realize I can't.

Not yet.

I can't put them in danger.

I won't.

I know that I don't have until March with Aiden anymore.

That his time bomb app just went off.

My biggest problem is the reporters, not my friends.

Because if they announce that I'm here, Vincent will come.

And I can't do that to Eastbrooke.

To the place I love so much.

I've been stalked and kissed and dated and loved, but now I can see it clearly on their faces.

Hate.

I hear the big metal doors behind me close and know that Peyton has made it safely out of the ballroom with the laptop.

I hate to do it, but I need to tell my friends one more lie.

Just one more lie.

And in order to do it, I'm going to have to give the performance of my life.

But I'll do it because I love them.

I stand up straighter, jut my chin out, and become the cold, uncaring bitch who takes whatever she wants from whomever she wants because she thinks she's entitled to it.

I peek through my fingers, finding Aiden.

He's the one I have to convince more than anyone.

I smirk, looking at him like he's a piece of trash, not worthy of my time, then shrug. "I came to Eastbrooke because I wanted to see if I could act. To see if I could pretend to be someone else. I lied because . . . Well, because I could. Because I'm a good actress."

AIDEN DARTS OFF the dance floor.

I turn around, my eyes following him.

Wanting to talk to him.

To tell him I'm sorry.

To tell him this isn't how I wanted him to find out.

My hand reaches out toward him.

He shakes his head at me, puts his hand up in the halt position, pushes his back against the exit door, and walks straight out of my life.

Tears spring to my eyes as Whitney grabs my elbow, pulling me close to her.

"Very slick," she says. "And *very* interesting. But don't worry, I have backups of the photos. Peyton's not getting out of this."

I hold my head high, still in bitch mode. "Yeah, she is. Because it just so happens, I have a few photos of my own."

I reach down, take my phone out of my clutch, click a few buttons, and send her the photo where she's lying across Coach Steele's desk.

When the picture pops up, the smug look slides off her face.

I wrench my arm away from her.

"If you *ever* try to hurt Peyton or any one of my friends again. If any of those photos *ever* show up anywhere, I will show these photos to the whole school. I'll tell them how you couldn't get Camden by sleeping with him, so you settled for his brother. I'll tell them that your relationship was a sham."

"What do I care? I'm going to college."

I give her a smug, bitchy smile. "Because I'll also send them to every Ivy League school you applied to. Camden kept *everything*. And there are hundreds of pictures and screenshots for me to choose from. I could release one a week for the rest of your life. If you wait until we're older, then I'll send them to your boss. Your parents. Your friends. Your husband. Because you can bet on this. If those photos *ever* see the light of day, I *will* destroy you."

For the first time since I've known her, Whitney looks scared.

She nods at me in understanding, puts her head down, and slinks off the stage.

Still shielding my face, I head off the stage toward Cooper.

I can tell he's pissed.

"What the fuck was that? What the hell were you thinking? There are reporters here. We've got to get you out of here now."

"No."

"What?"

"I said no, Cooper. I'm not going anywhere. Help me out by rounding up those reporters. I need to talk to them."

AS HE GOES off to speak to the reporters, Annie walks up to me and says, "I thought you were different. You made me believe that nice girls could be popular. I've mentioned your resemblance to Abby Johnston quite a few times. We saw her in New York! It would've been so easy for you to tell me the truth. Which means it was all just a mean game to you." She grabs Katie and pulls her into the conversation. "Katie and I are in agreement on this. We're not friends anymore. Although I doubt we ever were."

Her and Katie march away as I recoil slightly.

I wasn't expecting that from them.

I want to go after them and say I'm sorry.

But I can't.

I turn around and stare at the door Aiden just walked out of.

I want to chase him.

Beg him for forgiveness.

Tell him the rest of the truth.

But as I see Cooper and the dean herding the reporters into a room, I know that I can't do that either.

I remember Grandpa once telling me, *Sometimes you can't find yourself until you're lost.*

I thought it was just another silly Southern saying.

But I get it now.

I was lost.

And, somehow, throughout this whole ordeal, I found myself.

I know exactly who I am.

And if Aiden is the boy of my dreams . . .

If he really is my moon boy . . .

My fate.

Then he'll understand.

Someday.

The End

About the Author

Jillian is a *USA TODAY* bestselling author. She writes fun romances with characters her readers fall in love with, from the boy next door in the *That Boy* trilogy to the daughter of a famous actress in *The Keatyn Chronicles* series.

She's married to her college sweetheart, has two adult children, two Labs named Cali and Camber, and lives in a small Florida beach town. When she's not working, she likes to decorate, paint, doodle, shop for shoes, watch football, and go to the beach.

www.jilliandodd.net

94554573R00158

Made in the USA
Lexington, KY
31 July 2018